THE
FAMILY
STALKER

Also by the author

Death by Station Wagon
Sign Off

THE FAMILY STALKER

A SUBURBAN DETECTIVE MYSTERY

JON KATZ

DOUBLEDAY

NEW YORK LONDON TORONTO SYDNEY AUCKLAND

PUBLISHED BY DOUBLEDAY
a division of Bantam Doubleday Dell Publishing Group, Inc.
1540 Broadway, New York, New York 10036

DOUBLEDAY and the portrayal of an anchor with a dolphin
are registered trademarks of Doubleday, a division of
Bantam Doubleday Dell Publishing Group, Inc.

Designed by Joseph Rutt

Library of Congress Cataloging-in-Publication Data
Katz, Jon.
    The family stalker : a suburban detective mystery / Jon Katz.—1st ed.
      p. cm.
    1. Private investigators—New Jersey—Fiction. 2. New Jersey—
Fiction. I. Title.
PS3561.A7558F3 1994
813'.54—dc20   93-30638   CIP

ISBN 0-385-46903-9

March 1994
10 9 8 7 6 5 4 3 2 1

FIRST EDITION

To Marianne Goldberger

THE
FAMILY
STALKER

CHAPTER 1

When your office is on the second floor of a mall, even an aging mall with a mere eight hundred or so parking slots marked by faded white lines, you gain rare, sometimes unwanted, anthropological insights into the world of the American teenager, a culture in which nothing is as simple as it first appears. Along with sneakers, ankle bracelets, and T-shirts, for example, I'd recently been observing the sacred adolescent rites surrounding baseball caps.

When I was a kid, nothing would have been considered less fashionable or likely to attract the opposite sex than those felt things invented to keep the sun out of ball players' faces and worn by truck drivers and repairmen. But the whole ethic of being a teenager, I now know, is to confound and, where possible, irritate adults.

These days, of course, caps grow out of kids' heads as naturally as hair. They have nothing to do with baseball or the sun. In the four years since I set up my office at the American Way Mall, I've seen their prices shoot from four or five bucks to twenty. There's a whole wall of caps displayed in Murray

Grobstein's Shoe World, along with $120 sneakers with pumps, gels, and built-in rocket launchers. Sometimes the caps are worn with the visor forward, sometimes to the rear or the side. Sometimes the caps have team insignia or names, sometimes letters or random numbers. Sometimes the visor is bent up, sometimes down. Some kids cut it off altogether.

What I haven't made much progress with yet is exactly *when* the visor faces forward, and when it is turned to the rear. My son won't tell me, but from watching him and the kids in the mall, I notice it is quickly turned when (a) the opposite sex appears or (b) the wearer doesn't know what to do with his or her hands or (c) when a direct question is asked of the wearer. But why were the kids in the next booth at the Lightning Burger wearing theirs sideways?

Such baffling cultural observations, however, were interrupted by the businesslike woman now seated across from me. My first guess had been that she was from a law firm that wanted to retain me. My first guess had been wrong.

"I'm surprised and disappointed." Marianne Dow stirred her pale coffee with one of the Lightning Burger's garish yellow straws. "You'd look into this in a second if there were a body with a bullet or a blade in it. I'm talking about a kind of killing, and you're not *sure* it's something that's appropriate for you to undertake?"

I fumbled. "Well, it's a surprising concept, I guess." I winced even as I said it. Dow, who was a lawyer (at least I'd been right about that) and probably a good one, didn't waste any time making me regret how dumb I sounded.

"Mr. Deleeuw," she said firmly, "I'm not talking about a *concept*. This isn't a Hollywood pitch. I'm talking about a person who is trying to destroy my family just as surely as if she had a gun or a knife. It's been horrible watching my friends' marriages break up—kids seeing their parents torn apart, their lives shattered. One kid smokes too much grass, one is a ten-year-old bed wetter, one never talks. The adults are in therapy or drinking alone. There are wounds that may never completely heal, life savings squandered on lawyers and settlements, homes emptied and sold, pets put to sleep because they can't be moved to apartments. That's a lot of casualties. I won't have my kids added to that list. And I won't be on it myself."

When I'd walked into my office that Monday morning, my secretary—which seems too slight a word for someone as authoritative and iron-willed as Evelyn—hadn't even let me take my coat off. Without as much as saying hello, Evelyn had turned me around and sent me right downstairs to the Lightning Burger to meet Marianne, whom she'd gotten to know during Marianne's weekly visits to the library where Evelyn used to work. I was to see her immediately, Evelyn crisply directed, before I returned my calls, checked the mail, or even drank my coffee. Hiring Evelyn to handle the administration of Deleeuw Investigations has been the best professional move I ever made, if complete loss of control over my own work doesn't count.

At nine A.M. the Lightning Burger's customers are truant kids, the occasional salesman from the Toyota dealership next door, and the gray-hairs in pastel sweat suits and pedometers who enthusiastically trot each morning through the plastic palms of the the American Way for exercise.

At that hour the mall is a retiree's dream. The stores haven't opened yet, so the trotters can't spend any money; security guards make the place feel absolutely safe; and the walking surfaces are generous, flat, and smooth. There are plenty of benches for rest and conversation. At the Lightning Burger my savvy friend Luis Hebron had promptly glimpsed a marketing opportunity and offered The Manager's Early Bird

Breakfast Special—two croissants, juice, and unlimited coffee for $2.30.

Marianne Dow did not fit in, not as a regular. Her looks, clothes, and demeanor all suggested a consummate professional. Her brown hair was longish, but pulled back neatly with a tortoise-shell barrette. She wore a beige cotton blazer and a navy skirt. She looked fit, lean, and firm of chin. Her bright green eyes radiated warmth and humor, but there was nothing deferential or saccharine in them. She didn't root around for the right words, even if the subject wasn't pretty; she said what was on her mind. I understood immediately why Evelyn liked her. I liked her too.

When I'd entered, she'd stood, looked me in the eye, and offered her hand. "Mr. Deleeuw? Thanks for seeing me without an appointment. I'm so grateful. I feel like I'm about to lose everything I care about, and I don't know where to go for help. Evelyn said this was the place. And you know Evelyn —her suggestions seem pretty close to orders." They weren't pretty close to orders, I thought. They *were* orders.

Marianne Dow's story wasn't the stuff of *Rescue 911*, but it had far more punch for anyone whose family provided the central meaning in life, as mine did for me. I had never heard a story quite like it in my relatively few years as a private investigator, yet I never doubted that it was true. The question was, was her problem something I could possibly help with? I was far from sure.

These days I said "no" more often than I said "yes" to prospective clients. This was a sharp and luxurious contrast to my first years in practice. Then the only criterion for becoming my client was being able to dial my office number and sign a check that wouldn't bounce. And I was flexible about the latter.

The attention surrounding the Brown-estate case this winter—the murder of two teenaged kids by a camouflaged town psychotic—had given me the freedom to be a bit pickier. Now I turned down peeping cases; I no longer snooped after cheating husbands or wives. I still said yes—enthusiastically—to tracking down deadbeat dads who'd skipped out on their child support. I remained a sucker for kids in trouble—kidnapped by divorcing parents, stalked by sexual predators, hooked on drugs. I also continued to reap rewards from the modern private investigator's great benefactor, galloping insurance fraud. And with Evelyn de la Cretaz, the former Rochambeau town librarian, firmly in charge, my office was far less chaotic.

The rest of my life was about the same, however. I still got to my office early, grabbed a cup of specially brewed Lightning Burger caffeine, and gazed out at the swelling traffic on Route 6, a clogged suburban artery that runs alongside Rochambeau. I still raced back and forth across town after school and much of Saturday and Sunday, taking Emily and Ben to basketball games, dance classes, and friends' houses. The old Volvo's odometer had 112,000 miles on it.

The mileage piled on in spring. Every kid in town was liberated in late April, perhaps even a little more than usual this year after the fright of the past winter's murder spree, during which most of them were kept under lock and key, let out only under eagle-eyed parental escort. Now those days seemed about as relevant as the Civil War. Kids were outside on every street and in every town park until sunset, running, shrieking, blasting one another with giant water guns, playing in baseball and lacrosse leagues, building hideouts in trees. The notion of unequipped play has vanished. Rochambeau kids require an amazing amount of suburban paraphernalia: caps and hats, color-changing T-shirts, giant designer sneakers, pogo sticks, kites, roller blades and skateboards and mountain bikes on which to tear destructively over obsessively tended lawns.

Spring is the loveliest time in the old town, the growth so lush that on windy days you can see green clouds of pollen drifting onto your car hood. Every house is shrouded in oaks and maples, graced by dogwoods, azaleas, and cherry trees.

It isn't a quiet season, however. Spring marks the beginning of the roaring, howling, and growling of the vast armada of midsized machinery ruthlessly deployed for the next few months to beat back, beautify, and control nature, to throttle weeds, edge lawns, fertilize gardens, trim shrubbery, prune trees, and maim or kill rabbits and moles. (No rodent carnage in my house, though, in part because Emily would have shut down the block in protest, in part because our lawn was way past rescuing.) From now until late October, we would awaken to engines roaring to life, an activity recently and blissfully limited by town ordinance from eight A.M. to six P.M.

Each April my retired neighbor, Charlie Pinski, lovingly tucked plastic tarpaulins over his snowblower and leaf chopper and whirled out his even more formidable summertime arsenal. Once the danger of the last frost passed, Charlie took on the appearance of something out of Desert Storm. Most fearsome was his two-seater mower, which reduced his tiny lawn to Astro Turf and decimated any tranquillity that might have arrived with Saturday mornings. Worse, I was forced to repeatedly admire his machinery, even though I found it wasteful, polluting, and intrusive. But in suburbia, where today's enemy can provide tomorrow's school emergency-contact number, you offend your next-door neighbor only after life-and-death provocation.

Settled into a sleepier, warm-weather Rochambeau routine, perhaps Marianne Dow's story rattled me more than it would have a few weeks earlier. Beyond those meticulously tended lawns and gardens, I was more aware than most how many families had been or were being violently sundered by divorces, affairs, economic pressures, emotional problems, alcoholism, illness. In Rochambeau, I knew, families were, in fact, murdered all the time. And this woman seemed deeply convinced somebody was trying to kill hers.

"It's a horror story, Mr. Deleeuw. I'm as desperate as any suspicious spouse who ever walked into this mall and hired you. I've been to an attorney and a therapist. I've been to my minister. They can't help. Evelyn says you can, that you work wonders."

That took me aback. In my presence Evelyn was more likely to cluck about my sloppy record keeping or my even sloppier office.

"I love my husband very much," Ms. Dow went on, "cement head though he can be at times. I love the house I've been fixing up, that stupid dog Oscar, however much he sheds. I love being with my two kids—except for playing with Ninja Turtles and fighting about food, maybe. I read to them, take them to movies, drive them to music lessons and soccer. In a couple of years I'm going to return to my practice full-time, and I'll be ready to. But for now I cherish my life here. I want to fight for it. I need you to help me. I need you to stop her."

"You see, Mr. Deleeuw . . . okay, *Kit*. I go to an aerobics class. 'Buns of Steel' "—Marianne Dow had the grace to laugh—"the one in the old Women's Club. I'm there three mornings a week, usually. I don't know what it is about these classes, but there's a kind of community there. I think because we're all working hard to keep our bodies healthy. Most of us are in our thirties, went to college and started careers, but are pausing to take care of small children. At least, *I'm* pausing. I'm only working two days a week at my old firm in the city. It's a bite out of our income, my being part-time, but my husband Gil's with a successful small brokerage firm on Wall Street, and he can carry us until our youngest doesn't need an at-home mom anymore. She's five and our son is seven. A lot of the women in the class have kids about the same ages; that's another thing we share.

"There's no diddling about the class." She shot me a warning glance in case I wasn't convinced. "Some days when we leave, we feel like soaked rags. I'm surprised by my own attachment, but it's more than an exercise group. We look out for each other. We encourage one another to stay in shape, to keep at it. If somebody's sick, one of us will check up. We know if somebody's out of work, or having money troubles. . . ." She paused and took a sip from her cup. She seemed direct and open, neither melodramatic nor self-righteous, the way a lot of my prospective clients are.

Three elderly couples padded purposefully into the Lightning Burger in their cream-colored Rockport Walkers and claimed the orange booth across from us. They all ordered the Early Bird Special.

The mall ran seven days a week. It was never completely shut down, not even on Christmas Day, but it did take a breather in the early-morning hours. Now I could see and hear the mall beginning to stir, the normally invisible metal window grates rolling up, the fountains spurting to life, the lite FM wafting from the speakers hidden in the tropical plants, the scraping of tables and chairs being set up in the International Food Court. Murray Grobstein, suburban sneaker king, the right man in the right business at the right time, puffed past. He waved. Outside, the traffic on the highway would be starting to thin. The old folks would be leaving soon, replaced by harried young mothers pushing strollers.

"Naturally," Marianne went on, "some of us in the class have become friends. Our kids play together, and sometimes we shop or play tennis or just get together to talk about, well, anything on our minds. My kids are great—I feel I need to say that—but let's just say they're not all that stimulating to talk to. And despite all of our promises, my friends from the city and I just can't seem to stay in touch."

She sipped her coffee again and winced. She was less agitated than when we'd first met, but her sadness was more pronounced.

It's curious, but lots of people in the suburbs sound apologetic about it. Sometimes they complain about frivolous things—the produce in the supermarket isn't as fresh as the city greengrocers'. Sometimes they are bothered by the in-your-face wealth of certain neighborhoods, their fears about conformity, and the lack of diversity. People like Marianne would probably have stayed in New York City forever.

But kids seem to shatter whatever resolve all but the most resolute and resilient urbanites have to tough it out in the city. All of us put it the same way: here our kids can be free and safe. It's true enough, usually. Kids in Rochambeau lead as happy lives as kids anywhere in the world can possibly lead, even if they risk growing up mostly with people like themselves. (Rochambeau is unusually integrated for suburbia; mostly white, it has growing numbers of blacks and Asians and Hispanics. Nevertheless, almost everybody is middle class.) But some people never quite get over their abandoning-the-ship guilt. Others, of course, are delighted to forget the rest of the world exists, until a trip across the bridge or tunnel into Manhattan feels like a trek to Pakistan.

"Look, let me get to the point," she said. "This is not easy to be discussing with a stranger, believe me. God, in the past two years, five of the women in my aerobics class alone have gotten divorced. I always felt superior to them, so fortunate. . . . We pay for our arrogance, don't we, Mr. Deleeuw? The line between them and us can be crossed in a few hours or days, can't it?" She was watching my reaction, looking, I thought, for signs of discomfort or disapproval. It was too soon for any, but she sure had my attention.

She continued: "A little over a year ago, Gil and I began to have some problems. He seemed increasingly preoccupied. He started wanting to be alone a lot; he stopped asking about me or the kids. I thought he was losing interest in me, in almost every way, but I convinced myself it had to do with some financial troubles his firm was having. He was a million miles away sometimes, and whenever I raised the subject, he'd get annoyed, and then furious. Almost every couple has some problems, I know. Ours didn't feel like stuff we couldn't work out.

"I want to keep my marriage together, for me and for Gil, and for the kids. I want to fight for my marriage—" She was struggling to hold back tears, which made an impression on me. The lawyers I had known weren't given to losing control.

This woman wasn't just talking about marital sniping, that was becoming clear. She was grappling with something else, something she thought could unravel everything she cherished. But what?

"And that's why I've come to you. Because the survival of my family is at stake. She—" Bingo, I thought. I should have known there had to be a she.

"—She insinuated herself into my family. She became my closest friend; she got close to my children. She even walked our dog when we went on vacation."

The nine A.M. chimes went off from somewhere in the mall's ceiling, but the American Way had a timeless quality about it. You could never count the chimes for all the bad music piped in. Opening and closing were signaled by the gushing or stillness of the fountain. But the chimes gave Marianne a chance to steady herself.

"She made herself invaluable to me, a round-the-clock friend and confidante. . . . Then she went for my husband. I don't know—maybe Gil was flattered or confused or feeling vulnerable. I thought we could weather it. Then, in this crazy, fluky way, it all blew up. Gil and I have suddenly gone from having a few problems to seeing our marriage on the verge of collapse, our kids' lives utterly disrupted."

"Excuse me, Marianne, but this person, this woman, how do you know her? Is she in your exercise class?"

She shook her head. "No, not anymore. But she used to be; I met her there. People come in and out as they have kids, go back to work, get tied up in other things. I got more involved in work for a while last winter and dropped out myself for a few months."

I bit off a chunk of the cholesterol-laden home-fry patty that was a specialty of the Lightning Burger and that I was definitely not supposed to be eating. My internist is into grains and vegetables. She has a low opinion of anything fried.

"Marianne, excuse me, I'm not following. You know, I worked on divorce cases for several years. I don't mean to minimize the damage—I know it's horribly traumatic, and it would shatter me if it happened to my family. But people *do* have affairs all the time and split up. There have to be a half-dozen breakups a week in this town. Why do you need a detective? I'll be direct with you. I'm certainly sympathetic, but if you want somebody to snoop on your husband, I'm not your man."

She took a deep breath and considered her response for a good minute or two, struggling to be precise and to convince me of something.

"I'm not making myself clear, Kit. Lawyers are supposed to be clear, but when it's your own life that's falling to pieces, it isn't so easy. Let me try again. I am not concerned about an affair. I could handle that. I'd just give Gil twenty-four hours to end it and get into counseling with me or I'd throw him out. I'm not into being a victim. It took me a long time to see this situation clearly. People have this stereotype of suburban housewives, but I don't sit around all day yakking on the phone. I work hard taking care of my kids, negotiating with doctors, teachers, other parents, running the house, working part-time. So I didn't realize that Andrea—"

"Andrea?"

"Andrea Lucca. The so-called Other Woman. What I'm telling you is that there's something seriously wrong, that this goes beyond normal suburban adultery. Andrea's stalking us, she's going after my family in a dreadful, calculated way."

I remember leaning back a bit, as if to take Marianne in from a longer perspective. In my business you work hard to develop an instinct, a warning bell about people and their real motives. Was she paranoid? Obsessed? Vengeful? Private detectives don't have the greatest public image in the world, but good ones follow clear ethical guidelines. One is that you don't take on clients who are seriously disturbed. You might make some money in the short run, but in the long run it's not worth it.

If she was unbalanced, I thought, maybe I could jar her into showing it. Better to know now than later. "Look, I know I keep sounding skeptical. But what do you say to this notion: that you're a jealous, hurt, and shocked spouse twisting infidelity into something more menacing because it makes you feel better?"

She seemed startled by the question, and her look was long and appraising. "I'm a good mother, a respected attorney, a caring and attentive wife," she countered. "Aside from the normal neurotic anxieties about weight gain and child care, I have never had or been treated for mental disorders. If I had, I would not be ashamed to have gone for help, and I would tell you about it. I am convinced there's something considerably more menacing than a stupid fling going on here."

I nodded. She sure sounded rational. "Tell me again. Exactly what do you believe is going on?"

Marianne pushed her coffee cup aside. She looked very weary. "I feel like a target that she's picked out. She's after my family and I don't know what to do. She's worked herself into every part of my family life. My husband seems more erratic and unstable each day. I'm not just worried about whether my marriage will survive, but whether he will survive. My kids sense something terrible is happening. It's taking a toll on them. She doesn't just want Gil; she wants to rip our lives apart. I don't understand why. I just *feel* she's doing it; my instincts say she *needs* to do it."

"And you want me to find out if those instincts are correct?"

Her eyes met mine unflinchingly. "That's exactly right. I want to hire you to ask around about her. To look into her background, talk to other people who knew her. That's all. Then come back and tell me I'm right or I'm wrong. Because then I'll know. If she isn't disturbed, I am. Because I don't like the way I'm getting to feel. Sometimes I want to break into her home and shake her; sometimes I panic and want to move away. Sometimes . . . I want to kill her."

CHAPTER 2

I have mostly given up on moralizing. And on the majority of people who indulge in it. I have few answers to Life's big questions: God, love, the meaning of existence, the nature of death. But I will concede that on certain issues I am a passionate moralist, and Marianne Dow struck at the heart of one of them.

I believe families—the traditional American foursome, the single parent and kids, the gay couple or the survivalist commune—are sacred. I believe marriage and family constitute a contract that is horrible to violate and one that should be abandoned only after every plausible attempt to save it, especially when children are involved. This perspective is shaped by my work, a great deal of which involves sorting through the wreckage of families once launched in optimism and good faith. My code on this subject remains simpleminded in a complex world of nuance and qualifiers: if you have problems, get as much help as you can find as quickly as you can. If you can't work it out, part company as amicably and compassionately as you are able. But to cheat, lie, or sneak around on a partner—I can't stomach that. In my work I see the victims. My wife, Jane Leon, who is a psychiatric social worker, devotes much of her work to repairing the damage.

I suppose this code is why I never turn down a deadbeat-dad case. If the suckers can't be real fathers, they can at least help take care of the children they helped bring into the world. My most satisfying professional moments come when I track one of these guys to his spiffy new apartment and watch while he writes a child-support check. I have a distinguished batting average on these cases, or so the attorneys who hire me say.

Given my own, non-Republican views on family values, Marianne Dow's story got to me. If Andrea Lucca was, in fact, deliberately targeting the Dows for destruction, Marianne was making a plea from which it was hard to walk away. At the same time, I well understood the limitations of my profession. What can a detective do about a family stalker? Thirty years ago the hard-drinking private eye could have scared the hell out of somebody, even roughed a suspect up a bit. But I shopped, cooked, had two kids in the public schools, paid a mortgage and the bank loans on two Volvo station wagons. One well-drafted lawsuit would take care of my ability to pay for most of that. Not to mention what rough stuff would do to the image of a suburban detective. I have to stand next to neighborhood parents at soccer games.

"The problem is," I said as we stood and carried our trays to the trash bin, "I don't take cases I don't think I can deliver on, Marianne. Every day I see the dumb things men are capable of doing to themselves and their families. I know what happens. But I don't think I've ever heard of a man getting talked out of an affair. It's as if some of them have these amazing self-destruct buttons. Once they're pushed, they can't turn them off."

We walked out into the mall.

Even without the chimes that you could barely hear over the lush orchestral versions of old Four Tops hits, that I could have told that it was a little after nine just by glancing around the plant-bedecked, sun-drenched skylight that covered the walkway between the stores.

The window display at Cicchelli's Furniture is one of my favorites. Arnie Nicoll, its designer, is a frustrated artist. Arnie feels he should be doing Saks's or Bloomingdale's windows, but instead has been condemned to construct appealing living- and dining-room scenarios for "fat shitheads in polyester shirts and big behinds," as he delicately puts it. My own discreetly held view is that Arnie is precisely where he ought to be.

The Cicchelli family of mannikins is Rockwellian—a lacquer-haired Mom crochets while Dad sits reading the paper, and Sis and Chip play Parcheesi on the thick pile carpeting. Arnie's monthly efforts to enliven the nubby tweed sleep sofas and vaguely Maine-like landscapes on the fake walls are heroic. Here is the pioneer suburban family of the fifties, the family everybody thinks they are supposed to have, rather than the markedly more diverse and ungainly ones that stream endlessly past the plate-glass windows.

Cicchelli's windows are a reliable barometer of the economic climate beyond the mall, one I rely on more than the consumer price index. When things get rough, the coffee tables switch from brass to polypropylene, the upholstery from Haitian cotton to durable synthetics. Layaway plans proliferate. Right now the sign promised *Have a Brand New Living Room Tomorrow! Pay Nothing for One Year.* But the Cicchellis appeared content this morning. Their plaster faces were serene. They had no complaints; they were an oasis of stability and good cheer in an uncertain world.

Marianne and I walked over to a bench in front of the fountain—a green cement bowl shaped like a giant clam with three streams of tepid water bubbling up from its center—and sat silently for a moment. She looked discouraged; I wasn't all that optimistic myself.

"So you confided to this Andrea that you and Gil were having problems?"

"Yes, we had met once in aerobics class—the last time Andrea went, I think—and we had gone out to lunch and become friends. She was very sympathetic, or so she seemed. Things were so tense at home. . . . Gil had stormed out of the house for the third morning in a row. He was starting to drink, which he'd never done before, and was scowling at me and the kids constantly. He was like a lit fuse; almost anything could set him off. I was beginning to feel like I couldn't bear up much longer. Every time I started to feel better, things got worse. I was raw. One night I even thought he was going to get violent; he closed his fist as if he were going to. That was completely out of character. He didn't," she added hastily. "I think he knew there would have been no marriage the second he struck one of the kids or me."

The cart concessionaires began their morning parade through the center of the mall to set up their displays. Some marketing whiz had figured out that there was empty space in front of the stores in the mall and that lots of minor entrepreneurs—jewelers, T-shirt decorators, florists—who didn't do enough business to rent stores could set up in the interstices. In the highest traditions of mall ingenuity, all had cellular phones and took credit cards, and had become permanent fixtures of the American Way—Retail Gypsies, the mall merchants called them.

"Anyway," said Marianne, "Andrea sensed that I was on the edge when she called one day to ask me to lunch. She has a remarkable ability to tune into pain or tension. She said, 'Look, I can hear you're in trouble. Let's go get a cup of coffee right now.' Three hours and five gallons of tears later, there wasn't anything she didn't know about my marital life."

Andrea became her only confidante, Marianne said. From her Andrea learned that Gil Dow's brokerage firm was in trouble, that he was growing more distant and irritable—and drinking more. Andrea started calling Marianne several times a day, took her out for dinner once a week. She sent books by psychologists and toys for the kids. She plied Marianne with upbeat tales of successful marriage counseling, implored her to hang in there, relieved the stress with concert tickets and movies. A model friend, one who almost daily went beyond the call of duty. A friend to depend on, to trust.

A few weeks ago, Marianne went on, after another wrenching battle over Gil's increasingly abusive behavior, Marianne's car began sputtering and had to go into the shop. She borrowed Gil's. Crumpled on the backseat was the gray Vassar sweatshirt that Andrea always wore. She couldn't recall an occasion when Andrea would have been in Gil's car.

With that discovery Gil's increasingly frequent evenings at work abruptly acquired a different context. So did his lengthening early-morning and late-night "jogs," his long conversations behind closed doors on his work phone. Marianne fell silent. Then she said, "I told myself I was being paranoid, that there could be several perfectly good reasons why Gil would have Andrea's sweatshirt, but on some level, of course, my instincts told me otherwise . . . I just knew the truth. I've heard that most women in that position do.

"I know Gil sounds pretty awful, but he really has a lot of lovely qualities, Kit. He can be gentle and thoughtful and sensitive. He loves our children deeply. Maybe we can't work it out, but I have to make sure, before I inflict this damage on all of us. If we separate, I want it to be the two of us who decide to do it, not some, some . . . alien who breaks us up. Only a monster would do that to another woman." Her eyes filled with tears. She had a lot of betrayal to assimilate—her husband's and her best friend's.

Marianne's pain over her marital troubles was deep, naturally. Oddly, I felt a stab of envy. Men could feel betrayed by one another, but with no male equivalent of sisterhood, there is little sense of community to violate. I went back into Lightning Burger, ostensibly to get Marianne another cup of coffee, mostly to give her a moment to compose herself. By the time I returned, she could force a smile.

"Evelyn told me you would take this case." The lawyerly cool was reasserting itself. "She said you understand what a family means."

I nodded. I didn't think her comment was calculated, but even if it had been, it was pretty effective. "I appreciate that. But there's no guarantee that I can find out anything about Andrea Lucca that would be dramatic enough to shock your husband out of his infatuation. And even if I could, I assure you that people don't respond rationally in situations like this. I see how painful this is for you now, Marianne, but marital problems are quagmires. They require counseling, patience, trust—not investigative work. A detective learns that right off the bat." Especially, I thought, one who's married to a psychiatric social worker.

Simply inquire into Lucca's background, Marianne beseeched me, her voice low and controlled. At the very least it would help her understand with what she was dealing. Then she fished through her purse and tried to hand me a check. Two thousand dollars—Evelyn must have told her that was my retainer. But I wouldn't take it, at least not yet. I agreed only to check around a bit, without committing myself.

I admired her, though. Furious at her husband, stunned by a close friend's treachery, she was nevertheless prepared to try to slog through the pain to hold her family together. Under similar circumstances, I suspected that Jane, who loves me a lot, would have booted me out before you could say "sweatshirt."

When I returned to my second-floor office, Evelyn and I didn't exchange a word about Marianne Dow. Evelyn's look clearly said: *You'd better help this woman if you want to know peace.*

I was gone most of the day on an insurance-fraud stakeout, a juicy one, involving a twenty-nine-year-old alleged paraplegic who'd filed a twelve-million-dollar claim against a trucking company after a car crash but who had unaccountably ordered an Exercycle from the local bike shop three weeks ago. My computer mole Willie had come across the purchase during one of his computer searches, the details of which I didn't know and didn't want to know. If you put your ear to the shuttered window facing my "victim's" backyard, as I had for the past several mornings, you could often hear those tires whirring. Since the only other person in the house was eighty-three, my keen investigative instincts made me suspicious.

But my talk with Marianne kept nagging at me all day, all the more so when I went to the Lucretia Mott Elementary School to pick up Emily and ferry her to her modern-dance class. How could you not help somebody who was struggling to hold a family together?

Em came padding across the schoolyard, her head lowered, her gazillion-pound book bag bearing down on her shoulder. Rather than dash back and forth to her locker through the day to fetch the books she needed, she carried all of them around all the time.

Although Em was still two years from junior high, I was getting sad about what everyone warned me would be the beginning of some turbulent years. As it was, I was no longer allowed to sit next to my daughter in movie theaters or to remain in the room while she used the phone. As had happened with her older brother, Ben, her replies to questions had become more monosyllabic, her attentions focused more on her peers and their bizarre ways. She had lately discovered that Daddy wasn't a mythic figure of wisdom and strength, but a mortifying blockhead, albeit one with a car and a wallet. Meanwhile, the first boy had already called, tongue-tied and panic-stricken when not Emily but I answered the phone.

Ben, already in junior high and well along in this process, would rather slice off a toe than be seen with a parent, although he would open up occasionally and we would have wide-ranging philosophical talks about music and ancient times like the Reagan presidency. Most of Ben's politics revolved around two rap groups and a band from Seattle.

But Emily would still now and again fling herself into my arms with the sweetest, most absolute conviction in the world that she would be caught. I would miss her during these prickly adolescent years. But I knew that we were tight as ticks. She'd come back when she was ready; I'd be there.

During the first few years of Em's life I shuttled back and forth to Wall Street, busing her beautiful sleeping face when I got home, rushing around to zoos and movies on weekends to try to catch up.

Pleasures I'd missed until I came to private investigating via an unconventional route. Like everybody else on Wall Street in the eighties, my firm was making money faster than we could count it. Then one Tuesday morning, it seemed that the entire FBI had crashed into our brokerage. They hauled off everything we weren't wearing and a few of the things we were. My boss and colleagues were all indicted, tried, and convicted of insider trading. The U.S. attorney threatened to send me to jail forever if I didn't testify against my former workmates. The fact that I had committed no crime and wasn't aware of any being committed did not seem to slow the prosecutors down a whit.

My lawyer got me a deal: no testimony and no further prosecution if I agreed to abandon Wall Street forever. I refused to testify, and I didn't want to be hounded by the feds for the rest of my life, so I took the deal and became the most downwardly mobile wage earner on my block. The only other work I'd ever done was criminal investigations back in my army days, and now I grasped at it. Prosperity and security were out of the question, but survival seemed remotely possible.

Jane went back to work as a social worker in a Paterson mental-health clinic, taking graduate courses at night to become a psychologist. We learned the attraction of home-equity money and borrowed to the hilt, holding our breath and clinging to the notion that we would come out the other end with a roof over our heads and the appropriate sneakers for our kids. Lots of people learned that transitions like mine —from a Wall Street trader's job to the income of a private investigator with no clients—was like a jump from the top of a cliff with no parachute.

From the first, I loved my office on the second floor of the American Way Mall. I became fast friends with Luis Hebron, a once-famous criminal lawyer who had fled Castro's Havana and now managed the Lightning Burger ("Food In A Flash"), handling his reduced circumstances with admirable

dignity. I had more time for friendship now, spending at least
one lunch hour a week in the fragrant greenhouse behind the
Rochambeau Garden Center with Benchley Carrollton, its elderly Quaker proprietor and another of my assorted cadre of
pals and advisers.

Millions of people lost their jobs in the eighties and suffered, some of them terribly. But those of us who ended up
working without bosses wondered how we had ever survived
them as long as we had. I loved the freedom of being on my
own. I especially loved becoming the primary caretaker of my
kids.

If someone were out to bust up my family, I could barely
imagine how frightened I'd be.

My daughter and I ran through our after-school drill on
the drive across town.

"How was school?"

"Good."

"Any news?"

"Nope. Oh, one thing. Billy asked me out."

"What?"

"Billy asked me out." She squirmed out of her denim
jacket and wrestled her book bag onto the floor, accepting a
handful of dried apricots with a nod.

"Oh?" I said, my voice rising a touch. "Well, what did
you *tell* Billy?"

"Oh, nothing . . . Just that we should get together and
have lots of SEX!"

I couldn't pinpoint the exact moment Em totally stopped
taking me seriously. Maybe it was gradual. " 'Bye, Dad. Love
ya!" She smiled, got out of the car, and waltzed off into
Gotta Dance, where she would shortly be expressing herself
with a dozen of her artsy suburban sisters.

It was close to eight before we were all assembled as a

family in our decaying old frame house, and even when we were, everybody was too busy to do more than say hello on their way past one another. Monday was one of Jane's later nights at the clinic; Ben had basketball practice till seven-thirty; and Em had holed up in the basement after dinner to start painting her Popsicle-stick model of the Parthenon. I would look into Marianne's home-wrecker in the morning.

CHAPTER 3

I knew only two things about Andrea Lucca when I began investigating her. The first was that she worked as a graphic artist in an architectural firm just outside Rochambeau, and the other was that she'd once attended aerobic classes at Buns of Steel. When I called the architects' office, a yawning receptionist said Lucca was away and that she didn't know when she would return. "She doesn't tell us when she's coming in anyway," the receptionist said. Her tone suggested only an idiot wouldn't already know that.

The two architects Lucca worked for weren't in, either, but I made an appointment to see one of them later in the week. The receptionist didn't ask what the meeting was in reference to, and obviously didn't care. People like her were good for people like me; they let you come and go as you pleased. That left only one other logical place to start.

As I drove toward Buns of Steel, I decided there was nothing manipulative about Marianne Dow's appeal for help. She had challenged me directly enough, and right in the place it most counted. Despite my discomfort with a potential messy marital investigation, I couldn't quite find a rationale for refusing her. Check Andrea Lucca out, Marianne had asked, and if I found nothing to justify her suspicions, then drop it. It was fuzzy and unfamiliar ground. Here was a client I liked and instinctively trusted handing me a case I normally would avoid like the plague. The likeliest scenario was that Lucca was having an affair with Gil Dow. That was understandably profoundly upsetting for Marianne.

Yet she was unshakable in her conviction that there was something more sinister, more calculated, going on. That it wasn't just her husband Lucca was after, but her kids, her house. Her life. I didn't know what I would find, but my best guess was that Lucca would be a person whom I didn't like very much, but who was no more nor less sinister than any cheating husband's paramour who kept private investigators hopping from one rendezvous to another with motorized cameras and telephoto lenses.

Buns of Steel was located in the Rochambeau Women's Club, a monument to the genteel strangulation of early suburban life.

Not that the steel-bunned knew much about that. Since the suburbs tend to turn over every few years when the latest crop of the Child Obsessed arrive, fleeing their cramped brownstones and private-school tuitions, while their late-middle-aged and now childless predecessors shed their Colonials and Victorians for condos and apartments elsewhere, hardly anybody knows the history of the town. Benchley Carrollton, my Garden Center buddy, does. His family settled in this county shortly after the ink dried on the Mayflower Compact. Benchley had told me that the Women's Club building was more than a century old, erected when women's roles as tenders of the home and keepers of the hearth were as clear as they were oppressive.

Predictably, Jane reacted to the Women's Club the way an East German would have to the Berlin Wall, pointing out the sprawling clapboard building gravely to Emily whenever we drove past as a tragic reminder of a time when women's only break from the all-consuming task of serving and satisfying their irritable and demanding husbands was a quiet bridge game.

Jane would shake her head and commiserate somberly with the ghosts of women past. "But for the Grace of God," she always murmured, clutching Em's hand. As a consequence, I learned Em told her friends the club was haunted. And it was, I guess.

Rochambeau's upper-crust women—including my secretary Evelyn de la Cretaz's elderly aunts—had come there to lunch, to have tea, to play cards, to sew for the poor, and to compare food and fashion tips.

But much of that function had collapsed in the sixties and seventies. The women's movement hit suburbia and made such places anachronistic. The club had more recently become a sort of lifestyle mall. It was host to twelve-step and dieting programs, workshops in single parenting, and the Rochambeau Adult School, whose classes ranged from lectures on Matisse to imaginative bean preparations. And, in what had once been a dining room, to Buns of Steel.

I could hear the music thumping all the way out in the parking lot, featuring a voice of indeterminate gender urging me to shake that body. The double glass doors opened into a hallway papered with leaflets and announcements of community activities. A second door opened into a large room, in which it was hard to imagine that ladies ever nibbled finger sandwiches and sipped tea.

Two massive speakers thundered from opposite corners of the mirrored room. A statuesque, authoritative woman was marching ferociously in place and barking orders: "Knees up, pump those arms, *rev* it up, ladies!" Roberta Bingham's brown hair, escaping from a pony tail, was streaked with gray, and she'd made no attempt to rinse the streaks away. She looked to be nearly six feet tall, and her body was angular and terrifyingly firm. She wore hightop pink Reeboks, some sort of stretchy black leggings, and a T-shirt emblazoned with the motto "Sweat, Pain & Sacrifice." Underneath were the letters "BoS" and the class logo, a perspiring training shoe.

Looking around me, I felt a bit soft. So far I'd gotten by on genes. I'm tall, an inch over six feet, and I'm still on the thin side, although I know it's time to start thinking of some regular exercise. Jane says I look like a college history professor on the eve of tenure—attractive, informal, just a hair short of handsome. At least that's what she says. I think it's a compliment. But I did not have muscles like these women.

About fifteen of them—black and white, some young, some gray-haired, one very pregnant—marched and pranced, squatted and stretched, stepped and jumped along with Roberta Bingham. What would those meticulously coiffed, white-gloved Women's Club ladies say to this group? Roberta shouted a stream of paramilitary reprimands and corrections and incomprehensible exhortations to "grapevine" and "heeljack."

Like the ad says, this was no dance class. The students were sweaty and red-faced but fiercely determined. I could see calf muscles pressing against leotards, noticeable biceps, buns that were, well, as advertised. These women looked tough and healthy and well drilled, long past the point where I could have remained upright. I felt squishy and gone to seed. I wouldn't have wanted to run into any of them in a dark alley.

Fifteen minutes, many tummy crunches, and a cool-down

later, Bingham and I were facing one another in a Spartan office off the mirrored studio. "I'm sorry about how ugly this room is." She dropped into a patched vinyl armchair, wiped her face with a towel, and swigged from a Buns of Steel water bottle. "At night this place is the twelve-step capital of the world, a meeting place for the abused of the universe. Alcoholics, children of alcoholics, pets of alcoholics, people who've been hit, starved and beaten, suffered incest . . . You name it. Bright colors and comfortable chairs would be inappropriate, I suppose."

Her sinewy arms shone with sweat, but she was not out of breath. She might have been thirty-six or fifty-two or anywhere in between.

"You sound like you're not a fan of twelve-step programs."

"Not so," she said, gulping more water and leaning back in the chair. "You're talking to a recovering alcoholic. AA saved my life. Problem now is, the twelve-steps are overrun by people in pain in search of an addiction to go with it. In most meetings you can hardly find anybody hooked on booze anymore. They all want to get up and talk about how their uncles or parents or baby-sitters must have abused or frightened them. In this country everybody wants to be a victim, you know?"

I thought about it. The Buns of Steel group didn't look much like victims. More like some suburban commando unit in training, waiting for the call to liberate members of their gender from obtuse husbands and abusive bosses who didn't get it.

"So," she said briskly, with a glance at her watch she didn't bother to disguise, "I've got fifteen minutes before my next class piles in. You're looking into our little community, Marianne Dow tells me."

"She called you?"

Bingham nodded.

"I guess I'd like to know about Andrea Lucca," I told her.

She shook her head. "Yes, that's what Marianne told me. I'm not comfortable talking about the women who take these classes, usually, but Marianne was pretty forceful. . . ." She didn't look happy about it, though.

"And I guess I need to know a bit about your classes," I added, pulling out my notebook.

She wrapped the towel around her neck and scowled up at the ceiling. "I am very fond of Marianne," she reminded herself, the inference being that if she wasn't, I'd be starting up the Volvo by now. "Andrea, I don't know as well. There's something—" She looked troubled, as if something was bugging her but she couldn't quite put her finger on what it was. She shrugged it off.

"The reason I'm cautious is, this is a lot more than a job to me, Mr. Deleeuw. My history is brief and spectacular. If you're a detective, you'll find it out anyway. I was a housewife in Glen Ridge. I had let my teaching certificate expire. For ten years I spent my life on the phone with women who had nothing to do but call each other and get hysterical about chicken pox, snow days, teachers—whatever, it didn't really matter. We lived in phobia land. We even nicknamed one of us the Phobic Queen. She was afraid of ticks, street crossings, interstates, outdoor cats, planes, being alone, burglars, AIDS. Her kid had to fight to go to the bathroom alone when he was six. At the time, believe it or not, it didn't seem that odd. When you don't have a life, you hijack somebody else's, and your kids are handy and defenseless. They really can't tell you to get your own life and stop devouring theirs. I don't mean to say all housewives are wackos; if it's your calling and you genuinely love it, then you're doing God's work, and you know when to leave your kids alone.

"Me, I had three kids, and taking too much care of them all those years made me take a daily swim in alcohol. I screamed a lot, hit them now and then, lived in a fog. One night about eight years ago, I passed out while smoking. I burned the house down."

She paused. I stopped writing and met her gaze. "One of my daughters is still getting skin grafts," she added, watching to see how shocked or disapproving I would be.

I would not want to carry that baggage around, but if I had to, I hoped I would do so as gracefully as Roberta Bingham.

"My husband got custody of the kids—I didn't fight it— and moved them to St. Paul. I call every Sunday and visit them in the summer, but they don't want to visit me here. I don't blame them, even though I'm sober now. And I'm a feminist."

She stood and stretched the muscles in her right calf. "I'm middle-aged now, too. If I don't limber up, I'll go back out and cramp up like a pretzel."

She switched to her left leg. "When I finally got my act together, I decided to translate all of this into something positive. I decided to build a business and a community for women, a safe place where we could stay healthy, be strong, use our energy in positive ways, and maybe support one another a bit, as well. . . . It's pretty transparent, isn't it? They became my new family."

She had put her hands on her hips and was rocking back and forth on her heels. "They call me at all hours. When their husbands have affairs, when their kids get picked on in school or lock themselves in their rooms, when the boss is a pig, when they get crazy from having no lives of their own or having too many lives, balancing work and family and all, I hear them out. Mostly, though, I just try to keep them in shape. It helps, feeling strong.

"I care a lot about what happens to the women who come here, Mr. Deleeuw, and not just when they're jumping up and down out there. That's why there's a waiting list to get in. I take only twenty women in a class, and I run only three classes a day. I allow time after the workouts so we can talk and get to know one another. I know the name of every woman in each of my classes and usually a lot more besides. It does not make me happy to think that coming here might be harmful to any of them."

There was no doubting the conviction behind that statement. Her eyes had been boring into me as she talked, perhaps taking in my uniform: chinos, blue shirt, blue blazer. I do not possess a diverse wardrobe. On weekends and around the house or the mall, I take off the blazer. I wear L. L. Bean mocs every day of the year; I haven't put a tie on since I left Wall Street. Roberta Bingham was checking out more than my clothes, though. Women need to know just what kind of man you are these days, I guess.

I wasn't shocked by her story; even before I was run out of Wall Street, I knew bad things happen to good people. I considered myself one of them. I had seen a lot of people in the suburbs ravage themselves and those around them, then take their lives apart and glue them back together.

In that sense people in towns like Rochambeau are lucky; they have the education and money to change when they have to. Often the thing they don't have is the emotional support to do so. Maybe sweating with Bingham and her marching minions helped. In any case, she would be a great source for me. By her own admission, she knew much more than the physical measurements of the people who joined her class. But her loyalty was fierce. She'd need a lot of convincing.

"Ms. Bingham, Marianne Dow came to me for help. Did she tell you why?"

"No. She just said she needed your help badly and that you'd probably be calling or coming around. That she hoped I would help you as much as I comfortably could. We didn't go into details."

"Well, it's an odd situation, even by the elastic standards of my work. I won't go into it more than I need to, either, but what would be helpful is for me to learn something about Andrea Lucca. That would be helpful to Marianne, too. It's personal stuff, as I'm sure you've inferred. Marital stuff."

She nodded. "Anything I can," she said, again cautiously.

"Did you know Andrea Lucca well?"

"No. She seemed friendly; she worked hard. Some of the women who come here are in transition. For a lot of them, getting in shape is a metaphor for pulling themselves together. They've just had babies, they're trying to stay sober. Quite a few are divorced and suddenly in the dating game. Some are worried about staying attractive. And, of course, some are just busy women who want to keep their bodies in shape and stay healthy. But a lot of women who come here are needy. They talk to me or to members of the class. They hang around in the changing area or the parking lot.

"Andrea Lucca seemed to find these women, or they seemed to find her. She was a listener, not a talker. People came to her, and she was receptive, but she didn't seem in need herself. She rarely talked to me, for instance, whereas Marianne often made it a point to talk with me for a couple of minutes. I encourage that in my students, because it often tells me something that helps me design the right program for them. A recovering alcoholic should be treated differently from somebody who's just had a baby, you get what I mean?"

I nodded. But I knew I had only fifteen minutes, and five of them were already gone.

"Look, Ms. Bingham. Marianne has suggested to me that Andrea Lucca set out to wreck her family. Not just steal her husband, but deliberately demolish her family. Does that seem conceivable to you?"

Roberta Bingham was so guarded, I felt I had to shock her to get her to open up. Her eyes widened with that statement.

"Trying to get my attention, huh? Well, you sure did. I mean, I have no way of knowing whether Andrea would or wouldn't do something like that, but it's a shocking thing to hear about anybody. What a horrible idea—especially in a place designed to help women get healthy." But Bingham added quickly (too quickly?), she didn't know Lucca well and couldn't really be all that helpful. She thought Marianne Dow was honest, caring, and "exceptionally well grounded. If Marianne told me something, I would be inclined to believe it, I'll tell you that. I didn't like Andrea, I'll be candid about that. She seemed to be everybody's friend, which, to me, meant she wasn't anybody's. She seemed a little false to me, always so upbeat. But that's hardly grounds to think she could be so malevolent. . . ."

I persisted. "Look, this is important. Is it conceivable to you that Andrea Lucca could deliberately set out to bust up somebody's home life?"

She leaned back and locked both of her hands behind her head. She thought about it long and hard.

"There was something sort of calculating, sort of strained about her. She would never relax. You did get the impression that she was never quite real. But that's a far cry from what you're talking about. I'm sorry: guess the most honest answer is, I didn't really trust Andrea myself, but I just don't know."

I respected her for that. There wasn't any point in pushing it, at least not so openly.

"When did Andrea join the class?"

Bingham opened a drawer, leafed through some index cards. "About eighteen months ago."

"And Marianne?"

Marianne had been working out with the class for about seven months.

"But they met here."

Roberta fiddled with her index cards. "I don't really know. Their files show a brief overlap in membership, a couple of months, but I don't think either of them was attending religiously at the time, especially Andrea."

"What *is* Andrea Lucca like?" I asked, trying a new tack. Or maybe just the same one again.

She stretched her legs again. "She's striking to look at, quite appealing, thin, lovely, really. I remember she always wore bandannas wrapped over her hair. She always wore layers of sweats and shirts; she liked to sweat a lot, I remember that. Wonderful energy, probably the best stamina of anyone I've had in the class in several years. I do remember someone telling me that Andrea was always interested in what was happening to you, in your problems, but she never gave anything back. Never tired of wanting to know all about how you were, but when you asked how she was, she was always 'fine.' But that's really hearsay, I'm afraid. I didn't notice much. She wasn't here that often, and I didn't talk to her much."

"Were you aware of her friendship with Marianne?"

"Not really. I had a sense of her as a supportive, sympathetic person. But you know, in a community like this, I can only get so deep into people's problems. I've got more than one hundred fifty women coming here at various times on various days. When marriages start to rot or you see drinking or abuse, about all you can do is send them into therapy, help keep their bodies in shape to deal with the stress, then hope their friends will rally round. That's why I'm horrified by what you said about Andrea. It would be a gross breach of trust, a complete perversion of what this community is all about."

"Would you be willing to give me a list of women who've attended your classes in the past couple of years?"

Her hesitation was palpable.

"Here's why I'm asking," I hurried on. "In order to help Marianne, I need to learn as much as I can about Andrea Lucca. If Marianne is wrong about Andrea, I need to tell her so and straighten her out. Which I'll do. If she's right . . . well, I guess she needs to know that too. A marriage, a home, and two kids are at stake. It's important. I don't need to tell you that." I was never any good at pressuring people. But when I felt I was on the right side, I could be persuasive.

Bingham sighed and reached for her water bottle. "I appreciate that, Mr. Deleeuw, but there's no way I'm going to hand you a list. I can't have the women who come here being called by a stranger, a private detective at that, and being asked questions about other members of the class. They'd go through the roof, they'd have every right to. I'm sorry Marianne is having personal problems, but that's no justification for violating the privacy of everybody who comes here."

"Is there any way you can help me that you're comfortable with? Even the names of a few women who might have been Andrea Lucca's friends would be useful. I'll be as discreet as I can be. Look, Marianne is desperate, she's alone out there. She needs somebody's help—if not a detective's, then maybe a shrink's. If somebody's after her family in the way she thinks—"

Bingham cut me off. "Forget it, Mr. Deleeuw."

"Look," I said, speaking softly, but meeting her gaze. "If you think about it, you'll realize that I will get the names, one way or the other. Marianne can get me started, and I can take it from there. I would hate to jot down license-plate numbers in your parking lot, but I could do that, too. . . ." This was the part I wasn't good at, and I just hoped she didn't suspect it.

"And I could haul your ass into court," she snapped, her eyes blazing.

"Yes," I agreed, apologetically. "You could sue me, but I'm sure you don't have a legal fund any more than I do. I'm trying to help one of your people, not hurt anyone. Please, let's not battle with one another. Help me to help her."

We were both silent for a long minute. I tried to make my gaze as steely as hers, but I doubted that I succeeded. Still, I meant it, and I think, as smart as she was, she saw that. Logic was on my side. Bingham seemed to come to the same conclusion, even if she didn't like it.

"There's one thing I'd be willing to do, I guess. I'll give you a list of women I think were in the class at the same time, and who I think were Andrea's friends. It's better than your calling people up out of the blue. But I want you to promise me that you won't badger them. If they don't want to talk, that's it. In exchange you can tell them to call me if they want and I'll urge them to cooperate. That's the best I can do. And I promise you, Mr. Deleeuw, if you bug or hurt these women, I will take what little cash I have and sue your pants off. Deal?"

We shook on it.

The green sheet she gave me had eight names on it. Lord knows how I'd approach them. *Excuse me, I'm a private detective and I'd like to know if one of your dear friends is out to destroy the personal life of one of your exercise classmates?* Maybe something a bit more subtle.

Before I ran out of time, I managed to ask Bingham a few questions about the first three women on her list.

Gay Tannenbaum was a housewife who moved to Rochambeau from New York City with her lawyer husband. She'd joined the class at the same time as Lucca, then dropped out six months later when her marriage fell apart. Donna Platt, once an advertising copywriter, had signed up several months after that and stopped coming for the same reason. Diane Hathaway joined a month before Lucca.

Gay Tannenbaum had lived on Gateway Street, a wide tree-lined avenue, when she first joined Buns of Steel, Bingham told me. But she'd moved to Magnolia, which I recognized as one of Rochambeau's more modest streets, where several garden-apartment complexes had been built. Bingham had heard that Gay might be working part-time at a rehab hospital.

"Of this group, who still comes to the class?"

Bingham ran her eye down the sheet. "Lois Herman. Phyllis Seeger. Diane Hathaway. Gay and Donna, no, not since their divorces. I think they have to watch their pennies these days."

She'd called each of them, as she usually did when faithful exercisers went a week or two without showing up. Tannenbaum had burst into tears, stammered that her marriage was over, and hung up. Platt had never returned Bingham's calls.

"It's a damn shame, if it's true. This is supposed to be a healthy place for women." Her concern for her students was obvious, but I was disappointed. She hadn't really let me know whether she believed Marianne or not, and I was certain she had an opinion. I had some leads, but still no sense at all about whether Andrea Lucca was capable of doing what Marianne was accusing her of.

Bingham sagged in the chair and seemed, for the first time, deflated and a bit defeated. "I know it's ridiculous, but I feel partly responsible for what happens to them all. I've already destroyed my own family. These women come here to be healthy, and they trust me. Why would she do it? What could motivate a woman to turn on another woman that way? I expect that from—"

A man? "Well, one caution, Ms. Bingham," I said. "We don't know for sure that anything *has* happened. It could just be a rough patch in Marianne's marital life; she could be mistaken about Andrea. That's what I want to learn more about. That's why I appreciate your help.

"Can you see Lucca as a disturbed person, somebody who would destroy a family?" It's amazing how many times people will respond to a question on the third or fourth pass, after they've refused to discuss it. Roberta Bingham, however, wasn't one of them.

"Maybe," she said, reluctantly, getting up to join her class. "I don't mean to pretend I saw that quality you're describing in her. I didn't. But anybody who wrecks families in her spare time is a psycho in my book, if what Marianne says is true. Instead of a knife, she uses friendship and trust. Probably worse, don't you think?"

CHAPTER 4

To Evelyn's delight, some instinct prodded me to spend the rest of the morning and much of the afternoon at the mall, plowing through my paperwork and reports. A kind of deck clearing, just in case Marianne Dow's problem did translate into a plausible case. I guess in a way it already had; I just hadn't officially recognized it.

I had three reports to file in employee theft cases, a corporate security check to type up, two surveillance reports on fraud cases for insurance companies, and a deposition to prepare in a deadbeat-dad case.

I barely took a lunch break. Usually, the food court at the American Way, featuring such attractions as Totally Tacos and Lox Around the Clock, is a mecca for both people-watchers and fried-food aficionados. I'm both, but today I went downstairs just long enough to stretch my legs and grab a frozen yogurt. Then I waded in again.

Towards five I was actually caught up, or thought I was. "Good work." Evelyn beamed uncharacteristically. I could

count the times she had praised my administrative abilities:
twice, I think. Maybe never.

"But you still have seven calls to return," she continued
firmly, as if my businesslike diligence might evaporate at any
second. Disorder and procrastination, the cornerstones of my
administrative philosophy, were against Evelyn's religion. It
also made her a little nuts, I think, that I darted back and
forth on domestic errands all day. Evelyn had spent too many
years in the library to have much regard for children or their
demanding schedules. In a child-obsessed town like Rochambeau, I found this almost refreshing. Evelyn's nose would
actually wrinkle if I tried to tell cute stories about Ben or
Emily. Not that that stopped me.

"And the insurance company wants the report on the
Dineen case, and they want it ASAP. The case goes to trial in
two weeks."

So much for complimenting my diligence.

James Dineen had embezzled six hundred thousand dollars from a famous department store with a branch near Rochambeau. I had tracked him down; he was playing lots of
golf under an assumed name in Hilton Head. His lawyers
would surely negotiate a plea, but until they did, the attorneys
for Northern Life Insurance Company had to prepare to go
to court. To do that, they needed my report, which would
have to obscure the fact that I'd located Dineen through my
secret investigative weapon, Willie the computer freak. Even
Evelyn didn't know of Willie's existence.

"Evelyn, I'm sorry. I've got other things I have to attend
to. Just stall Northern for a day or two. Anyway, this your
goddamn fault. It's Marianne's case I've got to pursue. At
your insistence," I added huffily.

For once the tables were turned. Evelyn was left mumbling as I dropped my reports on her desk and went back into my inner sanctum. Flipping through the phone directory, I started calling the names on my Buns of Steel list.

No answer at Gay Tannenbaum's. Diane Hathaway hung up on me: "I met Andrea DeLucca in exercise class, never talked to her about anything, and wouldn't tell you if I had." O-kay, at least we're clear.

At Donna Platt's I got an answering machine. Something about her recorded voice sounded sad. On impulse I decided to drive over and see where and how she lived.

The address was 122 Bayview, in the older end of town. Here the Victorians were small, the shade trees old and huge, and real-estate values out of sight.

Donna Platt and her two kids were still living there, but probably wouldn't be much longer, Bingham had told me. Since her divorce Donna had begun working again in a Ridgewood ad agency, but only part-time, and her ex-husband Stan couldn't afford to support two households in Rochambeau. So she was thinking of selling the house and moving to a double-decker in Rosewall, a working-class town a couple of miles south. You could have a perfectly decent life in Rosewall, but the dislocation would be tough.

Rochambeau has lots of things for kids to attach themselves to—great schools, beautiful parks, ball. fields all over town, a child-centered culture that attends their every need for physical, creative, or social expression. There are droves of kids on Bayview, and the Platt children would soon have to leave their friends and their hockey league. It seemed the death of a kind of dream.

I could have found the house without a number. In Rochambeau house and lawn tending are the primary male hobbies, a matter of pride and recreation as well as considerable investment. Gutters are cleaned, porch steps repainted annually, trees pruned within an inch of their lives, autumn leaves whisked away in biodegradable bags within days of hitting the ground.

When a house is looking worn, when the paint is flaking and nobody has gotten to the hedges this spring or last fall, it is often a sign either that the family is broke or that the man has left or taken ill or died.

The house at 122 Bayview looked frayed. The grass was ankle-high, a supermarket circular was caught in one of the privet hedges, and last fall's leaves and twigs still cluttered the gutters. Adding to the sense of desolation, the blinds were all drawn. But the Platts were clearly still in residence: balls, tricycle, and a whiffle bat lay scattered by the front door.

I lucked out. A battered old Honda hatchback, cheaper cousin to the Volvos and vans that whizzed back and forth across town, was just pulling into the driveway. A young boy popped out of the passenger side and rushed toward the backyard. A younger brother in shorts and a "Wayne's World" T-shirt jumped out in hot pursuit. The woman yelled some caution in the familiar tone of Rochambeau parents: be careful about the street, about puddles, about large dogs, strangers, etc.

Donna Platt was short and stocky, with Dutch-boy hair and a big pair of square black eyeglasses, which seemed too large for her face. She'd probably hurried directly from work —she was wearing a black silk blouse and pants with leather flats—to the supermarket, to child pickup. No wonder she looked weary. A weathered briefcase tumbled out of the car onto the ground. She saw me sitting in my car as she was reaching in for a grocery bag. She paused, openly staring at me.

She could have been me, three or four afternoons a week. After work you run off to the A & P to pick up a few things for dinner, always startled that you've bought twice as many things as you'd planned, wondering how you could have forgotten half of what you went to buy, amazed at how much two children can eat and how quickly the pretzels, oranges, cucumbers, and carrots melt away.

You stuff the bags into the car, rushing to retrieve your kid after his or her lesson or game. You land in your driveway hoping you haven't forgotten anything essential. Dinner is a scramble. No matter how many dicta you lay down, everyone in the house wants something different.

At our house Jane is invariably late for supper, leaving me fuming over soggy green beans, limp pasta, or charred chicken. For me the goal of getting four nutritious, reasonably tasty meals in freshly cooked condition into four people at approximately the same time is rarely attainable . . . unless you have pizza delivered, which I do as often as I can in good conscience.

I had to decide whether to take off, or to talk to Donna Platt. Investigators don't have bylaws and training manuals to go by, as cops do; they have to trust their instincts. Mine said to get out of the Volvo and introduce myself, especially since she was likely to jot down my license number anyway and ask the police to check it out. That would bring a sarcastic call from Chief Leeming, who lived for those moments when he could tuck it to me. I got out of the car.

"Can I help you?" Platt demanded as I walked down her driveway. "If this is about a bill—" She ignored my outstretched hand.

"I'm not a bill collector."

"If you're from some charity and you're sending disadvantaged kids to the circus at the Meadowlands, I don't think I can help this year." She didn't smile.

"It's worse," I said apologetically. "I'm a private investi-

gator. Roberta Bingham gave me your name. I'd just like a
minute of your time."

I didn't think Donna Platt was going to invite me in. *I*
wouldn't have, if I'd just gotten home from work and had
two hungry kids racing around the yard and a meal to prepare. One of the boys glanced warily over his shoulder; the
younger one was openly staring at me. This wasn't a family
that seemed to expect good news from strangers.

"I'll be straightforward, Mrs. Platt. I'm inquiring about a
woman who used to be in your exercise class. Andrea Lucca."

Platt stiffened. "Who are you? What are you to her?"

She struck me as a plain-talker; I decided to be the same.
"My name is Kit Deleeuw. I have a client who's concerned
that Ms. Lucca might be interfering with her marriage. She
wants me to help her, and I'm trying to figure out if I can or
should."

"Deleeuw. Aren't you the guy they called the Suburban
Detective, the one who handled that murder case on the
Brown estate? You were all over the papers and TV."

"That's me, the Sherlock Holmes of Rochambeau. I'm
not BS'ing you. I need some sense of what's going on here,
so I can help my client or maybe refer her to somebody who
can."

A minute later we had carried the grocery bags in and
were standing in Donna Platt's kitchen. I was handing her the
last of the frozen food from the bag; she was putting it away.
A giant vat of water was being heated for the busy parent's
best mealtime friend, pasta—quick, healthy, universally liked.

The inside of the house showed more visible decay than
the outside. Stuffing pushed through the fabric of the once-
expensive sofa. The finish had worn off the oak flooring; the
carpets were worn and permanently stained. Charred logs and
ashes filled the fireplace and gave off a faint burned odor. The

kitchen linoleum floor had worn through in half a dozen places. This was a household hanging on by a narrow thread.

"I'm sorry if I'm bringing up a painful subject," I began.

"Me too." The water came to a boil, and she dumped in a large box of A & P spaghetti. "Andrea Lucca was my friend. The closest friend I ever had, at least briefly. We met in aerobics class, and we hit it off right away. We started sharing books, eating lunch together." She sighed.

"Andrea had this ability to always appear ready to listen. I'm usually worried about boring people, but she always acted as if every word was the most astonishing and insightful thing she'd ever heard. Funny how few people have that gift, of really wanting to hear what you think. My husband sure didn't. Stan and I didn't seem to have much to talk about anymore. We had become one of those couples you see in restaurants who chew their food very carefully and never speak."

I had reached into the refrigerator and almost unconsciously was putting together a salad. "I hope you don't mind," I said, my hands full of lettuce leaves. "I don't want to be presumptuous."

She laughed, and I realized how she might have sounded in happier times. "I don't turn down help, not at mealtime. Not anytime, these days. If you feel like baby-sitting tonight, just stick around; I'll skip the references and head for a movie."

"Did you work? Before the kids?"

"I was a copywriter for an ad agency in the city. I loved it. When I had Luke, I couldn't quite stomach turning him over to a day-care center, not at that age. So I took a couple of years off. Two years later we had Daniel. My maternity leave turned into a career, I'm afraid."

I had heard that before, talked about it often with Jane. In Rochambeau maternity leave can become a lifestyle, often without the mother quite realizing it. Sometimes it's a gift to the kids, and sometimes—when the mother suddenly finds herself rudderless, starved for something to do and smart people to talk to—it isn't.

"And now you're working again?"

She shrugged. "Stan was laid off; he's working part-time as a financial consultant. Anyway, I'm glad to be working. I wasn't really cut out to be a full-time housewife. Some women are, and they're terrific at it. They can do it without getting lost. But I wasn't one of them. I think that's why I was so happy to meet someone like Andrea. We talked half a dozen times a day. She was so interested in everything that happened to the kids, everything Stan was up to, everything I thought about books and movies and current events and life. There wasn't anything I wanted to say that she didn't want to hear. She was a godsend, I thought. Some godsend."

She sprinkled a few drops of olive oil into the pot, stirring, then moved to the silverware drawer. She pulled out three of everything. "Don't put mushrooms in that salad," she cautioned. "Luke will throw up right on the table." I opened the drawer next to the sink, found a serrated knife, and applied myself to the cucumbers. The boys, tired of tearing after one another in the backyard, were jumping onto their mountain bikes.

"Fifteen minutes," Donna Platt shouted out the window. "I don't want to have to go looking for you."

She turned back to me. "Single parents have to dispense with certain amenities. Like graciousness and manners. We use time economically. I have a conference with Luke's teacher and I've got to haul the VCR to a repair shop, since

I'm not available in the daytime when every repair person is. There's a shop in Walford that's open till nine, and that's only twenty miles away." She pulled a strand of pasta out of the pot for a taste test.

"Do you mind telling me how your divorce came about?" I prodded, sawing at the cucumbers. She gave me an odd look, then seemed to conclude there was no harm. She probably wasn't used to talking about it with strangers, even strangers who were helping her prepare dinner. It was a funny moment. My recent years of domestic chores gave us a kinship that I knew I wouldn't have had a few years earlier.

"I noticed that Stan was getting sort of distant and snappy, but he was under a lot of pressure at work. His company had been taken over, his new bosses were always on his case. He had a lot to be broody about. I felt guilty that I wasn't earning anything; the last thing he needed was more pressure from me. And frankly, Andrea and I were emotionally closer than Stan and I ever were. I know this sounds odd, but I think knowing her kept me from being lonely, or reacting as sharply as I might have otherwise.

"At first he used to make nasty remarks about Andrea— about her clothes or her hair, about something she said. He even suggested we were having a lesbian relationship. In some ways—not sexually—it did occur to me that we were in a kind of love. Then suddenly Stan dropped the subject. I guess I thought he'd accepted our closeness."

She fished another strand from the pot.

"Then last November I was taking Luke to his skating class. It was an unusually cold day, and the wind was so fierce, I cut around through the park to drop Luke off at the back entrance to the rink, where it's more protected. I was amazed —there was our car. Just like in some bad movie that's on at three A.M., there were Stan and Andrea sitting in the front seat holding hands. And even though they weren't kissing or any-thing, the intimacy was so apparent. . . ."

I began tossing the greens, which now had red peppers, carrots, and cucumber sliced into them. "But didn't Stan know you'd be taking Luke to the rink, that it was risky?"

"I don't think Stan ever kept track of where we were on a given day. But the thing was, Andrea knew. She knew my schedule by heart. When I'd walk in the door from a soccer game, the phone would be ringing and it would be her."

"Did you confront your husband?"

"Not right then, because Luke was there. I was just struck dumb. I rushed him into the rink and then sat there on the bleachers for an hour sobbing and shaking like a ninny. The other mothers thought I was having a nervous breakdown right there at the rink. They were right, I suppose. To make a long story short and bearable, Mr. Deleeuw, things promptly fell apart. I didn't trust Stan anymore. I tried calling Andrea, but she never returned my calls. I stopped going to class. That day at the rink I lost my best friend and my husband. The thing of it is, even though Stan acted like a jerk, I really loved him. We'd been together for eleven years; we could have worked it out. . . ."

The room fell quiet. I'd heard a lot of stories in recent years, but standing there in her kitchen, helping her fix dinner for her kids, the ghost of a fuller family seemed all around.

She pulled three glasses down from the cabinet and poured in the milk. Then she said firmly, "If some woman in my position is asking you for help, please give it to her. When you're alone in this town, people start looking right through you. You're standing on the baseball field alone, you don't fit in socially anywhere. Other people become afraid, like you've got something contagious. The kids . . . it's like half of their world falls away." She shook her head.

I wanted to put an arm around her shoulder, but thought better of it. "You know someone in the class named Marianne Dow?"

"Not well," she answered. "I think I saw her there a couple of times, although I'm not positive the person I'm thinking of was her. Some of the people in the class are good friends, they see a lot of each other, but I didn't make those connections. Except for Andrea."

"Donna," I said, "do you have any reason to think Andrea set out to bust up your family?"

"You mean, deliberately? Just in cold blood, decided to wreck my family?" She looked shocked. "I can't imagine that. I mean, look, I'll be candid, I daydream about her getting cancer, or worse. But no, it never occurred to me. You mean for kicks? Just for the heck of it? Or out of some weird compulsion?" She waved her hand, as if the very thought was impossible.

"I can't help you there," she added, shaking her head. She spotted her boys turning their bikes around and heading back to the house. A shadow crossed her face.

"You know, divorce is so common, you sort of forget how devastating it is." Her voice wobbled a bit. "What you lose. I get so lonely sometimes. I miss our vacations together, going to movies and dinner, our plans to buy a cottage on the Cape. Just having two people around to go to teacher conferences and share the shopping, to take care of the house. A lover, a partner, a father involved in the daily lives of the children. A whole life planned together. It's all gone, just like that."

I was surprised to glance at the kitchen clock and notice the time. I had a standing Tuesday-night pizza date with my own kids. I said my good-byes, thanking her for her candor and meaning it. Outside I sat in the Volvo for a few minutes before turning over the motor. Two families. Two affairs.

Donna Platt offered pretty potent evidence that Andrea Lucca was an immoral and cold-blooded person. But what about Marianne's sense that she was something more?

I think the kids would have missed our Tuesdays at Pepe's Pizza, although either would rather have died than admit it. It had become a kind of ritual. Pepe had our pies in the oven (one nitrite special with sausage and pepperoni for me and Ben, a plain for Em, and—if she got there in time—a Veggie Special for Jane) before we sat down in our usual booth.

To an outsider Ben and Em's grunting at me and sniping at one another might not have seemed like meaningful dialogue. To the eagle-eyed parent, though, it was a chance for some valuable temperature taking, to see if either kid was anxious, depressed, out of sorts in a way that needed further inquiry. It was at Peter's that I first noticed the preoccupation and discomfort in Ben that signaled his new interest in girls. And where I saw the tread marks on Emily's psyche after a group of friends-for-a-day had turned on her in gym class.

In any case, it kept the habit, if not always the reality, of conversation going. One day, a few years down the road, I had complete faith that communication would reassert itself naturally in our family. In the meantime, all I could really do was act as if we still always had it. Often enough, we did.

Even as Em called Ben a "jerk" for some infraction or other, I was conscious that night of our good fortune, especially when Jane joined us in midpie, bounding in with her files stuffed under one arm. When I thought of the ravaged family I had just left, it struck me that a family was an especially horrible thing to kill.

CHAPTER 5

"Triangulation."

Jane sighed, moving a towering stack of files to the side of the kitchen table to make room for the coffee mugs. Pizza bonding had nearly done her in, and after we got home, she still had two hours of grim paperwork. After several attempts one of her clients, a teenaged girl, had finally managed to kill herself that afternoon. It was about the only thing in her short, sad life she had succeeded at. No wonder Jane hadn't had much appetite.

Ben was studying in his room, concentrating on MTV, I suspected. With Jane's mediation we have worked out a healthy arrangement about his homework: I stay out of it. The irritating part is that he gets straight A's anyway.

Em was upstairs in her room grappling with Parts of Speech. Percentage, our loving, dim-witted black Lab (the Labrador is the Volvo of suburban dogs) had somehow wrapped himself underneath the table, where crumbs and bits of food occasionally fell from the skies.

"Triangulation," I repeated, hoping Jane could rise to the Häagen-Dazs Lite I was setting in front of her.

"It's a big thing in family therapy now," she said. "I was just reading about it. People think of love as involving couples, but couples can be infected or invaded—perhaps 'contaminated' is a good term—by a third party."

On top of the grinding work she did at her clinic in one of the poorest neighborhoods of Paterson, Jane drove into the city two nights a week to get her psych degree from NYU. Ironically, the collapse of my career had sparked the challenging process of building her own. She was frequently either exhausted or drained, and I tried not to bother her with my run-of-the-mill cases. But I had become dependent on her insights and training in trying to divine motives and behavioral patterns in some of my tougher marital and missing-persons cases, or when it came to analyzing which of five people in a clothing warehouse was likely to be feeding shipping information to a burglary ring. Given enough specific and accurate information, Jane was unbelievable, the brains behind the brawn, if you want to inflate my contribution.

"You know, there's little intelligent discussion of marital affairs in this puritan country," she mused. "We use these loaded terms—'infidelity,' 'betrayal.' Western culture has always been obsessed with adultery. But relationships aren't so simple. Sometimes marriages can be saved by affairs. They can buy time for the couple to work out their problems, to grow older and wiser. Some relationships are energized by affairs. Lots aren't, of course. In my clinic they sometimes lead to murder. Real murder, a knife in the chest, not just emotional dislocation. Still, for the family and the children involved, one can be nearly as brutal as the other, sometimes."

She sipped her coffee and took a swipe at the ice cream.

Suicides were devastating, but so was the brutality she dealt with on a daily basis. I was the detective, yet it was clear that Jane, not I, was really on the front lines. She worked so hard to reach her clients and pull them back. Overwhelmed by too many cases, too little time, too many problems, she didn't win many. There wasn't much I could do when she lost one, except to make sure the kids were in tip-top shape and to take comfort from the fact that she didn't have to worry much about the mechanics of running the household. (It had taken me four or five years, but I was getting pretty decent at it. It isn't easy to do well, believe me.) She never grew distant from our kids. It was a mother thing, I suspected, something I envied. When she and the children came together, their closeness was something they all took for granted. Fathers, I'd noticed, had to work harder at it. I could spend half the day rushing heavily programmed suburban children from one class or game to another, but when trouble struck—sickness, panic attacks—there was still nothing quite like Mom.

Maybe it was almost a welcome diversion for Jane to consider my case. I'd filled her in on my talks with Marianne Dow and Donna Platt, and she was already churning through theories.

"You know, Kit, there's a particularly insidious kind of triangulation. It involves mostly women, since they form close friendships more easily than men. There's a scenario where the woman befriends another woman, usually by being extremely supportive when the husband isn't. And how many men are?"

I refused to take the bait, mostly because I no longer disagreed. Jane was demonstrably appreciative of the fact that I shopped, cooked, and handled much of the child care, but she wasn't wild about my species. She frequently said her clinic would hardly be necessary if it weren't for men's drinking, abusing, stabbing, slugging, raping, and thieving. In a way, the same was true of Deleeuw Investigations.

"This woman attaches herself to another woman, insinuates herself into the household, and forms these extraordinarily deep connections. Sometimes the husband finds the friendship threatening, and that shakes the marriage. Sometimes the husband is drawn into a relationship with the friend."

"But would the friend be looking to destroy the marriage?"

She considered the question. "Not necessarily. Not unless she and the husband got too deeply enmeshed. All relationships are fragile, Kit, given the right set of pressures. If the third party became more intimate with one of the couple than the spouse was, that could cause problems. Or if jealousy or rivalry entered the equation. For better or worse, couples can hardly emerge the same when a third party gets deeply involved. Still, your notion of someone intentionally seeking to befriend a woman and destroy her family, that goes beyond triangulation, I think. That gets into something scarier."

I was surprised by Jane's last word. Like "crazy," it was a term she scorned now that she was studying psychology.

"Somebody that deliberate," she continued, "would have had to have been abused in some dreadful way, or traumatized early on. Somebody like that would really have to hate intact families and be drawn to breaking them up. She—if it was a she—would find functioning families unbearable."

I loaded the dishwasher and mulled over Triangulation. We'd known a lot of couples—too many—in which one or the other spouse had had a dumb, brief fling or even a longer, more intense one. Most of these marriages had, surprisingly enough, survived. But none seemed to involve someone pursuing a family with the intention of rupturing it.

Percentage woke up suddenly, one of the circuits firing in that great empty head, and banged his head on the chair, as he did about four times a night. Maybe, I thought, he started out half-bright and had simply suffered brain damage from so many thunks. I let him lick my ice-cream bowl.

Then Em stumbled down for assistance in diagraming a sentence, which wasn't exactly my forte, so Jane helped her sort out the pronouns and adverbs. "Oh God," Em declared, with the dramatic flair increasingly evident in recent months, "what is the *earthly* purpose of forcing *children* to diagram sentences?"

Watching the two of them pore over homework was one of my cherished domestic moments, striking ancient male chords that had to do with seeing one's family safe and secure. The last few years had often left me anxious about money and had sorely tested my conviction about my new paternal role, but when Jane and Em were together like this, performing the familiar rituals, things seemed right. Head-to-head, they were unmistakably mother and child. Jane had black hair cut shoulder-length, Em's was a shade lighter, but they shared a reedy, angular thinness—sharp chins and delicate wrists. Both of them had piercing green eyes and the terrifying ability to concentrate totally on the work in front of them.

Soon Emily went back up to her room, armed with a cuddle from Jane, a pat on the back from me, a brownie and a glass of milk, and accompanied by Percentage, who sensed the possibility of additional crumbs. That dog would abandon all of us instantly for a slice of toast. There was, in fact, no canine duty that Percentage performed well—not fetching, barking, guarding, or even romping. He did function superbly as a suburban symbol, however, sticking his big dumb, glossy head out of the station wagon's window, ears blowing in the slipstream.

Jane pushed her now-gloppy bowl of ice cream aside and frowned. "You know, at one of our classes this analyst was guest lecturer, the best we've had yet. He has a practice in the suburbs, Connecticut, I think. He mentioned triangulation, but he talked about it from a different perspective—he said he was treating an increasing number of abandoned women, as he put it."

"Abandoned by their husbands?" I asked. "That's more my turf."

"No, something quite different. He meant abandoned by their culture. They are liberated, he said, in the sense that they have education, careers, and ambitions. But they get snagged when they have kids. They get deeply enmeshed in their children, in their feelings about mothering, and they can't quite climb out and reenter the world. They lose their momentum, their confidence. They become sort of these lost women, he said, at sea, often chronically depressed or anxious. You know, like some of our mothers in the fifties, mired in the minutiae of their children's and husbands' lives. They dabble: take courses, work on one degree or another, volunteer a little in their kids' schools or maybe some civic organization. They aren't politically or psychologically suited to being housewives, because that is no longer an acceptable alternative in their world, but they can't quite disengage and regain more independent lives."

She held her cup up for a refill as I brought over the coffeepot. "They're ripe for trouble. He said he was seeing more and more women like that in his practice and hearing about them from other shrinks."

I had no trouble identifying the type, now that I thought

about it. Rochambeau has relatively few young housewives, in the traditional sense of women building their lives completely around home and family, but it has a lot of half ones, women who put careers aside when they have children. The shrink was right: in a way, these women are between cultures—feminists in their sensibilities and outlooks, something else in their daily lives. You can see them every morning in the school hallways, fussing at teachers about a kid's exclusion from a social group or pleading for more discussion of fractions, expressing a continuous stream of concerns to beleaguered principals. You can see them every afternoon, their wagons and vans lined up outside the schoolyards, ready to ferry their children to classes, soccer games, doctor's appointments, and play dates.

They describe themselves by their professions; they don't call themselves homemakers. They seem eager to make it clear that child rearing is an interlude, not a career. Yet they can't utter two sentences in a row without mentioning their children. A lot of them might not make it back. They drift through their thirties, wondering vaguely what they are going to be when they grow up, keeping their kids around and attached as much as they can for as long as they can. Marianne Dow had almost slipped into that category, in a way. So, certainly, had Donna Platt and perhaps, I thought, a number of other members of their aerobics group.

"You know, Kit"—Jane wagged a finger—"and don't groan, because you've heard this before—but the more I see of the world, the more firmly I believe that women have to have some source of achievement and identity beyond their families. It doesn't have to be a job in the traditional sense, perhaps, but there has to be something outside their homes, something more than the kids. It's just vital."

Jane was born believing that women had to and ought to

work. She had never found it comprehensible to spend life shopping, chauffeuring kids, tidying, and cooking. Thanks to my job, I could have given a pretty good lecture myself on the importance of women working. Any cop or private investigator will tell you that the notion of Idle Time being the Devil's Playground should be taken extremely seriously. But I did groan, not out of disagreement but because I *had* heard it before, about two million times. And in this case, Jane's passionate views might be coloring her judgment. What I had learned in the past few years was just how much kids need parents; how tough it was to be a good parent, and what an important and valuable thing parenting was to do. Still, I mixed it with other things. I probably would have gone berserk if I hadn't.

"Women working?" I needled. "There's a novel concept. When did you come to that?" She whizzed a pencil past my right ear.

Jane seemed to have skipped many of these identity crises. When I met her sixteen years earlier, she announced that she intended to be a therapist working with kids. She took six months off after each of our children was born, then returned to work or school. In those days we could afford a nanny. When my career fell apart, Jane uncomplainingly found a full-time position. She generated our mortgage payments, saved our home, and bought me a year or two, however impoverished, to establish Deleeuw Investigations. I took over most child care, fitting play dates and lessons into running employment checks and tracking deadbeat dads.

The year after Em was born, Jane had said never again, checked into the local hospital, had her tubes tied on a Thursday afternoon, and was back at her routine the next Monday. Now she moves through the suburban culture, living in it contentedly, but buying into few of its ethics. She can't abide child obsession, gardening, barbecues, malls, parents who scream at their kids during basketball tournaments, hysterical late-night phone calls about incompetent teachers, or parents whose twelve-year-old kids aren't ready for day camp or sleep-overs.

She has lunch or dinner with a couple of good friends whenever she can make the time and often goes to the movies with them. Otherwise, she is correctly perceived as self-contained, wrapped up in her family and her work. I love her more now than I did when we married, and she loves me *lots* more. The rearrangement of our lives has taught me what a real marriage is.

"Well," she sighed, "the workday continues into its fifteenth hour. Upstairs for some relaxing reading." She scooped up her thick manila case files and headed up to pore over them in bed.

I whistled for Percentage, who lumbered noisily downstairs as I took his leash out of the hallway closet. Because I had repeated this gesture nightly for seven years, I still hoped Percentage might eventually connect the sight of the leash with the concept of a walk. But he never had, and looked shocked and delighted when I opened the front door and called to him. We headed for our usual two-mile circle down the block and around Rochambeau Park.

At night, when you can't see the peeling paint, thriving weeds, or skewed roof tiles, our old gray Victorian looks proud and inviting, lit up like a funky ocean liner. In the springtime, late evening is my favorite time in Rochambeau. Its dark streets are an invitation to muse that's second only to my office window overlooking the mall parking lot. The street lamps peek discreetly through giant oaks and maples. Leaves rustle and whisper, sending shadows skittering back and forth across the lawns and sidewalks. Some front doors stand open, a marked contrast to the horrible weeks a few months earlier when the town saw its children struck down, its homes locked up like bank vaults, and police cars cruising nervously by every few minutes.

Down the block you could see raccoons lumbering into sewers, cats peering from under shrubs, the occasional rabbit on the trail of new garden shoots. Every few houses a retriever or shepherd went off, whoofing perfunctorily for effect, then giving it up as soon as was decent. The only thing you had to be careful of was stepping on squirrel carcasses, since many didn't survive their kamikaze dashes across suburban streets.

The silence was deep. Most Rochambeau homes are set back from the street, and you can almost never hear anyone speaking unless they are shouting, which is a rarity. If you look up into second-floor windows, you can often see shadowy moms and dads moving across kids' bedrooms, getting them into pajamas, reading them stories, cuddling and settling them.

Sometimes the neat lawns and cozy homes are a veneer, screening misery and pain. But lots of times they are the real thing, emblematic of lives as happy, advantaged, secure, and promising as any in this world, especially for children.

I was brooding about this triangulation business, about smart, accomplished, attractive, and vulnerable women who —although they wouldn't put it this way—are restless and depressed, married to nice but out-to-lunch men, and caught in a painful quagmire. They feel too much guilt and attachment to their children to return to work, but the culture has changed too much for them not to want to. They have gone too far to be fully content driving little kids around all day, but not far enough to make their peace with not doing so. Jane, busy and challenged, was often discouraged by the challenges she faced, but rarely depressed or lonely and never bored. She seemed so much less vulnerable to the problems Marianne Dow and Donna Platt were talking about.

I was as moved by Donna Platt's struggle as by Marianne's fears. The Platt home was a painful place, not in terms of furniture and lawn care, but in its permanent air of trauma. I knew many peaceful single-parent homes—often they were happier after philandering or deadbeat dad had finally split— but this one had the air of a place that had been shattered unexpectedly, before anyone in it had had time to prepare, much less understand why their lives were being brutally turned upside down.

If Jane was right and Andrea Lucca had suffered some sort of childhood trauma, it might be useful to find out what it was. Maybe I could talk to her, convince her to seek professional help. And maybe she'd tell me to buzz off and slap me with a billion-dollar invasion-of-privacy suit.

In the morning, I decided, I'd call in my secret weapon: Willie, a young computer freak working in a credit agency who could tell within milliseconds if any given Rochambeau resident was heating with gas or oil and how many CDs she had bought the week before.

Under a streetlight, I peered at my watch. I used to try to make it back from my walks in time to say good night to Em and Ben, but that seemed less necessary lately. There had been a shift in our house, subtle but profound, and in some ways sad. Now that Em had turned ten, and Ben was thirteen, we had come to the inevitable beginning of what Jane and I both knew would be an ever-widening fork in the road. Both kids would rather hang around with their friends than with us, rather talk on the phone than hear bedtime stories read, rather go to camp than sit around with us at the shore.

That, we told oursleves reluctantly, was just what we

wanted, what we'd worked so hard for—that they would learn how to lead their own lives happily and apart from us.

A year ago Em would have stayed awake until she got her good-night hug and goofy story. Now she was usually already asleep by the time Percentage and I walked home, or too immersed in some preteen novel to want to hear my tales. A perfectly natural development. The hard part was that you had to help it along, and you had to pretend to like it.

CHAPTER 6

The A.M. bedlam was at its height Wednesday morning when Jane, who'd gone out to fetch the *Times* from our front walk, announced that a moving van had arrived next door and that we ought to go over and greet the new neighbors.

Charlie Pinski, my snowblower / lawn mower / leaf mulcher–equipped neighbor on the other side, had been speculating for days about who the new residents would be. So had Ben and Emily. She wanted a girl, and so, Jane and I noticed with raised eyebrows, did he.

New neighbors are a significant event in a town like Rochambeau, one that could substantially affect the quality of your lives. Sometimes, when the chemistry is right, they even provide genuine friendship.

You want neighbors who will notice if an intruder carts your VCR out into a battered van, but who will also look the other way when you scream at the kids or at each other, who don't care that the crabgrass holds a summer festival on your lawn, and who can be relied on to pull pillows over their ears when sleepovers get too raucous. Life can get pretty tense otherwise. You hope for people as messy, noisy, and harried as you are. For obvious reasons, it is better not to have people who are quieter, neater, or richer.

Jane and I weren't especially social anymore. It seemed that was a trait we just could no longer afford, and I can't say I missed it. Our jobs left little emotional or physical energy for the bonhomie and good cheer that went into dinner parties and barbecues. More and more we treasured our time with the kids, which we were just beginning to realize was growing short, and we invariably preferred going out by ourselves for Szechuan and a movie. On those increasingly rare occasions when we all agreed on the same movie, or Ben and Em didn't have plans, we jumped at the chance to bring them along.

So our notion of ideal neighbors was people who happily watched for the UPS truck when we were out, brought over our mail when it was accidentally delivered to their house, shelled out money for the magazine subscriptions Ben or Em were continually peddling to raise money for their schools, looked the other way when Percentage relieved himself on their lawn, and otherwise pretty much left us alone.

The kids had a different view, of course.

Em, in her new melodramatic mode, had dropped to her knees and prayed. "Please, God, just one ten-year-old girl who likes to read and never wears dresses. And has a dog who's about to have puppies," she added. A tall order.

Ben was too cool by many degrees to debase himself by wishing for someone his age to move in. Ben was so cool, in fact, he was becoming our own adolescent equivalent of dry ice, no longer living *in* the house, but floating through and above it on his own ethereal plane, taking continual calls from unidentified young females.

Of all of us, Charlie Pinski, who was retired, was probably the most hopeful. Charlie pined for a fellow lawn-compulsive, somebody with whom to trade weed killers, jawbone over the fence, charbroil a few thick steaks in the summer, maybe even watch the game on fall Sundays. He was much too polite to say so, but Charlie found me sorely lacking in male attributes, since I never did any of those things.

"Gee, Dad," Ben offered, peering out the window, as the first pieces of furniture began to emerge from the moving van, "these people have sofas that don't have holes in them. They must be loaded." I watched him closely for signs of sarcasm, but he was more than clever enough to hide them.

"Nice sofas, but not rich people's," Jane reassured, joining Ben at the window. "Workbench, I think. Attractive and practical." She was relieved, having feared floral patterns.

Soon after that a purple van drove up and the side door slid open. A little girl with a dark complexion and jet-black hair bounded out and headed for the house. "Guatemala," reported Jane, who worked with Latins at the clinic. "Maybe Ecuador. Probably adopted. Let's go say hello."

Charlie Pinski had beaten us to it, bearing his wife Harriet's famous cheesecake, a staple at neighborhood block parties, graduations, bar mitzvahs, and anniversary celebrations. When we joined up with the clump of people on the sidewalk, he was already extolling the virtues of the neighborhood and looking around. His fellow yardaholic had not yet materialized. Two women had followed the little girl out of the car. "You got a supermarket just four blocks away," Charlie enthused, apropos of nothing.

One of the women was tall and thin, with short grayish

hair, dressed for moving in jeans and a work shirt. The other was shorter, her hair pulled back in a long braid. They both looked to be in their forties.

Charlie peered into the van, looked up and down the street, then toward the house. I realized that he was looking for the husband. I had the sense that he was going to be disappointed.

"Hi. I'm Jeannie Stafford," said the woman with the braid, who seemed the more outgoing of the pair. "This is Carol Goldman. That's our daughter Tracy who ran into the house." There was no more direct or graceful way to put it. She didn't want to hide anything, nor did she want Charlie ending up in intensive care. He stood rooted to the spot, like one of the ugly little shrubs he was always planting in his yard.

"We're very happy to meet you," said Jane smoothly.

"Welcome," I chirped. "It's a great neighborhood, and we hope you'll call us if you need any help at all."

Carol seemed to relax when Jane asked where Tracy was going to school, and whether or not they needed the names of day-care centers, pediatricians, or baby-sitters. They said they did, and the three women turned toward the house, which was rapidly filling with furniture.

Charlie stood stock-still, smiling weakly as they retreated, still clutching the cheesecake. "Everybody here? This all of you?"

"Yup. This is our family." Jeannie nodded, then headed into the house.

He turned to me. "There's no guy, is there, Kit?"

"Guess not."

"No husband. That means . . . Well, I guess there's only one interpretation."

"Lesbians," I said.

"Lesbians," he repeated. "Lesbians with a kid. Two women with a kid, just like a couple," he said. Nobody to bitch about the Giants with. No one to admire his armada of lawn equipment. "So, what do you call them? Miss and Miss? Ms.?" he wondered aloud.

"I think just Jeannie and Carol. They look like solid citizens, Charlie. I'll get you that book, *Heather Has Two Mommies.*" I would have given anything to have been in Charlie's kitchen when he got to the phone and dialed one of his bowling buddies.

"Can they do that? Can they adopt a kid?" He was still struggling to piece it together.

"Sure, one of them can. Maybe one of them even watches NFL football," I replied, but he looked even more rattled at that.

"C'mon, Charlie," I chided him. "They're respectable-looking, nice clothes, good furniture—that house cost three hundred thousand dollars, for God's sake. Try to relax, will you? They'll probably even let you run that monster snowblower over the walk."

Through the front window, as yet unobstructed by curtains, Jeannie and Carol were sitting down at the newly unloaded dining-room table. I headed toward our house, to put on another pot of coffee and bring it over.

One of the things I like best about suburbia is my sense—reinforced by my work, which takes me behind a lot of well-painted doors—that it is the site where the most remarkable cultural experiments and dramas are finally played out. In cities feminists or gays take to the streets to demand changes, parade in front of TV cameras, scream at city-council meetings. But it is in the suburbs where the changes become real, get played out in ordinary lives.

• • •

When I pulled into the mall parking lot a little later that morning, I was still chuckling about Charlie. He'd be all right, I thought; Charlie wasn't deep, but he was no hater. Ultimately, the new neighbors' views on lawn care would count more with him than their sexual orientation.

When I spotted the Rochambeau PD cruiser, I figured one of the officers had scooted off his or her beat just long enough to return a rented video or load up on charcoal briquettes.

So I was surprised at the sight of Rochambeau's beefy, cigar-puffing chief, Frank Leeming, jawboning with the head of mall security. Leeming spotted me coming in, nodded at Tim Leland, and headed briskly toward me. The chief and I'd had an uneasy relationship, at best, before the Brown-estate murders were resolved; Leeming had been warned by the feds that I was a dirty inside trader who had cannily eluded the law's righteous grasp. When I took on the Brown case, Leeming had huffed and bellowed and threatened me with extinction if I so much as wandered into his line of sight. That I was a town taxpayer, as well as its only private investigator, impressed him not a bit.

Fortunately, he was an ex–New York City precinct commander who had seen too much of everything, including too many FBI agents, and he made his own judgments. What he eventually decided was that I was sometimes amusing, mostly straight, and infrequently useful. And since I was no longer employable in my former world, I also wasn't going away anytime soon.

Our relationship improved dramatically when I helped break the Brown case, prying horrified townspeople off the chief's back and helping to preserve his daughters' college educations and his pension. He'd had several delightfully ordinary suburban months since, leaving ghostly murder behind him, searching for bicycle thieves, issuing traffic tickets, launching continual assaults on loudly partying teenagers, and hunting down burglars.

Suburbia is one big discount-appliance fest for anybody with a van and a little nerve, and its residents are loath to take precautions. It's as if alarms and grates and other devices undercut their idea of suburban life. "In this town," Leeming liked to say, "people *want* their kids to run around like the Brady Bunch." He had a point: people want so much to believe they've found utopia thirty miles outside the city that they simply ignore all evidence to the contrary, as if they're living in small-town Nebraska before the First World War. Half the doors in town are left open as soon as the weather warms, primarily so that kids can come and go as they please. Since almost every middle-class house has two or three TVs, a VCR, a stereo rig or two, a computer, a microwave, etc.—and dogs who welcome intruders as enthusiastically as their own family members—the pickings are often quite good. In return suburban burglars usually take pains to avoid encountering or hurting anybody. The victims carry plenty of insurance, and no one gets too excited.

While Leeming, like most professional cops, couldn't stand the notion of a private investigator mucking around in his town, we eventually came to respectful accommodation, if not intimacy. He was careful to keep enough distance so that he could yank my license, if need be, without too much guilt. Meanwhile, every month or so we had a cup of coffee and a freshly thawed Danish at Lightning Burger, where Leeming usually advised me to get into real estate or computer sales. Sometimes, when his guard came down and things were quiet, he would talk a bit about his days in a Brooklyn precinct, a world I doubted I would have survived for a month, let alone two decades.

"Deleeuw," began Leeming, without niceties, steering me up toward my office. "We got to talk. You hear about what happened this morning?" It was a pretty broad question.

We got upstairs just as Evelyn walked in from the opposite end of the hallway. I didn't know what the chief wanted, but his presence had undoubtedly saved me from the usual tongue-lashing I got over late files and letters. "Morning, Evelyn," Leeming said. "I'll buy if you'll bring up some of that Lightning Burger coffee. I know it's not in your job description, but Kit and I have some business and I'm in a heckuva rush."

"Because of the five-eleven on Hanover?" she asked coolly, startling him just as she had intended. Evelyn had shocked me a month earlier by buying a police scanner at Radio Shack (because, she announced, she was now in law-enforcement work, sort of) and becoming addicted to cop lingo and lore. Now she accepted Leeming's outstretched five-dollar bill, twinkling at me. He certainly had guts. I wouldn't ask Evelyn to fetch me coffee if she was sitting next to an urn. She and I alternated bringing coffee up each morning.

We went into my inner office. Leeming shut the door firmly as I flipped on the light and opened the blinds. Unless you peered out at the tops of distant trees or closely examined the string of fast-food franchises along the highway for Santas or jack-o'-lanterns, you really couldn't tell one season from another by the view from my window.

Leeming put his cap down on my desk, pulled out a notebook covered with scribblings, and rested both large hands in front of him.

"Kit, we may be back in shit soup again. At least I might. I might as well have stayed in Brooklyn. Hell, I take a job with the most boring department in the state and the town turns into Dodge City."

I felt my heart lurch. Surely the killer of two teenagers hadn't escaped from jail? "Is it the Brown estate case?"

"No. A guy on Hanover. Last night about one the volunteer ambulance got a call. Wife came into the bathroom to get ready for bed, found her husband in the tub, head under the bloody water, as close to dead as you can be above ground. The wife pulled his head up, and the volunteer guys did mouth-to-mouth. He's still alive, but in a coma, hooked up to a dozen fucking machines. Don't know if there's brain damage or not. Don't even know if he'll come out of it."

"Suicide attempt?" If so, why was he here?

"Don't look like it. The doc called me from the emergency room, said we ought to send some detectives down. He said the guy had a massive skull fracture, the kind you get from being whacked with a club or a baseball bat. He also had about a pint of whiskey in his blood, along with enough phenobarbital to kill a mule. We figure the guy had been drinking, took or was given pills, then climbed into the bath. Maybe he planned to sleep it off—who knows?" Nothing surprised the chief.

"It sure sounds like a suicide attempt, doesn't it?" I persisted.

He flashed his weary spare-me-from-amateurs look. "Maybe the pills and booze, Deleeuw, but I don't see how he whacked himself on the head with an object that has since vanished. Somebody must've come up behind him, cracked him with something, and watched him slip under the water— or pushed him."

"And the wife happened to walk in before he was quite dead?"

"That's what she says."

"You don't believe her?"

Evelyn came in with a yellow Lightning Burger sack. She took one cardboard cup of coffee, passing us the other two. Then she sat down in the office chair next to the water cooler. Leeming knew better than to ask her to leave, and I wouldn't dream of it. Evelyn knew as much as I did about my cases, and she was totally discreet.

My assistant looked every inch the small-town librarian that she had been for over thirty years. She was dressed in a nondescript brown suit; her hair was pulled into a neat knot. I had met her working on the Brown-estate murder case—she had recently retired from the Rochambeau Public Library, working only one morning a week. Librarians, I figured, spend their lives refusing to succumb to disorder and battling to create an atmosphere of quiet contemplation. So I asked for her help in locating some old files, and she wound up helping me break the case and moving into my outer office in the American Way. I think we both realized without ever saying so that each of us could make it possible for the other's work to continue.

In me she found a totally disorganized mind and manner. Piles of unfiled notices, reports, messages, Post-Its, newspapers, and magazines enveloped me wherever I went and filled every surface I approached. Jane wondered how I had ever been able to hold a job at all. In Evelyn I found my perfect opposite. An obsessive organizer, a compulsive keeper of files, she even filed my doodles. Most amazing to me, she remembered where every slip of paper was. She ruthlessly blocked my determined efforts at slovenliness and procrastination. During quieter stretches of the day, she read her beloved Dickens, sipped herbal tea, and knitted. Other than the Lightning Burger, I had never seen her enter a store in the American Way.

Without having to be asked, Leeming repeated to Evelyn what he had said. I pondered why he had come out to the mall to tell it all to me. The chief wasn't the sort to chitchat while a case was breaking.

"You don't believe the wife's account?" I asked again.

He shrugged. "I don't know yet, Kit. I don't like her story much. No robbery, no sign of forced entry or struggle. You telling me a burglar is going to stroll into the house, walk into a bathroom, and clock this guy with a bat while his wife's downstairs reading, then leave without taking anything? Why hit the guy? With that blood level, he had to be half under already. And how'd the thumper get past the wife?"

"Then why call nine-one-one at all?" I countered. "If she was guilty, wouldn't she have waited until she was positive he was dead?"

"Don't know," he said, again. "Maybe she thought he *was* dead or at least couldn't survive. We've just started the investigation. I don't like her story, that's all. Some of them you like, some you just fucking don't." He flushed. "Pardon, Evelyn." I marveled at a man who could spend decades on some of the toughest streets there were and lose it cursing in front of a woman. She nodded gravely.

Leeming sipped his coffee. He drank it black as any self-respecting cop would. I waited, wondering if the injured man was someone I knew, hoping it wasn't. But there had to be some point to this visit.

"There's something else going on that I don't like," Leeming went on. "Few days ago we get a possible missing persons report from a firm in town. A woman—an artist, I think—who works in their office hasn't reported to work or been home for a week and a half to get her mail or check her message machine. Okay, my guys tell me, so she ran off with somebody and will get around to giving notice when she feels like it, if she ever does. Face it: in this town when people disappear, they show up in Key West five months later with their sister's husband, not in ditches by the side of the road."

"Has she shown up in a ditch by the side of the road?" I could see by Evelyn's look of intense concentration that she had some sense of where Leeming might be headed. I sure didn't.

"Nope. No trace of her. But here's the thing. What do we find in our bashed man's bathrobe, the one he pads around the house in at night? A phone number. A local number. Even you, Deleeuw, have probably pieced together whose it is."

"Mine?"

Evelyn rolled her eyes. She had read a zillion mysteries and had a better sense than I did of how to behave.

Leeming took another gulp of coffee. "Jesus, Deleeuw, they must give PI licenses away like zoning permits for new porches. Don't you figure we would have called you right away if your fucking phone number turned up in some nearly dead guy's bathrobe?"

"Chief, this is all very exciting. I'm sure one of the networks will send a crew over here for their next *Supercop* episode to capture your brilliant investigative skills on camera. I'm also certain that a law-enforcement official of your stature working a serious case has better things to do than befuddle an ignorant ole detective like me."

Irony, as usual, was lost on Leeming. He looked like a football coach—short, squat, overstuffed, and tough. If he didn't want you to get past him, you wouldn't. His face, perpetually weathered, appeared preoccupied.

"Yeah, I do have to be moving on. Well, you'll never guess, but the phone number belongs to this artist, the woman reported missing. Lucca is the name. The thing is, the wife tells me in this surprisingly direct way that her husband knows this missing woman. That *she* knows this missing woman. And she didn't say so, Deleeuw, but it was pretty clear that the relationship these three people had had not taken a happy turn. You know how? Because on the MP's answering machine are three calls from the wife, and they aren't at all friendly. The way I see it, this woman is going to need help."

"Marianne Dow," I said.

Leeming ran an enormous hand over his graying crew cut. "Marianne Dow. Who tells me she's spoken with you. So what do you know?" He gave me a long, hard look that afforded lots of time to share my feelings about this case with him and suggested *lots* of trouble if I held back.

It was a pleasure to be able to tell the truth—almost.

"Nothing," I told him. "We talked for the first time on Monday. I haven't had a chance to type up a single report. But I do know this, Chief. Marianne Dow isn't nearly dumb enough to try and off her husband in her own bathroom, find the body before it's dead, then call nine-one-one in time to save him. Not if she wanted to kill him. Jesus, she's a lawyer, Frank. She's trained to think clearly. You're not only barking up the wrong tree, you're not even in the right forest."

The chief, as usual, appeared unimpressed by my keen investigative acumen. But something he said bugged me.

"One thing, though, Frank. As you know from what you found on the answering machine, Marianne Dow feels this Lucca woman was—is—hanging around her husband. She was concerned about it. Yesterday I called the architects' office where Andrea Lucca works. The woman who answered the phone didn't say anything about her being missing, she just said she wasn't there."

"You mean the teenage receptionist?" Leeming snorted

derisively. "I met her when I went over there. Lucca could have been lying across her desk and this kid might not notice. One of the partners in the firm called me five days ago. Lucca had missed several deadlines, which he said was real unusual for her. She hadn't come in to pick up her mail or check her messages. He went to her apartment and found her mail overflowing her mailbox. She obviously hadn't been there either. But he asked us to be discreet. He didn't want the police crawling around if she was off at Club Med with a boyfriend, or something. So the receptionist probably didn't know about it."

"Hmmm," I said. "But if she was, in fact, involved with Gil Dow, would she have another boyfriend? Maybe you ought to be scurrying around looking for her and leaving my client alone, don't you think?" I finished my coffee. I would go down to the Lightning Burger shortly and fetch another.

"Is Marianne Dow actually a client of yours?" Leeming smiled triumphantly. "She didn't seem sure."

"Yes," I said, having just made her one. I hoisted my empty coffee cup. "God, Chief, it's just so grand that we're working together again. You must be a just and deserving man."

He looked like he wanted some Mylanta.

CHAPTER 7

L ike a reporter secretly pleased by a juicy tragedy but uncomfortable about admitting it, I was excited to have a hot case, a hummer, even though Rochambeau might land back in the soup again. The chief, of course, intended to ensure that it wouldn't.

He'd said that the official police report would mention only that Gil Dow had sustained a head injury while taking a bath. That domestic accident wouldn't warrant a mention even in the Rochambeau *Times,* which preferred to concentrate on fender benders and stolen bicycles. The missing-person case might just as easily turn out to be a sudden career or lifestyle change. There was no evidence that Andrea Lucca had been harmed and much to suggest that she had wisely taken off before anybody could disembowel her.

The only danger, publicity-wise, was that the New York tabloids and TV stations might get wind of trouble reemerging in paradise and launch another orgy of suburb bashing. No story was more joyously pursued than Horror Lurking Behind Those Hydrangeas. Rochambeau would have a collective nervous breakdown if it attracted another wave of unfavorable publicity or thought for a second that another wannabe killer was hovering about its flagstone patios and velvety lawns. In my neighborhood the suburban dream wasn't some sociologist's notion; it was expensive and hard-won and taken seriously. Killers didn't fit into it. I didn't relish the idea myself. I was, after all, a father, husband, and property owner, however frayed the property was getting.

Marianne Dow's Volvo 240, a far newer and fresher version than mine (although Jane drives a new one), was parked in front of the slate-blue Victorian on Hanover Street in the North End, one of Rochambeau's gracious older neighborhoods.

Hanover Street is upper middle class. Here lawyers, young doctors, Wall Streeters just starting to see some serious money, enter Rochambeau. The houses, bigger than starter bungalows but less grand than the estates up on the hillside, are seventy and eighty years old, weathered, and full of character. The streets are edged with towering oaks.

Midmorning on Hanover Street, as in much of Rochambeau, was an odd, in-between sort of time. The commuters had already bustled off, kids were in school, and an uncharacteristic stillness cloaked the street. The ubiquitous tricycles and soccer balls were scattered across various lawns, and I heard the familiar halfhearted woof of a retriever inside the Dows' Victorian home. I also took note of a dark-blue Buick idling directly across the street with three aerials bristling from the trunk. A youngish man with clipped hair sat in the driver's seat sipping coffee and scanning the paper.

The door opened before I got to the bell. Marianne, so poised and articulate forty-eight hours earlier, now looked haggard and disoriented. Her hair was pulled back in a straggly ponytail, and she had thrown on a pair of worn jeans and a

sweater way too heavy for the pleasant day. They were probably the clothes she'd grabbed after the ambulance sped away
with her bloodied, unconscious husband.

She didn't seem surprised to see me. "I sent the kids to
school," she said, without preamble. "Now I can't decide if I
should pull them out or not. I thought it would be best for
them to go about their business, at least for today until we
know more about Gil. I shouldn't have sent them out, should
I? Maybe I ought to go get them. Do you think anybody will
say anything to them? I thought it would be horrible for them
to hang around an emergency room all day. I just got back a
few minutes ago to change and wash; I'm going back to the
hospital."

She was frantic—understandably so—about her husband
and about how to deal with her kids. I'd had some frightening fantasies myself about what my children would do if Jane
or I got sick or hurt. It did seem strange to have sent them off
to school, until you considered the impact of their hanging
around the house or a hospital waiting room all day, possibly
waiting for their father to die. And Marianne, visibly traumatized by the previous night's events, was obviously in no position to deal with them calmly. Was this a person who could
have taken a blunt object to her husband's skull? She could be
faking her shock, but it seemed more likely that she would
carry the scars of what she had seen last night to her grave.

"Whoa." I clasped her wrist, which trembled. There was
still dried blood under the fingernails. "Calm down. The kids
are better off in school. It's the right decision. If you want,
you can call the school and I'll go pick them up early. But
right now I need to ask you to do three things that will be
difficult, but you must do them right away. First, you've got
to call a lawyer." She looked astonished; I plunged on. "Then
you need to tell me every detail of what happened last night.

And I need to see the bathroom; it's crucial if I'm going to help. Okay? I know you're terrified, but we have to do these things first. Then I can leave you alone and go out and help. Okay?"

I was talking as slowly and clearly as if she were a preschooler, but I still wasn't sure I was getting through. When she didn't respond, I steered her inside.

The Dows' house looked more buttoned up than Donna Platt's, despite the footprints of the cops and ambulance attendants who had tramped in and out during the night and a disquieting trail of dried bloodstains. With two adults, two kids, and a dog, a house that had no pet hair on the carpets or dustballs in the corners enjoyed either a full-time homemaker or a maid.

As in a lot of Rochambeau homes, the living room looked the least worn, probably reserved for grandparents' visits and holiday parties. The brocade chairs seemed barely sat upon. I noticed two decent-looking watercolors and some pencil sketches signed M. Dow.

With a living room so neat, there had to be a playroom, in our town known as the designated Hell Room, littered with Nintendo cartridges, Cabbage Patch dolls, comic books, and unrecognizable body parts of old My Little Ponies, Smurfs, games, and toys. The Dows', I saw, was off the kitchen. From it a golden retriever bounded joyously up to me, rammed his nose into my crotch, and dropped a slobbery rubber ball at my feet. I recognized the same useless, undeterrable good humor as Percentage.

"Look, Marianne, I know you haven't had any sleep, I know you're in shock, I can see you're right at the edge. I want you to go change your clothes, then go into the kitchen and give me five minutes in the bathroom. You're an attorney, right? You've had training, right? Remember it. You're a professional person. This is a crisis. You need to stay especially calm and clear-headed, for your kids as well as for yourself. You need to pull yourself together while we sort through this, okay? I will do everything I can to help you."

My speech had its effect. Marianne was a trained and, I suspected, skilled public-interest attorney. She specialized in harassing corporations, Evelyn told me.

She understood the importance of holding on under troubled circumstances. It was exhaustion that was probably unraveling her as much as anything else, that and the fact that her partner in an increasingly troubled marriage, the father of her two children and a man she said she loved a great deal, was in a deep coma from which he might never emerge. She had to be tough just to be walking around. I'm not sure I would have been.

She nodded, then headed upstairs, coming down shortly thereafter with an armful of clothes. I waited until she went into the downstairs bathroom, which adjoined the kitchen; then I climbed the stairs. The Dows had a standard Rochambeau upstairs for a home that age. To the left of the staircase were two smallish kids' bedrooms, then a larger room set up as a study, which probably doubled as a guest room. Straight ahead was a bathroom for the children and for guests. To the right was the larger master bedroom, with a queen-sized brass bed and a couple of reading chairs and brass lamps. The carpet was a light blue, its color nearly obliterated by boot marks, the universal signature of cops or rescue workers called into a neat home in the middle of the night. An antique patchwork quilt was all scrunched up on the bed. Across the room I could see a small dressing room with women's shoes, a tie rack, and closets and shelves; beyond it was a green-tiled bathroom, post-War sturdy, with a thick porcelain sink with polished metal faucets, and an enormous claw-footed tub. I felt a little creepy going in, then remembered that Gil Dow was still alive, which for some reason made me feel better.

The green-striped vinyl shower curtain had been torn down, either by Marianne or the cops struggling to lift Gil out of the tub. The water had been drained from the tub, which, judging by the smell of cleanser, had been scoured heavily. I wondered when she'd had the time, although I sympathized with the impulse; I wouldn't want Jane's bloodstains in the tub while my kids were hanging around the house.

There were still some splatters, though, on a couple of tiles near the rear of the tub and along the floor beneath it. This would have been, I guessed, where somebody cracked Gil's skull as he languished in deep, warm water. The tub was almost half again as large as a modern bathtub. It must take half an hour just to fill it, I thought. The soap rack held a thick bar of expensive soap, a bottle of men's shampoo, and a small plastic vial of conditioner from a hotel in San Francisco. You were supposed to take this stuff home these days. I jotted my observations down in the small notebook I always carried, wondering if Gil had seen the intruder reflected in the beveled mirror above the old sink. Even if he had, he might not have had time to get up. I suppose if I were in Leeming's shoes, I might be thinking that perhaps the face Gil saw was familiar, so that it didn't occur to him to get up.

Leeming's investigators, of course, would have photographed every corner of the room and the tub, but they didn't always see everything. Suburban cops didn't have much experience with these kinds of cases.

In fact, I noticed something I'm sure they *did* see, but didn't care that they saw. Wedged under the drain stopper were the remains of one of those scented bath-oil pellets that Emily insists on taking into the tub with her. They are pretty irresistible, turning squishy and soft before dissolving, releasing their pungent scent into the water. Remembering Sergeant Mize, my army CID instructor (who else did I have to seek inspiration from?) and his dictum about evidence—"see everything, save everything, write down everything"—I stashed my notebook and scooped up the gooey green remains of the bath ball, wrapping a piece of notebook paper around it and stuffing it into my jacket pocket. This would drive Evelyn, who liked to hoard evidence, berserk. Would she open a Squishy Bath Ball file? Back at the mall I had a box filled with even less savory odds and ends from various investigations. One day one of them might prove important. I went downstairs.

Marianne had changed into work clothes—a white silk blouse, navy blazer, and gray slacks—which seemed to settle her a bit. She had called the hospital. Gil was still comatose, she was told; no change at all in his condition, but the nurses' station would call if there was. She said she would be there shortly. She next called a local criminal attorney we both knew named Eric Levin (he coached a soccer team) and made an appointment for that afternoon. I made a note to call Levin myself, to be sure he was comfortable with my working on the case. Sometimes criminal lawyers have their own investigators, but I had done some work for Levin and doubted he'd have any problems.

She also called her kids' school. While I was upstairs, she had obviously made plans with her baby-sitter to pick the two children up at one P.M. She told the school it was all right to release them. She was getting it together.

We sat on the screened porch, sipping from the mugs of black coffee I'd prepared while she was on the phone. The view from the porch was at odds with the air of tragedy inside the house. New Jersey has ten truly beautiful days a year, five in the spring and five in the fall, and this was one of them: temperature in the upper seventies, a crisp breeze, the sun streaming through the old maples shrouding the Dows' backyard. This was as pretty a picture as most people get, and none of it counted a whit. Life inside the house, already unraveling for unknown reasons, had been horribly shattered a few hours earlier, probably for good.

But Marianne was calmer, as though having help and a plan for her kids eased her sickening sense of life's spinning out of control.

"Now I see why there's a squad car across the street. I thought they were protecting me." She laughed joylessly. "Kit, how on earth could they suspect *me?*"

"Look, Marianne, it's a cop's job to suspect everybody, especially people right in front of them who have means and motive. That's a good cop's first impulse, and Leeming is a very good cop. You found Gil's body, you were alone in the house with him, you left angry messages on Andrea Lucca's answering machine. People have been arrested for less. As the cops come across other people in their investigation, they'll suspect them too. Now I know you want to get back to the hospital, and you have an appointment with Levin at three. So I'm going to turn on my tape recorder, and I want you to walk through what happened last night. Anything you think I ought to know."

She took several deep breaths, clearly dreading the recounting but understanding why it was necessary. Yesterday she was a woman battling to keep her family intact. Today she was in danger of being accused of destroying it. She had courage and dignity, and I admired her forthrightness, but I had been misled many times, as recently as the Brown case. Marianne had some explaining to do.

"Usually I go to my aerobics class in the morning, but

Tuesdays I take the evening class with Roberta. It's a late class, nine P.M., designed for the commuters who come home from the city, have dinner with their families, see the kids off to bed, change into their tights and sneakers, and are ready for a workout. See, that's the sort of thing Roberta would think about, the women who can't exercise mornings because they're on the train. Roberta takes no prisoners Tuesday nights, not that she's lenient anytime.

"I got home about ten-fifteen, sent my sitter home. Gil got in just as I was stepping out of the shower. I could see by his face he'd had a dreadful day. He said a deal he'd been working on for six months had fallen through and that he was getting the blame. Now he wouldn't be getting any midyear bonus, so our money troubles would only get worse, and he thought he'd be lucky to have a job at all by Labor Day. He said he wanted to be alone, to have a drink and a sleeping pill, maybe take a long, hot bath. That was his way of relaxing."

Marianne stopped. Her way of getting through this, I could see, was to pause periodically and collect herself. I leaned over and scratched the retriever behind the ear; his tail waggled gratefully. He would have moved in with me if I'd invited him.

She forced herself to continue. "This was getting to be a pretty familiar pattern with us. The kids were in bed, he was upset, he didn't want to talk about it, at least not with me, and he was heading straight for the Dewar's. He needed some solace, and I wasn't providing any, so the Scotch would. At least Gil thought it would. And maybe Andrea was . . .

"I had some legal papers to go through—a toxic-dumping lawsuit brought by some Ocean County farmers who have cancer in their families, a horrible case. So I went into my downstairs study to plow through my briefs for a couple of hours. Lately I've tried to give Gil the space he says he needs.

It seems to drive him crazy when I offer to help or to talk with him. Sometimes I get the sense my very presence makes him want to jump out of his skin." She struggled here, then took a ragged breath.

"I'm sorry. This has all turned to such a nightmare. Poor Gil." I thought she might cry, but she went on, her voice almost crisp. "This is going to be the hard part, Kit. I'm going to rush through it, okay? Then I have to go over to the hospital. Then I can't talk about it anymore, all right? Promise?"

I promised. Looking out from the porch, I could see two young women and their toddlers playing on a blanket on the grass in the yard behind us. They were staring at the house, at the porch, at us. They might be clucking in sympathy or titillated by scandal. Marianne didn't seem to see them. She'd better get used to it; people might be staring at her a lot now.

"I must have fallen asleep," she continued. "Something woke me up around one, because I remember being shocked when I looked at my watch and saw how late it was. I got up, let Oscar out, waited for him to come back, closed up down here. I remember feeling both sad and, I guess, irritated that Gil hadn't even come down to say good night. I remember thinking, 'This feels like we're divorced already.' I went upstairs, stuck my head into Alan's and Susie's rooms the way I always do, then came into our bedroom.

"Gil wasn't in bed, which puzzled me. He never stays up so late. He has to be on the six forty-five train in the morning. A couple of times lately, he has drunk himself to sleep in the upstairs den, but I had passed by the den and the lights were out. Then I noticed that our bathroom door was closed."

She cupped her shaking hands around the coffee mug as if they were cold. Her knuckles were white.

"Kit," she said softly, "it was the most awful thing I've

ever seen. I can't imagine that I'll ever get over having seen it, let alone dealing with the police, the kids, Gil—"

I nodded. "It must be dreadful, Marianne, but I've got to hear it while it's fresh."

"Okay," she said, closing her eyes, speaking in a monotone. I knew I would have to come back for additional details or clarifications, but if it helped to say she had to tell it only once, that was a pardonable fib.

"On the way upstairs, I thought I'd heard a splashing sound. As I said, Gil likes to take late-night baths, and once in a while he drifts off to sleep in the warm tub. That was my first notion. But then I saw the water. . . . I guess I thought one of the kids had dropped some paint into the tub, but then I saw . . . He was lying on his side. The upper part of his head was above the water."

"His nose was above the water?" I interrupted.

"Maybe," she said flatly. "It could have been. I don't really know. I think I screamed, then I remembered the kids and forced myself to shut up. I rushed forward and pulled him up. It was then I saw the gash. It was horrible. Blood was still pouring—" She gagged, spit her coffee up onto her slacks, began to sob. I pulled my chair over next to hers, put my arm around her. I said nothing. She pulled away and quickly resumed. Marianne Dow wasn't the type who was comfortable falling apart and being comforted.

"I opened the drain, tilted his head back, then ran into the bedroom and dialed nine-one-one. I ran downstairs and opened the front door so they wouldn't have to waste time breaking it down, ran upstairs and started mouth-to-mouth. Gil was making this horrible, gurgling sound, and his eyes had rolled back into his head.

"I remember hearing the sirens, and I was shouting, 'Up here, up here,' and the paramedics and the police were there, pushing me aside, putting a mask on Gil. I called my sitter, a lovely elderly woman who lives down the block, and asked her to come back to be with the children. She came running over in her robe. Then we were at the hospital, and they kept asking me a lot of questions."

Sweat slicked her face. How much more could I ask her to endure?

"Marianne, you mentioned hearing a splash. Could you be more specific?"

She shook her head. "Not really. It sounded like somebody moving a bit in the tub, that's all. I didn't hear anything else. No shout, no noise, nothing."

"And Gil never said a word?"

"Never. The wound is so dreadful, I can't imagine that anybody could survive it. Look," she said, beseechingly, an unspoken plea for me to stop.

"That's enough for now," I agreed. "But there's something Levin will ask you, and that I have to know. Chief Leeming says Andrea Lucca has been reported missing. He tells me there were some messages from you on her machine and they weren't pleasant. You didn't mention that at the mall the other day."

She shuddered. "I'm so embarrassed. . . . I told you I tried to call her. On a couple of those messages, I said something like 'Andrea, I don't know why you're doing this to me, I can't believe we were so close and you're betraying me and my family.' I told her to stop. I said I would fight for my family, not just sit back and watch it fall apart. Something like that. I was pretty angry."

"How angry can you get?" The implications of the question were surely not lost on me. But I'm a one-man band. I rely a lot on intuition, and to have any, I need to see someone react to difficult, even provocative questions and situations.

"Kit, I don't know if I can really explain this to a man. Given the species, you seem a pretty receptive one, so I'll try. But put yourself in my place if you can. I'm a logical person. I know the law. I'm not going to go over to her apartment and punch her out, as a man might. Yet she's violated me in the most personal way imaginable. She's invaded my house, befriended my children, almost surely slept with my husband. Nothing can quite be the same again. How am I to react to that? Sometimes I'm furious. Sometimes I feel like I'm about to fall apart. Sometimes I just can't fathom it. During one of the angry moments, I called her up, not to threaten her but to reason with her. Do you understand?"

I said I did, insofar as I could. But my job wasn't just to sympathize. And neither one of us had time for me to play therapist. "Would someone like Leeming interpret those messages as threatening?"

"You mean would a jury?" she asked bluntly. "Maybe. I was enraged at the time. I wanted Andrea to know that I wasn't going to let her do this to me. I wanted her to understand that if she thought I was just going to throw up my hands and run, she was terribly wrong. I owed Gil and my kids more than that. I believe in the family, Kit, in people coming together and trying their damnedest to stay together. I *was* threatening her, in a way, with the fact that I was going to fight."

"How hard?"

She stood up abruptly, avoiding my eyes. "Not that hard, friend. I was wounded and angry and ready to slug her, but the truth is, I couldn't hurt a tick. Unless he was on a witness stand." She smiled. It wasn't much of a smile, but it was the first one I'd seen from her this morning, and it was slightly reassuring.

Marianne walked into the kitchen and returned with the two-thousand-dollar check I had rejected two days before.

"Thanks," I said, accepting it. "You're my client now. I've even earned a bit of this already. Look, do you know a woman in your aerobics class named Donna Platt?"

Marianne seemed lost for a second. "Oh, sure, Donna. Short with brown hair, big heavy glasses?" I nodded. "Why?"

I explained about the visit to Roberta Bingham, and my calls to two of the women on Roberta's list. I told her what Donna Platt had told me about Lucca and her husband, about the Platts' divorce and the dispirited house I'd seen. As I spoke, there was no expression of vindication, no look of I-told-you-so on Marianne's face. She looked as if someone had punched her brutally in the stomach.

"Andrea's a pretty active little friend, isn't she?" she said, after a bit. "I can't believe it. I can't believe I could have so misjudged somebody. My God, poor Donna. But now you believe me?"

I got up. "Well, maybe not yet, not the way you want, Marianne. Lucca may have had an affair with Gil. And maybe with Stan Platt, too. It's pretty disgusting, but it happens. I can't yet look you in the eye and say, 'Yes, I believe that this woman set out to destroy your family.' "

Her look was controlled but cold. "And what would it take to convince you?"

"I need to find out more about Andrea, I guess. I just need to know more. I'm on it, I can promise you that. I'm clearing my desk; you have my full attention, believe me. And my support."

She acknowledged that with a brief nod. "I'm sorry for slobbering, Kit. I don't like it. It's a nightmare I haven't had time to assimilate. I've got to get over to the hospital now. I hope my sitter can be flexible. She usually works thirty or thirty-five hours a week, but it will be more this week. Do you need anything else from me?"

This was no time to be a pussycat. If I had any doubts about Marianne, I had to resolve them. I could see from the way she steeled herself that she knew what I was going to ask.

"Did you have an argument with Gil last night?"

"No."

"Did you hit him in anger?"

"No."

"Punish him in some way?"

"No."

"Did you hit him accidentally?"

"No."

"Did you try to kill him?"

Some silence. "No." She whispered. "I swear on my children's lives, I didn't harm Gil in any way."

"Have you talked to Andrea or seen her recently?"

She shook her head.

"Do you have any idea where she is?"

"No. I just hope it's far away and unpleasant."

"Can you imagine any way in which anyone else could have entered this house, gone into your bathroom, attacked Gil, then left the house without your noticing or hearing a thing?"

This time her answer was quick and direct, her gaze unwavering.

"No."

CHAPTER 8

During the fifteen-minute drive to the mall, I decided it was time to activate my Suburban Detective Action Team. Not the stuff of comic books, exactly, but it worked for me.

The team consisted of a computer mole working deep inside a credit agency, and my only real cop source, Sergeant Tagg of the New Jersey State Police. My plan was to start them both trawling for information on Andrea Lucca, her background, financial history, and current whereabouts. When I arrived at the office, Evelyn was looking especially prim, which meant she would momentarily mount a let's-catch-up-on-paperwork campaign, but I ignored her long enough to contact my commandos, saving Tagg for last.

I had met Bill Tagg only once—in a courtroom where a teenaged client I'd yanked from the clutches of a drug dealer was testifying. Tagg, who had made the arrests using information I'd supplied, was a short, sour-looking man in a rumpled suit who'd made it clear that while we could occasionally do business, we weren't going to be buddies. That was fine with me.

On the phone, where all contact now took place, Tagg had a knack for sounding bored while actually being extremely alert. He had no taste for small talk about how I was, made no pretense of caring, and responded to inquiries into his own well-being with a noncommittal "unnnh." I had been of intermittent use to him, handing over drug dealers preying on affluent suburban teens, and he would be of intermittent use to me. I hoped this was one of those times.

"L-u-c-c-a comma A-n-d-r-e-a? Lemme see." I heard the clicking of a computer keyboard. "Bingo. There's a missing-person's alert out on her from Rochambeau PD. No details." Interesting. The chief had somehow neglected to mention this to me.

Even if my little network succeeded in dredging up such information, it might not reveal what I really wanted to know: was Andrea Lucca merely a garden-variety slut or the Ted Bundy of suburbia, as Marianne fervently believed? Was Lucca being scapegoated for other people's self-generated marital woes? In a tightly woven environment like Rochambeau's, weren't paranoia and finger pointing possible or even likely? Perhaps Lucca was being branded the scheming Other Woman because she was single. It was a wariness not unheard of in a couple-dominated town. I had to get a better bead on her, and fast.

I thanked Tagg, who grunted in reply; then I called to check on Marianne. Her baby-sitter said she was still at the hospital and gave me the number.

Gil's condition hadn't changed. "I can see by the doctors' faces that they're pessimistic," Marianne reported dully. She sounded utterly drained. "I have to prepare Alan and Susie.

He could make it, but I don't think he will. Though"—a burst of hopefulness seemed to seize her—"sometimes people do come out of comas, don't they?"

I didn't respond. I'd learned the hard way not to get too close to clients. And as much as I instinctively liked Marianne, I could only guess at whether she was capable of braining her husband with a blunt instrument or not. My guess was no, but other people had different instincts.

There were now, she added, two unmarked Rochambeau police cars parked in front of her house, according to her unnerved baby-sitter. What if the children noticed them? How could she explain? The lift in her voice flattened again.

I tried to be soothing, mumbling some inanity about the cops taking precautions, in case whoever attacked Gil returned. I didn't tell her that I took the arrival of the second car as an ominous sign.

"I have a dreadful feeling about this, Kit. I'm scared sick about Gil, then I worry about the kids, then I worry about me. I have this sense that things are moving all around me that I can't see or understand. I know the police are suspicious of me. I love Gil and I'm so worried about him and so furious with him—"

"Marianne," I interrupted. "Don't talk about this on the phone. Let's see what we can find out. I've checked around and I'm going to try to see another member of your aerobics class now. Then I'll start trying to locate Andrea myself. You just worry about Gil, the kids, and yourself. Talk to your lawyer this afternoon. Don't talk to anyone else. I'll visit in the morning."

There was only one reason Leeming would have cops keeping their eyes on both the front and side doors. One police car was usually plenty for deterrence, unless Leeming was expecting Saddam; two meant that the chief was making sure his suspect didn't bolt before he could clap handcuffs on her.

We agreed to call if either of us had any news.

"Kit," said Evelyn firmly when I hung up. "The claims investigators want their reports. I assured them they would have them." She sat down, steno notebook in hand. Half an hour later she had them.

Since I had some time before I had to load Em's science project into the Volvo for the annual Lucretia Mott Elementary School Science Fair, I decided to swing by Gay Tannenbaum's apartment.

Magnolia, only two blocks long, is one of the few drab streets in Rochambeau. Gay Tannenbaum's modest complex was a series of boxlike red brick apartments. The paint was beginning to peel from the window trim, and the grounds suggested neglect despite a couple of spindly trees planted out front. The lawns were pocked with brown patches, the gardens overgrown with weeds—rather like mine. Naturally, the place has rustically been named Lake in the Pines.

The street was crammed with kids, roller-skating, playing catch, spraying each other with giant water guns, racing back and forth like kamikazes on bikes. I was surprised by the population density. Most of Rochambeau feels spread out—broad streets, houses with lots of room between them, wide lawns, and leafy backyards. The sounds of children playing are constant but distant, dreamy background noises. Magnolia Street, however, was more urban, more condensed. That is to say, more poor.

"G. Tannenbaum" was written neatly in ink on a yellowing piece of cardboard taped over the bell of Apartment 1A. I pushed the buzzer three times, until a cheerful voice crackled back.

"Yes. What is it?"

"My name is Kit Deleeuw. I'm a private investigator—"

"A what?" squawked the voice.

"I got your name from Roberta Bingham at the aerobics class."

The buzzer bleated. Apartment 1A was in the basement of the building, down a hallway that reeked of food, a sign of cheap ventilation. The woman who opened the plywood door was quite different from Marianne, Roberta Bingham, or the other women I had encountered thus far on this case.

For one thing, she was working class, not unheard of in Rochambeau but unusual, given housing prices. Her hair was teased and frosted, Jersey-girl style. Beneath a sturdy coat of makeup, her face looked cheerful but pasty, as if she didn't get outside much. The oversize floral-print blouse she wore didn't match the striped jeans below it. She was slender but a bit soft, as if she no longer exercised much. I had the sense that she was probably quite a looker a couple of years ago, but no longer had the time or money to keep up the effort. In another setting, I would have taken Gay Tannenbaum for a stressed-out community-college student, crashing for finals while juggling a receptionist's job.

Behind her, towels and clothes were draped thickly over the chrome-and-vinyl dinette chairs. The place was far from a slum, but it was a pretty jarring contrast to the graciousness of her former address.

"May I come in?" I asked in my most cheerful and trustworthy tone.

Gay Tannenbaum shook her head without apology or ill will.

"No, I'm sorry, but I don't think so. I don't know you, and I'm not clear what you want. And my kids are here. I don't know if I want to talk in front of them, and I don't want to leave them alone. Before," she said with a slight smile, "we could have gone into the sun room. But as you can see, we don't have a sun room anymore. So just ask me what you want to know. I have to go on shift soon, so I don't have that much time."

"On shift?"

"I'm a nurse at the Meadows Rehab Center down near Neptune. I work with brain-damaged children: car crashes, bike and skateboard accidents, a few gunshot wounds to the head from New York City."

"That's got to be rough work."

"It is, but I love it, if you know what I mean. You might stagger into bed at night, but you know you did some good, at least most days. But you didn't come here to talk about my work, right? And given the state of my social life, I can't imagine what brought you here."

Tannenbaum had the easy air of a person with an un-troubled conscience. When you introduce yourself as a private investigator, words that still emerge haltingly from my mouth, lots of people get a panicky look as they mentally run through all of the things you might be visiting them for.

I offered her some generalities. I was working for some-one in her former exercise class, I said, somebody whose mar-riage had been undermined. She didn't seem to want or need any additional explanation; she just looked puzzled, wonder-ing what all this had to do with her.

She yelled over her shoulder to her invisible children that she would be busy for a few minutes. She said that they could turn on the TV and have a few pretzels and some milk, but nothing else. I heard a thundering of feet, which in my house meant siblings rushing to snare the best seat on the couch in front of the television. Then I heard a thump and a shriek. "Kevin," she shouted, barely turning around. "You hit your sister again, and you won't see the TV for a week." There were impassioned denials, then countercharges, then silence.

"I guess you could say my marriage was badly shaken up, too," she said, turning back to me. "We split. It's just me and the kids now."

"I'm sorry," I said. But I wasn't surprised.

"No bad feeling, though," she added quickly. "Bob and I, we're still friends." We were still standing in her doorway. She wasn't hostile, but she hadn't invited me in either.

"That's an accomplishment," I said. "I can tell you from my work, that isn't the norm. The bad blood . . ." I didn't need to spell it out.

She shrugged and crossed her arms over her chest. "This wasn't anybody's fault, you know? It just wasn't right. Bob went to an Ivy League college and a top law school, and I studied nursing in Jersey City. We both thought it would work anyway, but when we moved out here, I don't know . . . we were just too different. And my work, not a lot of men could live with what I bring home." A bit of elated pride crept into her voice.

She had a right to feel proud. I knew how hard it was for Jane to stagger home after what she heard all day long, then transform herself to be the loving wife and mother. "I'll bet." I was sincere in my admiration, but I also saw a way in.

Gay nodded. "I mean, last night Ishm—well, this kid from the city who fell, or maybe was pushed, out of a third-floor window and broke his back? He moved his fingers for the first time in a month. The whole ward went crazy, like he'd won the lottery. I was still crying when I got home." She shook her head. "Maybe in six months or a year he'll move his whole hand."

My own work felt remarkably cushy by comparison, irregular income aside. "You deserve a lot of credit for that. But,"

I prompted, "you weren't in rehab work when you moved out here?"

"Oh, no. I quit nursing for a while when we moved from the city. I had two little kids, and I didn't like the idea of turning them over to a nanny. I mean, what's the point of having them if someone else is going to take care of them all day? And they're not little for long, I'll tell you that." She didn't have to tell me. But most women talked to me as if I couldn't possibly know such things.

I let it pass, though. If I stayed quiet for a bit, she might lead where I wanted to go—toward her divorce.

"But, you know, that house we moved to across town on Gateway, it wasn't my speed. I've got no reason to complain —lovely neighborhood and all—but I just didn't feel comfortable. If you wore polyester, it was like you'd broken one of the Ten Commandments. I'm just a reverse Cinderella. Grew up in Jersey City, then moved to a castle with a prince, then figured out I belonged in fucking Jersey City—excuse me. Bob sure tried. He still does. Anything the kids need that I can't give them, I just ask. He's taking them to Orlando this summer. In a way, we still appreciate each other. It's just better if we don't live together, I guess."

If I read her right, this woman was far sadder about the way she hadn't been able to love what was supposed to be a great life than she was about leaving it.

"But at least," I said, nudging her back toward the issue of Andrea Lucca, "there was no horrible quarrel, nothing that would keep you from having an amicable relationship."

She shook her head. "No. I know he was just trying to give us the American Dream. When I was a kid, I would never have dreamed of a house like that, you know what I mean? The backyard was like a park, with two huge trees and a little valley that was the kids' secret place. My place was on the second floor, a room facing south, full of plants and flowers; when I wasn't taking care of the kids, I was repotting and misting those plants. But most of the time I did take care of Kevin and Melissa. I drove them to play groups, to the park to feed the ducks, to doctors and dentists, to Toys "Я" Us, to museums." She paused, remembering. "I was sure my mom would think I'd flipped out when I told her I was splitting. But she just said, 'Gay, you seemed like you were living out of your own skin and inside somebody else's.' She was right."

"While you were living there, you joined an aerobics class, right?" I none-too-subtly interjected.

She flashed me a wan smile. "Yeah, that was a kick. Nice people, and I was in great shape for a few months there. In the neighborhood where I grew up, the idea of women jumping around in spandex pants for kicks, well . . . But Roberta, the lady who teaches the class, she was a killer. A *killer*. She really cared about getting everybody in shape, and you got in shape." I was struck at the way Tannenbaum, whom I already liked, talked about her former existence the way a middle-aged person recounts a postcollege trek through Europe. "Thing is, you have to have time, as well as money, for that. I don't anymore."

Gay asked if I wanted a Diet Pepsi. I said yes. She disappeared into the apartment, then came back with two from the fridge, yelling to the kids that she would be out front. Cans in hand, we walked the few steps down the hall and out the apartment's front entrance, where she lit a cigarette and settled herself on the top step. I kept trying to keep the conversation aimed at her split-up and any connection Andrea Lucca might have had with it.

"Some people really loved that class," I prompted.

She looked at me strangely. "For me it was just an exercise class. Some of the other girls were good friends, but I just sweated my ass off—excuse my French," I shrugged; I could take it.

"Some of the women there called themselves Recovering Moms. You gotta love the name. But where I come from, heavy-duty personal conversations are between family or old friends. Here you jump up and down with somebody for twice a week, you're practically sisters. I just wanted to keep from sagging. You wouldn't know it to look at me at this moment, but I was in terrific shape."

She wasn't complaining. Tannenbaum's philosophy seemed to be that some things work out and some things don't. The world had expected her to be happy on Rochambeau's affluent, upper-middle-class track, and she was bewildered but relieved to find that she was happier now. Like me, in a way. Sometimes you end up finding yourself almost by accident.

The sun was beginning to lower over the apartment buildings across the lawn. The rhythms of the street changed, as kids filtered into the buildings for dinner. Gay went in to check on the kids, then returned with a colorless beige sweater over her shoulders.

"Did you make any *special* friends in the class?" I was losing any pretense of subtlety.

She watched me closely, knowing I was edging toward something, too smart to talk much until she knew what I was after. "Yeah, I did, as a matter of fact. After a few weeks in the class, this incredibly nice person, a single woman, came up and introduced herself. She said she couldn't help noticing my energy, and she asked me out to lunch. We hit it off right away. She seemed to find me the most interesting person on earth."

"Did that strike you as odd? I'm sure you *are* interesting, but—"

"No need to explain." She smiled ruefully. "I understand what you're asking. But when someone with no conceivable motive for bullshit appears and tells you how fascinating you are, well, it's a good start as far as I'm concerned. I loved those lunches. They were among my best memories from the Gateway Street time."

"Did your buddy ever meet Bob?"

Gay shook her head. "We talked once or twice about having dinner, but never got around to it. I think I was a little jealous of her, you know what I mean? I didn't want to share her. She understood me. Like she knew it was okay for me not to want that life, that it wasn't me. She was really supportive when I left. She was a great friend. I owe her a lot. But she never met Bob, at least not that I know of."

She put the soda can down on the stoop, cocked an ear to pick up any untoward child noises, then looked pointedly at her watch. Her patience was wearing thin. "So what's this about, anyway?"

I ran my hands through my hair. This calm account of the disintegration of her marriage wasn't what I had expected. "I'm talking about Andrea Lucca," I said. "Are you?"

She nodded, wary eyes on me.

"You still talk to her?"

"Not for months," Gay said. "My schedule makes it crazy. And . . . I don't know, she got busy. We haven't kept up. I'm like a cop now—I can really only relax around other rehab workers and social workers. Andrea's an artist. But she's good people, I'll tell you that, pal." She said it softly, but with conviction.

She flicked her cigarette out into the bushes, reached into

her pocket, and lit another. A voice from inside yelled something about pretzels, and Gay yelled over her shoulder in that strange way, as if she were talking to the apartment rather than any person within it, "Yeah, six each. No more."

I laughed. "Will they stick to six each?"

Her face broke into a sly smile. "You've got kids?" I nodded. "What do you think? But a limit will keep them from eating the whole bag. Maybe."

She took a long drag on the cigarette. I saw people smoking so rarely these days that the action struck me as almost eccentric, a statement of distress. But that was probably because I was surrounded by relatively affluent people. Lots of the people who paraded through the American Way in sneakers and stonewashed denims smoked.

"Is Andrea in some sort of trouble?" Gay asked finally.

I hesitated. I had to be careful. "Look, Gay, I appreciate your talking to me. I can see that you're a person who would take loyalty to a friend very seriously. But I need to ask you a tough question. Please, don't take it as a reflection on your friend, or your husband, or anything. It's just something I have to ask in connection with this case I'm working on." I looked at her beseechingly.

Her expression didn't change. "Mr. Deleeuw, in my work, I learn to take just about anything. You're not going to shock me and you're not going to scare me, not unless you got bad news about my kids. Do you?"

"No. But is there any chance at all that Andrea was involved with Bob? That they had something going behind your back? That she contributed in any way to the breakup of your marriage? I should tell you I have no reason to assume that she did, but she's been accused of things like this. . . ."

For a second I feared I might get knocked right off her

stoop. But Gay took a couple of deep drags on her cigarette, probably scanning back over the months before her divorce.

"Shit, that's a kick in the gut. That's one I wasn't prepared for," she murmured.

"I can see that," I said, as gently as I could.

She took another drag. "Hey, who the fuck can ever say for sure, one hundred percent? But I think I would have guessed. And I don't think Andrea would do that to me. I mean, she was such a good friend when I needed one, it hurts even to think about that."

I leaned back on the stoop. "But is it possible?"

"Jeez, anything's possible. I'm an adult, I know what goes on." She was mulling it over, looking sorrowful, maybe a little disturbed. "Bob did act funny before we split up. He'd disappear for a few hours here and there, come home late without a reason. . . . But, Christ, screwing around with Andrea? Nope, I don't think so. Not that he would admit it if he had, I suppose. He knows I wouldn't think a lot of a guy who cheated on his wife and two little kids."

I tried again, in a couple of different ways. Gay thought about it some more. She couldn't imagine an affair in the first place, and couldn't imagine not having discovered one in the second. But an impossibility? She wouldn't go that far. "And I have to say, I never heard from her much after we split up," she added. "But that isn't proof, is it?"

I shook my head. "Not at all." We sat without speaking for a while, until the soda cans were empty. Then I stood.

"Well, look, I gotta go. I've got to get my daughter and her project to the science fair. I can't thank you enough for your time."

Gay Tannenbaum ground her cigarette under her heel and got to her feet. "Good luck on the science fair. I hope you don't have to do the bread molds. Every year it's either bread molds or the goddamn ant farm." She wafted back toward her apartment, looking, I thought, troubled and confused. I liked her a lot. I hoped I hadn't infected her relationship with her ex, but she didn't seem as certain about things as she had earlier. Still, she'd been right about one thing: no proof.

As I headed home, Marianne's almost desperate question kept echoing in my head: what would it take to convince me that Andrea Lucca was out to destroy people's families? I still didn't know. Donna Platt's story was a good start. But Gay Tannenbaum had a somewhat different take. If Andrea had broken up the Tannenbaum marriage, she had done it differently—more discreetly, less malevolently. Maybe Gay didn't want to know the truth about her marriage. Maybe it was better to see the divorce as a sad but healthy act of mutual parting, rather than the kind of betrayal that had torn Donna Platt's life apart.

In the couple of years since I took over a lot of the child care, I've come to see the experience of being a parent as so extraordinary and absorbing and emotional that you can't comprehend what it's like before you have a kid and can't quite recall the details afterward. That's why couples with teenagers can't bear their friends' toddlers and why grandparents and parents often have so much friction, I think. None of these groups can quite relate to the others, even though you've all been through the same experience, more or less.

When your kid comes into the world, you are up at bat in probably the most profound way you ever are. Not that having children is the only meaningful experience in life—I know that's not so—it's just that for most people child rearing is the time when your successes and your mistakes so clearly and visibly affect, enhance, damage, or even destroy a helpless person's life. It's your turn to put your instincts, values, and experiences on the line. With little real training or preparation, you suddenly have all these choices to make about school, bedtime, TV, religion, toys, chores, allowances. How many water guns to buy, how much reading to require, how much civil conversation to insist upon, how much to trust them alone, how much punishment (if any) when rules are broken. When they can cross the street by themselves, go to sleep-away camp, pierce their ears, or stay up for *Saturday Night Live.*

The list goes on forever. And you don't know for years, maybe decades, how it's really going to turn out. Still, you can hardly help measuring your own children constantly, comparing them to others' to gauge how they're doing. And, to be truthful, how you're doing. The Great Suburban Sweepstakes.

In our house the idea of an iron-willed dad putting his foot down would be met with incredulity and howls of laughter. Almost all decisions are debated endlessly in daily discussions. Jane likes the kids to be involved in sports, although she can't bear to watch the other parents at games. I don't really care if they have milk at every meal. She likes bedtimes to be regular and fixed; I don't care if they stay up reading till midnight. She can hardly say no to Ben; I can rarely resist Emily's sustained pleading. Ben is smart and slick enough to manipulate me when he wants to, but Em doesn't usually have to bother.

Still, Jane and I have rather little to fight about when it comes to raising Emily and Ben. We share the same basic values about family, responsibilities, education, and courtesy. Once we agree on a policy, we try to project a united front, and we sometimes even succeed. The kids find lots of our decisions ridiculous, but they're pretty good about accepting them, which is all you can ask.

To me it is this process, this endless dialogue—a complicated tapestry of decisions, regulations, sensitivities and ethics, conversation and negotiation—that is at the core of parenting and determines what kind of people our children become. It never occurred to me that our family could be threatened, even devastated, by the sudden appearance of someone like Andrea Lucca, an outsider with the obscene power to wreck us emotionally. Anybody who ever turns on a TV sees the things that can derail a family: random violence, illness, tornadoes. But the kind of thing that had happened to Donna Platt (and maybe, without her knowing it, to Gay Tannenbaum)? It never crossed my mind.

That's why this case was beginning to haunt me, I thought, as I lugged Emily's science-fair entry out of the Volvo and into the gym later that evening. I could see curious parental eyes trying to scope out what I was carrying. This was, after all, the big moment. Parents and kids slaved for weeks, even months, on their science projects.

For parents anxious to demonstrate that they have produced superior children—and are therefore superior parents—the school system, like the athletic leagues around town, is a license to kill. Parents are not supposed to get involved in science-fair projects, a rule that produces knowing chuckles among public-school veterans as they race back and forth to hardware and art-supply stores, install wires, play with filaments, handle rats doomed to sacrifice their lives in the interests of science.

One such experiment last year proved a turning point in Em's political life. We'd traveled to Grove Station, a dingy factory town west of Rochambeau where, at a pet store named Danny's, you could find anything from pythons to Vietnamese pigs. The cages reeked and flies dive-bombed the patrons. We left with three white mice, to whom Em and her friend and science partner, Blair, planned to feed Snickers and sugar water for eight weeks to measure the effects of sweets on weight and health. On the fifteenth day, however, we came downstairs to three dead mice. Em buried them in the backyard and cried for ten minutes or so, after which she and Blair became vegetarians and fanatic animal-rights activists, surviving ever since exclusively on pasta, pizza, peanut butter, carrots, beans, and fruits. They now write angry letters to furriers and study the labels of shampoo bottles as if they're the Dead Sea Scrolls to make sure the stuff wasn't tested on bunnies. The kicker was that their mouseless project won second place that year, the judges being happy to honor any evidence that sugar must be fatal.

When I found myself at home after leaving Wall Street, I seized upon such projects, not only to give me something to do but to demonstrate that I could be a good father. Em has nearly forgiven me for dragging her to Creative Expressions (Rochambeau's wondrous child arts store) for glue, paint, and papier-mâché, from which we constructed the largest, loudest, and most disastrous volcano outside of Kilauea. Our first science project together was four feet tall, the outside covered with genuine dirt, mud, pebbles, and grass, with a deep center crater. At the bottom of the crater, we'd secreted a small well of lighter fluid to send flame and smoke out from the top. For added impact, I'd obtained a few small firecrackers to throw in from time to time for sound effects, figuring the judges would certainly marvel at our dedication and ingenuity.

I'd smugly noted the anxious gazes of parents and kids as

I rolled our huge mountain past rain forests in fish tanks, countless mold-on-bread displays, and hapless house plants exposed to repeated doses of Metallica and Mozart.

"Jeez," said our tablemate as I heaved the giant volcano onto the table, then tossed a match down the center. Most of the children screamed when the thing went up. So did a lot of the parents and teachers.

"Please move calmly out of the gym," rasped the bull-horn-armed principal with considerable authority as smoke billowed from the top of the volcano and supersensitive smoke alarms went off all over the building. The piercing wails of a score of sirens permeated the nervous titters of children and muttering of parents as everyone filed out of the gym and the firemen came pouring in.

"Thank God the sprinkler system didn't come on," Jane said later that night, sitting me down at the kitchen table and delivering the first of a score of lectures on being supportive without taking over, allowing children to take responsibility for what they do, finding my own creative outlets, etc. It's taken me a couple of years to really get it, but in the meantime Em has never let me do more than carry her project into the gym, under the suspicious gaze of the principal. Sometimes—like this time—I didn't even know what it was.

She'd been threatening to enter a project demonstrating that cheerleading caused brain damage, a notion she'd been chuckling over ever since she'd read a statistic in *Sassy* magazine about how many cheerleading-related injuries occur in American schools each day. But that was a joke. I think.

CHAPTER 9

Between Monday and Thursday, what had appeared to be a marital problem that really required a counselor had mushroomed into a bizarre and complex case, different from anything I'd ever handled or even heard of. Private investigators these days don't exactly resemble Philip Marlowe and Lew Archer. We deal much more in computers and balance sheets than in actual snooping. We hunt for the hidden assets of deadbeat husbands, follow the computer traces and trails of insurance fraud, and pore over warehouse inventories to figure out how VCRs and microwaves disappear.

But this was uncharted ground. I had wondered if Marianne Dow had her head on straight, especially after I had talked with Gay Tannenbaum. I don't run into a lot of people who take responsibility for their own troubles these days. When your business fails, when the *New Yorker* doesn't want your brilliant short story, when you get fired, and especially when you get divorced, it is always somebody else's fault. Many times it *is* somebody else's fault. But I'd feel better if I met just one person somewhere along the way who said, "I'm in trouble because I screwed up." Or "I messed up my marriage, not Andrea Lucca."

Donna Platt and Gay Tannenbaum were both dream witnesses in any court. Marianne's and Donna's stories were shocking and powerful. These were among the most fortunate and entitled women there were: attractive, articulate, educated, skilled. They had worked hard to build families that were important to them. And yet they both claimed one woman—somebody I had yet to lay eyes on—had brought them and their lifetime game plans crashing down. Yet this was the same woman that Gay Tannenbaum assured me had helped her regain control of her life.

I couldn't wait to get a look at her. If my client was to be believed, Andrea Lucca was chilling, a flash of good old-fashioned evil, of malevolence far beyond infidelity. The question was how to find her. I had to track down her friends or family, or else find some credit-card or travel expense that would tip me to her whereabouts. That part *was* in my line of work. At breakfast I jotted three things down on yellow Post-Its and stuck them to my arm. When I got into the Volvo, I would transfer them to the rearview mirror, unless I forgot about them, in which case Evelyn usually spotted them when I got to the mall.

I could not survive a day without Post-Its. Jane thinks this is all preparation for my being a dotty old man, but I place these stickum notes right up there with Velcro and running shoes as landmark American inventions of the twentieth century. I stick my canary-yellow reminders to refrigerators, windows, the inside of the Volvo, sometimes even my forehead. It isn't a foolproof system: I occasionally find Post-Its from months ago stuck here or there. Periodically, I sweep through the house wiping the slate clean, shocked at how much I still manage to forget.

Jane is more organized. Over breakfast she told me she'd gone to the NYU library to do some reading on obsessive, triangular relationships. Part of what she was learning did seem to come right out of Andrea Lucca's life, or what I had been hearing about it.

"One study I found deals with the triangulation I was telling you about; that's what I suspect you're dealing with," she said, wolfing down her second slice of honey-smeared wheat toast and her second cup of Kit's secret coffee blend. "As usual, it's more complicated than our stereotypical notions of it."

We didn't have much time to chat. Thursday was Jane's nine A.M. to ten P.M. day at the clinic, thirteen straight hours of neglect, abuse, violence, abandonment, and hopelessness, as she put it.

We were interrupted by the frantic and thunderous appearance of Ben and Em, scrambling to get off to school. My only kid chore that afternoon was to drive Em to the library so she could research her school paper on ghosts and spirits. I scribbled another Post-It and slapped it on the back of my hand.

Ben didn't need driving much anymore. His hobby these days was being cool, researching how to be cool, buying and ordering things that looked cool, experimenting with things that might prove cool, avoiding whatever appeared uncool. This involved endless, mysterious efforts and rituals that made baseball caps seem a snap. Sometimes his jeans were high on the hip, sometimes down so far he could barely walk. Strange new words—"hype," "fly," "phat"—popped out as greetings or responses to questions. The more puzzled you became by all this, the dumber and more out of it you seemed. "That's okay," I assured him. "I don't like you much either."

What fascinates me is how they all know at the same moment what's in and what's out. Is there, I wonder, some secret fax service, whose existence is automatically forgotten when you turn eighteen, which flashes the word about the latest sneaker, whether denim shorts should be cuffed or frayed, which T-shirt is hot? And if so, how can I subscribe and rake in some of the zillions that Murray Grobstein is making in his sneaker store?

What was uncool, on the other hand, was perfectly obvious: being seen anywhere with parents, describing much of anything about one's day, speaking in complete sentences.

Jane assures me this is appropriate, even healthy behavior for a boy Ben's age. He has to become independent, she says. He can either do it this way or in less appealing ways, which in Rochambeau means drugs or liquor. I like his way better.

In sporadic moments when no one is looking, he can abruptly and mysteriously open up like a flower in the sunlight for a few delightful minutes and chat about friends, schoolwork, the family, or even politics. One day he announced he was going to play football; on another he disclosed that he was volunteering one lunch hour a week in a soup kitchen. Although I often missed him, I could not begrudge him his autonomy. Our job as parents was, after all, to make ourselves obsolete.

Jane and I pored breathlessly over the more voluble moments like Kremlinologists, back when people cared what folks in the Kremlin were up to. But our morning moment with Ben had just passed.

" 'Bye," he said, ricocheting off the wall and out the door for the school bus as Jane and I waved, then laughed. "Nice talking with you," she yelled.

"Yeah," he shot back with a straight face. "It was good for me, too." At least he hadn't lost his sense of humor.

"So," said Jane, looking at the clock and shifting to less domestic subjects, "this is what I've read about triangulation that might be relevant." She shrugged into her linen jacket, then stopped and looked at me strangely for a moment.

"Lots of people have the desire to stray from time to time," she said. "That's why people are sometimes so suspicious of their spouses: they know potential infidelity exists within *them*, so they assume it's within their partners as well. Sometimes jealousy isn't based on any specific act or fact but on the idea that we know what *we* might do, what we're capable of."

I glanced protectively at Em, who took a later bus, and who'd been rummaging through the cabinets. But she was slurping down a bowl of Cheerios, absorbed in reading the box for the five-thousandth time as if she were a Russian scholar happening across an undiscovered Tolstoy manuscript. Frosted Flakes and Wheat Chex packages were also reading favorites.

"What are you telling me, Jane? Are you suggesting that these women might have been imagining friendships or relationships? That they were projecting their own feelings onto Lucca or their husbands?"

Jane shrugged. "I don't know these women. I can't diagnose people based on what they say to you. It's just a caution. Remember that Lucca seems like an evil schemer to you now, but you don't know anything about her other than what you've heard from others.

"I've asked staff people around the clinic and my professors. Everybody has heard of or is familiar with case studies of psychotics, of people who hate women enough to stalk them, hurt them, even rape or kill them. But nobody I asked has ever heard of a woman like you're describing, of a family stalker who deliberately insinuates herself into families, then systematically destroys them. I'm not saying it's impossible, or even untrue. Just be careful about accepting other people's interpretations of emotional events and their descriptions of somebody else's motives. We know nothing about Andrea Lucca. We do know there are lots of unhappy marriages out there, and you've certainly stumbled across a few."

Not too many private eyes have a shrink-in-training on their staffs. It would have been dumb not to listen. I was already uneasy about this case, and Jane had put words to my uneasiness. Part of my discomfort came from one of the first things Marianne Dow had told me when we met in the mall. I think her exact words were, "Sometimes I want to kill her." Chief Leeming would love to hear that line, and if subpoenaed and deposed, I'd have to pass it on; I wouldn't lie. But I was getting paid by Marianne Dow to help her. She deserved the benefit of the doubt. My own shattered career was powerful testimony to the fact that the authorities didn't always go after the right person. It had been one of the great shocks of my life, but an instructive one.

"We do know something about Lucca," I countered. "She's missing. I've spent the last two days talking to a bunch of women who would love to see her obliterated, and one of them might have even arranged it. If I read Rochambeau's beloved chief law-enforcement officer right, he figures Andrea Lucca may have come to harm, and he has surrounded my client's house with a good chunk of the department's detective bureau. That's a lot of mistaken people, if you're right."

She picked up her briefcase and kissed me good-bye. "Or the other way around," she said. "*They* might be one hundred percent right. Until you know more about Lucca, you can't know. Seems to me she has lots of good reasons to take a long vacation, or even to leave town permanently. I wouldn't get ready for any homicide trials just yet. Men are always quick to tag women as scheming sex demons."

"True," I conceded. "And by the time you get home tonight, I *will* know more about her, superior suburban sleuth that I am. Maybe even where she is. And you're forgetting one other event not covered by your wise caution."

She raised an eyebrow.

"Well, somebody snuck into Gil Dow's house after midnight Tuesday and took a heavy object and smashed it down on the top of his skull while he was sitting drunkenly but peacefully in the bathtub. I don't know who did it. Maybe Lucca. Maybe Marianne, for that matter. But it does suggest that we're not dealing solely with people's skewed perceptions here. We're dealing with at least one person who is willing to kill."

She frowned. "I hadn't forgotten that, exactly. I'm just absorbing that you're on a possible murder case again. Be careful, okay?"

I nodded, though I was making even myself edgy. I couldn't help feeling a lot of trepidation when my work took me near death or murder. If robbery wasn't the motive for the attack, then what was? What would people kill for? For money. For love. For their families. To protect them. To seek vengeance on those who would destroy them. The hatred generated by divorce cases was sometimes breathtaking. What might somebody do who was betrayed by a spouse and a best friend at the same time?

Today's Post-Its said B.C., LEEMING, COMPUTER CHECKS. And EM TO LIBRARY. Translation: first I was going to stop at the Garden Center to see my friend Benchley Carrollton, who had called and pointedly reminded me that I hadn't stopped by in several weeks.

"What are you up to?" he asked on the phone. "Your seat in the young tree grove stands ready, along with some cool cider."

"I'm knee-deep in a weird case," I replied. "I'm not quite ready to lay it out for you, because I'm not one hundred percent sure about my client. But the basic mission is to check out somebody who kills families for kicks."

"Kills whole families?" Benchley gasped.

"Not with guns or knives. Not like that. Somebody who gets off on befriending the husband or wife and busting up the family. No blood, but the family still dies. Then again, it might not be quite that heavy. It's creeping me out, though. I'll let you know if it gets more serious."

Benchley clucked, horrified, I was sure. Benchley is a mystic, a spirit who can read a simple organism like me at will. If something is happening in my life, his Deleeuw alarm goes off.

That had been true from the start of our friendship. Five years earlier, when I'd found myself suddenly at home with tons of time, a rapidly shrinking bank account, and no prospects that I could imagine, I took up gardening to keep from sticking my head in an oven. Benchley invited me back to his little rain forest for long talks that sometimes were the only thing that kept me going. I have no idea why he thought I could possibly make it as an investigator—life in Rochambeau bore little resemblance to the army that had trained me. I don't know why I believed Benchley when he said I could. What would a Quaker gardener know about detective work anyway? But I got my state investigator's license, bought a gun (which I quickly locked in a safe and then lost the combination to), and started sending fliers out to lawyers.

Ever since, Benchley has become the father I never had (mine died years ago) and the close friend few men ever have.

Benchley seems to know without being told when I am worn-out, frightened, or discouraged. My nature at such times is to go off and brood; Benchley reels me in.

The "tree grove" is actually a greenhouse behind the Rochambeau Garden Center, filled with maples, pin oaks, Bradford pears, weeping willows, and half a dozen other varieties of young trees, soon to be purchased and deployed in the never-ending struggle to make every square inch of Rochambeau shady, atmospheric, and aesthetically pleasing. A score of misters hiss on and off all day and night. My "seat" is next to the central mister control panel, from which I can adjust volume and speed of spray and have fun clicking back and forth. The Lord of the Environment, Benchley needles.

The place feels like a hidden jungle. The soothing sound of water spraying and dripping down onto the leaves, the pungent smell of burlap and soil—it is my favorite place in town. Benchley and I spend countless hours there sipping tea or cider, downing the muffins he loves to bake, talking about my cases or mulling politics, religion, or general observations about Life. Sometimes we just read or sit in silence. I am not a religious person, but I know the tree grove has become a sort of church for me. As for Benchley, who *is* deeply religious, silence comes naturally to him.

He can be outspoken in defense of his trees, though. To buy one, you have to submit to a rigorous adoption process. He wants to know about sunlight and drainage, dogs, the dryness of soil, the use of road salt, whether cars or buses idle nearby, whether you'll water it and how much.

If he isn't happy with your answers, you don't get the tree. He isn't self-righteous or unpleasant about it, just determined that his trees find a safe and appropriate home. Out-of-towners and strangers are incredulous at this tall, elegant, white-haired man who refuses to take their money for a plant.

"They won't let you take a kitten home from an animal shelter if they aren't sure you can take care of it," he explains, not a bit defensively. "A tree can live for a hundred years, grow sixty feet tall, or perish from neglect; why wouldn't you be at least as careful?"

Once he had driven past one of his new Zelkovas withering on someone's lawn from lack of water. He got out of his pickup, grabbed a shovel from the back, and took the tree back to the Garden Center, leaving a frostily polite note behind. He mailed the customer a refund, inviting him back when he felt ready to "undertake a more serious commitment" to shade trees.

No moping about old age or loneliness for eighty-one-year-old Benchley. When he isn't selling, planting, or rescuing trees, he is running the town Historical Society, driving the elderly to supermarkets and doctors' appointments, and visiting nursing homes. I want to be just like him when I grow up. In fact, I want to be just like him right now.

I almost always filled Benchley in instantly on my toughest cases, especially when I got mired, but this one was still too embryonic for much scrutiny.

Benchley was smart, thoughtful, and had an amazing perspective on the town, since a garden center, even more than a school or hardware store, is a suburban common denominator. Some people have kids and some don't, some fix their houses up themselves while others hire contractors, but everybody needs a garden center at one point or another. The Carrolltons have been in the town forever, and Benchley knows most of the people in it. Although he is much too discreet to tell tales, he does occasionally deign to nudge me sagaciously in the right direction.

I'd called Marianne from the house, but the baby-sitter said she was at the hospital. Both police cars, she reported anxiously, were still at their posts. When Marianne had last called in, she'd told the sitter there was no change in Gil's condition. I needed to tell my client what I'd learned about Andrea Lucca, but I wanted to be careful about how and when I talked to her. Marianne wasn't in great shape, and I didn't want to give her any reason to do something dumb with Leeming's bloodhounds sniffing around.

It was eight forty-five—just a few minutes before the Center opened and our quiet little retreat would become less quiet. Benchley came bouncing out the back door, his shock of white hair crowning his tall, angular frame. His retriever, Melody, as discriminating in her affections as Percentage, came bounding joyously over to slurp at my pants leg. Benchley once suggested that we mate our two retrievers, but I feared offspring too dumb to stand up.

"Kit," Benchley said, grasping my hand and eyeing me closely. "You have your 'I'm on a big case' look. Is this your family-destroyer?"

"I'm still in the preliminary snooping stage. You'll know when I move beyond that, psychic that you are."

"Well, I do have supernatural powers, you know that." He'd already set up a tray of cider and muffins in the greenhouse. We sat on the wicker chairs amid the young trees, the misters hissing and spitting all around us. I filled him in a bit. We were close enough now that we both knew the drill. I didn't need to ask for help; he would give as much as he could.

"I know the Dows, especially the husband," he said softly when I'd finished. "They bought a number of white pines for their backyard when they moved in. Platt and Tannenbaum don't ring any bells. Now, Roberta Bingham, she does quite a bit of gardening. I like her a lot. She believes in what she's doing. And it's funny—"

He had thought of something. He frowned, held up a finger, then walked off toward the house and, no doubt, the dining room that he had turned into a study after his wife died a decade ago. He kept his Macintosh there. Benchley had resisted the computer age as long as he could, but I finally had dragged him to a computer warehouse, and now, of course, he was like some teenage techno-wiz in front of a Super Nintendo.

Sure enough, in a couple of minutes he emerged with a printout. "I knew it," he said as we heard the first car pulling into the lot. "Andrea Lucca. I couldn't remember her face, but the name struck me as familiar. She charged a bunch of things on her MasterCard." He paused. I could tell he was mulling the ethics of showing me her bills.

"Look," I said. "If her husband dies, Marianne Dow may be charged with murder at any moment. I need to know as much as I can about this woman. We're talking house plants, aren't we? Not personal letters or data."

He pondered the idea a second longer, then handed me the printout.

"Not house plants," he said. "Trees."

"Trees? She lives in a condo. What would she want with trees?" The invoice listed the purchase of three maples exactly a month ago, each for sixty-five dollars, as well as lesser purchases of plants, seeds, and pots.

Benchley vaguely remembered discussing the maples with her—he always wanted to know where his trees were going—but they hadn't talked long.

I couldn't resist. "I'm amazed, Benchley. Didn't you make certain the trees were going to a happy home?"

"I can't interrogate everybody," he said, a bit primly. "I remember that she wanted them for shade trees. A lot of towns don't like maples for that purpose, because there's been a lot of disease and because they often grow up forked and require more maintenance and pruning. But they provide the loveliest canopies over streets or in backyards, next to oaks. That's all I remember, selling her those maples."

He stared into his cider mug, talking more to himself than to me. "It's terrible to think of Gil Dow being attacked that way. Lord, we've had enough suffering in this town. Although when you read the papers . . . Anyway," he said, snapping out of the sad look he got whenever he contemplated the bloodshed in the world, "they were a quite attractive couple. I'll pray for them. For her, too—Andrea Lucca I mean. I recall her as lovely, very warm. Nice to think of trees going to people like that."

Maybe not, I thought.

I was sure Marianne and Andrea both remembered Benchley fondly too. A remarkable number of people came in and out of the Garden Center, and a considerable proportion of the women seemed to go away sighing about Benchley. I needled him constantly about the number of times women had told me how cute he was, and he flushed like one of his Christmas poinsettias every time.

"Benchley," I said, after a swallow of cider, "who was the last person in your life you met that you *didn't* like? Thinking critically doesn't come naturally to you." It was true; his historic perspective was invaluable, his judgments of people utterly useless.

So Andrea Lucca had bought some maples. I made a mental note to check with Marianne, Donna Platt, and Gay Tannenbaum to see if she'd bought the trees for their yards. If not, there might be a fourth family in Rochambeau about to disintegrate.

What, I wondered, was I supposed to do with a fourth family even if I identified one? Warn them about Lucca's past record? I got the shivers again. If Marianne was correct, this woman had left a lot of suffering in her wake.

I let Benchley tend to his first customer of the day and headed for the police station, intending to try Marianne again, afterward, to check on Gil's progress. What a horrid spot for her if she was telling the truth and really did love Gil —the worried wife a suspect in the near-death of her husband. But it would be even more awkward if she was lying. For one thing, what if Gil recovered, or even regained consciousness for a short while? Did he know the identity of his attacker? Had he seen someone in the mirror? Had the intruder said something? And what would *I* take for the headache that had just started pounding away?

A crumbling red-brick former elementary school now serves as the Township of Rochambeau's Public Safety Center. The town fathers and mothers want the police to be unobtrusive, and if their headquarters had been any more so, it would have collapsed altogether.

Suburban communities are embarrassed even to have police departments, since there isn't supposed to be any crime. Officers aren't supposed to stand out in any way. They are encouraged to keep out of sight while making absolutely certain every auto, stereo, and mountain bike remains unmolested, and they do it with too little backup, for a salary of peanuts. An impossible job, in my view. In Leeming's too— he once conceded he was just hanging on long enough to get his two daughters through college and be eligible for his pension.

A half-dozen marked cruisers were parked along the Center's driveway, mixed in with three or four unmarked cars and a few squat little traffic carts.

Inside, the place looked like my office at the mall before

Evelyn had arrived to bring order to my life. Piles of newspapers, files, and folders were stacked on every visible surface. We had a long way to go in Rochambeau before we tapped into modern law-enforcement technology. In fact, the local PD was one of the few places in contemporary society where you could still hear the clacking of manual typewriters, as cops jabbed out arrest reports with three sheets of carbon paper between the pages.

A computer screen was visible through the dispatcher's window, however. The department had to have some way of running checks on license plates and suspects' records.

I had to wait five minutes for a meeting in the chief's office to break up. He groaned when I came in.

"Downtown merchants," he muttered in explanation, after the five well-dressed men had filed out. "Too much shoplifting. Fuckers are the first ones to get up in town-council meetings and scream bloody murder when I ask for a couple of new slots every year. But let some kid pocket a candy bar, and it's Gotham City versus the Joker. But *you'll* brighten my day, Deleeuw. You always do. Jesus, sometimes I miss Brooklyn." He rolled up a paper ball and tossed it neatly into the wastebasket.

I doubted that his last remark was true. Leeming had done twenty years in New York City, where he'd fought countless battles, many of which seemed indelibly etched onto his face and reflected in his weary eyes.

"Marianne Dow still your client?"

I nodded. I didn't usually share the view that an investigation client was a big secret worth getting roughed up to protect, a philosophy of which I informed prospective clients right away. I didn't want to work for people who had things to hide, and in cases like this, the police could make life unbearable if you didn't tell them.

"Well, here we go again." He scowled. "I know if I warn you off this case, you'll give me an I-told-you-so because you lucked out on the last one." He still thought I was far better suited to selling vacuum cleaners than investigating crimes.

"Deleeuw, I don't think you have yourself another winner here. I could be wrong, but your client is looking sour. My guy at the hospital says her husband is a long shot to make it through the weekend. There's motive—those phone calls to the Lucca woman support it—and there's opportunity. And no shred of evidence that anybody else was in the house."

"None?"

"Not a thing." I couldn't tell whether Leeming was helping me out or trying to scare me off. "No other footprints or fibers in the shag, no fingerprints that can't be accounted for, no sign of forced entry, no open windows. The old lady next door has called nine-one-one about seventy-five times in the past year, every time some teenager with a loud radio drives by the house. She heard nothing. The dog didn't bark. What the fuck do you think happened, man? Some ghost slid through the walls and bonked the hubby, then melted away? Give me a fucking break.

"And where the hell *is* this Lucca? She didn't tell her employer or her landlord that she was going away. She didn't empty out her refrigerator or make arrangements to have anyone take in her mail. She's just gone. You heard your client's messages to her?"

I wouldn't have told him if I had. Since he knew damned well that he hadn't played them for me, my having heard them would mean I had a source in the Rochambeau PD. I didn't, but I did have one in the New Jersey State Police. Leeming sensed I had access to some police information, and it drove him half-mad trying to figure out how.

I shook my head. Maybe this was going to be a lucky encounter.

"Well, you ain't hearing the messages here. The DA would have my hide, and my pension would follow. I'll tell you this much. They're angry, and they're nasty—"

"Fuck you," I said. I'm not good at male blustering. It cracks my family up whenever I try it at home, but if you want to be a private detective, it's supposed to be part of your repertoire. "What did you want her to say, Chief? 'Thanks for diddling my husband and threatening my family? Please consider halting your offensive practices?' My client tells me she begged this woman to stop wrecking her family. What kind of a phone call would you make if that was happening to you? Let me tell you something, Chief, this Lucca is no citizen of the year. She's bad news."

Leeming kicked his chair back and stood up. A beefy, imposing man, I suspected he had glowered many a tougher ne'er-do-well than I off a street corner in his time. "A jury might have to decide that, Deleeuw. I think they would find those phone messages pretty threatening. That's how they sounded to me. I know it's out of character for this Dow woman. Believe me, it always is. I never arrested anybody for murder in twenty years where almost everybody close to them didn't tell me it was impossible.

"But, listen. This is a mess. I got guys guarding Dow in the hospital. I got a team watching the Dow house. And we're tearing the town apart looking for Lucca and we can't find her. She may be the Wicked Witch of the East, but she's got no reason to run that I know of. If every spouse in Rochambeau who got caught with his pants down took off, we wouldn't need traffic lights here. So where is she? You know, Deleeuw, this ain't Manhattan South. I got nobody available to cross the kiddies at school now. You better pass on any

goddamn whiff you have of Lucca—assuming you get one—
or I'll have your license for breakfast. Got that? I gotta go. We
got a grand-jury sitting."

Our warm little chat was over. Leeming didn't look subtle, but he was. He firmly believed Dow had tried to kill her
husband; he was beginning to think she'd succeeded in killing
Lucca as well. He was about to tell a grand jury as much. I
didn't have lots of time; Marianne had less.

Why *would* Lucca take off? Leeming had gotten to me on
that point. As slimy as the woman might be, she had no reason to bolt.

I decided to make a few calls from a pay phone close to
my house. I checked Lieutenant Tagg, my state-police buddy,
who had run Lucca's name through the NJSP computers, to
see if he had any new information, but he wasn't in. I had
better luck with Willie, my electronic mole in the credit
agency, probably one of the few sources Leeming didn't have
access to unless he got a warrant.

"Hey, Martin," Willie said, coming on the phone right
away and using our agreed code name. If he got caught, he'd
lose his job and probably end up in front of the same sort of
grand jury the chief was about to see; disclosing personal financial information is against the law.

But no investigator ever had a more reliable, better-wired,
or more enthusiastic source. Willie is a genius at electronic
sleuthing. He relishes the challenge of it. The giant credit
agency he works for maintains a vast data network handier
than the CIA for tracking purchasing and dining habits. Let a
soon-to-be-divorced and ostensibly impoverished father, on
the run from support payments, charge a single CD or a fifth
of Johnnie Walker, and Willie will be on his trail in an electronic beep.

"You do anything but sleep, you gotta leave a trail for the Tracker," Willie always tells me, using his own code name for himself. The Tracker sees himself as a modern-day Natty Bumpo, using computers and modems rather than broken twigs and footprints. Willie likes to know a bit about the people he is looking for. By now he knows that deadbeat dads often secretly play the market with out-of-town brokers or need stereos and furniture for their new apartments. If the case is interesting, Willie will really wade into it, working for hours at no extra charge, tapping into one data base after another. What he can't find, his electronic buddies all over the country can, scouring computers through the night and swapping information and messages, sometimes in code. At the end of each month, I leave an envelope under the door of his studio apartment in nearby Westfield—two hundred dollars in twenties for each case he's worked on. He is worth much more.

"Got a MasterCard hit. Providence, Rhode Island," he announced promptly. "Address 6889 Douglas Avenue. Lucca, Andrea. You can run anywhere in the world, but you can't hide from the Tracker."

"When?"

"Ummm . . . let's see, hold on. I got it. Sunday. Four days ago."

"Restaurant?"

"No. Looks like a market."

"A market? You sure you got the right name?"

"Yup. And I can match the card against previous charges. Same card. Rochambeau address. Maybe somebody lifted it, but I never heard of somebody stealing a credit card and then charging thirty-six dollars' worth of groceries on it. Di Gregorio's. D-i-g-r-e-g-o-r-i-o-s Produce. Plus the CVS drugstore on Thayer Street—eighty dollars for surgical supplies. There's a delivery fee on this one. Whatever she bought, she had it delivered." Willie knew what I could and couldn't use.

"There's no other charges—oops, wait a minute. Garden State Parkway Exxon. Saturday. Fifteen dollars. Looks like a fill-up. Enough gas to go to Providence, right?" Willie chuckled, a rich, mysterious sound. His voice, husky with a hint of drawl, sometimes led me to wonder if Willie was black. Believe it or not, he and I have never met. I'd like to—I often picture him in thick bifocals and a vinyl pocket protector—but it is safer for both of us if I don't. That way I can swear I don't know who he is and almost be telling the truth.

Willie was bequeathed to me when another local investigator, Dan Ferrante, suffered a heart attack and retired and moved out west two years ago. Ferrante had never met the Tracker either. But like me, he was fond of Willie and trusted him implicitly.

I considered calling Chief Leeming, who, if he ever caught me withholding information, would turn me into the state licensing commission in a flash. But I pondered for only about five seconds. It didn't sound as though Lucca had been kidnapped or was in danger. Medical supplies, gas, and groceries? That suggested something else. To help my client, I needed to prove Lucca was alive. Maybe Gil Dow had decided to dump Andrea Lucca, and she had crept into the house and brained him? She knew the dog as well as the house and its layout.

I called Jane, drove home and left a note for the kids to order pizza for dinner, went out to the car, went back inside to leave them money to pay for the pizza, then drove toward the Parkway North. Em's library visit would have to wait. I had never been to Providence, but that would change in about five hours.

CHAPTER 10

I-95 rips through the middle of Providence like a surgical scar that will never heal. As I entered town, I braced myself for more of the grime and blight visible as you first approach the city. Instead, I was brought up short by a gracious old neighborhood. Meticulously preserved Federal homes mounted the hill. I was following a map guiding me toward Brown University and Thayer Street, where Andrea Lucca—or someone with her credit card—had been shopping less than a week ago. The charming, brick-and-stone downtown had clearly been torn in half by the highway.

What could people in cities like this have been thinking of when roads like this were built? Were they thinking at all? Did they have a clue what would happen to their communities? Where were all the savvy, far-sighted mayors and congresspeople? Not only did residents have to watch helplessly as the government spent millions for the middle class to drive right out of town on the sleek new highways, they saw their own beautiful neighborhoods and business districts destroyed for good measure in the process.

I spotted a Days Inn off the highway and pulled in. Already worn-out from the drive, I had no idea how much walking I was going to have to do, and I wanted a place to get messages and make calls. The smile on the desk clerk's face froze just a bit when I wrote down Deleeuw Investigations. It always seems to me they check your credit card just a bit more carefully after the I-word, but that could be my imagination.

Evelyn picked up on the second ring, which was unusual. She usually had this thing about letting the phone ring at least four times so that clients would assume we were busy.

I was further alarmed the minute she opened her mouth. In case I haven't mentioned it, Evelyn has nerves of iron. If, in fact, she has any nerves at all. "Hello?" Her anxious greeting was a marked departure from the customary "Deleeuw Investigations," spoken in a tone that conjured up leather waiting-room sofas, original art on the walls, and dozens of hyperefficient associates.

"Hi, Evelyn, it's me. I'm in Providence, at a motel near the harbor. I'm just—"

"Kit," she quavered. "Are you sitting down? I'm afraid—"

My heart started to race. "Evelyn, is Jane okay? The kids?"

"Oh, Kit, they're fine. It's not your family. I just don't know how to—well, it's Roberta Bingham, Kit. I know you saw her Tuesday." She choked. I waited as she struggled to get it out. Whatever had happened, it was dreadful, and it wasn't the normal stuff on a former librarian's plate. Or mine, for that matter.

"Oh, Kit, Roberta's dead. She was found in her office in the aerobics class by one of the women coming to take the lunch-hour class. Usually, she's out warming up when the class gets there. I took a few of her Stay Fit classes for seniors, you know." Of course, I didn't know, and probably wouldn't have believed it if I'd heard.

"The woman peered through the blinds in the office window—this is according to the police—and saw the body."

I didn't want to interrupt, but I did wonder how Evelyn happened to be talking to the police.

"It was just terrible. Her face was unrecognizable. There was blood all over everything. The woman ran and called the police."

"God, Evelyn. I just saw her—" I was stunned. I couldn't picture the smart, warm, tough woman I'd spoken with just two days ago as a battered corpse. When I thought about the fire that scarred her daughter, the troubles she'd overcome, I thought I was going to start crying right on the phone. I took a deep breath, not because I was ashamed to cry, but because, like cops, I get paid not to freak. I get paid to take bad news in stride, analyze it, act if necessary. Falling apart is unprofessional, if tempting.

"Her clothes had been torn off, Kit—oh, I can't talk about those details. I can't remember anything like this in Rochambeau. Never." She was sobbing softly.

I had to ask. "Evelyn, I'm so sorry. This must be so upsetting, to hear about this. But how did you happen to be talking with the police? You didn't know Roberta well, did you?"

She cleared her throat. "No, Kit. A detective was here. Detective Drake. They found your name in Roberta's appointment book. Drake said she taught her normal class yesterday—he wanted to be certain you understood that you weren't considered a suspect."

That was generous, I thought. If Chief Leeming represented the best in suburban law enforcement, Charlie Drake, his lumbering serious-crimes head, was a candidate for the worst. I wouldn't trust Charlie to write up a traffic ticket, which is probably why they assigned him to felonies, which in Rochambeau so rarely happen. Homicides are generally investigated by the state police, while local detectives like Charlie gather routine testimony and tie up loose ends.

"Detective Drake was curious to know what you and Roberta Bingham talked about, he said, and whether or not it might have any bearing on her murder. He said they thought she had been killed around noon, probably just a few minutes before she was found. Then, after Drake left, Chief Leeming called. He said for you to call him the second you checked in. I told him I had no idea whether you would be reachable or not, and that was the truth, so help me."

I had to think. "Okay, Evelyn, you don't know where I am. That's true, Evelyn, 'cause I haven't given you my hotel or phone number. Right?"

"Well, I guess—"

"Good. If I'm successful, I'll be home tonight. If not, tomorrow. But I'll call either way. I'll get back to the chief in a few minutes, but there's a call I have to make first."

I hung up. Evelyn was loyal, but she wouldn't lie for anyone, not even me. That, she'd said, was an absolute condition of her coming to work for me, and she meant it. So sometimes I didn't tell her things so she wouldn't have to, which drives her crazy.

I put the phone down and sat in the upholstered armchair. Out the window, I could see what my map identified as Federal Hill and its beautiful old clapboard homes. Evelyn wasn't totally accurate about Rochambeau's criminal past: there *were* occasional murders in town, maybe one every couple of years. Usually, it involved some troubled kids falling apart, going over the edge and attacking a family member. That was the difference: in Rochambeau you were not likely to get offed by some stranger for five bucks, and your toddler wasn't going to take a stray bullet meant for a drug pusher.

Sometimes a divorced husband or wife would grab a gun and go after an ex-spouse or lover. Once in a great while somebody would get shot during a robbery or bungled burglary. And of course, more frequently than anyone liked to admit, there were teenage suicides, suburbia's hidden shame.

But this savage killing would surely hit an especially raw nerve. Aerobics classes weren't just about exercise, as Roberta had pointed out. They were a kind of community, a place women went to take care of themselves and one another. Every other woman in town probably knew Roberta Bingham or someone who knew her, and lots of aerobics-class attendees had enough time on their hands to pummel an overworked police chief about their slain leader. Leeming would have his big hands full.

I dialed Marianne's home number. She answered. She was just getting ready to go back to the hospital. No change in Gil's condition. She was sending the kids off for a couple of weeks with their godmother, even though it meant missing some school. She dreaded having them around to see their father die or watch their mother hauled off in handcuffs, if it came to that.

She took a ragged breath. "I heard about Roberta. It's horrible. What's happening, Kit? All she did was help people, make them better." I thought I heard her crying quietly.

"Marianne," I said, "don't misinterpret this but I must ask. The police will—"

"You're forgetting, Kit, that I have the best alibi in the world. Two detectives sitting outside my house." I exhaled in relief. So they were still there. Good. It *was* as good an alibi as you could hope for. "And Sandy, my best friend from college, has been here with me," Marianne went on. "She stayed on the sofa bed in my room last night, because we were up late yakking, like we always did in school. Sandy was with me the whole time; she just left. God—"

"The cops are going to pester you more than ever, Marianne, because they're really confused now. I'm just glad you had somebody with you." My client's credibility had just gotten a considerable boost. Not even the most suspicious law-enforcement mind could come up with a solid motive for Marianne to kill Roberta Bingham. Now Chief Leeming had really better locate Andrea Lucca, if not for the reasons he had originally thought.

"Where are you, Kit? Have you found her?"

"I'd rather not say exactly, not on the phone. I think I do have a lead on her, or at least on where she was last weekend. I don't know if it'll pan out or not. Just keep the faith, okay?"

"I don't have a lot of faith left, I'm afraid. Gil is in a coma, our marriage is a mess, the kids are totally freaked out, and I may be indicted for murder. I don't know what to feel." Marianne sounded terrified. I had lots of empathy but little time to exercise it. I had to get going; all hell would be breaking loose back home.

"Look," I said. "Don't give up on yourself. I've learned some things about Andrea Lucca in the last couple of days, and you may have good reasons for feeling what you feel. I'll tell you all about it when I see you."

"So you don't think I'm crazy?"

"I don't." I realized as I said it that it was mostly true. The fact that Andrea had seemed a good friend to Gay didn't mean Marianne wasn't right. Bad people can do good things. What didn't figure at all was Roberta Bingham's murder, unless it really was a random robbery or act of revenge. Maybe somebody was afraid Bingham possessed—or would reveal—some damaging information. But I ought not kid myself either—all I'd really found out was that Donna Platt thought Lucca busted up her marriage and Gay Tannenbaum didn't know.

Suppressing a shudder, I dialed the Rochambeau PD. Withholding information in a murder case is license-revocation stuff, not the kind of thing a smart detective messes with. Leeming and I may have become grudging friends, but he was a rock-hard cookie when he needed to be. If he thought I had critical information in a murder investigation, he would nail me in a second.

Leeming came on right away. Sounding harassed, he sputtered when I told him where I was and that I had reason to believe Andrea Lucca was in Providence. I don't know why, exactly, but I told him about the charge at CVS and left out DiGregorio's Produce. Withholding some information from the police just becomes instinct after a while. I wouldn't say how I had learned of Lucca's purchase, something Leeming vowed to pursue later. He also cursed and threatened to turn me over to the DA, who would, he assured me, roast me like a suckling pig on a spit.

In turn Leeming refused to tell me much about Roberta Bingham's murder except that her body was warm when the ambulance arrived. She appeared to have been hit repeatedly, viciously, on the head and face with a heavy object. It sounded creepily familiar.

"You connecting this killing with the attack on Gil Dow?" I asked.

"I'm not prepared to say. This doesn't look like a sneak attack. Somebody could have waylaid her in her house, or outside the exercise place, if they'd wanted to. But there was no robbery, nothing missing we can make out. Look, they're already howling for us to find the killer by dinner. You have any information I could use, Deleeuw, I want it ASAP. I'll even take any crackpot theories, not that they'd be worth much."

I laughed—to myself. This was assuredly the closest Frank Leeming would ever come to asking for my help. But I wanted to establish something first.

"At least this murder gets Marianne off the hook. As you know, she had your guys watching her all night."

Leeming said nothing.

"I don't see her as a killer, Chief." Why no response? Was he embarrassed?

"This is not appropriate for us to discuss," he snapped. He was right to be ticked. Murder charges, right or wrong, are brought on the basis of evidence, not pleas from private detectives. It was a bush thing to say.

"Until I have some evidence otherwise, I don't see these two events as connected," he continued. "Your client still had the means, motive, and opportunity to kill her husband. One has nothing to do with the other until we find something that connects them."

"Well, I think Andrea Lucca connects them."

There was silence. I looked out the corner window at two huge oil tankers anchored in the middle of Providence Harbor.

"I'm listening."

"Lucca had possible motive, too. Gil Dow was probably breaking up with her to save his marriage. Lucca knew the house, probably had a key or could have easily enough gotten one. And she kills families. It's her thing. Roberta Bingham was onto her, was furious with her for targeting the women in her class, in fact. I know another one who caught Lucca with her husband and hates her plenty. Bingham and Lucca could easily have had a fight. Lucca has worked out at the class, she's younger; she would be a match for Roberta. Bingham told me Lucca was in terrific shape. And she's missing. Maybe it's because someone stuffed her in a shallow grave, as you and the DA obviously suspect. Or maybe it's because she's on the run. Look, Chief, I don't know who attacked Gil Dow or who killed Roberta Bingham. But you ought to at least take a good hard look at Lucca." I wanted to get off the phone, more for dramatic effect than anything else, and also to keep him from asking directly whether I was withholding information.

"Great, Deleeuw, and where is your hot suspect? Probably lying under a pile of leaves off I-Eighty. I'm not going to debate a murder case on the phone with you," Leeming barked. "My hunch is Marianne Dow has to be involved in this one way or another. That's what works for me. You prove something else, I'll be happy to hear it."

Leeming had focused on Marianne like a rottweiler on a bone. He had his reasons, and I couldn't shake him. If I wanted to get him interested in Andrea Lucca as a suspect, I had to prove that there still *was* an Andrea Lucca. When the police think they have a case all tied up, they like to move on to the hundreds of cases that aren't tied up. It takes an earthquake to change their minds; I didn't have one.

"The women in Bingham's classes are having a meeting and a vigil tonight outside town hall," Leeming added, moving out of his bellowing phase. "You can bet your ratty old station wagon that by the end of the vigil they'll be denouncing the incompetent police investigation." His tone suggested that he was prepared to be assaulted by a phalanx of physical-fitness fanatics shrilly demanding justice. It wasn't that he blamed them, just that he was going to be busy as hell.

I gave it a final shot.

"No record of appointments? I know she wrote my visit

down on her calendar." There was a pause. "C'mon, Chief, I told you about the credit-card charge up here. Give me a break."

The chief snorted. "Well, it's harmless enough. Bingham had two names written down for today—no times attached, just the names. *M. Dow. A. Lucca.* Nothing else. What the hell do you make of it?"

I didn't know. But as my son had taught me to say, it creeped me out.

Thayer Street coursed through the Brown University campus the same way I-95 cut through Providence, but with considerably more pleasing results. I couldn't help looking around at Brown and considering it a possible college for Ben or Em; with its graceful old houses and brick dorms, it was beautiful. The narrow street was thronged with pricily dressed-down students cruising the boutiques and cafés that offered asparagus salads and water at two dollars a bottle. Maybe too beautiful, I thought. Brown was probably not an affordable destination for college-bound offspring of private eyes with multiple mortgages.

The CVS drugstore, where Lucca had charged the items Willie uncovered, was across from a whole-grain-looking muffin shop called A Currant Affair. I mulled my options. I could walk into the CVS, claim to be A. Lucca, and ask a clerk to verify my weekend purchase, claiming I'd lost my receipt. But if her credit card carried her full name, that obviously wouldn't work. I could talk to the manager. Or I could charm one of the cashiers at the counter into looking through the credit-card slips for me. Detectives who don't know how to charm people shouldn't be detectives. As it turned out, that was the wrong option.

"Excuse me, miss." I beamed at a twentysomething

woman neatening up a skin-moisturizer display. "I was wondering if you could help me. I need some information on a purchase made a few days ago."

A man appeared out of nowhere at her left shoulder with a "manager" tag over his heart. A crisp white jacket added to his air of authority and cleanliness. "May I help you?"

The CVS manager was a courteous, poised young pharmacist type with rimless spectacles and the perfect combination of earnestness, sobriety, and diligence. CVS should feature him in its commercials. He took exactly eleven seconds to shake his head firmly and show me the door. The company did not under any circumstances discuss purchases with any person other than the one who made them, unless a judge or subpoena or person with a badge—none of which had materialized—ordered it to. The very notion was out of the question. If I wished, I could call company headquarters and speak to CVS attorneys. I knew how far that would get me.

DiGregorio's grocery was six blocks away. I decided to leave the Volvo parked in front of the muffin shop and hoof it.

I am lax about many of the details of investigative work, but my army supervisor, Sergeant Mize, had drilled a few into my head. *Always, always check to see whether you're being followed when you're working a sensitive case,* he said. *It's the easiest thing in the world to forget and one of the most important to remember.* Sergeant Mize was full of sayings like that, and he would fall over in a dead faint if he knew that somebody had remembered a single one of them nearly twenty years later. None of them made enormous sense on deeper consideration, but he offered them with such authority and repeated them so often that they stuck.

Imagine my amazement, as I walked briskly down the block, then stopped suddenly and turned, to see that Sergeant

Mize had been right. A dingy brown Buick (detectives on routine cases always drive grimy American sedans; federal agents have theirs washed) with two bulky men in the front seat braked suddenly, inched forward while horns sounded impatiently behind them, then pulled over to the curb. The two men looked at the stores, at one another—everywhere, that is, but at me. I was as delighted as I was stunned. This was one of the most detectivelike things that had ever happened to me. I had never been followed, nor, to my knowledge, given anybody any reason to do so before.

I walked coolly back toward the Buick, now idling awkwardly in a no-parking zone twenty feet behind me. "Oh, shit," I heard one of the men say through the open window. Both looked to be in their midthirties, had pleasant, cheerful faces, and wore casual slacks and sport shirts. The one behind the wheel had a receding hairline. As if to compensate, he'd grown a thin mustache.

"Detectives," I said cheerfully, bending over and putting both hands on the driver's door. "How ya doing?"

The driver put a finger to his forehead in respectful greeting. "Mr. Deleeuw, right? Your friend the chief said you wouldn't spot a tail if an elephant was attached to it."

"Please let my friend the chief know he was wrong."

The man riding shotgun chuckled. "Oh, I surely will. Might I impose upon you to show me a piece of paper or something with your face on it?" he asked amiably.

I took out my license and investigator's shield. His comparison of the pictures with my face was unnervingly more than cursory. Then both men stepped out of the car.

The driver offered me his hand. "Lieutenant Grossman. This is my partner, Detective Gleklen. You carrying? 'Cause that's against the law here, carrying without checking in with us."

I assured him that I wasn't.

"That's right, you're from Rochambeau. Guess they don't need guns much there."

"Not much. Though lately we've had our share of excitement."

"So Frank tells me." Grossman nodded grimly. "We worked together in New York for a while. My wife wanted to come up here, back home, so here we are. Has its ups and downs, but it's pretty pleasant compared to Brooklyn. I owe Frank a lot of favors. He's a good guy. Don't go giving him a hard time."

"Believe me, I am on his side," I said fervently. "He's just sometimes slow to recognize it."

Around us streams of students parted in waves, as though we were boulders in a stream. None of them seemed to pay us any mind, even when Grossman managed to glide his hands around my armpits, waist, and backside without seeming to be frisking me at all.

"So," he said, "the CVS people must've tossed you out on your ear 'cause you weren't in there long enough to buy an aspirin. Maybe we'll have better luck, although they usually make us go get a court order. Leeming said you weren't exactly street smart. Where you going, my friend?"

"Back to the motel, I guess. Then home. This was the only lead I had, and I didn't get anywhere."

"Good idea," said Detective Gleklen amiably. "But you don't want to be walking in this direction. You want to turn and go back to where your car is parked. Don't you?"

It didn't seem like an invitation that ought to be refused. Both men looked cordial enough, but I could see they were hard and slightly harried. When I hesitated, fantasizing about telling them to buzz off, Grossman took the offensive. "Look, Mr. Deleeuw, we don't want to hassle you. We've got lots of work to do, all of it more important than baby-sitting you. But don't go yanking our dongs, or we'll go yanking yours, only harder. Don't let this ivy throw you. Providence ain't no suburb. Either tell us where the fuck you're going or get in your creaky old Volvo back there and get the hell out of town." Or words to that effect.

" 'Bye, guys," I said promptly. "Take care of the college kids. You've been just wonderful."

I was surprised that they didn't follow me. Maybe they really were too busy to waste any more time on me. Maybe they thought they were so fearsome I wouldn't dare disregard their wishes.

But if nothing else, Roberta Bingham's murder left me feeling that nothing was going to shove me off this case now. Once out of their sight, I parked the Volvo down near the Brown gym, then cut back on foot, darting through side streets and around corners and in and out of stores twenty times to make sure I wasn't being followed. I wasn't. Good old Sergeant Mize. I ought to drop him a note. He would be delighted to know that at least one of those old saws had worked.

DiGregorio's Produce was a relic of a different time and culture: croissants and artichoke salsa would have seemed bizarre here. The neighborhood, identified by the street signs as Fox Point, looked far less yuppified than the university and environs. Here bodies weren't sleek and hip, but wide and tired. DiGregorio's was on the ground floor of a wooden house that looked two hundred years old and probably hadn't been painted in almost that long. The MasterCard decal by the door glowed with incongruous brightness.

Inside, two fans rotated slowly under a tin ceiling. Creaky, worn old planks covered the floor. Until I saw the bread in simple white bags labeled Providence Portuguese Bakery, I couldn't place the language I was hearing. The neighborhood was Portuguese, sprinkled with graduate students. The proprietors were Italian. It was a yeasty mix.

Mrs. DiGregorio stood at her post behind the cash register, making change and greeting the old women who trickled through the aisles picking up bread, milk, cheese, and meat. Mr. DiGregorio sat on the other end of the counter in a beat-up wing chair, joking with the customers and leafing through the sports section of the *Providence Journal.*

He was a big man in a wide-brimmed straw hat, his short-sleeved white shirt straining over a world-class belly. His garrulous, welcoming old face looked accustomed to talk and laughter. A cane rested on the chair's arm; a giant mug of coffee sat on a table next to his chair. He was my man.

"Hello, hello," he said in jovial greeting as his wife gave me a hard look from down the counter. "You're a stranger. Have a seat." He spoke in a broad, working-class Rhode Island accent.

Pasquale DiGregorio probably liked most of the people who dropped by to break up his day.

"You're from New Jersey?" He guffawed, as if that in itself were amusing. He offered me a cup of coffee, which his wife sullenly brought over. From her vantage point, I suspected, I was bad news, no matter where I hailed from.

We chatted about the weather, about kids (Pasquale had five), about the old days in Providence when nobody knocked you on the head for two dollars, about the college kids who came in looking to buy bottles of water— *"Water,* can you believe these fuckin' kids? If it was their own money, they'd drink from the fuckin' *tap"* —and about the taxes that kept going up as said kids made inroads on Fox Point.

"I'm glad I'm gonna die soon," Pasquale declared, "before the taxes push me out." He was chuckling, but I knew he meant it. He talked about the Red Sox, how they always broke his heart, and asked about the Yankees, since New Jersey was in the vicinity of that hated team. His wife didn't seem to find any of this amusing. Maybe she'd heard it before.

But there came a point when we both knew it was time to move on to business and when Pasquale, I could see, was growing curious to know just what the business was.

The thing was, I liked him a lot—that's why we connected. You can try to charm people all day long, but the best trick of all is to encounter somebody you genuinely like (take that, Mize). It doesn't happen all that often.

"Mr. DiGregorio," I said, "I'm looking for a woman named Andrea Lucca. I have reason to believe she was in this store last weekend and made a few purchases."

Pasquale's face gave away nothing. He didn't say he knew her. He didn't say he didn't. Over by the register, his wife stopped bustling and stared at us.

"I am a private investigator." I took out my ID and handed it to him. "A client of mine is in trouble. Ms. Lucca might help me get her out of trouble, if only we could find her. But she is missing. She hasn't been at her job or her home for days, and we don't know where to find her. She's mentioned you to me, time and time again, so I thought to come here. I swear to you that she is not in any trouble that I know of. The police are looking for her. If I found out she came here, so can they."

Pasquale DiGregorio looked briefly at his wife. Almost imperceptibly, she shook her head. She wasn't buying a word of it; I don't think she bought much.

But he waved a defiant hand and said, "I don't see no harm in telling you about Andrea. You can find out anyway, a smart guy like you. You couldn't know about this store if she hadn't told you. And you look like a decent guy. I've been wrong about lots of things, but never about that, eh?" He shot a defiant glance at his wife, who shrugged skeptically and turned her attention back to the cash register.

I leaned forward. "She *was* here, then? Andrea. On Sunday? So you do know her." I spoke too eagerly. Slow down, boy, I reminded myself. I would dearly love to make the telephone call that advised Leeming where to find his supposed murder victim.

Pasquale swigged from his coffee mug. "Know her? Brother, I know Andrea for most of her life. She went to Fox Point Elementary. Took a piece of candy from that candy counter every day after school—all the kids do. She spent seven or eight years living across the street. Her aunt and uncle are still there. Joseph and Catherine Lucca. They can't even walk up and down the stairs, but they're still where they have been for fifty years. Half a century. We send food up to them every day—our delivery boy takes it up. Poor people. He's got arthritis. She's got the cancer. Andrea comes up once, twice a month, brings them food, medicine, helps out. A great kid, Andrea, a wonderful woman. She was always in here, right, Marie?" His wife ignored him. "She's not in any trouble, right?"

I shook my head. Maybe she ought to be, but as far as I knew, she wasn't.

"When did she leave here? Move away, I mean."

"Oh, she was born down your way—in Jersey. I don't know the town. She came to live with Joseph and Catherine all of a sudden. I don't know why, I wouldn't tell you if I did." He stopped, his mind drifting back. "It was something horrible," he said quietly. "They never said what. I never asked. My wife thinks she's got the curse on her, Andrea. Can you believe that? Stayed here a few years, till she was outta high school, then she moved back. Broke our hearts when she moved. But she said she would visit every month, and she has. Brings us presents from New York City. A wonderful child. Tough life, but a wonderful child."

"Why do you say a tough life?"

"To be taken away from your momma and your poppa when you're little? That's tough. Although Joseph and Catherine loved her like she was their own. But it isn't the same. You have children. You know."

I nodded. I did know.

"You wouldn't happen to have a picture of Andrea, would you?" I looked around hopefully. Aside from having practical reasons, I was dying to see what she looked like.

"No, no picture at all." He shrugged, and looked up at the clock on the wall. Time to move along before my welcome wore as thin here as it had with the Providence police.

"Look, Mr. DiGregorio. Two favors, if you would. One, would you call the Luccas and tell them I'm on my way up to see them? Also, there are two policemen who may come around. It's up to you what you tell them—"

"Are they from the neighborhood? No, of course not. Then fuck them!"

I'm not exactly off these streets myself, I thought, but I kept that notion to myself.

I got no farther than the doorway of Catherine and Joseph Lucca's apartment, on the third floor of the classic New England triple-decker opposite DiGregorio's.

The hallway beyond was a trove of religious statues, family photos, and china bric-a-brac. It smelled of disinfectant and decay. Joseph Lucca was emaciated and frail; moving even a step or two was obviously painful. He remained in the doorway, mumbling something about not inviting me in. He said he couldn't disturb his wife, who was getting her first sleep in days in the living-room-turned-sick-room.

"She's in so much pain. She doesn't want to go to a nursing home. I promised her she wouldn't. Poor thing; she doesn't know where she is."

I apologized for intruding, said I was a friend of Andrea's, and asked if she was there.

"No. No. Andrea went home. She comes on weekends. Don't know when she's coming back. She has her work . . . uh, painting, I think. God bless her. She comes very faithfully. I don't know how we would get by without her. We'd have to leave." He turned as his wife cried out, maybe in her sleep—I couldn't tell. As he shuffled away to check, I moved a few steps into the hallway. On the oak table near the door, a scrawled note lay atop the lace doily: *Poppa Joe. See you Sunday. Love, A.* I reached out, folded it and slipped it into my pocket, and stepped back.

The Rochambeau phone number her uncle had for her was the same one I had. So was the address. Joseph Lucca was struggling to be polite, but was obviously fading. I didn't know how far to push it.

"Mr. Lucca, can you tell me why Andrea came to live here when she was a child?"

Abruptly, his whole demeanor changed. He became confused, frightened, then angry. "Who are you?" he cried. "Why do you come here? What do you want? I don't have to talk to you!"

"I'm just a friend of Andrea's. Mr. DiGregorio called to tell you that."

"No, you're not," he spat. "You're a liar!"

I heard a door open on the floor below. "Joseph," came a

frail voice. "Is everything all right?" But the Luccas' door had already slammed shut. I figured I'd better get out of there, before somebody called my friend Grossman.

It wouldn't have taken him long to arrive. The good lieutenant was sitting in his dirty Buick right in front of the Lucca house looking supremely disappointed in humankind, especially the part of it represented by one Kit Deleeuw. Sergeant Mize did warn against underestimating people.

He opened the car door, walked up to me, and his right hand shot into my belly so suddenly and so hard that I doubled over. I couldn't remember feeling so much pain so fast. My face broke out in a cold sweat, I gasped for breath, then knelt by the side of the curb to vomit. I was as astonished as I was uncomfortable. The gracious old neighborhood had taken on a new cast.

"Jesus, Grossman, who do you think you are?" I gasped, clutching my stomach. "This isn't what Leeming had in mind, believe me. It's not his style. Isn't this a little out of line? You can't—"

"This isn't Leeming's town, cowboy, this is mine. I told you to get the fuck out of here and you didn't. You thought we were rubes from Iowa or some fuckin' place, so you could do what you wanted. That we couldn't follow a fucking amateur like you. I want you out of here. This time we're going to follow you to I-Ninety-five, and I'm going to call ahead to the state police to make sure you make it through to Connecticut. You want to stop by the civil-liberties office, they're right nearby. I'll take you there, you can file a lawsuit, then drive back up here a dozen times to testify."

He helped me up, brushed off my jacket. The odd thing I was thinking was that this wasn't meant to be sadistic. It was a message, delivered with no more nor less force than Grossman thought appropriate. But it *hurt*.

"Nothing personal, friend. You just pissed me off. Lucca up there?"

I just stared at him. By now I was as ready to get out of town as he was for me to go.

"No matter. I'll talk to these friendly folks myself."

Good luck, I thought. Across the street, Pasquale DiGregorio was watching Grossman through his store window. The old man's look was pure hatred. But I really couldn't tell if it was for Grossman or for me.

:alled home from a rest stop on the Connecticut Turnpike. I told Jane about my trip, including the fact that a Providence cop had punched me in the stomach, but that I was fine. Other than a sharp intake of breath, she didn't say a word. Jane was smart about things like that. She trusted me to tell her if I was okay, and she knew getting excited wouldn't make either of us feel any better. And in a couple of hours, she could see for herself.

She'd left the clinic early to cover for me, something she rarely did. I figured it was because she would be worried about how the kids would take Roberta Bingham's murder— the fourth in Rochambeau in just six months, the first three all related to the Brown-estate case I had worked on. I wondered if Rochambeau would go berserk, as it had the last time.

"The town seems pretty calm about it, from what I can tell," Jane reported. "Living in America in the nineties, what's just one violent death? God, it's so awful. Are you okay? Was the trip successful?" Jane and I both were on the run so much, we had developed a kind of code. We frequently checked in to see that the other was alive and well, but waited until nights or weekends to fill in the blanks.

"What's the buzz on the killing? Or is it too soon?" I

knew without asking that Jane would have asked around a bit, and that between kids and phones, various versions would already be competing with one another.

"According to the radio, the police are saying that a considerable amount of cash was missing from one of Roberta's file cabinets and from her purse. Everybody's seeing it as a robbery, probably committed by somebody who knew her or worked around the Women's Club."

"Robbery?" I said, ripping the cellophane off some peanut-butter crackers. "Who on earth would rob an aerobics instructor, outside of a junkie?"

"Hey, I'm not the police. I'm just telling you the word they're giving out. You can check it out when you get home. Harriet Pinski says she heard Bingham was an ex-alcoholic who lost custody of her kids. That makes her feel better, I guess. Safer."

"Did you tear her throat out?"

"No. I just said in my most professional voice that if every recovering alcoholic on the block vanished, the Pinskis wouldn't have enough people to get a barbecue together."

"How about you?" I asked. "Tough day?" I could usually tell by the edge in her voice. I was worried about Jane's job, which raised everyday stress to levels beyond my experience. But she could certainly take care of herself, and intended to, no matter how much I worried.

"Yeah," she said wearily. "The more they cut back federal programs, the more casualties I see. Kids left alone, people evicted, drug stuff. I feel like I'm standing beneath an erupting volcano with a cork.

"But the kids are fine," she said, cheering up. Jane wasn't much for whining. And I didn't know how to cheer her up after the things she saw all day. Other than making sure I wasn't adding to her problems. "Em's been invited to Hershey Park Sunday. I hesitate to say yes only because I don't know the kid who invited her or the parents."

"I'll call," I said. My rule, to which I adhered pretty firmly, was that I had to know or talk to at least one parent one time before either of my kids could go over to another kid's house, certainly before going away on a trip. I just thought I should make contact with an adult, make sure he or she sounded sane and alert, that I had a name to ask for if my kid vanished. Given that my schedule was more flexible than Jane's, this was one of my tasks.

Next, I tried calling Marianne Dow, but there was no answer. That made me mildly apprehensive. She'd said she was sending her kids off, but I've never heard of lawyers or insurance salespeople who turn off their answering machines. Or mothers with two kids who aren't home, for that matter.

CHAPTER 11

So far that Thursday, I had breakfasted with Jane, visited Benchley in the Garden Center, gone to see Chief Leeming, talked to Willie, driven to Providence, checked into a motel, gotten the news about Roberta Bingham, visited CVS, DiGregorio's, and the Luccas, been sucker-punched in the stomach, decided at the advice of Lieutenant Grossman to cut short my visit, and headed back. A routine day at the American Way seemed like retirement. I was depressed, uncomfortable, confused, and exhausted.

I pushed the speed limit all the way back from Providence, making it in less than four hours, haunted by Lucca's elderly relatives as well as Bingham's sad end to a life of struggle. No violent death makes any sense, but surely she was entitled to a longer stretch of peace. Once again the real world was invading and shattering suburbia's comfortable pretensions. Once again things that happened only elsewhere were happening here.

I had especially admired Bingham, during our few minutes together, the way she had taken responsibility for the messes she'd created, climbed out of a black hole to rebuild her life, and tried to help people in the process. Now all of it was snuffed out. "I will never grasp the logic of violence," Benchley used to say, whenever he read about some grisly New York City crime. Maybe there wasn't any.

I spotted the big sedan parked by my front door the minute I rounded the corner onto my block. I had to peer through the dark for just a few seconds to recognize it as a U.S. government car, the kind of four-door Chrysler used to ferry federal agents around.

My heart sped up. I harbored no more unpleasant or fearful memories than the ones this car conjured up. As I got closer, I could see that it had a New York plate and aerials sprouting over the trunk and roof. Two mirrors protruded from either side. The men inside were probably struggling to see me as I was struggling to spot them.

You can usually tell a federal law-enforcement car on routine business. The FBI can be invisible when it wants to be, but much of the time its agents aren't trying to be invisible. The cars are used much less than city patrol cars, so they don't have many nicks and bumps. They are cleaner than police cars too, since they're washed regularly at a government garage. And they're the straightest-looking cars you can find; nobody but a dentist in Topeka would voluntarily ride around in one.

Even before I pulled into my driveway, two tall, lean men in dark suits were climbing out of the car. In the street lamp's glow I recognized the face of Van Morfey. None of the reasons I could come up with for his visit were good. Was he reopening the insider-trading case? Coming to pressure me once again to give evidence I didn't have against friends and colleagues? Suggesting one more time that I get a *good* attorney, because I was really going to need one? It seemed I'd had every right but the right to keep my career, which they'd had little trouble taking away. Maybe the right-wingers were right, and the police had had too many of their powers nibbled away. But as far as I was concerned, they still had plenty left over.

I pulled the Volvo into the garage, turned off the ignition, took a deep breath. If there was any single person likely to rattle my composure, it was Van Morfey. He'd done it a dozen times before. I reminded myself that he was just doing his job; that he sincerely believed I possessed a trove of incriminating evidence against members of my former firm; that I had squirreled away millions in illicitly obtained funds in Bahamian or Swiss banks until I could sneak out of the country to retrieve them.

Van Morfey was as mean-spirited as a pit bull, and as tough to shake off.

He used to press his face as close to mine as it could get, his mint-scented breath all over me. "Deleeuw," he would whisper. "I think you smell and I think you have things to tell us about other people who smell. If you don't tell me those things, you're going to spend the rest of your life looking over your shoulder, waiting for me to come with a piece of paper in my hand to take you away from your pretty little suburban house to some dirty basement where they'll take your fingerprints and drag you out in front of the TV cameras."

Was this that time?

My face was covered with a sweaty film: my stomach churned. I pulled the Post-Its down from the mirror and dashboard, stuffed them under the front seat, climbed out.

Jesus, I thought, what if they arrest me? What about the kids? Who'll get them to the ophthalmologist and to keyboard lessons? I worried more about the kids seeing my mug shot on TV, as Morfey probably knew.

I took my deepest breath, emerged, and headed down the dark driveway toward the men. What you've got, I told myself, is the sure knowledge that you did nothing wrong. Remember it. Morfey was coming toward me, as promised, but without a piece of paper in his hand, which might be hopeful.

When we met on the front walk, twenty feet outside the door, I was astonished to hear Percentage's continuous, angry barking. Good boy, I thought. There are a few instincts left there. Or maybe he'd climb into the car and go home with the feds.

Morfey didn't offer his hand, and I didn't offer mine. At least we wouldn't have to go through that school / kids / real-estate chatter. The agent looked the ex-marine he undoubtedly was, a bit over six feet, with a graying crew cut and razor-sharp blue eyes. He was in his midfifties now, I guessed, and perhaps pondering retirement.

His case had actually not gone that well, from what I'd read in the financial pages. Most of the senior people in my firm got off, and the few who were convicted drew light sentences. That must have made Morfey crazy. He loathed the Yups in my firm who were raking in hundreds of thousands of dollars in their early thirties. Of course, so did I. But I suspected he blamed me for the case not being more solid.

From the disgusted expression on his face, Morfey's view of me hadn't changed. He still locked onto my eyes, the way he used to, alert for the slightest wavering or sign that I'd break.

His partner looked much younger and markedly less intimidating. He was chubby, with his hair creeping rakishly over his collar, something Morfey would never have permitted himself. Morfey probably pined for Hoover.

"You know me, Deleeuw," he said without pleasantries. "This is Agent Driscoll." The younger man pulled out a leather case and flashed me his shield. I nodded. It didn't feel as if I was under arrest. He would have gotten right to that, unless he was a complete sadist, wouldn't he?

"Hello, Agent Morfey. As you can see"—I gestured toward the battered garage with its loosened roof tiles, the overgrown shrubs, and the venerable Volvo—"I haven't made it to my secret Swiss bank accounts yet."

He didn't smile. "When you do, we'll be waiting for you."

They probably didn't train agents to be malleable or resigned. But there seemed a bit less conviction in his voice than there had been a few years earlier when I was his own personal Dillinger.

"Lonely for the good old days?" I suggested. "Drive all the way from New York and sit in the dark for hours, just to talk about the great old times we had together?"

"Not far for me, Deleeuw. I'm in the Newark office, now." So his career wasn't skyrocketing either.

"Agent Driscoll drove out from New York. When I saw your name in the file, I thought I'd come along for the ride. Since we have a relationship. If you will." Morfey would have sounded droll if it weren't outside the range of his personality.

"The police here in Rochambeau asked for our help. They don't know whether they're dealing with an interstate flight or a kidnapping or a murder conspiracy. And once again, as luck would have it, you're the man in the middle, the man who knows more than he's sharing."

I braced for a round of threats and warnings, even though I could see how much steam had gone out of Morfey since our last confrontation. Maybe he was having second thoughts about his conviction that I "smelled like cowshit," as he so incisively put it. His opinion of me didn't much matter to me anymore, so long as he didn't have any arrest warrants to go with it. I had no money squirreled away in my pants pocket, let alone in Switzerland, and no respectable career to lose.

"Mr. Deleeuw, you're working for Mrs. Marianne Dow?" Agent Driscoll seemed to have little patience for this ancient history. "You've been making inquiries about an Andrea Lucca?"

"You guys want to come in?" I asked wearily. I'd had a long drive, I hadn't eaten, had barely stopped for a breather all day, and my abdomen was still throbbing from Lieutenant Grossman's little warning. I'd had enough cops for a month. But I didn't want them to come back.

Driscoll seemed uninterested in the interior of my house, but Morfey took in every detail: the comfy but fraying living-room furniture, the piles of comic books and stuffed animals, the playroom devastated by years of Ben and Em and their pals. Percentage had cast aside his brief moment of watchfulness and reverted to his usual crotch sniffing and slobbering. I was chagrined to see he was especially drawn to Morfey, the wretched animal. Upstairs, I could hear Jane moving around, tucking in Emand, tactfully calling good night to Ben.

To my own surprise, I wanted Morfey to be there, to see it. I was in many ways happier than I'd ever been. But I had paid. Morfey had won, in a sense, when I wearied of being hunted and agreed never to work on Wall Street again in exchange for the government dropping its investigation of me. There followed months of boredom and isolation, when the phone wouldn't ring and no company an-

swered my résumés. ... ars of financial grief, of watching our
savings and expectations dribble away until there was nothing left and we were living off home-equity loans. Long,
hot summers for the kids—no camps, no weeks at the
shore. Long nights sitting up wondering how on earth we
could get Jane back to school, keep the house, clothe the
kids. We still weren't sure we could. People suffered far
worse, but it was hell enough. I was glad that I still didn't
have enough money to buy carpets or replace the bubbled
wallpaper or the chairs shredded by Em's kittens. The walls
and furniture gave testimony to what my family and I had
successfully faced. In a way, they were the most eloquent
witnesses to my integrity. Morfey was taking all that in, I
could see. What bizarre vindication.

"What do you guys want?" I asked, after they had prop-
erly declined refreshment. Driscoll was scribbling officiously
in his notebook—what, I couldn't imagine. "Look, I'm not
going to hide that I have a lead on Lucca in Providence." I
had to tell them most of what I'd found out; these guys
would haul me in front of a grand jury before Ben could
change his sneaker style. Besides, by now Grossman would
undoubtedly have talked to Leeming.

So I filled them in on the older Luccas, declining to spec-
ify how I had gotten onto them. "She might return there. I
don't know. Can I ask if this interview means you are considering Andrea Lucca as a suspect in the attack on Gil Dow?
That you want her for interstate flight?"

Driscoll ignored the questions. He asked me about my
interview with Roberta Bingham, and then the two stood.

"Morfey, I think it's a fair question," I persisted. "I do
have a client to represent. Are you here because you're looking for Andrea Lucca?"

Driscoll replied, making me realize that he, not Morfey,

was in charge here. "The police here would like to talk to Miss Lucca," he said impassively. "There is also the possibility that some harm may have come to her. She is missing, as you know, and we could become more actively involved if she was harmed by someone who crossed state lines to perpetrate an injury against her." Now wouldn't that be a treat, I thought. Up against Morfey again.

Driscoll closed his notebook, handed me his card.

Morfey was still peering intently around my house.

"We're not here looking for her, Deleeuw," Morfey said quietly. "We're here looking for your client."

I gurgled something incomprehensible. "Marianne?"

"Yes, Marianne Dow. She's skipped, too, it seems. She dumped her children with a friend in New York City, eluded the police who were watching her house here, and has been gone for six or seven hours now."

I vaguely remembered her telling me something about arranging for the kids to visit their godmother, but I hadn't been paying much attention. Had I missed something important? I was utterly stunned. How could she go anywhere without telling me? "But I talked to her this afternoon." Marianne gone? Not possible.

"Yes, we know. The phone records confirm that," Driscoll put in. "Right after that she went to her bank here, cleaned out her account, then slipped back on foot, packed some luggage, clothes, jewelry, and personal effects, took her husband's car out of the garage, and left. The local police were back at the bank watching her car." Leeming would be berserk. I thought Morfey wore a slightly what-do-you-expect look. "The Rochambeau PD had warned her not to leave the area, of course, and have sought a warrant seeking her arrest on interstate flight to avoid prosecution for murder."

"Murder?" I repeated, sounding to my dismay like some shocked garden-club matron.

"Yeah," said Driscoll as they headed for my door. "Her husband died at three-fourteen P.M. this afternoon. I don't think you have a client anymore, Mr. Deleeuw. Sounds like you're off the case."

When my heart stopped pounding, I wondered if I *ought* to be off the case. Suddenly I had that sinking feeling I got every now and then when a case seemed to need more than a semipro working out of a mall.

CHAPTER 12

Rochambeau was saved from another splattering by the happy-to-bash-suburbia New York press at a horrid cost—a plane crash at La Guardia left thirty people dead and fifty critically burned and injured. Assessing blame—reporters were swarming all over the airline and pursuing the traffic controller who'd guided the plane in—would consume the media for weeks. They took perfunctory note of Roberta Bingham's murder, but the story was not nearly as graphic as the plane crash; the coverage didn't even approach the lurid headlines the Brown-estate killings had sparked.

That had been a realtor's nightmare, as a horrified Rochambeau found itself branded the "Town of Death." Bingham's killing was labeled a probable robbery-turned-murder, shocking in the suburbs, but unfortunately not that big a deal in a metropolitan area where babies and old ladies are shot through apartment doors as they sleep.

The media weren't making any connection between Gil Dow's death and Bingham's—yet. The local paper would pay more attention but could be relied upon to remain subdued:

Leeming couldn't kill the story, but he could contain it for a bit.

Within Rochambeau's borders, too, the freak-out seemed less intense than the last time. For one thing, nobody was preying on our kids. For another, the gossips got hold of Bingham's past, and although no one said so out loud, you could almost hear people thinking that the woman's death must somehow be connected to her troubled life. And maybe it was.

Locally, word spread quickly that there might be some connection between the two recent deaths in Rochambeau, that the police were seeking Gil Dow's wife. The art of rationalizing—nearly a religion in suburbia when it comes to violence and trouble—was making it possible to put the deaths in comfortable perspective, if not to dismiss them entirely.

Chief Leeming and I both knew that the comparatively mild response provided only a few days' grace. He needed to get a suspect behind bars before the next township council meeting, when the ubiquitous enraged taxpayers would appear in droves screaming for his hide. People in Rochambeau pay a lot of property taxes, and they want nothing less than paradise for it.

Township managers, police chiefs, and sanitation commissioners who don't or can't oblige these demands are quickly gone. Municipal executives are one of suburbia's lost tribes, drifting from community to community to confront the next set of impossible expectations and loud complaints, to grapple as long as they can with the unbreachable gap between what people will pay for and what they demand. You don't dare raise taxes, but cut one helmet from the school football program and your head will roll all the way to the George Washington Bridge. The five-year-old police cruiser with 150,000 miles on it can make it through one more year, but the officers had better be in the driveway five seconds after the loud party next door is called in.

I felt overloaded after the previous day's revelations and Morfey's visit. I was reeling from Bingham's killing, and now from the fact that Marianne had apparently fled just after her husband's death. My response had to be to keep moving forward, to keep searching for answers, not to sit around clucking in shock. In between I had a household to keep an eye on, refrigerator shelves to keep stocked, homework to be overseen.

Was there any real question now that Marianne Dow was guilty of something? Leeming wouldn't even consider any other possibility. And for that matter, was I even on the case anymore? Yes, I told myself quickly. Marianne had given me a check, she hadn't told me to quit, and in the absence of that, I wouldn't. Besides, I had awarded myself another client: Roberta Bingham. Somehow I felt her death must be connected to Gil Dow's.

I had called Marianne's attorney at home, after the feds left, to see if he knew more than I did, but Levin hadn't heard from her. Neither, he told me, had the lawyers at the firm in the city where she worked part-time. "I don't like it," he said. "When a client runs, it usually isn't because they're innocent." That tended to be true in my work too.

Marianne hadn't even called the godmother with whom she'd parked her children, Levin reported. If everyone was telling the truth, it was time to worry. I couldn't see Marianne being out of touch with her kids for long.

Levin probably hoped he'd never hear from her again. The local attorney handled mostly wills and real-estate closings, there being little in the nature of criminal activity here. We both knew that if Marianne was actually charged, he'd bring in a big firm from Newark. He probably wouldn't be happy being too closely associated with somebody who might have offed two Rochambeau citizens in less than a week, one of them a hardworking, commuting dad of two.

"Under the circumstances, Deleeuw, if you want to bail out, I'd understand." Levin had obviously lost faith rapidly in his client. "This behavior is inexplicable and, frankly, disturbing. She didn't even contact me. I don't know what to tell the police, to be honest."

But he misunderstood the nature of my business, where being associated with spectacularly unsavory types was a boost, not a drawback. He also misread my own notions of loyalty.

"Nope, not yet," I told him. "It's an ethic among us private eyes. We're not off the case until the client stops paying or tells us we're fired. Or dies." Possibly my bravado fooled him, but Marianne had knocked me off my pins. I've never felt more like the naive pretender that Chief Leeming assures me at every available opportunity I am.

I'd begun the eighties like most of the other men around me on Wall Street. There was more work than we could accomplish, more money around than we could ever seem to scoop up. Without quite realizing it, we had become pigs at a trough that never emptied. We were so busy feasting, we didn't pay much attention either to the rest of our lives or to the many warning signs that we were engaged in the frenzied building of a house of matches.

When it collapsed, and I found myself wandering about, avoiding what I thought were the curious glances of the gainfully occupied, almost every fundamental reality of my life had changed. Before, I'd felt I had no choice but to work like a demon. Then, no choice but to stop. Before I was even forty, my career was over.

I would never go back to that kind of life. I couldn't. In my new existence work and home were so tangled, I never could completely extricate one from the other. I was always juggling, and there were new meanings to it I couldn't have fathomed. I actually knew my kids' friends as opposed to struggling to recall their names. I didn't have to cluck sympathetically and ask a lot of questions when Ben and Em recounted their spills, social traumas, and squabbles; I was there. I wouldn't ever give that up.

These days it was Jane who faced tough choices about work. One of her clients had taken a savage beating from her stepfather and was in intensive care, just two hospital floors up from an unsuccessful suicide. A multiple personality—the nasty one—had smashed all the glass in the house, and a teenager with AIDS was failing rapidly. Jane's contract with her clients was simple—she would not let them down the way the rest of the world and the bureaucracies they encountered so frequently did. Often she couldn't make their lives much better. But they clung to their weekly appointments, and she to her responsibility to be there for them. My contribution, which I took extremely seriously, was to make sure she didn't have to look over her shoulder when she did. Jane kept telling me this was rare in men, but I suspect there were many of my sex who would have done it if they felt they could.

Still, as dedicated as she was, she needed lots of reassurance. "God," she muttered for the thousandth time as I woke her the morning after Roberta Bingham's murder and she struggled to sit up in bed. "There's this huge part of me that asks, 'What the hell kind of mother isn't there when her daughter has a fever of a hundred and two or her son plays a championship soccer game?' Won't Ben and Em be asking the same questions?" She groaned.

"You seem to be living with it," I replied calmly. "You

can't go back any more than I can. You're the kind of mother who's going out into the world and doing something important, something you care about," I added, pulling her over for a hug. "Look at the gift you're giving them. You're showing them women don't just cook and drive their children to their lessons, and you're letting me show them that men can get kids off to school, too."

"With a balanced lunch?"

"Always. But don't whine about your anxieties today. Mine are bigger. I am once again up to my nose in the Big Muddy." We had a scant fifteen minutes to catch up before the kids were awakened and the breakfast chaos underway. She shifted gears instantly, asking me about the case, sifting through the grisly and puzzling information from Providence and Rochambeau.

She frowned when I told her about Dow's disappearance. "She isn't necessarily running out of guilt, you know, although that is what the police would conclude."

"Why else would she take off, Jane?"

"She could be frightened of something, or she could be heading off to do something. To take care of something. Maybe even prove her innocence."

"But that's why she hired me."

"I understand, sweetie." She patted my shoulder reassuringly. "But, you know, I believe this more every day: people can hide huge chunks of their lives. You only know about Marianne what she's chosen to share with you." Yawning, Jane stood and pulled her bathrobe on, heading to our bathroom. "To be honest, I'm more drawn to Lucca. She's stuck in my mind."

"Why?" I was following her.

"Because she becomes more fascinating by the day. She's clearly—perhaps subconsciously—enraged at healthy, functioning families and has this intense need to smash them up. She's a very powerful, complex person. Strong enough to befriend people at will, seduce lovers whenever she wants to, seemingly indifferent to all the suffering she knows she must cause."

"You'd love to treat her, wouldn't you?"

"She sounds over my head. Until I get my degree, that is. Even then, of course, I couldn't see her because of your involvement. It would be unethical." But Jane sounded wistful.

I felt a bit wistful myself. "Why don't we meet for lunch somewhere up on Route Forty-six? There's a new Chili's we could check out. Might be a nice break from your parade of misery." Like other couples when both parents work and there are two young kids, our moments alone together are far too few.

"Thanks, sweetie. But I'm having lunch with Pam. I told you about her, didn't I?"

"Pam?" I sort of remembered Jane exulting over someone she'd met just a few days ago.

"Yeah. She's helping the clinic put together an ad campaign, a sort of outreach thing for women. She's done a lot of nonprofit work, and she's donated some of her firm's time. And her own."

"That's great. What's she planning?"

"She's putting together some brochures and designing a knockout poster. I met her at a staff meeting, where we all kicked ideas around and described our work in the clinic. We connected right off. I want to have her over, if we ever again have time for dinner guests in our lives." She sighed.

I gave Jane a hug. "HouseHusband can do it. New chums are precious. I've made my best ones in the last couple of years. Let's try to do it."

"Yeah," she said, looking at the clock and speeding up

her routine. "We should. Pam has great friend potential." We had come to the point in the day when we plunged along our separate paths. We probably wouldn't reconnect till bedtime. I was glad Jane had a new friend—she didn't find them all that easy to make—but I would have loved to have seen her at midday. Although when I thought about it, it was doubtful I'd have much time anyway. I had a lot of unscrambling to do.

Each day that passed, more things happened in the Dow case and I understood less about them. Why had Marianne run, if it wasn't to avoid facing her own guilt?

Was Andrea Lucca lying in the woods waiting for some deer-stalking orthodontist to trip over her shallow grave and lose his lunch? And how could I reconcile the two images of Lucca: the doting niece who drove two hundred miles to bring her dying relatives medical supplies and food—Gay Tannenbaum's supportive friend—against the cold-blooded family killer who shattered one household after another? The case had kept me awake half the night.

Willie had left a message at the house the night before, asking me to call him in the morning—a Post-It had gone up on the back door to remind me. Maybe he'd discovered something more about Lucca and where she was shopping these days. I was desperate to get my hands on something tangible, something that could bring this specter to life.

Meanwhile, I couldn't imagine the authorities would have much trouble catching up with Marianne. She was hardly a seasoned criminal, and they had the description and license number of Gil's car, which proved her amateurishness and, to my mind, her innocence. Wasn't that really what shook me so much, now that I thought about it? My inability to see this straightforward, open woman as a killer? And my inability to see Lucca at all?

But school buses come whether clients are truthful or not, whether bodies are found bludgeoned or murder suspects give cops the slip. Breakfasts have to be served, jittery adolescent nerves calmed, social-worker spouses sent off with bagels and briefcases. Lunches have to be overseen.

I stormed into the kitchen, trying to rouse my sullen, lumbering family by sheer force of personality and will. It hadn't worked yet.

"Protein!" I yelled.

"Check!" Em yelled back groggily. Ben was much too cool to respond in actual verbiage, but he did look into his lunch bag to make sure some cheese or egg or turkey sandwich lurked within.

"Vegetable."

"Check. And fruit," Em responded, before I could ask.

"What's dessert?"

"Two cookies."

"Got a spoon? Napkins?" Em nodded. Ben sullenly went over to the drawer for a plastic spoon.

"Kids, I'm going to be a little crazy the next few days. Actually, I'm going to be a *lot* crazy. You're going to have to watch out for each other. I'm working on this murder case."

Em yawned. At ten, murder is simply not a part of the comprehensible universe.

But Ben perked up. "The kids are all saying the cops have a suspect. That there were two, maybe three, murders, and the same person did them, that it wasn't a robbery at all."

I was surprised, but not astonished; I had seen this phenomenon before. Kids have an amazing grapevine. In towns like Rochambeau, hundreds of prying eyes and alert ears pick up the scraps of information and speculation dropped by town officials, lawyers, cops, and gossips.

"Well, I am working for the person the police think did at

least one of the murders," I said, a trifle haughtily. "And I don't believe she hurt anybody. You know, we learned last winter that the police aren't always right."

I shut up, as I heard my own conversation drift into a lecture. It was a mistake I often made with Ben. The common perception—that I was a Wall Street felon who happily and illegally took part in the economic rape that characterized the eighties—had made life tough for my son and put severe strains on our relationship. Things had gotten better, but I undermined that progress every time I drifted into the reflexively didactic mode that characterizes so many fathers' conversations with their sons. I think the hardest thing I ever learned as a parent—and I hadn't got it yet—was to shut up. So I just squeezed his shoulder before he loped out toward the bus stop.

The American Way was suffering through the kind of day its tenants loathed: warm spring sunshine drew even the most devoted shopper to a park or the backyard or a stroll with the kids. The mall merchants prayed for inverse weather. "Great forecast," one would yell to another. "Drizzle and rain all day."

The Cicchelli window family was as sunny as the weather outside, suddenly sprouting mocs, polo shirts, and canvas tote bags. Summer was just ahead, and this was one family prepared to enjoy it. Rattan and wicker chairs appeared in the eastern corner of their glassed-in living room, and a pitcher of refreshing iced tea stood close at hand. Daddy Cicchelli looked wise and benign, like his suburban predecessors on fifties TV shows. Nobody would brain anybody in this family, or have an affair or do anything hurtful or dumb. I waved to them, bought Evelyn some coffee, and sat down at my unnervingly tidy desk to clean up the mounting paperwork and plan my next move.

Then Evelyn reminded me that it had better be a visit to the architect for whom Andrea Lucca worked, and it had better take place at eleven A.M. I had, of course, forgotten. That's what happens when I neglect to put important engagements on Post-Its. Outside, Route 6 was quiet. The rush-hour roar was down to a steady hum, punctuated by the occasional tractor-trailer that whined by like some sci-fi mosquito.

Willie, whom I *did* remember to call before I left, sounded unusually mysterious.

"Call me this afternoon at this number," he ordered, giving me a different one than we usually used. "A friend's office. I won't talk now." He sounded as if he had something for me, or at least expected to.

I'd pay him extra for this assignment. I was queasy enough about our secret arrangement. He'd be fired in a flash if his employers ever got wind of his free-lance electronic sleuthing; at least he should be better compensated.

At ten forty-five I was heading to Andrea Lucca's office.

Peter Babst & Associates was built on stilts right into the side of a hill that hung over Route 22, a highway fronted by county parklands in Rochambeau which quickly degenerates into a five-mile stretch of fast-food joints, car dealerships, and those ubiquitous minimalls filled with office-furniture suppliers and party-goods stores. From the renderings in the entrance hall, it seemed Babst & Associates concentrated on designing those small, reflecting-glass office complexes that now sparkle all over the hinterlands.

The indifferent receptionist I had encountered three days ago on the phone practically yawned in my face. She was so like I had pictured her, I had to suppress a laugh. Her blond hair was teased and sprayed, she wore a billowy yellow blouse, and her sleepy eyes peered out from behind a crust of eyeshadow, liner, and mascara. A copy of *Self* lay open on the desk in front of her. She was in her late teens or early twenties and fortunate not to be behind the counter at Lightning Burger. Actually, she wouldn't last there; Luis would run her off. Without a change in her bored expression, she buzzed Babst, then pointed the way in by waving one highly manicured hand as she turned the pages of the magazine with the other.

The window behind Peter Babst took up the whole wall. Unfortunately, the view was of traffic inching its way along the highway. He introduced himself and launched into a practiced explanation of his firm and its virtues.

"We specialize in residential housing and, as you probably noticed, smaller, technologically advanced office space." I thought he was about to hand me a brochure, when he abruptly seemed to remember that I was a private investigator and changed his patter.

Babst was in his late thirties, although his hairline had receded about ten years ahead of schedule. He wore rimless granny glasses, a rust-colored gabardine shirt, and a knit black tie. A thick gold bracelet glowed from beneath his right cuff. The look was a strange sort of cross between academic and developer. He was a touch more gaunt than seemed normal, as though he should have been chunky, but wasn't, from which I inferred he was a runner. A picture of his wife and two smiling kids was prominently propped before him on the oversize desk.

I doubted he had ever met with a private investigator before. He was jumpy. His fingers began drumming on the desktop, his intelligent eyes darting away from mine. He obviously had a comfortable practice and no appetite for being drawn into a murderous scandal, especially one, as he quickly made clear, that involved a part-time employee.

"Andrea went to Pratt in Brooklyn. As I told the police *and* the FBI," he added with some exasperation, "she answered an ad I put in the *Star-Ledger* about a year and a half ago. I need an artist to prepare sketches for clients. Because we're a small firm—there's only myself and an associate—we need somebody only part-time, two afternoons a week or on a pay-per-drawing basis."

Something about Babst bugged me, although I couldn't put my finger on it. I could see his being irritated by all the cops traipsing through his office, but why jumpy? He kept checking the photo of his wife and kids every few seconds, as if he expected them to evaporate. I had a great nose for twitchy people: it's one of the few positive legacies of my Wall Street days. As a commodities trader, you deal with a lot of twitchy people. If he was so uncomfortable, why was this guy seeing me at all? Babst had already given his story to the cops and FBI; he couldn't possibly want a private investigator hanging around.

"So she didn't work regular hours?"

"No, not at all. I would leave blueprints and sketches for her, or my associate would, and Andrea would come in whenever she felt like it, more often than not in the evening or on weekends. All I cared about was that she make her deadlines. Her sketches were terrific, and as you might imagine, they're critically important in my work. Someone isn't going to go ahead and authorize the construction of a million-dollar home or new office if it doesn't look beautiful." I bet, I thought, while Babst talked on about integrating structures with the environment. Andrea's sketches probably made each project look like Valhalla. I was increasingly conscious of not liking this man.

"I paid her seven hundred and fifty dollars per sketch, and we do five or six a month here. Usually, the quality sketches we use go for a thousand apiece, but we gave her the use of an office in the back in exchange for the reduced rate, plus the use of the phone and of Jennifer, my receptionist. I know she accepted other free-lance work from other architects as well and did sketches for the advertising departments of local department stores, that sort of thing. But I didn't see much of her. I mean, technically, she didn't really even work here. She was a tenant."

"So you didn't pay for benefits, or anything like that?"

He shook his head quickly, horrified at the notion.

"You think she did pretty well. Financially, I mean?"

"Yes, especially for a graphic artist these days. She probably did better than fifty thousand dollars from me over the year. I don't know what she made from retail concerns. But she was quite good, very creative and stylish and scrupulous about meeting her deadlines. I was very happy with her work. But she didn't hang around here and never stopped by to chat or anything like that."

"Never?" That didn't sound like the attentive and sympathetic listener who had attended Buns of Steel.

"No. Never."

So now I guess I was figuring out what was bugging me about this guy. "You sleep with her?"

"What?"

"Did you sleep with her?" I enunciated carefully. This kind of questioning wasn't usually my style, but Peter Babst's unease and Lucca's history were coming into focus, at least enough to gamble on. Since he claimed to know nothing, I had nothing to lose.

"How dare you, Mr.—"

"Deleeuw," I answered. Any faithful spouse in that situation would have shown me the door on the spot. But he didn't toss me out. The only conceivable reason for his sitting there hissing and steaming like a forgotten tea kettle was that he was desperate to know what I knew. As usual, I knew squat.

"Look, Mr. Babst. I used to work on Wall Street. I never really meant to be a detective at all. I'm not a rough guy and I'm not a sleazy one. I don't care about your personal life, just about finding Andrea Lucca. She was as friendly as a retriever puppy, from what I know about her. She was interested in everybody, she had friends all over the place. People she'd known for a few hours poured out their life stories to her. I also know that the standard rate for architectural sketches around here is five hundred dollars. They're not full-color art; they're treatments. Lots of architects do them themselves. Only takes a few hours. She was getting five hundred dollars for her sketches from other firms, and I have documentation on that," I lied smoothly. "Why would you claim her work was worth double that, and pay her fifty percent more than the going rate? You were sleeping with her, weren't you? You had a relationship with her."

Babst cursed and huffed and stonewalled for nearly ten minutes—but there's this curious phenomenon that I'd already encountered a hundred times in my brief detecting career: minor miscreants are relieved as hell when their dirty little secrets come out and they can stop dreading the moment when they will. You just have to wait them out, let them work it through.

"Look." He got up to make sure the door was closed tightly. I couldn't imagine Jennifer stirring herself to walk over and eavesdrop or giving a shit if she heard. "Here's the truth. I swear on my kids. You can believe it or not. A year and a half ago, Andrea Lucca met my wife at a reception at the county museum. They became inseparable, talking on the phone all day, going to movies together—I hate movies—and working out—"

"At an exercise class?"

"Yes, you know about that?"

"I know about it. Whatever else you can say about Andrea Lucca, she's gotta be in dynamite shape."

He pulled out a handkerchief to wipe his face.

"And then you slept with her?" I prompted.

"One night she came over looking for Cindy—that's my wife. Cindy wasn't home. In fact, she was at a meeting at the museum. I was surprised Andrea wasn't there herself."

Not me.

"But instead of going away, she asked if she could come in. She burst into tears, told me how attractive she found me —well, I don't think you need all the details. We did . . . we had . . ."

"Jesus, Babst, you can say the words. I'm a big boy. You went to bed with her."

"Yes," he said. "Okay. But just once. That was the incredible thing. We did sleep together. Then the next morning she called, told me an intimate relationship was inappropriate, that she had too much affection for Cindy. Besides, she said, we had been discussing her working for me part-time. Which was true."

"So, Babst, are you telling me she slept with you so that she could get work?"

"No, not at all." He sounded shocked at the idea that

somebody would climb into bed with him for any other reason than his being devastatingly attractive. "Andrea didn't need to do that. She had plenty of talent. I think she meant it. I think she was drawn to me, we both got carried away one night, then she realized it would be a disaster. So did I," he added hastily. "So I suggested this arrangement where she used my office as a base."

More likely, I thought, she was toying with busting up your family, but realized that with one night of mediocre sex she could control you, have a base from which to launch her little strikes, and bust up your family later when she got around to it. Andrea had gone through this cluck like a cleaver through Play-Doh.

"And it worked out," he said firmly. "It worked out. There was no more . . . involvement, if you will. Course, I was about to point out the impropriety myself, just before she did." Right. And I was about to replace the Volvo with a Jaguar. "She did excellent work for us. And she got an office and the facilities here."

"Were you ever tempted to get involved with her again?"

I was expecting a lie, or more charitably, serious denial. But he surprised me here.

"Sure. I found her attractive. But it was striking—once we came to this arrangement, she seemed . . . transformed. For one thing, I was scared to death. I mean, I love my wife and kids and all." He looked abashedly back at the photo on his desk. "And then Andrea stopped seeing Cindy, or even talking to her on the phone. She never spoke to me much, either, other than to wave or say hello if we ran into each other here in the office. It was as if we had never been intimate at all; our relationship became strictly business. My wife was badly hurt, though; her best pal suddenly vanished."

"How about you? Were you hurt?"

He looked out at the stream of cars and trucks. "Half-relieved, half-hurt, I guess." Well, he had some integrity at least. Unlike Lucca. This woman was working her way into my dreams, and not pleasantly.

"Was your wife suspicious?" I wondered, ever on the lookout for suspects other than my client. "Did she recognize that the friendship ended exactly when Andrea moved in here?"

He shook his head. "No. Cindy isn't the suspicious type. And I didn't give her any reason to be. After all, the relationship did become completely professional. I never saw Andrea socially again. I hope it wasn't a big mistake to talk to you," he said hastily as if the idea had just occurred to him.

"Mr. Babst, I don't think you have anything to fear from me. What you told me will remain with me. Let the police think Andrea answered an ad. You have to build houses that don't fall down. I have to protect people who speak with me. But what I need," I said pleasantly, showing him my inevitable hand, "is information on where I might find Andrea, where she might have gone, who she might have turned to—"

"The police seemed to be suggesting that she might be in some sort of trouble, even . . ." He shook his head, unable to complete the thought.

"Yes, I know. She's taken off, and they think somebody might have taken her off. Other people may be looking for her, and I need to find her first. For her sake. I know you probably hope she'll disappear, but believe me, this could be a life-and-death matter. And I know you're a decent man." If Andrea had flattered him so easily, no reason why it shouldn't work with me.

"I'd be happy to help you, but I honestly don't know

how." He shrugged. "I told the cops what I knew. I have no idea where she went or who she was close to."

"Did she write you any letters? Leave any address books behind? Get any mail?"

He shook his head.

"Did she ever mention family? Friends?"

Nope.

"In her conversations with your wife, did she talk about people or friends or family outside of Rochambeau?"

"No. In fact my wife used to say that Andrea was a wonderful listener, but she didn't share much of her life." Those words again. There sure were a lot of people out there who needed somebody to talk to.

"Did she ever have to fill out any papers for you? Anything—employment forms, bonding, insurance . . ."

He snapped his fingers. "Wait a minute, there might be something." He pushed a button on his phone. "Jennifer, bring me the file we keep with North America, the insurance company." Pause. "It's under 'insurance,' Jennifer. Begins with *I.*"

He got up and went outside into the reception area.

"Here it is," he said, returning a few minutes later. "We have additional liability insurance. The company was nervous because we built on the side of a hill, worried about rock slides and the stilts collapsing and such, so we had to pay a bigger premium. I remember that an adjuster came and made a big deal out of everyone signing these liability forms. They say we understand we're on the side of a hill and that there are some slight risks, you know, things that probably wouldn't mean a thing in court, but which insurance companies like. We all filled one out, including Andrea, I'm sure. Here it is."

Babst was so relieved to be able to help that I saw just how frightened he was that I might betray the secret I had wormed out of him. I wouldn't. Trapping people into admitting affairs wasn't my notion of brilliant detective work. Maybe I was a sleazier sort than I liked to admit. Thing was, I desperately needed a break in the case.

It was a standard liability form, commonly used by insurance companies in a losing battle to discourage claims. I'd had to sign one to rent my office in the American Way. Babst was right; these forms were useless in court. But useful to me. Under next of kin, where I had expected to find the old couple from Providence, I found instead the name Ruth Murray, at 1780 Woodland Avenue, Millville, New Jersey. There was even a phone number attached to it.

Finally, an honest-to-God break in the case.

Twenty minutes later I pulled into my driveway to let Percentage out of the house and drop off the food I'd picked up at the Wawa en route. I tried never to shop at pricey convenience stores for groceries. I almost always made it to the supermarket—and didn't need a list, a point of pride, although it had taken a few years to reach that milestone. I left two frozen pizzas out on the counter with a note for Ben and Em to heat them for dinner, along with something green, in case I wasn't back. I headed back outside for the Volvo, and the short trip to the American Way and a visit with Luis Hebron.

Charlie Pinski came charging up to me as I unlocked the car.

"Hey, those les—those *girls* next door aren't so bad." My next-door neighbor was huffing and puffing from the unaccustomed exertion of walking.

"It's okay, Charlie. They don't mind being called lesbians, that's what they are."

"Well, whatever they are, they weeded those flower beds like every last blade of crabgrass was a personal insult. It hasn't looked that good in ten years." To Charlie this was the finest character reference there could be. It didn't matter if you methodically slaughtered paper boys in your basement, as long as your lawn and garden met his standards.

"Gotta run, Charlie. I'm on a case—"

"Sure, sure," he boomed. "It's just that somebody dropped this off at my house this morning." He pulled an envelope out of his shirt pocket. "It was in the mailbox. Has your name on it. Obviously they got confused."

I waited until he was out of sight before I ripped it open. The note inside had the name "Marianne Dow" engraved across the top of the paper and was written in a distinct but shaky hand. *Kit,* it said. *I'm sorry to head out like this, but I have no choice. Keep the faith. You'll hear from me. Marianne.*

That was it. *Keep the faith.* I shook my head in disbelief. If the scene had been a cartoon, my jaw would have scraped the ground. The strange part is that I was not only surprised, I was stung. I liked Marianne. She'd come to me for help and I was killing myself to provide it. Why had she communicated through a note? Why hadn't she called me or come to see me at the mall or at home?

But then, I couldn't imagine why she was doing any of the things she was doing—running, hiding, leaving her kids at a devastating time. There was only one good reason I could think of—she'd murdered Gil. That would explain all of it. And that would prove me the amateur I felt like at the moment. But that sure didn't feel right.

I slipped the note into my pocket and drove to the Lightning Burger. Luis was interviewing teenagers for part-time jobs, which is what he spends 70 percent of his time doing. He was always looking for kids to run the machines and clean up the tables, gently but firmly exhorting his largely adolescent staff to new standards of courtesy and responsiveness. But the chain itself is a turkey, one of those sad fast-food franchises that somehow never quite take off but still manage to hang on to their greasy, smelly existences.

Luis always chuckles when he talks about Lightning Burger. "May I show you our wine list?" he likes to say when I come in for coffee and a chat. But of course, he *would* see the irony of it. Luis had been one of Havana's top criminal attorneys before he defended the wrong person, and a friend in Castro's police force warned him to get out. He did, fleeing Cuba in the smelly hold of a fishing boat and ending up in Newark with a ballpoint pen, a useless law degree, and the equivalent of twenty-five American dollars. Lost in America. His wife eventually followed, but his two sons did not. He never volunteered the reasons, and I, seeing the sorrow and pain in his eyes, never asked.

Luis was the courtliest, most gracious and savvy fast-food manager I would ever encounter, conjuring linen suits, oceanside verandas, and cool rum punches rather than burgers and fries.

In many ways I was as close to Luis as I was to Benchley. But there were rigid, unspoken boundaries around our relationship. Luis had never invited me to his apartment. He had politely declined my invitations to dinner at our house. But when cases got complicated—as this one was—he was an invaluable source of wisdom and experience.

He was programming his bank of microwaves for the new burrito dish his chain was offering in its effort to be less cholesterol oriented. This ploy was particularly distasteful, since he knew what Latin food was supposed to look and taste like, but he took it with his usual good humor.

We sat in the manager's booth—always reserved—where

the Lightning Burger manager sipped his black coffee and looked out at the mall lot, thinking thoughts I imagined to be exotic, tropical, and nostalgic but would probably never decipher.

It took me fifteen minutes to go through the case.

"You've got to find this Lucca woman," he said at once. "And quickly, Kit. The police have a terrific case against your client. She had the opportunity, a provable motive. And now that she's left their jurisdiction, she looks even guiltier. I've lost clients on less. Although these days . . ." He didn't have to say it. Fidel. Luis couldn't speak the name. He ran his fingers through his silver hair. Luis would look distinguished anywhere, even here. He always wore a cotton dress shirt, with a dark tie. I put him at past sixty, his handsome face dark-skinned and gravely lined. He chain-smoked one unfiltered cigarette after another. If he had taken off his manager badge and nameplate and slipped on a jacket, I could picture him charming the socks off the toughest jury.

"Frankly, Kit, I find Marianne Dow's flight disturbing. And inexplicable. Why run? She knows the legal system; she has resources. She could have gotten a top-drawer lawyer. She had you. She didn't even press to know what your information was when you called. That's quite significant: you go to Providence, find out that this Lucca woman has been there recently, and Marianne doesn't even wait to know what you've learned. Doesn't seem to want to speak to you directly, even on the phone. It's as if it didn't matter, as if she didn't care." Or already knew, I thought with a chill. But how could she?

"Your only possibility"—he extinguished one cigarette and lit another—"is to find Andrea Lucca, establish that she is alive. She might have motives, too. And perhaps she fled as well." But I could see he didn't really believe that. He believed she'd been killed, but didn't want to further discourage me. He smoked in silence for a moment. I waited.

"I'm thinking about how confusing all these changes are among American women, especially in affluent communities like yours. They have so many more choices than Cuban women, so many additional ways to live. But it's difficult, still. The path remains clearer for men. If men work, that is what they are supposed to do. If they take care of their families, then they are warm and caring. But for women, it still seems so complicated. If they work, people blame them for abandoning their families. If they don't, then they are seen as old-fashioned and dependent. I feel for them, these women you describe who stay at home. They can be victims, ready for someone like this Lucca creature to prey upon." He sighed. "I don't know what to think. But I will consider it, and perhaps we can talk again tomorrow."

This has to be a mess, I thought as I headed up to my office, if even Luis is befuddled. But he had gone to the heart of it, of course. This case was completely entangled with women, with the ways in which they've changed.

The women I know who work full-time and unequivocally, women like Jane, seem to me to be on firmer ground. She sometimes feels guilty when she isn't around for the kids, but there is no doubt about her basic choice: she has chosen a career and is intensely devoted to it. The women who choose from the outset to tend their children and their homes also seem surer of themselves, better able to enjoy their routines and build a community for themselves. But the ground in the middle is clearly a tar pit for many, easy to enter but hard not to get stuck in.

At my desk I took a swig from a bottle of mineral water and dialed a number I'd scrawled on a Post-It and stuck inside my wallet.

Willie picked up on the second ring.

"Okay to talk?" I asked. I wondered, as always, what he looked like, but didn't ask; better not to know. I gave him the name and address Babst had given me and heard some furious keyboard action as he fed the name into whatever he fed names into. He assured me it would take only a few seconds. I could imagine the piles of *Mondo 2000* and *Wired* and other cybermags scattered around his keyboard.

"I got some other stuff. But it's confusing," Willie said.

"Shoot," I said. I had closed the door, which was uncharacteristic, and waved to Evelyn as she looked at me curiously before heading home. Her job technically involved twenty-five hours a week—nine A.M. to three P.M., with an hour off for lunch—but she usually worked thirty or more. I think she hated to leave me alone in the office for too long, certain I would lose a critical document at a critical time. It had happened.

"Well, without going into details, I've gone to visit a friend who works for one of the big credit agencies. He's an awesome hacker, and we—well, you don't need to know this."

"I'd love to, but it's just as well that I don't."

"Well, Martin"—our code name for me. I never used a name for him—"I figure that everybody out there has to do three things at some point in their lives. Get a car, get a house or apartment, and buy insurance for those things and the things inside them. That means credit checks and stuff. I can get onto 'em, man. Now your Ms. Lu—" I interrupted to suggest we not mention her name either. Now that the FBI was involved, phones might be tapped, something the Rochambeau PD didn't have much appetite or budget for.

"Well, I got onto her right away. Two years ago she used a car company credit program. When car sales were down, they offered all those rebates and she bought a Corolla. Got a good price, too. Bought it at this dealership in eastern Pennsylvania, place called Kaplan's Toyota, in a town called Mizpah. Found some other charges out that way, too—a couple at a restaurant and at the Holiday Inn." He gave me the addresses and phone numbers.

"Were the food tabs large?"

"You mean, big enough that there was more than one person? Yeah, they're for forty, fifty bucks. There's actually three or four of them. That's about standard for two."

"Anything in the last few days?"

"Nothing since Providence. I'm into a lot of computers, though." I wondered how he did it. "If she buys anything or stays anywhere, I'll spot it. But here's the thing that's weird. The other person, Mrs. D, the one you said had taken off and you needed to find her? She popped up, too. And in the same town. I tried to call you, but you always tell me not to leave my name. . . ."

"Right, you did the right thing. You've got to be careful. But what did you find out about D?"

"Well, she bought fifteen hundred dollars in furniture yesterday afternoon. It surprised me to find her out shopping, since you seemed kind of worried about her."

My stunned silence went on long enough for Willie to interrupt it and ask if I was still on the line.

"Willie. Would you repeat that?" He did. Twice. I still had trouble believing it.

"Willie, are you lost in cyberspace? Your brain waves altered by too much screen time? Are you positive? It's not possible, what you're telling me."

I heard furious clicking and clacking as, at my insistence, Willie put Marianne's name back into the computer and ran it through again. Again he came up with the same impossible information. Marianne Dow, whose husband had been savagely attacked, who was under suspicion of murder, whose kids had been parked with a friend, who was fighting for her literal existence, was buying furniture? In the same town where Andrea Lucca had bought a car and frequently gone out to dinner with somebody? Had Willie lost his mind? Had I lost mine? I made him run it through again. It came out the same way a third time. I accepted it, but I still had trouble believing it. And I sure as hell couldn't come up with any conceivable explanation for it. But Willie was great, terrific at what he did, and absolutely confident about his information. He had never failed me—I considered making him my first junior associate—it had to be true. But dear Lord, was I blown away.

"Shopping? You *sure* it's the same person?"

"This is the fourth time you've asked me, Martin." Willie sounded exasperated. "I'm one hundred percent. You can bet on it, man. Have I been wrong yet? Unless somebody swiped her credit card. And people don't tend to buy furniture with stolen cards, Martin, because, like, when you have furniture delivered, the furniture company has all the time in the world to check on your credit and all, then call the cops."

I said I understood what he meant, embarrassed that he'd thought of that and I hadn't.

"And this stuff was purchased in Mizpah? It isn't possible she ordered it somewhere else? Like around here?" I still couldn't bring myself to accept it.

"No, that's the thing, that's what I'm telling you. She bought it in Mizpah, the same town in Pennsylvania."

I felt as if I'd turned on the evening news to see Marianne skydiving over the World Trade Center. The first thought that popped into my head was this: if she was out buying furniture, perhaps she was setting up house, and if she was setting up house, then maybe there was another man in her life, and if there was another man in her life, Chief Leeming would have yet another juicy motive for murder, and he already had more than enough. But if there was another man in her life, surely she wouldn't be out ordering sofas while her husband lay dying or when the police were seeking her in connection with his murder.

And the other stunner here wasn't just that she was buying furniture, but in a town Andrea Lucca visited regularly for some reason, a town where Lucca stayed in a motel and had lunch or dinner with somebody. Had Lucca contacted her and arranged for some sort of meeting? Was Marianne planning to kidnap Andrea and torture her on some new couch? Was she planning to hide out in Pennsylvania? If so, wasn't it beyond reason to charge all this furniture on a credit card? Surely if Willie could, my buddies in the FBI could trace her to Mizpah. I was spinning.

I had a renegade client, somebody who had bolted from the police and from me, somebody who could very well be indicted and tried on murder charges. Everything she had done since hiring me had shocked me. I could find no intelligent—or even stupid—rationale for anything Marianne was doing. For the grizzled, hard-boiled private eyes of yore, this would have presented little problem; their self-assurance was unshakable. But I didn't have any such reservoirs of confidence; my detecting was tentative and highly shakable. My client had left me so bewildered that I thought I should be selling sneakers in Shoe World, not on the second floor taking responsibility for people's lives.

Get a grip, I told myself. I was still a detective, and Marianne was still my client, wherever the hell she was and whatever the fuck she was up to.

So I made some decisions. I would make a serious effort

to stop mumbling to myself. I would attend tonight's memorial for Roberta Bingham. And then in the morning, I'd head straight for Mizpah, Pennsylvania. To do my job, I didn't have to understand it all at the moment. I just had to understand it fast.

Willie had put me on hold. He came back on after a few minutes, sounding puzzled. "Martin, I'll keep scanning, but the name and the address you gave me are bogus. No Ruth Murray in Millville, and the address shows up as a diner. No residence at that address. I'll check more, but I betcha it's a phony."

Why wasn't I surprised? Nothing about Andrea Lucca's life seemed accessible. Nothing in this case was going to come that easy.

On the way home, absently fumbling in my jacket pocket for the car keys, I came upon the gelatinous remains of a green bath-oil ball. I tossed the goo into a trash can in the parking lot.

CHAPTER 13

Roberta Bingham's memorial service required the largest room McPherson's Funeral Parlor could offer, the one usually reserved for former mayors and beloved English teachers. Probably it had once been the ballroom of this old fieldstone mansion, a huge parquet-floored room with a massive chandelier and curving windows draped in plush red. In the front of the room, a woman in a black suit now stood at a lectern, preparing to read from her notes. A hundred women ranging in age from midtwenties to indeterminate old age crowded the rows of gilt chairs.

What a contrast to the group that would have gathered here just a few decades ago, hostesses and canasta competitors in ruffled shirtwaists, considered athletic if they played golf once a week. They probably would have had men sitting alongside them, too. Few of these women did.

Among the suited professionals and arty-looking gypsies in Birkenstocks, I could pick out some friends and colleagues from Roberta's other life—the twelve-steppers, probably members of her AA unit, and scattered friends. They stood out—noticeably less fit, marked by slumped shoulders and creaseless pants—from Buns of Steel's well-toned legions.

A few reporters had slipped in, too, with notebooks on their laps or peeking from pockets.

The woman at the podium read a brief eulogy. I guessed she was from the AA side of the aisle. Her face was weathered, her eyes sad; she was attractive, but not athletic looking. Her talk was as honest and touching as Roberta Bingham herself had been.

"Roberta failed at some of life's most important tasks. She could never manage marriage, and she felt she had never managed parenting. You all know of the tragedy that afflicted her family. There are no members of her family here today. That speaks to her greatest sorrow. Perhaps one day her children will be able to see the other side of Roberta Bingham's life, the side represented in this room. She would not have wanted me to whitewash her history. You all know that. But this crowded room is evidence that she had succeeded in building a new and better life, one from which all kinds of people drew help and inspiration."

I noticed Chief Leeming drift into the back of the room. He scanned the crowd, perhaps hoping Marianne Dow would be overcome with emotion and stop by. He would have no such luck.

I felt a flash of fear when the chief turned his eagle-eyed stare on me. He had a genuinely steely gaze when he wanted to apply it—it went right through you and suggested that any deception or evasion would be instantly apparent. I intended to share my experience with his Providence buddy, Lieutenant Grossman, although I didn't think for a second that Leeming would have approved of Grossman's tactics for getting me out of town. Still, he'd owe me one for a stomach that was still sore, and he'd get an earful about it.

I knew I really ought to tell him what Willie had dug up about Andrea and Marianne. But I didn't know how I could without compromising Willie. And I was reluctant to help Leeming get his hands on Marianne—he'd charge her with murder one on the spot—if I had any chance at all of locating Lucca. That wasn't what Marianne was paying me for. Solid rationales—but the chief still scared the hell out of me. I had lost one career already. I wasn't sure I had it in me to recover from the loss of another, not after legal fees and suburban life itself had wiped out my savings and I was still so far from covering Ben's or Em's college.

Jane and I joked that we would both end up working at Lightning Burger, but it wasn't a completely farfetched fate. If Leeming found out I had withheld information on the possible whereabouts of a murder suspect and possible victim, he could pull my license. Under the law and in the eyes of the state attorney general's office, he'd have every right to.

But my obligation was still to my client, even if she'd run out on me and all but hung a poster in her bathroom window saying, *"I'm guilty."* Looking around me, I wondered what kind of a turnout there'd be for her husband Gil, about whom I knew so little and had little time now to learn more. His family had insisted on a private ceremony and burial in his Massachusetts hometown, Evelyn had told me.

"In AA," continued Roberta's eulogizer, "Roberta was a voice—a firm and caring one—that led a lot of us back from the hell we found ourselves in. Nobody will ever know how many lives she touched, how many of us she pulled back from the dead by sheer force of her will and her love. In her work she helped women to get healthy and to stay healthy. That is no small achievement. As we struggle to build our lives, and find work, and balance it with family, many of us need a place to go to for encouragement and support in learning how to take care of ourselves, especially when we often get so little support from our families or lovers or bosses. Many of you found this support in Buns of Steel, which Roberta always saw as a haven where women could feel safe and strong. I was planning to join." There was some laughter at the procrastination. The woman smiled and went on.

"I guess I see Roberta as something of a hero. She would laugh at that. But she was a hero to me. She couldn't live up to the expectations of domesticity, and she hurt some people in her life very badly—herself included—in the process of accepting that. Through Roberta's life, at different times in different ways, came women in all their complex guises and under all of the pressures of our culture. Roberta understood our doubts and our pain. God bless her for her compassion and her courage." The woman turned away, unable to go on.

A handful of other women in the room were crying, too. The reporters were now openly taking notes. Chief Leeming, I noticed, had not altered his sour expression. God help Roberta Bingham's killer, I thought.

The mourners kept arriving as an all-female string quartet in one corner of the ballroom played something in a minor key. People drifted in, signed the leather-bound guest book, and tiptoed to the rear of the room in search of seats. Two men, two older women, a trim young one who might have been a junior instructor at the aerobics class. And a woman who caught my eye.

Maybe it was the scarf she'd tied over her brown hair that provided a slight air of mystery, or the tinted glasses through which no one could see her eyes. In the crowd I could make out only the scarf and the glasses and a dark trench coat she wore over a white shirt buttoned at the neck. She stood in the back, about as far away from the rows of Buns of Steel members as she could get, holding herself proudly, almost regally.

Her face looked stricken, although I couldn't tell if she'd been weeping or not. She looked as though she belonged among the exercisers, several of whom stirred when they spotted her. One waved tentatively and was frostily ignored. Maybe her apartness made her stand out, but this woman appeared striking, even in a room filled with attractive women.

The music ended and a neighbor of Roberta's got up to read a poem I had never heard before. I twisted around to get a better view of the newcomer. A woman in front of her shifted positions, and the visitor and I were suddenly looking right at one another. She nodded ever so slightly, and it seemed to me she smiled as well, although I couldn't swear to it. Had we met before?

A minister stepped up to the podium. He asked us all to bow our heads for a moment of silence and prayer. Then, with the announcement that burial would be the next morning at St. Stephen's at ten, it was over. There was gridlock as everyone stood to leave. I made my way to the back of the room to look for the latecomer, but she was gone.

I pushed through the crowd toward the narrow doorway. I'm sure it was easy enough to get in and out of McPherson's when a family of five or six lived there with their servants, but not when 150 people attempt to exit all at once. I squeezed through, apologizing every step of the way. Outside, probably spotting the look on my face, Leeming excused himself from the scribbling reporter to whom he'd undoubtedly been spouting reassuring platitudes, and came over.

"What's up, Deleeuw?"

"Chief, did you see a woman, midthirties, black scarf, dark glasses, trench coat, just come out of here?"

"Yeah, as a matter of fact. She was a good-looking . . ." The chief looked around, recollecting perhaps the political sensibilities surrounding him. "She went past me and out toward the parking lot. Why?"

"I'm just wondering who she is. Something about her . . ."

He was already moving back toward the funeral-home lobby, reaching into his pocket for his walkie-talkie.

I gave the parking lot a look as we headed in, but with three exits leading to surrounding streets, it was emptying quickly. Anybody who wanted to be gone would have been.

"We'll check the log," Leeming commanded, as if we were suddenly on the same side. "McPherson stands guard and makes sure everybody signs in, because the families want to send thank-you notes and that stuff."

He moved quickly past me to where the stragglers were collecting their coats from the checkroom and saying farewells. The red leather book lay open. "I noticed she came in late," Leeming said, running a stubby finger down the names. "If she signed in, it will be on the last page."

"Shit." He snapped the book closed and took it from its carved stand. He pressed a button on his walkie-talkie. "Central? This is the chief."

"Read you, Chief."

"Get somebody from the detective bureau and a squad car over to McPherson's. Code four." Everybody who watches TV knows that means pronto.

"Can you give us the nature of the call, Chief?" asked the dispatcher.

"Yeah. Andrea Lucca just signed in as a guest at the Bingham memorial service."

Jane had put aside her case notes and files, stacked in a foot-high pile on the kitchen table, and was calmly listening to me rant.

"So what kind of person does that?" I demanded. "What does it say about her? She must know that everybody in Rochambeau is looking for her. The cops have been through her apartment, the FBI has been to her office, and so have I. What kind of person strolls into a funeral parlor, knowing she's going to be recognized, then signs her goddamn name in the register? Do some shrinking, would you? I'm sinking like a cement block in the ocean here."

I was pacing. I was also mortified. If I'd reacted just ten seconds more quickly, the police or I could have stopped Andrea Lucca, could have talked to her. Instead, she vanished from the face of the earth once she walked out of McPherson's. Three Rochambeau PD cruisers had appeared quickly to look for the new blue Toyota Corolla she drove. But nobody saw her. Leeming looked as rattled as I was.

Lucca's behavior had suggested at the very least that she had something to hide. Maybe a fear of being lynched or run over. At least three—maybe four—women in town that I knew of would have been pleased to drown her in the municipal swimming pool, and most juries would be hard-pressed to convict any of them. But at least for the moment, Lucca was very much alive.

"You can't be one hundred percent sure it's her," Jane cautioned, unperturbed as usual by my bellowing. "You've never met her. Have you ever seen a picture of her?"

"No one seems to have one," I said grudgingly.

"So you don't really know what she looks like?"

"Well, some of the Buns of Steel women seemed to notice her. One even waved," I retorted, pulling a can of diet soda out of the refrigerator and popping the top. "C'mon, Jane, give me a break. I'm not an idiot."

"You said yourself she didn't get close to any of these women. That she stood as far away as possible. She had a scarf and glasses on," Jane said, sipping from the herbal tea I had poured her.

"Advise me, wise and trained one," I pleaded, trying to keep from panicking at the fact that my case was hurtling in a dozen different directions while I watched helplessly.

"I think she's an interesting person."

"That's the report from the psychologist-in-training? That this family-killer is *interesting*? Oh, please—"

Jane held up her hand. "Patience, please. You lay types are forever fitting people into the narrowest compartments. I don't know much about this woman or her motivations. But I think she went to this gathering tonight out of genuine regard for Roberta Bingham. Because she was attached to her and sincerely wanted to pay her respects. It was a brave and classy thing to do. I know you think she's a monster, and there are obviously plenty of people in this town who hate her and might give her cause to flee or hide. But why, if she was guilty of some awful crime, would she take a risk like that? There's nothing in her behavior to suggest she's irrational. Quite the contrary. She might be destructive, even vicious, but she's chillingly rational, from everything I've heard. So there."

Not what I wanted to hear. For me to feel comfortable pursuing this case, Andrea Lucca needed to be an unalloyed demon, not a complex case study with submerged noble instincts. If she wasn't a monster, what did that make my client? Aside from self-interest, I just didn't buy what Jane had said. Surely, people *are* complicated, and good and evil are simple-minded notions. But the Lucca I'd been hearing about was cold and arrogant enough—perhaps even cruel enough—to invade somebody's funeral and play the part of the grieving friend.

"None of this makes any sense to me if Andrea Lucca's

capable of classiness," I protested. "There's lots of contrary evidence, I remind you. I just have to keep trawling until I have a clearer fix on her, one way or the other. By the way, speaking of good guys, how was your lunch with . . . uh . . ."

"Pam," said Jane, clearing some of her flotsam and jetsam from the table. "It was great. We got a sandwich near the clinic. You know, she's in the same spot I am. She's committed to her work, feels vaguely guilty about not spending more time with her kids, and suspects they'll hate her someday for it. But she's going to keep working anyway. You'd like her a lot; she's funny and interesting. She asked all about you, and our 'partnership.' She says I'm a lucky woman to have a husband who isn't threatened by my working so much and providing the health plan."

I sniggered. "Well, gee," I said, "I like her already. I never heard *you* say that" (actually, I had).

Jane ignored me. "You know, the last few years have been so hectic, I haven't really had time for new friends. I'm going to have lunch with her again in a few days."

I went over to turn on the dishwasher. "What did you say she does?"

"She runs an ad agency, one that specializes in nonprofit groups. She's working for our clinic gratis, which is great. You can ask her yourself when I get her over here one weekend." Wow, I thought, Jane must really like this person. Between my irregular work schedule, her studies, and her patients, I could count the number of people we'd had over in the past six months: none.

"I will," I said. "I hope by then I know whether my client is a murderer or a victim. Or for that matter," I added glumly, "where the hell she is."

CHAPTER 14

Iwas disoriented when I felt a tug at my pajama sleeve in
the dark and heard the unmistakable sound of a daughter
sniffling. But nothing wakes me up faster.

The digital clock said 5:45. Jane was still sleeping, exhausted by case-file updating that must have gone on into the
wee hours. "Daddy," Em whispered. "Please come into my
room. It's . . . oh, it's terrible." The hall light was bright
enough for me to see the tears streaming down her face.

I pulled on my robe and followed her to her room. Em
occasionally wakes us in the middle of the night when she
can't sleep, when bad dreams dog her, if she's sick. But on
those occasions she calls out from her room. Fetching me in
tears happens rarely.

"Daddy, look. Percentage brought it to me."

Well, it turned out that our national poster dog had
caught himself a mouse, something that actually impressed
me. The only explanation I could think of was that the mouse
had staggered out of its hole and had a massive heart attack,
then keeled over dead in front of Percentage's nose. But he

had picked it up and then thoughtfully retrieved it for his beloved charge, Emily. Now here, I thought with a touch of bitterness, was a canine who wouldn't bring a ball back to you if your hands were slathered in gravy. But catch a dead rodent, and he would of course warmly present it as a gift to the person in the house least anxious to receive it.

"You shithead," I hissed as Percentage thumped his tail against Em's dresser, expecting a shower of pats, biscuits, and compliments. I gave Em a reassuring hug, then picked the carcass off the rug by its tail with a paper towel and wrapped it in several others.

A few minutes later we were embarking on my last domestic chore for the next three days, although I would have been shocked to know that. My daughter and I convened at the Rodent Graveyard, the patch in the southwest corner of the backyard, covered with heavy stones—to keep out inquisitive dogs and cats—where all of Emily's beloved and deceased pets are buried with appropriate ceremony. That usually means a short tribute, a few seconds of silence, and when we get around to it, some flowers.

I might be off by one or two, but I believe there are three gerbils interred there—Bobby, Randy, and Don. Four hamsters. Plus a dozen or so mice, all named after ice-cream flavors—Raspberry, Vanilla, Chocolate, etc. Four hamsters. And a few other species (all purchased not at a mere pet store, of course, but at the Rochambeau Domestic Animal Center, which not only sold creatures but offered workshops on their history, care, and place in the great food chain): newts, an iguana, snails, various snakes, and countless fish. In our little ceremony, Em remembered every single one of the creatures, recalling their odd little eating habits and cute traits. I mumbled some hypocritical banalities about this undomesticated mouse having had a good and free life and our honoring its memory.

"I love you. I'll remember you the way I remember my favorite mouse, Vanilla," Emily intoned somberly—and then added, for good measure, "I'll always love you, Vanilla."

I thought you were disgusting, Vanilla. I hated you from the first moment I realized how bad you smelled, the way your cage stunk within minutes of my having dragged it to the sink, rinsed it out, and replaced all the litter on the bottom. The squeak your lousy little wheel made as you scurried around in it all night and drove me nuts. The way you bit my thumb when I took you out of the cage. Vanilla, I fantasized about letting that enormous stray tomcat who hung around the neighborhood for a couple of weeks, until the Rochambeau Animal Shelter nailed him, pry the top off your cage. I hated you too, Celery, you evil-tempered iguana, and the way you hissed and snapped your tail around whenever I reached into the cage to give you your damned pureed spinach.

But that was the kind of honesty that had no place in our household. Em would have been scarred for life, her grief mocked and dismissed.

She laid the wrapped corpse into the freshly dug hole, a look of mild revulsion mingling with sadness. This mouse, after all, was a stranger. We'd shared no tender, smelly moments with the Deceased. I looked back to the house to see Percentage staring intently from a second-floor window. Finally, after ten years, a kill.

The Mizpah Holiday Inn clerk was a cherubic young man in a spit-spot maroon blazer, white shirt, and slacks. He actually chortled aloud when I handed him my card with two crisp twenty-dollar bills tucked beneath it and asked if he would mind running Andrea Lucca's name through his reservations computer. I was interested in the address she'd given. And in any phone calls she'd made or visitors he remembered.

"You mean, like, a bribe? That's just like in the movies." He slid the cash back. "I can't take that. We don't give out information like that. I'd be happy to call the manager, but he'll tell you the same thing, and he might call the cops to boot. I don't think he gets to the movies much."

He flashed me a wide, white-toothed smile. "Just like Raymond Chandler, huh? Aren't you supposed to say 'Maybe *this'll* jog your memory, pal.' Or something like that?"

Give me a fucking break, I thought. Six years ago I was making $150,000 on the commodities floor in New York, and now I'm driving my rattletrap wagon all over the Northeast looking for people who don't want me to find them.

I left him smiling and chuckling, while I glanced around sheepishly to see if anybody had overheard. Okay, maybe the times called for greater subtlety. These days forty bucks probably wasn't worth risking your job for. But I wasn't experienced at bribing people, and I didn't have a Pinkerton budget behind me. I wasn't even sure I had a client.

From the phone booth in the lobby, I dialed the café where Lucca had charged some meals, according to Willie.

"Morning. Cielo's," said a friendly female voice.

"Morning. I'm in trouble. I'm supposed to meet a friend at your place—I'm from out of town—and I can't remember if the reservation was for dinner or lunch. And I've lost her phone number too." The woman laughed sympathetically. Most people really were instinctively nice, something I must keep reminding myself of in my line of work. Trusting, too, I thought with a stab of guilt. "She would have made it in her name. Andrea Lucca."

"Oh, Miss Lucca. I know the name. Let's see. . . ." I

heard some pages ruffle. "No, there's no reservation for Miss Lucca today. Are you meeting her brother too?"

"Well, to tell you the truth, I'm not sure. I think so."

Brother?

"That's who she usually has lunch with when she visits. Frankie."

"Frankie Lucca?"

"Right. Would it be helpful if you called him? I don't have his number, but he lives over on Shepherd, I think. I'm sure he's in the book."

There he was. *Frank Lucca, 78 Shepherd St.* Sometimes it's so hard; sometimes it's a stroll in the park.

Before heading to Shepherd Street, I decided to put a quick call in to Emily to see if she'd recovered from her early-morning tragedy. My son answered.

"Hey, Ben."

"Yo."

"What's up?"

"Nothing. You want Mom?"

"No, actually, Em, if she's around." The phone clunked down. Fine, Ben, and how are you doing today, I mumbled to myself. It would probably be four or five years before I should expect anything approaching a real conversation with my son. I could make it if he could.

"Hi, Daddy." Em was as chirpy as Ben was monosyllabic and remote. "I just won Wordtris. I beat Liz." Wordtris was one of the small number of home-entertainment games I liked: no bombs or bodies, just letters.

"I just called to see how you're doing."

"Oh, fine." I should have known. Early morning was like a forties movie in black and white to a ten-year-old, ancient history. "Dad? Guess what? I'm going into New York this afternoon. Mom's friend has an extra ticket to the Little Orchestra"—that was the kid's wing of the New York Philharmonic, I recognized—"and her son can't go and she has a daughter who's ten and she invited me. I'm gonna get dressed up, I guess." A shocker: Emily got dressed up only at gunpoint. "Mom says I should because it's Lincoln Center," she explained. Good for Mom.

"Who's Mom's friend?"

"I don't know her, but Mom says she's really nice. Her daughter's name is Annie. I gotta go. 'Bye."

Well, Em had certainly recovered from the trauma of the morning. Casting the desk clerk a withering glance in a final, futile effort to restore my tattered dignity, I headed out to find 78 Shepherd Street.

"See ya, pal," the clerk said in his best Bogart, which wasn't that bad, cocking his thumb and forefinger like a pistol and mouthing "bang."

Mizpah is one of those grimy, half-abandoned old eastern Pennsylvania coal towns. The main street was at least a century old, lined with two- and three-story brick buildings. It ran about four blocks, with a fourth of the storefronts standing empty—a sure sign that a big mall was now within easy driving distance. The tiny old movie theater was shuttered, a closed-up department store in the middle of the block still advertised a sale that had ended years before, and the few surviving stores looked bedraggled. The only really well-maintained building was a towering, white-spired Methodist church at the edge of the retail strip.

The houses were small and stood close to the street. Many were covered in aluminum siding or fake-looking formstone —a rarity in privileged Rochambeau.

I rarely felt privileged these days, since there were almost never more than two mortgage payments in my bank account. With a wife studying to be a psychologist, I might possibly end up with three members of my family in college at the same time. But driving through this ugly little town, I realized just how pleasing an oasis Rochambeau was.

Number 78 Shepherd Street was a tiny white wood-frame cottage with a shingled roof and freshly painted shutters. A plywood wheelchair ramp ran from the front door to the driveway. Two ersatz brass lanterns hung on either side of the door. Something about the house suggested a retired school-teacher. A small white American-made sedan sat, spotless, in the driveway. It had either just been washed or wasn't used much.

I could see the mailbox and the letters "F. Lucca" from the car. Nobody had mentioned any brother. Not old man DiGregorio in Providence, not her ailing uncle, not the architect she worked for, not Marianne or the other women with whom Andrea had once been close. He hadn't shown up in the credit-card check Willie had run on her, either.

I thought of the scarfed figure I'd seen dart in and out of the funeral home the night before. Talk about elusive and mysterious. Here was a person who had made close friends who knew nothing about her, and who had bits of a family tucked away in odd places all over the eastern seaboard. Andrea Lucca had at least three incarnations I knew of. She was the loyal friend, always ready to listen. She was the dread Family Stalker, raiding one family after another. She was the dutiful niece, faithfully tending to her sick elderly relatives. Was I about to uncover another? I hoped whoever was in the house would help explain her a bit. That might in turn tell me why my fugitive client would be buying furniture here at a discount warehouse ninety miles from her home, when scores of them lined every highway out of Rochambeau.

Two distinct, loud chimes sounded in response to my finger on the bell. A voice crackled over the intercom. "I'll be there in just a second. Please wait." The intercom wasn't there to guard against intruders, I realized, but to explain to visitors that the person inside might take a while to get to the door. That squared with the ramp.

A few minutes later, the bolt slid and the door swung open. The man in the chair looked about my age, judging from the way his short hair was graying on the sides. He was wearing a white shirt, with a dark sweatshirt draped over his shoulders. His right leg ended at the knee, his khakis neatly folded at the bottom. His left arm hung limply at his side, and the side of his face bore a callused red scar running from his forehead to his chin. Even with the scar, it was a handsome, interesting face.

"Frankie Lucca?"

He nodded, peering up at me over reading bifocals.

Although I am not a believer in sizing people up at a glance, I believe most people will level with you if you are straight. I am lousy at fake cover stories. I can lie if I have to, but it doesn't come easily to me, and in most cases, the truth is the most daring and innovative gambit you can take. I hate most of all lying about who I am, maybe because it has taken me so long to start figuring it out myself.

So I held out my ID. "My name is Kit Deleeuw. I'm a private investigator. I work for a friend of your sister's. Maybe a former friend would be more honest. I've even visited your aunt and uncle in Providence—did you live there too?" Sometimes if you presumed cooperation, you got it.

Frank Lucca shook his head. "No. Our household . . . well, it split up. Andrea went to Providence. They couldn't take more than one of us. I came here, to live with a cousin and his wife. This was their house. They've both passed on. Is my sister in trouble, Mr. Deleeuw?"

"I don't know," I answered. "*I* think she might be. The police were worried that she might be dead. Now they think she might be a witness in—"

"In a murder investigation," Frank finished. "She told me."

"May I come in?" I asked when I got my breath back.

He nodded, backed up the wheelchair, and whirled it around, beckoning me with his good hand to follow him into the kitchen. It wasn't a modern kitchen, but it was well maintained, bright and neat. I saw two boxes of sugary cereals out on the counter and a pile of tape cassettes, universal signatures of the adolescent, but the house was quiet.

"I want to be polite, Mr. Deleeuw," he said, when we had both settled around the table, awkwardly fiddling with bottles of spring water. "But I'm not having much luck in thinking of reasons why I should cooperate with you. You could be out to harm my sister, maybe even blame her for something she didn't do."

I glanced at his immobile arm.

"Vietnam?"

"Nope," he said without further explanation. "Tell me again why you're looking for Andrea."

"Okay. Mr. Lucca, do you have a family?"

"I've had and lost a couple of families. I have a child, but she lives with her mother in Philly now and spends alternate weekends here, and some vacations. My daughter is thirteen. The handicapped—or do we say physically challenged now?— can lead normal lives, sometimes, but the people around them can't always."

I asked about his daughter, told him about my son. They

were both at the same weird age. "Has he stopped sitting with you in movie theaters yet?" Lucca asked. I nodded. "You let him date?"

"Not yet," I said. "He's got plenty of time for that. I let him go to the movies with a bunch of kids if he wants."

We both liked talking about our kids a lot more than we would like talking about his sister.

We swigged water for a couple of minutes in silence. Tolerating silence is one of the most valuable and underutilized skills of anybody who depends on information for a living. In our culture people aren't used to quiet. They tend to fill it, sometimes even with the words you need to hear.

Frankie and I were already at ease with one another, something that doesn't happen very frequently with men and would, in a way, make the process harder on both of us. This man had a lot of dignity and grace, given what he had evidently been through.

I set my bottle down with a clink. "Okay, I'll be honest with you. My client's husband was murdered. The police think my client killed him because he was having an affair with your sister. In checking around, I've found two other nice middle-class families that split up when your sister became involved with them. There could be others."

Frankie didn't respond. He looked to me as if he were bracing himself. He certainly didn't need any more trouble in his life.

"I don't think my client is a murderer. She's a loving parent, an attorney. You never know, but if this person wanted to kill her husband, I think she could find a more intelligent way than to walk into the bathroom while he was in the tub, smash his head in, and call nine-one-one. I'm not saying your sister is a killer, either. But I do think Andrea has hurt a lot of people. She's missing, and the police thought at first that my client had a terrific motive for getting rid of her. That's why they were surprised and I was relieved to see Andrea—at least, I think it was Andrea—at a service last night in Rochambeau, for another murder victim."

I stopped and took a breath. It was getting pretty convoluted. Frankie's face didn't reveal what he might be thinking. I went on. "The second victim ran an aerobics class that my client and your sister both attended. So, by the way, did two of the families your sister got tangled up with.

"I don't know who did what to whom, to be honest. Rochambeau isn't a town where you get exposed to a lot of murderers. I think your sister might have some answers for me, perhaps answers that will help my client, perhaps not. I don't know if Andrea is on the run, or if there is something else going on. I don't understand why she's vanished if she's done nothing wrong. But my client has vanished too. And both of them have been here in Mizpah, I am amazed to find out. More than amazed. I'm in shock. I got onto you through the restaurant you and Andrea go to."

"How did you find out about that?" he asked, surprised.

"Secrets of the trade. I came here to ask you to tell me about Andrea and if you're in touch with her, to urge her to call me. There's been a lot of damage in our town, Frankie. You're a family man, you obviously love your daughter, you know the kind of pain that can come when families break up. I mean, it's a case and I'm getting paid for it; I'm not a social worker. But it gets to me, seeing the damage. You must know something about that kind of damage. I need you to help me. I don't have any slicker pitch than that."

By my standards, and those of my craft, it was a lengthy speech. And I meant every word of it.

A cat startled me by slithering alongside my leg and hopping up into Frankie Lucca's lap. I heard a train rumble somewhere in the distance. But otherwise, the only sound was the hum from the refrigerator.

Frankie wheeled himself over to the refrigerator for two more bottles of water, pausing by a kitchen cabinet to pull out a box of cookies. When he returned to the table, he seemed to have decided.

"Deleeuw, I'll tell you everything but where Andrea is. Let's say I don't know. Coming forward is her decision, not mine. I'm not going to make it for her, and I don't want you pressing me about that."

"Agreed. Although you have to understand I'm going to keep looking for her. I will find her, or the cops will, you know. Sooner or later she's going to trip up."

Lucca let the warning pass. "God, I'm tired," he said. "Sometimes I'm bushed just by being me. I've only begun telling this story for the first time in the past year or two, and then only to people I know goddamn well—my shrink and a guy in my support group. I'm not good at telling it; every time I do, I'm all fucked up for days. I'm actually going to have my first date in a long time tonight, and I'd rather not be any more fucked up than I already am. So I'll make it quick. I'm only telling it because it helps explain Andrea. And she needs a lot of explaining."

I nodded and took out a notebook, to which he paid no attention. "You probably noticed that I didn't say, 'My God, Andrea could never be involved in what you're describing,' because I know too well that she could. You're not the first person to come to me with a tale like this. She's told me some of them herself. She wants to be part of a normal family real bad, sometimes too much. I know it does a lot of harm, but she has her reasons and she's not a monster. She's been as loving and caring to me as anybody could be. I could sit here all day and tell you the things Andrea's done for me—visited, called, sent packages and books, paid for operations, helped me get into therapy. So much more than she had to."

He shook his head regretfully, resurrecting memories he would obviously have dearly preferred to forget.

"There were three of us. I'm thirty-eight, Andrea's thirty-five, Dana would have been thirty. At the time, Dana was five, Andrea was ten, and I was thirteen." He held up a hand. "I'm only able to go through this once, Deleeuw, and I know you have a lot of questions, but my advice to you is to hold off. Let's see if I can do this." He drained his mineral water and fetched another from the fridge.

Things had changed with some men, at least. Twenty years ago he would have been pulling at a bottle of Scotch, and we wouldn't have traded behavioral anecdotes about our beloved teenagers. He sat back. He was ready.

"We grew up in Hollandale, New Jersey, in the central part of the state, about an hour or so from you, Mr. Deleeuw . . . okay, Kit.

"Our father died a year after Dana was born. He just keeled over in his truck cab and lay there at a truck stop all night till some state trooper came across him. I remember him a bit, and I guess I'm haunted by the way he died, but the girls didn't remember him at all. He was a cold, tough SOB, James Lucca, but he was Santa Claus compared to what came after him.

"My mom couldn't raise three kids on a waitress's pay. Things got really bad. The electricity was always getting turned off, or the phone. We had cereal for dinner lots of nights. We got clothes from the thrift shop. Andrea and I joke sometimes that we were homeless in a home. We slept three to a room for almost a year, until this guy proposed to Mom.

"He had been a fireman, but retired on disability. He claimed to have been injured in a fire, but his real sickness was booze. I think Mom knew he was bad news, but we were hungry much of the time, and being a middle-aged mother of three, she didn't exactly have a line outside her door. Pete was a psycho drunk. Not one of those good people who get mean when they drink, but one of those people who drink all the time, 'cause otherwise they couldn't live with themselves. I saw him slug her a couple of times. He was a sadistic man."

I'd put my notebook away.

He raised his good arm and rubbed his right temple with his thumb. "I got a headache already," he said, then squared his shoulders and resumed.

"Anyway, after they were married, Pete went at Andrea and Dana in the most disgusting, brutal ways. My sisters were too scared to tell Mom, and then, when she got breast cancer a couple of years after she remarried, well, it was clear she was in no shape to help. She probably didn't really even want to know.

"So Pete was all we had. Our source of food, shelter, medicine, everything. Not to mention that the sight of him almost paralyzed us with fear. There was no doubt in any of our minds that if we seriously crossed him, if we answered the questions about the bruises that some of our teachers and friends asked us about, he would kill us. Or worse. There are worse things." He scowled.

"Andrea brought a kitten home one day. She'd found it on the way home from school, half-starved and looking chewed up a bit, maybe by a dog. She gave it milk in a dropper, snuck it food, nursed it back to life. You know girls and pets. Under the circumstances, that kitten meant more to Andrea than the rest of the world combined. She hid it from Pete for maybe a week, until it got loose one afternoon and tore up his favorite sweater. He came home and found it shredded and went berserk.

"He dragged Andrea and the kitten into the bathroom, filled the sink with water, slapped her face, made her beg him to save the kitten, promise she'd never do anything without his permission again. Dana and I crowded in, too. Remember"—his voice cracked here—"I was the big brother, I was the only protection they could possibly have.

"I could see Pete was enjoying himself, loving the way we were all hypnotized with horror, crying, pleading for the cat. He held the kitten there, lowering it into the water while we all screamed and shouted at him to stop. As beat up as it was, the little thing—it was black with white spots—yowled and struggled.

"Then he tried to make Andrea help him. He told her to come and take the kitten, and when she did, he grabbed her hands and pressed them down on the cat. She begged and cried and wanted to close her eyes, but he said he'd break the kitten's neck if she didn't look. Then he took her hands and with them pushed the kitten under the water again. It took him a long time to kill it. Afterward he chased me out of the room, and he . . . well, he just beat them and beat them. It was . . . God, I felt so guilty that I couldn't stop him. I'll never stop feeling guilty. He did other things to us—some of them even worse—but I don't feel right talking about them."

That was okay. I'd heard enough.

Frank Lucca took a cookie, broke it into four pieces, and ate each one, chewing and swallowing carefully. Would it make him feel better, learning to tell his story to others? Or did it just invite the pain again? He was doing this for his sister, for the little girl he couldn't help then but just might be able to help now by baring the secrets from their ghastly past.

In my work I've seen people do incredible things to each other, even in a town like Rochambeau. Those pretty houses can be gilded prisons for the kids of alcoholics or wives trapped with abusive husbands. Yet I couldn't really picture this happening there, at least not these days. Teachers are too attentive, neighbors too alert, the kids themselves too savvy. There are counselors in the high school, abuse hot-line numbers posted all over town, Oprah on TV. The Lucca kids were stuck in a different world. They'd had nowhere to go, no one to turn to.

Frankie's face was ashen. This was taking a toll, a journey down a path he really didn't want to travel.

"Things really fell apart about a year after that, when I was going on fifteen. Mom was in the hospital. The cancer had come back, she was on radiation, she was wasted. One afternoon after school, when she'd gone back into the hospital, Pete came home so drunk he could hardly talk. Andrea knew the look and tried to run out of the house, but he dragged her into the bedroom. I heard some screams . . . and then I snapped. I was big enough by then. I went into the bedroom, pulled Andrea out, and kicked the shit out of him. Dana ran and called the cops. So did the neighbors. Finally, Pete went to jail. My mom couldn't take care of us, of course; she never did leave that hospital. Andrea didn't speak for two, three months after that day." He was clearly coming to the end of his tolerance for recalling this, and frankly, I couldn't take much more myself. He gathered himself for what remained.

"Dana was such a mess, they put her in a home for emotionally disturbed kids. Andrea wound up with our relations in Providence, and then went to art college in New York. I know she went back to school again even after that. Seemed like she was in school forever. I came here." He took a deep, quavering breath. "I didn't figure to tell that story today. Ask away, but do it fast, man."

I took out my notebook, saying a quick prayer that my kids would never go through anything like this. I had heard enough such stories from Jane to know that they were not nearly as rare as most people in Rochambeau liked to think. But that didn't make them comprehensible.

"Dana?"

"Killed herself nine years ago. Three bottles of sleeping pills, two bottles of vodka. It was her fourth attempt. Nobody who knew her was surprised. She never really wanted to live. Not for a single day, not after the years with Pete."

"Your leg and arm?"

"I became a drunk. Hit an embankment on the Pennsylvania Turnpike at ninety miles per one morning at two A.M., then flipped over into a ditch. Like my dad, I sat in the car half the night. My wife had tried to stick it out, but that, plus all my other baggage, was too much. So she left and took the kid."

"So Andrea—"

"She visits me as often as she can. It's a miracle that she can hold a job or even get dressed. We don't talk about those days. Mostly, she listens. You see, all Andrea could do after that time was listen." He shook his head. "She can pick up somebody's pain like the most sophisticated radar in the world and tune right into it. It's weird. I mean, she'll hear anything you want to say, but she never gives even a little piece of herself to anybody else. Do you know what I mean?"

"I know that's what everybody says about her, Frankie. That she wants her friends to spill everything, but she doesn't reveal a thing."

"That's her," he said, nodding soberly. "That's her."

"Frankie, whatever went on between Pete and Andrea—

in the bedroom? I'm not trying to pry, but is that something I need to know about? I've got a client looking at a possible murder rap."

Frankie looked drained but far from rattled. I was not on the top-ten list of frightening things he'd had to deal with in his life. He didn't respond.

Jane's voice seemed to float through the neat kitchen. *You don't know anything about Andrea Lucca. You need to know more.*

I changed my tack. "Has Andrea told you why she's running?"

He cleared his throat. "She's told me that she's afraid for her life in that town. She kept forming friendships with people that got too close, and she got involved with some men whose wives found out. She said that she got some threatening calls"—I winced; some of those had to be from Marianne. "Some people there wanted to hurt her. When this guy Gil got whacked, then the instructor got murdered, she got frightened. She realized that somebody in town had gone beyond threats."

It didn't wash. "But she took off before Gil Dow was attacked and before Roberta Bingham was murdered," I objected. "She disappeared four or five days before that, the police say. Why?"

"I didn't know. Maybe one of these men or women got to her. I really don't know. Look, I'm not justifying what she did or didn't do, Kit. I'm just saying that a threatening call to Andrea isn't the same as a threatening call to other folks. She knows what it's like to be hurt, and she doesn't believe anybody will protect her. There are cops, neighbors, teachers, friends, and social workers out there, but some guy can tear you apart for months, years, and nobody comes. That's what she learned the hard way, and that's why she runs."

His story shook me. There is so much talk of abuse—substance, physical, sexual, emotional—that I confess to having become somewhat numbed to it—until now.

"I'm sorry, Frankie. Jesus, that's rough. I thank God my kids never had to go through something like that. Your telling me this, well, I promise you I'll make it worth your pain. I appreciate it."

"There's nothing you can say, or need to say," he answered. "I have part-time work; I'm a programmer at the GM plant. I see my daughter and my sister. I have a lot to learn about having normal relationships, I guess, but I have a life."

"Frankie, I'm not asking you to be a shrink, but do you think it's possible that Andrea hates families? Was striking back in some way?"

"Anything's possible," he said dully, shrugging. "All our lives we wanted a normal family, Andrea and I; I'm not surprised she would hang around other people's families. Could've made her sad, I guess, or maybe angry."

"Don't misunderstand the question. But you're about the only person in the world I can ask: is she angry enough to hurt people? Is she angry enough . . ."

"To kill them?" he asked, exhausted now. "Isn't that what you're asking? Christ, man, I've just taken my guts out and put them on the table. You can at least be honest."

"Okay. Could she kill somebody?" If she couldn't, that left one person I knew of in this equation who must have—my client.

He leaned back and looked up at the ceiling, massaging the back of his neck with his hand.

"Look, Kit. With what Andrea has been through, I think she might be capable of violence, sure. Wouldn't you be? If she thought somebody was going to hurt her the way she'd been hurt, sure. But she and I love each other very much. We've walked through the fire with one another, and that's a kind of closeness that rarely comes to siblings, or anybody else. It's the kind of relationship where we always know what the other is going to say. The question really isn't do I think she could kill somebody, but do I think she *did* kill somebody? And the answer there is no. Absolutely not. Andrea has been here, called, written. We've talked. She may have a problem with these friendships and, like you're saying, with these nice suburban families. I don't know, really. But if she'd killed somebody, she would have told me. In fact, she wouldn't have had to; I would've known. But the truth is, I guess to really know what she's capable of, you'd have to know what happened in that room twenty-odd years ago."

"And she's never said?"

He shook his head, then laughed a bitter laugh. "But you can find out. You can ask our stepfather."

"What?"

"Pete's still alive. He still lives down there. He spent eight months in jail for what he did to us, then was on probation for a few years. I lost track of him for a while. When I looked him up, I was thinking that if he was alive, I wanted to find him and kill him. I could've done that, killed him. Gone to jail happily for it. But he's a doddering, sick old man, wasted away by all that booze and hate. He's in his seventies, living in some nursing home. I get letters from him every now and then begging for money. You want to know what happened to Andrea in that room, ask him!"

A few minutes later he handed me a much-folded envelope postmarked six months earlier. Frankie's name and address were on the front, scribbled in barely legible letters with a red felt marker. The return address said *Pete Scronziak, Maple Shade Nursing Home, Hollandale, N.J.* I don't know which made me shiver worse: Frankie's story or the prospect of meeting the creature he had described.

I took the envelope and said good-bye. As much as I liked Lucca, I couldn't wait to get out of the house. I felt for Jane. She heard these kinds of stories all day long. Lord, the things people could do to one another.

The Modern Furniture Warehouse was three miles from Frankie Lucca's little white house. Half a city block long, it was stuffed with sofas, lamps, rugs, and low-budget bedroom suites and dinettes. Nothing looked particularly attractive or well made, but I'm no furniture expert, and it seemed in better shape than the battered stuff my family sat on at home. It was surprising that Marianne—who, judging from her clothes and home, had impeccable and expensive taste— would come here. This stuff was for newlyweds looking to buy on layaway.

The second salesman I talked to, a genial guy in a cheap brown suit, remembered her right away, though. "Yeah. Dow. I remember it because I follow my stocks on Dow. You looking for some furniture?"

I explained that I was looking for her. The guy didn't even blink, as if it were quite routine for people to come in looking for his customers. He went back into the office, then returned with an invoice.

"She bought a sofa, a chair, two tables, and a lamp," he said, showing me the form. She had signed the order and given her correct address. But he continued, the furniture wasn't delivered there.

"She had a truck come over and pick it up yesterday afternoon. One of those rental trucks—I didn't see which kind, 'cause I wasn't here," the salesman reported, looking eagerly over my shoulder at a live sale. No, he said, reluctantly going back to ask and then returning, nobody in the warehouse had noticed anything about the truck. No, I couldn't go back and ask the loading-dock guys myself. No, they had no idea where the shipment was going.

I made him repeat it three times, just to make sure I wasn't losing my mind or stumbled stupidly into some other person's life by mistake. Why on earth would Marianne be purchasing furniture? And why out here, when you couldn't throw a rock outside the Rochambeau town limits without hitting a discount furniture place? And where had she taken it? It was inconceivable that there wasn't a connection between her shopping in Mizpah and Andrea's brother living here. The case had careened off on a crazy course of its own, with me hanging on for dear life.

Cases were supposed to go the opposite way. You were supposed to understand more, not less, about them each day. Behavior was supposed to be clearer, not ever more inexplicable.

Did I have the skills and experience to understand developments like this? To keep on top of it, let alone explain it? I drove out of town in a daze.

I doubted I'd seen the last of Mizpah, but I'm not sure I was ever happier to see the American Way Mall when I finally pulled into the lot around four P.M. The mall was full of kids celebrating the weekend with doughnuts and new sneakers. Luis was interviewing sullen, gum-chewing prospective employees, as usual; I waved through the glass at him. Evelyn had left me a list of things to do, most of which I wouldn't.

What I did do was make a phone call and demonstrate what I called "telephone gall." Which, loosely translated, means having the guts to do things on the phone that you don't have in person.

" 'lo. Modern Furniture."

"Hello, this is Charlie Dow. Look, I'm pretty ticked off. My wife Marianne bought fifteen hundred bucks' worth of furniture from you Thursday. The condition was that she could have it picked up yesterday afternoon. Well, the truck came to get it and it wasn't ready. Now it's a day later, the big party is coming up, and we still haven't gotten it."

The voice became immediately apologetic and switched me through to customer service. "Sorry, sir, do you have the invoice number?"

I read her the one I had memorized from the invoice. Only one number was off. The voice on the phone corrected me and put me on hold.

"Excuse me, sir, but our records show that order was picked up yesterday at five-thirty P.M."

"What?" I sputtered with a theatricality my daughter would have admired. "By whom?"

"Well, according to the dock form—furniture has to be signed for, you know—it was picked up by Haul-It, a company in Bordentown, near Fort Dix. Haven't you received it?"

I grumped about having to call my wife, then hung up. Haul-It was in the phone book.

"Marianne Dow?" repeated the thickly accented Hispanic voice. "Yeah, we made the pickup. Stuff is here. Hold for storage until instructions. You ready for it?"

Not yet, I said. Just wanted to make sure it had arrived safely.

Back to the Volvo. On the way out, Luis gestured with a coffee cup, but I pantomimed back, throwing my arms into the air to show that I was too busy. I threaded my way out through what seemed like acres of baseball caps with bears, bulldogs, and cheetahs on them.

No one was at home when I walked wearily through my

back door, but an urgent message from Chief Leeming was waiting for me. I kicked myself for not calling to check for messages before tracking down Marianne's furniture. The chief had called in two hours earlier.

"Deleeuw. This is an above-and-beyond call. You'll owe me. I think you will want to be at your client's house at five P.M."

CHAPTER 15

Marianne Dow's house was about fifteen minutes from mine on a normal day with average traffic. I made it in ten. The Volvo doesn't exactly have rapid-fire acceleration, but once it gets up a head of steam, it is formidable.

A dark blue state-police van was parked in the Dows' driveway, along with the Rochambeau PD crime-scene cruiser. Behind them were two black Chryslers, which looked federal: the men in suits with whom Chief Leeming was talking were FBI agents, beyond doubt. Four or five other officers in navy windbreakers with oversize yellow lettering marched conspicuously up and down the sidewalk and through the manicured backyard. A cluster of photographers and reporters and a TV cameraman stood watching across the street; at the end of the block, half a dozen teenagers had parked their bikes and skateboards and openly gaped.

Too bad I hadn't chosen the police fashion business over private investigating. Everywhere law-enforcement personnel went these days, they were graphically and fashionably attired in windbreakers with FBI or Customs logos, jumpsuits with DEA insignia, caps with impressive initials announcing affiliation with this or that tactical squad or strike force. Was there a cop shop somewhere in Manhattan, I wondered, where your unit could pick up the perfect jacket or shirt? I loved the two guys waddling around Marianne's driveway in heavy pullovers with foot-high RPD: CRIME SCENE letters stenciled on them, ignoring the fact that it was seventy degrees outside.

I parked the Volvo across Hanover Street and walked toward the chief. He broke off his conversation and came over to meet me.

"Hey. You think these guys might be members of a crime-scene unit, or something like that?"

He ignored the crack and glanced around to make sure we were out of earshot. I saw detectives carrying shovels into the backyard. They were digging around some bushes and beneath several slender young maple trees, the kind of activity that would have made Benchley nuts.

"Thanks for the tip," I said quietly. "What's up?"

"Your client returned last night. She's in our custody, inside the house. She's been read her rights and is under state charges of homicide in the second degree and federal charges of interstate flight to avoid prosecution. Seems she went out of town during her little spree."

I swallowed the impulse to say something smug like "You mean to Pennsylvania?" and merely nodded. "You mean she surrendered?"

"No. She snuck in through the back gate. She'd parked her car around the corner. We and the FBI"—I thought he slid over that part a bit too quickly—"had the house under pretty close watch. She didn't make any effort to hide her presence once she got in there. She turned the lights on, put on a pot of coffee. The guys on the scene called me, and we decided to move in. That's really all I can say right now."

"So you figure she's looking for the murder weapon? Or are *you*?" Not hard to figure out, with all the excavating going on in the backyard. Unless they were looking for another body. Like Andrea Lucca's . . .

Leeming was purposely vague. "Deleeuw, you know we don't have a murder weapon. We would like to find one. This is our third time around this goddamn yard. I know every pebble in it. I just thought I ought to call and tell you that your client, whose whereabouts were unknown to you, showed up. I worry about you, Deleeuw. If your agency falls apart, I'll have a vagrant on my hands. I gotta go."

"Wait. Why'd you let Marianne sit in the house all night and today? Why didn't you move in right away?"

"I can't tell you that, Deleeuw. Don't you know jackshit?"

I probably did know. They had bugged and wired the house like the CIA, hoping for an admission of guilt, perhaps something that would lead them to the murder weapon or other evidence, before moving in. Maybe they got what they wanted, I thought, listening to the digging and scraping going on in the yard.

"Can I see her?"

"Nope."

"Talk to her for just a second?"

"Nope. She's called her lawyer. The prosecutor will try to get bail denied, but I hear her lawyer has brought in some hotshots from Newark. If they can convince a judge she won't bolt again, you might get to talk to her then. Of course, you can always visit her in the county jail."

"Right. While you tape our visits."

"Tape *your* visits? On my fucking budget? I could buy half a police car for what it would cost to tape and transcribe you. And it would be a much better use of the money, too." Then he turned serious. "Deleeuw, don't break my balls, okay? *I* called *you*, remember? This is a federal rap. I can't let you have private chats with a murder suspect before she's even formally charged. Wave to your client, then get the fuck out of here. She's going to be moved out now, the FBI guys just went in to get her. She'll be arraigned in Newark, first on the state murder charges, then the federal interstate flight rap. Her kids are still staying with a friend in New York City. Their grandparents are flying in to take care of them."

"Have you had any luck in tracking down Andrea Lucca?" I asked, pushing it. "With all these cops and all these jackets, surely one little old person in a Toyota couldn't have slipped out of town."

"Fuck you." Then, cagily, "Do *you* have anything on her?"

I told him I'd tracked down a brother in Mizpah, Pennsylvania. He didn't even jot down the name.

"We knew about the brother. It was in the state adoption records. It's illegal to give that out. But if you know their story, it's understandable this woman would take off when she got Marianne Dow's threats—"

"Isn't 'threats' a little strong? Didn't she just warn her to lay off her husband?"

"We'll see what a jury says, Deleeuw. Does the brother know where she is?"

"No. He told some pretty horrible stories about the family's early life, but he claims he doesn't know where she is. Are you going to talk to him?"

He shrugged. "The feds probably will. But I'll be honest with you, Deleeuw. My major concern with Lucca was whether she was alive or dead. Now we both know she's alive, and after her appearance at the funeral home last night, so does half the town. I'd still like her to prove that your client had a motive to murder her husband. We'll want Lucca's testimony, but I wouldn't say it's immediately crucial. We'll find her, anyway. Dollars to doughnuts that she was hiding from your client, in fear of her life, and now that we've got Dow, Lucca won't have much to be afraid of. Funny woman, your client . . ."

"How's that?"

"Well, she won't talk to us. She seems disoriented, although that might be just an act, a warm-up for an insanity plea. But she sure looks spooked. Her running away doesn't make any sense, especially her being a lawyer and all. She's gotta know that no matter what, running away hurts. She won't say a word about why she ran, or why she came back. I mean, Jesus, she had to know we'd be watching the house. Lawyers can be dumb as anybody else—worse most of the time—but that lady didn't seem dumb."

He was fishing, hoping I would explain her. His case looked airtight: the opportunity, a documented motive, guilty flight. But Leeming was too smart not to be troubled by out-of-character behavior. On Monday this was a buttoned-up attorney and suburban homemaker doting on her two kids, fighting to keep her family whole. I didn't know what she was any longer, aside from my client.

The door opened, and two agents came out. Marianne, in a cardigan and dark slacks, walked between them, her hands cuffed in front of her.

She looked at me, started to raise one hand, but couldn't. She had aged a decade in a week. Her bone-white face was haggard, her eyes sunken, her hair scraggly and unkempt. She didn't try to shield her face or eyes from the news cameras

that had materialized around her . . . either out of resigna-
tion or dignity, I couldn't tell. But I knew she would care,
very much, how she appeared to her children. Something had
given her an incredible jolt.

The cameras flashed and Marianne blinked as a woman
with a microphone started shouting at her. The agents
nudged her toward the car. One of them reached forward to
open the door and gently guided her into the seat, as the
photographers darted back and forth for better angles and the
reporters circled.

"Mrs. Dow," they yelled, "do you have any comment?
Are you a murderer? How do you feel about the police accus-
ing you of your husband's murder? Where are your children?
Are they safe?"

I realized, of course, that the reporters simply wanted to
provoke Marianne into making some statement. It was no
worse than the slimy tricks I employed to get people to talk to
me, but at least I didn't quote the First Amendment so much.
No matter how provocative the shouts, Marianne seemed not
even to hear them.

I had a few questions I wanted to yell myself: *Why did you
run away? Why did you come back? Why didn't you at least call
me? What were you doing in Mizpah, Pennsylvania? You must
have been following Lucca or known she was there, right? But
what earthly reason could you have had for buying fifteen hundred dollars' worth of cheap furniture in Pennsylvania, then
storing it in central New Jersey? And what were you doing
sneaking back into your house without talking to your investigator or your attorney?*

There was one clear explanation for all that behavior, one
that squared perfectly with the haunted way she looked: she
might have had a complete breakdown.

The only word that came to mind when I stared at Marianne's face through the police-car window was confusion. She didn't look angry, mortified, or frightened. She looked bewildered, as if she could not grasp what was happening to her. That made two of us. The car made a U-turn and sped off.

I heard a dog bark. Her retriever? But it was the state police's K-9 unit, two shepherds whining and sniffing around the yard. Through the hedges I could see one of them running in circles, stopping to paw at one of the young trees.

Several of the men in windbreakers scrambled toward the dogs. One of the officers snapped a picture as two others leaned down and pulled something out of the ground. I heard one of the handlers curse, shake his head, and urge the dog on. Several uniformed Rochambeau officers cajoled the reporters and TV crew back to the front of the house, sealing off the street.

It might have been my imagination, but the cops looked tired, discouraged. I didn't think they were getting anywhere. Neighbors shook their heads at the scene around Marianne's house. This was evening-news stuff, not what we wanted to see in Rochambeau as we drove along our shaded, wide streets each day.

Discouraged, I drove home. Jane's Volvo pulled into the driveway right behind me. "Hell-o!" I bellowed. "Good timing."

"Hey there," Jane called. Em slid out the passenger side and came bounding toward me, as she still did occasionally despite her advancing years.

"Hey, sweetie," I said, hugging her until she groaned. "How was New York?"

"Oh, she didn't go," said Jane. "I took her cheap-o shopping with me."

I grabbed a shopping bag out of the backseat. I knew I would get my own fashion show, as I did whenever the girls in the household managed to hit the discount outlets. Jane believed it was a sin to buy any garment that didn't have at least one red slash through the price tag.

"What a shame," I said. "That would have been neat, to see the Little Orchestra. What happened?"

Jane frowned. "Well, it was strange. Pam called this morning all excited about this extra ticket. Then a couple of hours later she called back, very upset. She was in tears. I couldn't figure it out. She insisted nothing was really wrong, but that she had to cancel. She hung up before I could even ask her anything."

I parked the packages inside the back door. Ben was lumbering around upstairs, heedless, as always, of domestic activity. Percentage was probably asleep. "What's her last name, this Pam?" I asked casually.

"Brittain. Why?"

"Just curious. Have you got her phone number?" Jane dug her address book out of her purse and handed it to me, watching me curiously.

"What's up, Kit?"

"Nothing, maybe. I just want to have it."

Jane saw I didn't want to talk in front of Emily. They went upstairs to prepare for my fashion show. I went into my study and dialed the number Jane had given me. After four rings, a recorded voice crisply announced, "This is Andrea Lucca. I can't come to the phone right now, but if you leave a name, a message, and a number I'll get back to you as soon as I can."

CHAPTER 16

Jane and I were speechless for probably the first time in our sixteen years of married life. For a few minutes after I told her, we stared at one another in mute incomprehension, imaging the almost's and might-have's. Wordlessly, she clasped my hand.

But I didn't have time to descend into the appropriate level of sympathy for Jane, who had been excited about her new friendship, or shock at what seemed to be the Family Stalker's sudden intrusion into our family—I had to get to work. Jane, I was sure, would be terrified, mortified, and hurt, and in that order.

"Oh, my God," was all she allowed herself. "How could I have been so stupid? I'm supposed to be the shrink." I felt a tremor in her hand. "This is the creepiest feeling I've ever had in my life. Do you think she would have hurt Em? Or us?"

"Sweetie, I just don't know. There's no evidence she's physically harmed anybody, and kidnapping seems out of her league. Maybe she just wanted to send me a signal. Maybe I was getting too close, although I'll be damned if I know how.

She's brilliant at sizing up people's vulnerabilities and befriending them. Better, I guess, than I am at being a detective . . ."

"Or me at psychology."

We hugged, more in immense relief than anything else. We could conceivably have been having a very different kind of conversation. What, I thought, if we'd made this little discovery while Em was in New York—or who knew where?—with Andrea. How could we have endured that level of fear? Andrea was as deft as Marianne had described.

"Until we know more, Em has to stay inside with one of us, or be under the care of an adult at all times," I said.

Jane nodded. "Should we call the police?"

I mulled that one. "I don't think so. We don't have much to tell them. She didn't actually pick Emily up or harm her in any way. I think she meant to frighten us. And she sure did. But lock the windows and be careful about answering the door. I've got to go back out there."

I called Em downstairs and wrapped my arms around her tightly.

She eyed me warily. "What's the matter with you?"

"Nothing," I said. "Can't a guy hug his daughter?"

"Yeah, but you don't have to squeeze her to death."

In the car I shook my head to clear away the terror and shock. Suddenly, I sympathized with Marianne in a completely new way. Now I understood what it felt like to be stalked by an intelligent, malevolent presence who could penetrate the defenses of a shrewd near-psychologist and a private investigator in the middle of a baffling case that should have put both of them on the alert. I felt as stupid as I was lucky, but Marianne didn't have time for that either.

Why would Andrea risk her cover to come at us this way? I must have blundered near some truth she didn't want me to know. She had responded, either seeking psychological revenge or warning me to back off. But she hadn't gone through with it. I started running through all of my conversations in the past week, hoping to recognize whatever it was I had stumbled on that had provoked her.

I must have gotten closer than I knew. In a way, that was even more frustrating.

This smarmy intrusion on our family galvanized me. I meant to see that she regretted it. There had to be a way into this case.

One of the differences between cities and suburbs is that out here, everything about your life is seen, heard, or learned quickly. Even though people are jammed together more closely in the cities, one of the great truths of suburban life is that ultimately, there is no privacy. In Manhattan you can be anonymous if you wish. Here no one can hide.

It was Benchley who had first alerted me to this on one of the long, sweet evenings in his steamy greenhouse, where we sipped cider and pondered Life. The theory seemed nonsensical in a community that had had a one-house-per-quarter-acre zoning law for fifty years, where most houses were shrouded in trees and hedges behind fences and azaleas. But I had learned a thousand times since that Benchley was correct, and it was good for me and my work that he was. The reality he had taught me made me certain there was a way to crack this case.

In the suburbs people's lives are threaded together inextricably and irrevocably at back-to-school nights and in car pools, on dog walks and at tax-rate hearings, during encounters at hobby shops and pediatricians' offices, on the sidelines at soccer games and in the clogged aisles of the local market on Sundays when you and the rest of the town simultaneously realize there's nothing for the kids to make tomorrow's lunches with.

There are no secrets. Coaches and teachers live here, too. Their kids hang around with your kids; their neighbors talk to your neighbors. Anybody can drive by and ascertain your financial status by the paint peeling off the porch. The elderly housekeeper who comes to your neighbor's house after the divorce next comes to yours, shaking her head at all the domestic squabbling those poor kids had to endure, or perhaps at all the beer cans she put in the recycling bin.

Your lawyer plays golf or tennis with others and is, of course, careful to avoid confidential details of the divorce or the will but is slick enough to let the broad outlines slip. Your insurance salesman knows everything about everybody on your block. Even the dog walkers who thoughtfully take in your mail as they take out your Labrador while you're out of town will cluck sympathetically at one minor scandal or another.

Out of this diverse but relentlessly compiled social tapestry a detailed portrait of your life emerges for everyone else to consider, an astonishingly accurate one, in my experience. Somebody had to know something about Marianne Dow or Andrea Lucca that would help me sort out a lethal mess that no longer felt abstract.

So I drove right back to Hanover Street to look for somebody who knew something about my client that I didn't. I was having trouble shaking the awful sight of Marianne being led away in handcuffs. She'd looked shattered; she was losing it.

Keep the faith, I cautioned myself—she's your client. She deserves the benefit of your doubt, your energy and hard work, right up until the jury gives a verdict. And remember Benchley's notion: somebody, probably somebody standing

around watching the police poke through the Dows' backyard and knock over their new maples, knows or saw something that might help.

I dismissed the kids still hanging around the corner. They
were only Ben's age or a little older, at a point in their lives
when hormones rage and the only adult activity they can relate to is someone driving them to the video-game parlor. But
I had noticed two prospects across the street: a nanny playing
on a lawn with two little kids and an elderly woman peering
from the safety of her porch a few doors down.

The nanny, it turned out, was Bahamian, imported for a
two-year look at America for virtually no money. I hoped
looking at America was worth being imprisoned with two
preschoolers who tugged incessantly at her leg and com-
plained continually of boredom. Her employees were in the
city seeing something shattering and seminal at the Public
Theatre.

"Nah," the nanny said, shaking her head forcefully. "I
don't see anyt'ing." I didn't want to press her. She looked no
more than eighteen, but she was surely better informed about
life in these United States than to exchange confidences with
a middle-aged stranger driving a battered old Volvo.

The woman in the house next door was more direct. In
her midthirties, with a young boy peering from behind her
knees, she looked at my ID and began to close the door. "My
husband would kill me if I talked with you. And I don't know
anything anyway. We've only been here six months, and we
mind our own business." *As you should mind yours,* her tone
clearly said.

The elderly woman was still on her porch, taking in my
unsuccessful journey down her block, curious to see whether
I was a door-to-door salesperson, a reporter, or perhaps a
cop. Fortunately, for me, the reporters, like the cops, were

mostly interested in talking with one another across the street. Later they would get their little sound bites, I was sure. *She seemed like such a lovely woman,* the neighbors would say. *They were a good family.*

I had seen this woman walking her little chow around this neighborhood, and I bet she was the neighbor Marianne had mentioned to me; the one she'd called to come over to be with her kids while she rushed to the hospital with Gil Tuesday night. I couldn't fix her age, though I would've guessed eighty if pressed, but she was aging well. There weren't so many elderly people in Rochambeau year-round. Most retirees took off, either for Florida or the Southwest or the new, well-patrolled, red-tile-and-stucco condo communities that had sprouted all around central and southern Jersey. For some reason this woman had decided to stick it out. She stood with her arms folded, looking mournfully at the activity across the street, too dignified to walk up and gawk like some of her neighbors, yet not too embarrassed to come out for a closer look.

The house was a brown-and-white Tudor, its gardens lovingly and meticulously tended. She had thrown a plaid shawl over her shoulders to fend off a nonexistent evening breeze. She quieted her yapping chow with a sharp "Shhh, Albert," as I climbed up the stairs and introduced myself.

"Well, well." She looked curiously at my shield, then my face. Her eyes were a startling blue beneath a cap of white hair. "A private eye. This is just like TV. I don't think I've ever been approached by a private eye before."

"Well, I never have, myself," I said. "You can see by my ID that I live about a half mile from here. Marianne Dow—the woman across the street who was just led away by the police—is my client. Do you know her?"

"Yes, I know her. I know Marianne quite well." I

thought her gaze flickered a bit. She introduced herself as Sarah Lawson, motioning me to take one of the white wicker chairs behind her. Down the street, the excitement was winding down. The TV crew was pulling away, heading back to New York to make the late news. The crime-scene technicians in the backyard were pulling out, apparently having found nothing for the umpteenth time. If Marianne had killed Gil, didn't the weapon have to be in the house or on the grounds? Or nearby?

"When Jim—my husband—became ill a few years ago, Marianne came by almost every night," Sarah Lawson said. "Sometimes she drove me to the hospital or the market. She helped me with the laundry and the dishes, picked up Jim's prescriptions, all of the things you have to do when somebody is sick, things that can get hard for people my age. It wasn't easy for Marianne either." She shook her head. "She had small children. I kept telling her that I could take care of myself, that she had lots of other things to do, but Marianne is one of those people who just show up and help. Not many people do—though you can't blame people for having lives, just because yours is slipping away, now, can you?"

Sarah said this cheerfully, without any trace of self-pity. And she couldn't know how much I needed to hear that description of my client. Just as I did, Sarah liked and admired Marianne Dow. "So you see, I know quite well that that woman is not a murderer. No matter what they say. And I'd be happy to help you in any way. But I can't imagine how. I never even met Marianne's husband, only saw him from a distance going in and out, or working in the backyard."

"And your husband?"

"Jim passed on a few months ago, in the nursing home right over on Chestnut. A blessing, really; he'd been failing for so long. One reason I stayed in our house was so that I could visit him every day. I rent out the two bedrooms up-stairs to students at the state college. They help out with some of the chores." She looked about the same age as Benchley, perhaps a bit more frail. Hmmm. The last time I'd tried to fix Benchley up, he'd almost had a nervous break-down. He was old enough to arrange his own social life. But maybe I'd just mention Sarah to him.

"How is it, living here?"

She considered for a moment. "I still love being in my own house, but it can be something of a prison. I don't drive much and I never go out at night. Can't stay up late. But this house has lots of memories, Mr. DeLeeuw. Our children are gone, far away and happy, as it should be. But the house is full of them, of course; there are all these reminders of the time when I was so engaged in taking care of them and worrying so about them. I have time to read now, more peace in my life, and the satisfaction of having done a good job as their mother. And there are lovely things about this neighborhood. I love the sounds of children, the school buses driving back and forth. I used to wait for the bus with my daughters every morning right there in front of Marianne's house. But people here, well, you get the feeling they don't really want to see you when you're old. . . ."

I felt a bit of a pall. Waiting with Em and Ben for the school bus the first few weeks of elementary school was one of my cherished memories, too. I was still frantic with the pres-sures of child care, pets, after-school appointments. Talking to Sarah Lawson, I saw how piercing the loss would be when the time came that I wasn't. Would I ever have bothered to talk with her if not for this case?

I suspected life for her in Rochambeau was a lot tougher than she was acknowledging. This was a place where you worried about school, camp, Cub Scouts—where life begins and flourishes, not where it ends.

Sarah Lawson was somebody to keep in mind when the time came to deal with growing older, though. If I could do it half as gracefully as she or Benchley had, I would be happy.

But back to my case. "Look, Mrs. Lawson, to be candid, I'm stuck. The police have an overwhelming body of evidence against Marianne. They have a motive, the opportunity. There's the fact that she ran away. They've been tearing up her yard looking for a murder weapon. I have the same sense that you do—I can't accept Marianne Dow as a person who could sneak up behind her husband and bludgeon him to death."

Sarah Lawson shook her head and placed one thin hand over her heart. I thought I saw fear as well as sadness in her eyes. She seemed twitchy again, once we moved beyond small talk and focused on Marianne and the murder. Was I imagining this?

"I spotted you as a potential source of information because detectives learn to look for retired people," I continued. "They're around and they see things. If you want to help Marianne, then please try to remember if you saw or heard anything unusual, anything out of the ordinary that night or any night recently."

"What night? You mean the night her poor husband was attacked?"

I nodded. Across the street I saw one of Leeming's badly dressed plainclothes underlings scanning the block. He'd spotted my Volvo and, after looking around, had located me on the porch. He frowned. I expected Mrs. Lawson would get a visit from one of his colleagues before too long.

"Well, Mr. Deleeuw, I have told this to the police," Sarah

Lawson said in her soft, firm voice. "And I do have to be leaving shortly." Really, I thought. Didn't she say she didn't like to go out at night? Don't spook her by asking about that now, I cautioned myself. Be cool.

"There was that car. I reported it to the police. I suppose you know all about that."

"No, I don't."

"Well, it was just after midnight on Tuesday. I had been up watching the eleven o'clock news, then I had fallen asleep as I usually do. Most of the time one of the college girls upstairs will come in and wake me. This time Albert started barking. Well, it's true what you say about old biddies in a neighborhood; we do pay attention to things, it's one of the ways we can be useful. I've seen several kids fall off bikes or skateboards and get hurt; I call their parents. One time a German shepherd, a stray, had Jason down the street stranded . . . well, anyway. Pardon me, Mr. Deleeuw, I can see you're a patient man, but one does stray when you get to be my age."

She sighed. "I heard a door slam, very loudly. I went to the window and I saw a man running from the Dows' house, jump into a car, and then race off. It wasn't their car, I knew that, so I tried to see if I could get a look at the license plate, in case it was a burglar. I watch out for burglars; we've had a few around here. But I couldn't make out the number."

I pulled out my notebook. "Did you see the man?"

"Not very well. He was large, wider than you, and tall. But it's too far for me to see, and I didn't have my regular glasses on. I told the police this." Needless to say, Leeming hadn't passed it on.

"Did you actually see him leave the Dow house? Run out the door?"

"No. The officer asked me the same question. I didn't see

him leave. I only looked after I heard a noise, a door slamming. But where else could he have been coming from? He was running down their walk, right near the streetlight, which is why I could see him at all. And then the car made a U-turn, much too fast, and passed right by my door. I still couldn't read the license plate, but I did see, or at least I think I did, that he was driving an old Honda station wagon, a brown one. I know nothing about cars, but that was the car my husband Jim swore by, and the kind I still drive, when I drive. I didn't know anything was wrong until Marianne called me and asked me to come over and be with her children while she went to the hospital with her husband. I was there for a half hour or so until her baby-sitter could get there."

She smiled sadly. "I wish I could have seen more. Is it important?"

Now here, I thought, Sarah Lawson was being coy, and coyness wasn't her natural style. She was far too savvy not to know that what she'd seen was important. You're hiding something, I thought.

I shrugged. "I don't know. Even if the police did ID the car, nobody can say for sure where he came from. And there are a lot of brown Hondas in this country." But I had the sense that I had seen one recently.

I'm not the world's best-organized person, but one gift I do have. If I see something twice, or if somebody gives one version of events one week and another the next, a little bell goes off. It might take a while for the contradiction or connection to become clear, but it will eventually rise through the fog. One great benefit of my years in the commodity trading pits was that you had to keep a lot of things in your head at once, without Post-Its. Where had I seen a brown Honda wagon? I thought I knew.

But it was time to make my move. I didn't have much

time. I leaned forward in my chair and took one of Sarah Lawson's pale hands in mine. She was startled, too polite to pull back, too sharp not to know that something unpleasant was coming.

"Mrs. Lawson, I like you very much. I can see you're a decent person and a good friend to Marianne. But I'm also a good friend of hers, too. She's in terrible trouble. She's being arrested on murder charges. If I can't help her, she'll go to jail for the rest of her life. I truly believe that I'm her only chance of avoiding that, at the moment."

I paused. The silence was overpowering. Sarah Lawson was taking in every word, her blue eyes blazing in concentration, but she said nothing. I kept her hand in mine and kept silent, too. Two can play this game.

"Marianne is so dear to me," Sarah said softly. "She helped me when I desperately needed help, and even my own children didn't think to give it. I can hardly repay her." Certainly not, I thought, by betraying her.

"Mrs. Lawson. You said you rarely go out and you can't stay up late. Marianne told me when I talked to her earlier this week that you came rushing over to her house in your robe that night, sometime after midnight. I don't think you were up that late dozing in your chair. I think you saw the Honda, took note of it because of all the burglaries, then went to bed. I think Marianne called or came by and woke you up, told you she was in trouble and needed to leave something here. I think she begged you to say nothing, and you felt you owed her that much. After all, it wasn't really even lying. It was just silence."

She sat stock-still in her wicker chair, watching me closely, trying to figure out what to make of me, how much I really knew. There was as much fear as caution in that proud, kind face.

"I do owe her," she said after a few minutes had passed. It was a kind of acknowledgment. She pulled the plaid shawl closer around her shoulders, shivering slightly.

"Mrs. Lawson, please understand. I have to pass this information on to the authorities. I don't think you need the Rochambeau PD swarming all over here like they did Marianne's backyard. And Marianne, it seems, is either severely disturbed or desperately in need of all the help she can get. Either way, I have to know everything; surely you can see that? I don't know if she's guilty or not. Frankly, I'm so confused by this case, I'm not sure of anything. But I do know I can't fight for her blind. I've got to know what happened here that night. Please, please tell me." It was a good speech, and I believed every word of it, something I prayed Sarah Lawson could see.

"She came over here, didn't she? The night of the attack? That's why there was no murder weapon in the house or in the yard. Marianne brought it here, didn't she? In a package or a bag?"

Tears welled up in Sarah Lawson's eyes as she nodded. Poor thing, she must have been living in such fear and confusion. All alone, just months after her husband's death, with such life-and-death decisions to make. I truly felt for her. I, too, didn't want to see Leeming and his troops rampaging through her quiet house.

"You're her friend? You're working for her?" she said, her voice trembling.

"I swear it. On my two children. I'm working for her. Mrs. Lawson, you're in no trouble. She brought a package over, and you probably had no idea what was in it. . . ."

"I'm not worried about me," she said sharply, and rightly. "Let them try to put an old lady in jail for helping a friend. Jail would be interesting at my age." She pulled a tissue out of her sleeve and dabbed at her eyes. "I have no idea what's in the bag. I can't even lift it, it's so heavy. I love Marianne dearly. I couldn't bear to get her in trouble. . . ."

I leaned forward and patted her hand reassuringly, Albert the chow watching my every move from his spot beside her chair. "She's in lots of trouble, Mrs. Lawson. You didn't put her there. I'm just trying to get her out."

She nodded, as if she'd come to a decision, then stood, wordlessly leading me through the house to the pantry behind the kitchen. The glass-doored cabinets held an array of pans and supplies: flour, cereal, cans of soup and vegetables. On a bottom shelf behind the vacuum cleaner—in a hiding spot the cops would have uncovered in about three seconds—was a red-and-black gym bag. I pulled it out. Whatever was inside weighed at least ten pounds.

This discovery would seal Marianne's fate as far as the chief was concerned. I was torn between elation and anxiety. Had I helped or doomed Sarah's friend?

"I need to use your phone, Mrs. Lawson."

She nodded.

I called Jane, who said Em and Ben were in their reading chair and at the video-game controls respectively and that Percentage was downstairs guarding the entrances.

I made a second call. "Hey," I said when Willie picked up his home phone. "This is Martin. I want you to put another name in your computer. Actually, two of them. A couple, recently separated, I don't know if the divorce is final." The heaviest computer trails, I had learned from Willie, were left by mortgage applications, bankruptcies, and divorces, which meant that in Rochambeau there were lots of trails.

Willie called back in under five minutes to tell me he needed more time, just as I was finishing the tea that Mrs.

Lawson had brought me and was chewing on one of her peanut-butter brownies. I told him I'd call him later.

Then I called the police. Leeming was at home, but the switchboard patched me through to his house when I insisted it was urgent. "Oh, dear," said Sarah Lawson as four squad cars—two unmarked—came screeching up to the house within minutes.

I'd left the red-and-black gym bag where I found it. Leeming didn't ask me to leave as he carefully unzipped it and pointed a flashlight inside.

"Aerobic hand weights," he announced. "About five pounds each, I'd bet." I peered over his shoulder and the backs of the two detectives who were kneeling on the pantry floor. I glimpsed a green-striped towel—like those I'd seen in the Dows' bathroom, but this one was stained with several large rusty-colored spots.

Leeming exhaled. After grumping a bit at Sarah Lawson for not telling the authorities about the bag—a lecture even the chief quickly gave up when he saw her terrified face— Leeming turned to me and nodded.

"This was the right thing to do, Deleeuw. But I appreciate it. There's some that wouldn't have." I was very nearly one of them, but that would have been too far over the line. I preferred to be able to look Ben and Emily in the eye and say I hadn't broken the law and expected the same of them. Just to be on the safe side, I told Leeming about Andrea Lucca's aborted effort to take Em into the city. He whistled at that one, then said he'd have a cruiser hang around the house for the next couple of days. I was grateful.

And I was miserable. I feared I had only further imperiled my client, however virtuous my intent, and time was running out for me to do her any good.

I thanked Sarah Lawson, reassured her that she had done the right thing (had we?), and drove to a phone booth a few blocks away, by now thoroughly depressed at handing over to the police what could be the final nail in Marianne's coffin.

"Got something on the couple," Willie announced happily. Good old Willie. He didn't even have to be in his office to access the world's secrets, only near his trusty little modem. "Still have the same MasterCard account. But they each have their own supermarket cards, and separate banking."

It amazed and frightened me that Willie could pick up this stuff in minutes, without days or weeks of passing out twenties or whispering in informants' ears. If I was in a hurry, he would just put the phone down; I could hear the keyboard clacking and then the not-so-private lives of people I needed to know about would appear miraculously in front of him. It made me queasy, not only because we were invading people's privacy but because there were stringent laws against this sort of thing. And I thought the police were getting pretty proficient at cracking down on the Willies of the computer world. Guess not.

But Willie was the most valuable information source I had. In most private investigations, as in most police work, cases were cracked not by derring-do or gun play, but by information. Thanks in large measure to Willie, whom I wouldn't know if I ran into on the street, Deleeuw Investigations had a pretty good track record. I really ought to raise his case fee from $200 to $250, though he would have worked for free if the electronic chase was challenging enough. God knows what he does for fun. Like a lot of the more ethical hackers, Willie draws the line at damaging or destroying other people's computer files. But he believes information ought to be free, and he does his part to keep it that way.

"What about cars?"

He clacked for about twelve seconds.

"Well, the guy is living in Hoboken. Stan."

"Okay," I said.

"The wife Donna is in Rochambeau, right?"

"Right."

"According to this, there's just one car. A Honda hatchback, 1988, bought new at Suburban Honda."

"I don't suppose you can tell me the color?"

"Sure, man. It's brown. They paid fourteen thousand dollars. Payments were three-ninety a month. Good car, too. Not many repair bills."

Donna Platt answered on the third ring, sounding as harried as when I'd first met her earlier that long week.

"Donna, it's Kit Deleeuw."

Silence.

"The private detective . . ."

"Oh, shit, yes. I should remember the name—you helped cook dinner. In fact, I saw you at the memorial service. You didn't see me, you were too busy looking at our friend Andrea, just like I was," she added sourly.

"Listen, Donna, I have a quick question. It might help me a lot. You have a brown Honda, right?"

"Yeah, that's right. You saw it the other afternoon. Why?"

"Does anyone use your car but you?"

"Yes, Stan does sometimes. He lives in Hoboken, and he takes the train into the city. But once or twice a week, usually to take the kids out to dinner or to go somewhere himself, he borrows my car. I can get a ride to work with some people at the office when I need to. It's in our agreement that I will make a good-faith effort to share it, because he claims he can't afford to buy one. Why?"

"A neighbor says she saw the car outside Marianne's

house a couple of times," I said cautiously. Even ex-wives don't want their kids' fathers linked to murder. "A big, tall man was seen driving it. I just wonder what your car was doing there. Is Stan tall?"

"He's six three, but, Jesus, you're not suggesting Stan had a thing with Marianne Dow? That's inconceivable. Look, he may be a scum, but he's not . . . oh, my God. What *are* you suggesting?" Donna's voice was climbing upward in pitch.

"Please, Donna, you can imagine what Marianne's going through. I'm not suggesting that Stan is a killer. I'm just wondering what he might have been doing there. I plan on asking him myself, believe me. Was he friends with the Dows? Did he know them?"

"Not that I know of. Maybe you ought to ask him yourself. He gets home from work at eight or so, and he's supposed to call me tonight to discuss the kids' summer plans. But I don't think he would have any reason at all to go over there, unless Andrea Lucca was hiding in a closet."

Maybe she was.

"I'm driving over to Stan's apartment," I told her, keeping my excitement out of my voice. "Please don't tell him about this. I'm not the police. I'm just trying to help Marianne. He might not even have been there, and if he was, he probably has a very simple explanation. Give me a chance to find out, okay?"

Donna Platt said yes, and sounded so stunned that she seemed to mean it.

CHAPTER 17

S tan Platt lived in Divorced Dadland, turf I know well from my countless searches for separated or divorced fathers who can't make their child-support payments or who desperately try to hide assets, but who often leave a rich trail of stereo, carpet, and leather-sofa purchases for Willie to find.

I dislike those people as much as thugs who rob old ladies. In a way, they are worse. They rob their own spouses and children, depriving them of rent money so that they can stock their new bachelor pads.

When I find them—and I almost *always* find them, since they are almost never prepared to live the way a true fugitive has to, to avoid detection—they bellow and whine and bluster and complain. But once I explain that the courts will order marshals to come and pick up the new shag carpeting and CD player by nightfall if I don't leave with a check, they always pay up.

Platt lived in a spanking-new apartment building in Hoboken, twenty stories high, with gleaming tall windows separated by red brick. The view across the harbor was stunning, looking directly into lower Manhattan with twice the space and at half the money it cost to look directly into Jersey from Manhattan.

Platt was not a deadbeat dad, I reminded myself sternly as I parked the Volvo across the street. As far as I knew, he paid up. But I wasn't prepared to like him. His wife seemed warm, smart, even loyal despite his sneaky affair with Andrea Lucca, and I had a low tolerance for men who tore their families apart just to prove their own virility. Still, I had to be careful. It's always dangerous to make moral judgments about others. Outsiders never really know everything that's going on inside a marriage. Besides, Andrea Lucca seemed to have the power to detonate marriages at will. Why should Stan Platt be less vulnerable than many other married men in Rochambeau?

My latest theory, one I wanted to bounce off Jane if I ever saw her again, was that Lucca had a knack for spotting weakened rather than healthy marriages, that she could sense stresses and fissures in a relationship and slither in. That could explain why she was so successful: if there was a problem to begin with, she noticed it or was told about it and promptly made a move. That would make her no less destructive, but a little less mythic.

The night had turned dark and chilly. A stiff wind was coming off the Hudson, bearing a variety of rich New York City odors whose sources I really didn't want to think about much. On the street in front of the apartment building, well-dressed couples headed for the train station en route to cafés in Tribeca and obscure films at the Museum of Modern Art. The once-decaying waterfront towns of Jersey City and Hoboken had become magnets for singles, artists, and kids driven from New York by skyrocketing rents and crime, a juxtaposition that sounded contradictory but somehow wasn't.

At first I couldn't place the sound I was hearing as I searched my pockets for quarters to feed the meter. I thought it was a truck backing up, but the beeping was too close. Then I realized what it had to be and flipped open the glove compartment. There, buried under a pile of Post-Its, was a beeper I hadn't seen or heard from in months. Like a gun, it wasn't equipment I was comfortable with; unlike my gun, which I hurriedly locked in my office safe four days after I'd purchased it, it seemed useful to keep around for emergencies. I was astonished to hear it functioning at all; somebody had probably dialed the wrong number. Still, the thought that Ben or Em might be in the emergency room or that Andrea Lucca had surfaced sent me scurrying for a corner phone booth.

"Hey, sleuth," Jane answered. "Everything's all right. I was worried the beeper might not work anymore. The batteries should be dead by now. Have you calmed down yet? Are you ever coming home?" Jane usually sort of liked my being a private investigator. She thought it suited my previously suppressed odd ways and quirky nature. And she had come to love the freedom it gave me to keep an eye on our kids. My getting shot on my last big case had rattled her for a while, but she seemed to have overcome her fear—or maybe wasn't letting me see it. I had worked hard to convince her that 99 percent of my cases were about as dangerous as picking up a pizza. But Em's recent brush with Andrea Lucca might have shaken that claim for good.

"Soon, I hope," I told her. "What's up? At eight P.M. you can't be beeping me for anything good. Your buddy 'Pam' hasn't checked in?"

"No," she said, almost sadly. I hadn't had time to think it through, but in addition to being scared out of her wits about Em, Jane had lost someone whose friendship she had high hopes for. "But Marianne Dow's lawyer did call. He said she's asked to see you tomorrow afternoon, right after her bail hearing. Either she'll get out or she won't, but apparently you can see her either way."

"That's why you called?" It didn't seem urgent enough for only the second beep of my detecting career.

"Also, a man called, sounded like a kid actually, and said he had information you might need in a hurry. He wouldn't leave a name, just the initial *W*. Sounds quite mysterious." Willie, of course, and he was right. I called him right away, and it *was* particularly timely.

"Who is it?" barked the voice on the apartment intercom after I'd buzzed 16D.

"Mr. Platt?"

"Look, if this is a salesman, I'm busy. I have company. . . ."

"I'm Kit Deleeuw, a private investigator. I'm working for Marianne Dow, and I'd like to ask you a few questions." I thought I heard a woman's voice murmur. He snarled something I couldn't quite make out. He did not sound like a gentle man.

"What do you want?"

"I want to talk with you, Mr. Platt. I don't think this is something I ought to discuss standing in your lobby."

"I'm busy, and I don't think this is something I want to discuss at all. Why don't you call later? I'll give you my phone number. . . ."

Time to shift gears. "I want to know why you were in Marianne Dow's house the night her husband was attacked and, as it turns out, murdered. And why you haven't told anybody, especially the police, that you were there."

There was a brief silence, then a verbal explosion. "Hey, fuck you, Jack. Who the hell do you think you are, coming to my apartment? I'll call the cops and have your ass hauled out of here."

I couldn't tell if Stan Platt was talking tough to impress his girlfriend or if he was trying to scare me off, and frankly, I was beginning not to care. "Platt, my name's not Jack. Either I come up and talk to you, or I drive right to the Rochambeau PD and tell them about your visit to the Dows' house at almost precisely the moment they think Gil was attacked." I didn't really know if that was true or not. "I don't really give a shit. Since I'm here and you're here, it sort of makes sense for you to stop puffing up like a hot-air balloon and take five minutes to talk with me. Believe me, the cops'll be less gentle than I am if they have to drive over here."

He buzzed me in without another word. When I got off the elevator on the sixteenth floor, he stood waiting for me in the hallway.

Stan was a beefy guy. He looked to be pushing forty-five, and judging from his snug jeans and the muscles bulging underneath his dark-green polo shirt, he spent much of each day at a gym. His eyes were so eerily blue that I suspected tinted contact lenses. He was steaming.

Apparently, I wasn't going to be invited inside to meet his new girlfriend, who, if experience taught me anything, worked in a low-paying menial job, was twenty years younger than he was, and deferred to his maturity, wisdom, and Gold Card.

"Who the hell are you?"

"Deleeuw. Kit Deleeuw." I handed him my card, then showed him my ID. It sometimes cooled people off. "I was hoping we could sit down, Mr. Platt. Lord knows I don't want to crimp your social life, but we are talking about a murder investigation, and this doesn't feel to me like a hallway conversation."

"Well, I don't really care what this feels like to you. Aren't you that guy from the Brown murders? The Wall Street thief who got off?"

This kind of talk no longer got to me. People I didn't care about could believe what they wanted. People I did care about knew better, although I had recently and painfully learned that, as always, the reputation had filtered down to kid level. Ben had gotten and given several bloodied noses over it. "That's me. Aren't you the guy who ran out of a house where a man was murdered and didn't report your presence to the police?"

His face reddened, and he kept clenching and unclenching his fists, as if he were just waiting for an excuse to slug me. "That's crap. Why do you say I was there?"

"I can prove you were there. You borrowed your wife's car that night and you were seen." Platt had actually already revealed more than he'd meant to. Obviously, he hadn't been with Marianne that night, or he would have assumed that's how I'd learned of his presence. So he sneaked into the house while she was working in her study. Why would he do that?

"You're lying, Deleeuw. If you could prove I was there, you'd have gone to the cops already. You're just fishing." A weak bluff. He was either desperate or dumb, and if he was that dumb, I couldn't imagine why someone as sharp as his wife would have married him in the first place. Of course, I probably should have turned on my heel at that point and gone straight to the police. But the police had their case, and it was growing stronger by the hour. I needed to find an alternate one to hand them. Watching the muscles in Platt's neck bulge, I hoped I hadn't made a mistake.

"I'm sure there was some innocent purpose for your being there. I'd just like to know what it was."

We were fencing, and with as much grace as a dump truck unloading. I wanted to know if he was hiding something; he wanted to know how much I knew. Thanks to Willie, I knew quite a bit, but I wasn't sure how to play it. This guy was a coiled spring.

He didn't have a clean conscience, or he would have made good on his threat to sic the cops on me. So there we were in classic male posture, belligerently fluffing our feathers at one another. I would have to make the first move.

He stepped back as a door opened across the hall and a woman came out with her poodle on a leash. The three of us nodded and cleared our throats (the poodle yawned) until the elevator blessedly arrived.

"What do you want?" he demanded, edging closer, within easy striking distance. I felt vulnerable and edgy. He had a lot more muscle than a part-time financial consultant had any need for. "I'll give you two minutes."

"Were you at the Dows' house that night?"

"No. Anybody who says I was is mistaken. Why would I go there, anyway? You're not suggesting I hurt him, are you?" The threat in the last statement was not implied. He was probably thinking that I hadn't gone to the police because I didn't really have anything. And it was true that my evidence was slim: Sarah Lawson was an eighty-year-old-plus witness watching from across the street in the dark. She never saw his face. There were probably only about two hundred thousand Honda hatchbacks in the country at the moment; maybe a fifth of them were brown. A defense attorney's daydream. But this was the only hook I'd been able to latch on to that might help Marianne.

"Maybe you were there to talk about the lien Gil Dow was putting on your special account in the city. The one you had probably not only hidden from him, but from your wife as well. . . ."

I suppose I always knew what he was going to do, although not the vigor with which he did it. He brought a knee up into my groin. As I doubled over, he brought his left elbow up into my nose, then drove his right fist into my left eye. I crumpled to the floor, instinctively balled in a fetal position. He kicked me as hard as he could in the small of the back. Through a rush of pain, I contemplated getting up on my knees and slugging him as hard as I could, but that would just expose me to another beating. I could hear Jane: "As dangerous as getting a pizza, eh?"

He kicked me again, as close to the kidney as he could get. I rolled over onto my back, avoiding another kick, then lunged up, pounding my right fist into his testicles. He was caught in a bad position, shouted in pain, then doubled over. I rolled into his legs and he fell alongside me. The only good thing that happened was that I vomited all over his shiny black cowboy boots, then struggled up and hit the elevator button.

Blood was streaming from my nose, soaking right through the handkerchief I'd pressed against it. My groin and kidneys felt as if someone had shot me. I don't remember ever being in that much pain. I ought to call Donna and ask if she was sure her husband wasn't a scum. Did she deliberately avoid telling me about Stan's temper, or had he hidden it from her? Or had he been driven to the wall by something she didn't even know about?

I held the elevator door open with one bloody hand. "Look, Platt, this is stupid. It tells me you have a psycho's temper, and it tells me you have things you want to hide. I know you owed Gil Dow twelve thousand dollars in brokerage fees for orders you placed. I know he filed for a lien against your city account five days before he was attacked. You're already broke from having been laid off and divorced. You've got motive, and I can place you at the scene." The only thing I couldn't figure out was why he hadn't killed Dow with one blow. I'd be willing to testify in any court he sure had the strength to do it.

"You repeat a word of this shit, and I'll have my lawyer up your ass," he hissed from the floor as the doors closed.

"I'm glad you're getting a lawyer," I shot back, fighting nausea. "You're going to need one." But I was already down to the ninth floor, explaining to the terrified woman who'd just gotten on that I had fallen and was headed for a doctor. At least I'd put a crimp in his sex life for a few days.

My hands were shaking as I climbed into the Volvo. The bleeding from my nose had stopped, but half of my body was swelling. I didn't want to walk into my house looking like this. "Gross!" I could picture Em shrieking. I'd drive to the mall, I decided.

Willie's information must have been correct. Trawling through his computer system, he'd discovered the lien—the sort of thing credit companies would know about. It was no big deal to learn that Stan Platt had placed a bunch of buy orders with Gil Dow's firm that he couldn't cover. Platt probably knew Dow from around town and had done something stupid when his financial woes mounted. I'd seen it before: men who have worked hard to acquire some money can't stand to see it whittled away, not even for their kids. They'll do almost anything to keep it, hide it, or, as probably happened here, get more.

Did Platt go to Gil's house to argue with him? To beg for more time? A lien probably would have meant he couldn't make his alimony payments and child support, and then he would have really been in a bind. But if his purpose was aboveboard, why hadn't he simply rung the doorbell? Why hadn't Marianne seen him?

I peered into the rearview mirror. Drying blood caked my upper lip and cheek. My left eye was turning purple and would soon swell shut. My testicles were on fire. Maybe Wall Street had more going for it than I realized.

I didn't make it to the mall that night. I made it barely two blocks from the apartment. There two Hoboken police cars stopped me, one pulling in front of the Volvo, the other blocking me from the side, both with lights flashing. Platt was playing it safe, filing assault charges before I could, I guessed.

Police brutality was a big issue in New York at the time. And even though these officers—two men and a woman— were quite polite, the humiliation of being hauled out of my car and spread-eagled over the hood of theirs was piercing. They eventually let me park the Volvo, offered to drive me to a hospital (I declined), then frisked and handcuffed me and drove me to police headquarters. I was wrong, it turned out; Stan hadn't called the cops, the woman in the elevator had.

When they saw my ID, they got curious. But I found I was slipping more and more into the habit of not talking to the police. I have a law-abiding nature, and I even like Chief Leeming. But there were so many things happening and I understood so few of them that it seemed more prudent, and more in my client's interests, to keep them to myself for the time being. Basically, I wouldn't say anything because I didn't have to, and because we weren't really on the same side and never would be. That's the lonely thing about being a cop; the only people who are ever really on your side are other cops.

Besides, I knew there were going to be no charges pressed against me. Sergeant Jerry Poluszny, detective on the night shift, had to pretend that he cared about what I was doing in his town. I had to pretend I was considering telling him. The exchange bored both of us.

I called Jane and said that I was at Hoboken police head-quarters collecting information. She took the news in stride, until I unwisely told her that this had been one of those ex-tremely rare moments when my new career and the real world had collided a bit violently. I warned her about the bloody nose and bruises and insisted I didn't need to go to a hospital or get X-rays. I knew she'd make me go when I got home.

Sitting outside the detective bureau waiting for a cab ride back to the Volvo, I tried to figure out where I was with all this. I'd paid dearly for it, but maybe I had a genuine suspect, somebody Marianne's attorney could put on the stand and make squirm.

Platt was more brutal than I'd expected, which bothered me for more than the obvious reasons. This kind of rough stuff really was out of character for a middle-class Rocham-beau male. We hurt each other with lawyers, not fists. My other problem was that while twelve thousand dollars was a lot of money to me, especially these days, it wasn't much of a motive for murder, not in the suburbs. Plenty of people had stereo rigs worth as much and cars that cost three times that. The money might have been cause for bad blood, even threats, but was Stan Platt so hard up for cash he'd kill for so paltry an amount? Even if he would, bumping off Gil Dow wouldn't eliminate the debt; the brokerage firm would simply pick up where Dow had left off.

Maybe it wasn't money alone that brought him there. Maybe there was something else as well. Perhaps when my head stopped throbbing and stomach stopped turning, I might be able to figure out what.

CHAPTER 18

With the blood washed off my face, the only visible injuries were a gash above my left eyebrow, where a fist had landed, and a swelling on the bridge of my nose, which, miraculously, wasn't broken.

Jane tried for an hour to persuade me to go to the hospital emergency room, but I told her it looked a lot worse than it was. Besides, the first thing they'd do in the hospital would be to call the police, and I didn't want to tell Leeming everything I'd learned, not until I was sure I couldn't go any further. Jane was furious, and though she didn't come out and say so, she was rattled. First, the discovery of her friend Pam's real identity, now this. I looked, she said, like one of those multicolored terrain maps. I promised I'd go see our family doctor if I didn't feel better tomorrow.

But, next day, my ribs still incredibly tender and one swollen testicle giving me a gait like Charlie Chaplin's, I wasn't at a doctor's office. I was at a pay phone a few blocks from my house.

Willie and I had a prearranged telephone rendezvous we

had worked out for emergencies and special occasions. If he called up and left a message saying I had just won a car in a magazine sweepstakes, I was to call him at a phone booth at ten P.M. or ten A.M., whichever came first. If it was particularly urgent, he said I'd won a Buick, and then I was to call him— also from a pay phone, never from my phone—every hour on the hour until I got him. He'd called at seven that morning, advising me I'd won a shiny new Buick—my third or fourth, actually. Anybody eavesdropping over the past few years would have wondered why I was driving a Volvo that might have once transported hula hoops.

"Yo, Martin?" he said, picking up right away. I could hear cups and plates clanking in the background and supposed he was calling from a diner.

"Yo, W. Do you spend all weekends at the keyboard?"

"Well, Martin, I go to every movie at the eight-plex, I hit the video-game parlor with my buddies. But otherwise, yeah, I'm at my screen." It sounded to me as if Willie was always near a screen. "I'm hooked up to one of those interconnecteds. I talk to other hackers on my monitor half the night. I'm addicted to it, I guess."

"I don't think I could really imagine. I'm starting to want to meet you. Anyway, I want you to know you're doing great work, and I'm raising your assignment fee by fifty dollars."

"Hey, thanks. I appreciate that. I could use the dollars."

"W, you're over eighteen and have a job and everything, right? I mean, you're not some sixteen-year-old whose parents think you're up in the room studying algebra, are you? You are an adult?"

He laughed. I heard silverware crashing behind him. Someplace on Route 4 with bottomless cups of coffee and ultrahigh cholesterol breakfasts around the clock, no doubt.

"I'm on the up-and-up," he assured me. "I'd like to meet you, too. You sound okay. Even when you're stressed, you're always polite and considerate. Whenever you want, you can buy me a drink, okay? I'm old enough."

"Okay." I felt a little easier. At least someone over twenty-one was taking these risks. If Willie could tap into every computer in the world, couldn't lots of others tap into him? But this was not the time to consider the ethical implications of my major investigative resource.

"Hey, here's why I'm calling, Martin," he continued. "I don't know what you're working on, but I've been feeding names into my network, you know, gas and food purchases, credit lines, that stuff. Your friend Andrea showed up early this morning, on a credit check put in yesterday at ten A.M.— it was processed overnight, like they do, at a central clearinghouse. Realty company asked for it. She put down twelve hundred dollars as a deposit on a two-bedroom apartment. I never heard of the town, but my computer says it's about an hour south of here."

Bingo. Lucca was moving, flushed out of hiding, perhaps having found another suburb with some troubled families ripe for infiltration and destruction. I guessed she'd done this before, moved from place to place until the list of enemies and casualties grew so long she had no choice but to head elsewhere. I could feel the adrenaline hit. I'd wanted to find Andrea Lucca all week, but after the business with Em I had to admit my need to see her had taken on a personal nature.

The police were looking for her, but there was no warrant out for her arrest and they didn't suspect her of any crime, so they weren't looking all that hard. In fact, once Leeming had seen with his own eyes that she was alive, I think he stopped worrying about her at all. His real interest in her, he had admitted, was as another murder victim. If she wasn't dead, she probably had little to offer. After all, they had a great case against Marianne without her. And maybe he was right.

Maybe it was time for me to let go of my stubborn and increasingly lonely notion that my client was innocent. I wasn't even sure *I* believed it anymore. When I saw her being led away in handcuffs, she looked so disturbed and disoriented that she was probably capable of anything. And her sneaking over to Sarah Lawson's house with what had to be the murder weapon sure seemed to seal it up. If there were any other explanations, why hadn't she told me or the police about them? And why, in God's name, would she have taken time out in the middle of all this to shop for furniture? That one had completely crossed my circuits, making me suspect the only two real options were that she was deranged or a killer. Maybe both.

My work for Marianne was now a matter of loyalty and professionalism, of trying to do my job and earn my fee. Whatever else, I wanted to feel clear that I had done everything in my power for my client, even one that I suspected hadn't come to me in good faith.

This was the part that still bugged me the most, that she'd come to me at all. Why would she hire a private investigator to dig up evidence on her husband's lover if she was planning to beat his brains in? To draw attention to another suspect and deflect it from her? If so, she'd wasted her money. Simply to spatter dirt on Lucca? But she could sully Lucca herself, with a few well-placed rumors at soccer practice or at Buns of Steel. Anyway, if the person I'd first met in the mall nearly a week ago was a deceitful killer, then I had some serious work to do when it came to judging human beings, a critical matter in my line.

"Martin? You there?"

"I'm sorry, W. I'm just trying to make some sense out of this case. Look, I'll let you go. Where did you say the town was?"

"Hollandale, man. Central Jersey. You know it?"

A shiver ran from the base of my neck right down to my butt. "Holy shit. No, I don't know it, but our friend Andrea does." Hold it, I cautioned myself. This isn't a case to kick around with some hacker I've never even seen.

I thanked Willie profusely, reminded him to keep rummaging through Stan Platt's finances, hung up, and placed another call. A teenaged girl who had been sitting on a bench in the adjacent bus shelter waiting to use the phone flashed me a murderous glance, then looked taken aback at my swollen, misshapen face. You didn't see a lot of fist fight injuries among Rochambeau's middle-aged dads. Why on earth would Andrea Lucca rent an apartment in the town where her sadistic stepfather lived? None of the obvious answers were comforting.

I called Marianne's attorney at home. "Bail denied," Levin said, obviously irked at having to work on a weekend. "The judge said that she'd run once, and he wasn't going to give her a chance to do it again. We argued that she returned voluntarily, but the judge wasn't buying it. We'll try again tomorrow. But she's spending the weekend in jail, that's for sure. I feel lousy about her kids. Their father's dead, their mother's in jail, they're not even living in their house. It's like their whole world fell apart." That's right, I thought, and if their mom was convicted of second-degree murder, their lives would fall further apart.

I relinquished the phone, took a pack of Post-Its out of my jacket pocket, and wrote:

Hollandale. It was time—past time—to confront the mythic, mysterious, and perhaps deadly Andrea Lucca and her even creepier stepfather Scronziak.

Stan Platt. I was so busy wincing that I hadn't given much thought to Platt's motives for drubbing me. Perhaps his machismo had been pierced, interrupted by a private investigator moments before he was about to jump into the sack with his honey. The connection to Gil Dow was fascinating, but didn't really add up to murder, unless there was more to it than we knew. Willie was plowing through one computer file after another to see if there was. Platt's secret visit to the Dow house the night of the attack might have significance beyond money.

The pouty girl had vacated the phone surprisingly quickly. Without her accusing eyes on me, I called the Rochambeau PD and asked to be patched through to Leeming, who, sure enough, was in his office.

"Well, happy sabbath, Deleeuw. I've been trying to call you. The Hoboken cops tell me they didn't know what the other guy looked like, but you looked like you'd spent the weekend with Jason on Elm Street. Is this related to our case, or were you cruising the bars picking fights with bikers?" He *tsk-tsk*ed. "You know Dow's been denied bail, right?"

"Yes, I know. Your concern is touching, Chief. Look, I want to tell you what I found out, before you haul me up before the licensing board. I was in Hoboken to talk to Stan Platt. His wife is Donna Platt; she lives on Bayview. Lucca busted up their marriage."

"That's one for the tabloids, Deleeuw, but I don't see—"

"Look," I said, a bit sharply for me. My head was throbbing. "Here's the thing. Stan Platt and Gil Dow had another connection, besides Andrea Lucca. Platt owed Dow's firm money—not major bucks, about twelve thousand dollars that I know of. And Sarah Lawson, whom you met the other night, told your people already that she saw somebody who fits Platt's description driving a car like Platt's away from the Dow house on the murder night."

"You thinking maybe Marianne Dow and Platt had a thing?"

"No, Jesus. I knew you'd say that. Can't you see any information on this case as anything but more evidence that Marianne murdered her husband?" I still hated to see Marianne as anything but a straight, loyal woman of character. Because it was so, or because I wanted it to be?

"Because that theory works for me, Deleeuw. You see, here's the difference between you and me: I don't believe your client when she says somebody came into the house, walked right past the room where she was working, waltzed into the bathroom, beat her husband nearly to death, then left without her hearing or seeing a thing. I think she's lying. She's always fit. She was home, she walked into the bathroom. Naturally, he doesn't try to run or fight because it's his wife. She brains him with the exercise weight—which the medical examiner confirms is our murder weapon, by the way —then runs up the block and leaves it with the sympathetic old lady. Couldn't get much tighter, pal." The only thing I could think of that he was missing was a videotape of the attack. Why wouldn't a jury convict after hearing all that? Especially when the cops tracked down Andrea Lucca and she swore that she and Gil Dow were having an affair.

"Lord, Deleeuw, I know you haven't handled a lot of homicides, but there's a big difference between being loyal and being just plain dumb. Have you thought about this fucking case? The only truthful thing this woman's told you is her name. My hunch is she was probably having an affair with

Platt. Maybe they did Dow together. I'll send a couple of detectives over there now."

I pondered, then repressed, several nasty responses. Maybe Leeming was right. Platt seemed absolutely the last man in the world Marianne would be attracted to, but stranger things happened all the time. And a visit from the chief's men would at the very least wreck Stan Platt's morning; I didn't want to discourage that.

But something he said stuck in my mind. So did something I'd seen in Marianne's house. Still at the phone booth, I made two more calls, one to Willie, one to Benchley. Each one was given a task, which I had no doubt would be superbly executed. I drove the Volvo over to the gas station in the middle of town to fill up, then over to Marianne's, where I saw what I wanted to see without having to get out of the car. Then, over to the Parkway: I wanted to be in Hollandale by noon.

The Maple Shade Nursing Home was on the left as I pulled into downtown Hollandale, ten miles east of the Jersey Turnpike exit. Some of Rochambeau's gracious old mansions had been converted into small nursing homes. But Hollandale wasn't a shady suburb; it was a tiny, run-down old farm town south of Fort Dix, its tacky main street thickly lined with video stores and bars.

If Maple Shade had taken its name from actual maples, they were nowhere in evidence. The nursing home was a long, low white building on three sides of a broad asphalted courtyard. It might once have been a good-sized motel servicing soldiers and families from the base, which had been eviscerated by the recent rounds of military reductions. A dozen elderly men and women in wheelchairs sat out dozing on the pavement in the midday sun.

I parked out front and walked toward what looked like the former lobby. The place was even dingier inside than out. The lobby had been converted to a combination lounge and administrative area. There were too many people for too little space, and the sight, sounds, and smells were oppressive and depressing. A score of old people, several of them laced into wheelchairs or strapped onto gurneys, had been arranged around a couple of small TV sets in wood cabinets.

I was frightened. Pete Scronziak had never done anything to me, and his living here meant he was not likely to do anything to anybody else again. But somebody who could have done what Frankie Lucca had described was clearly missing several of the minimal ingredients that go into being human. Jane tells me there are lots of people who fit that definition, more than our suburban culture wants to know about. I was fascinated by the prospect of meeting such a person, and repelled, in roughly equal parts. But I was scared, too. I would rather slug it out with some musclehead like Stan Platt than sit down opposite somebody who would scar children the way this man had.

But he was the link I'd been scrounging around for, the bridge to Andrea Lucca. He had to be the reason she was nearby. If she was renting apartments yesterday, she was around today. I wasn't leaving this sour little town until we finally met.

The receptionist at the desk glanced at my bruises (I had toted ice packs down in the Volvo with me, but I still looked like one of the gargoyles on Notre Dame) and asked if I was a relative of Mr. Scronziak. I said no, but I was a friend of Andrea Lucca.

Her pale eyes were impassive. "So you're not a relative of Mr. Scronziak?"

"Look," I said, "I'm a friend of the family. If he doesn't

want to see me, fine. But the sign outside says nursing home, not prison. If he's able, I'd like to talk to him, and I don't see why it's anybody else's concern."

She yawned. I reached into my pocket, folded up two twenty-dollar bills, and slid them over. She took them, unfolded them, and tucked them in her pocket. I was thrilled. Finally, a bribe working the way it was supposed to.

She drifted into the office adjoining the desk and closed the door. A few minutes later she came out and told me to have a seat. "Nurse Brabham will bring you back."

Nurse Brabham was a tall, young black woman with a grim demeanor. She didn't look sullen or resentful like the receptionist, who clearly thought she should be doing more important things—just tough as nails.

"Ten minutes," she decreed. "He's not well."

"Is he lucid?" I asked.

But she was already leading me down the hall. No sweet-talk for visitors here. As we got to the room, she turned and looked me directly in the eye. "I don't know who you are or what you're doin' here, mister, but let me tell you that this man is just as mean as if he was twenty years old. Only difference is, he's got an old body, cancer, and a heart condition. I know it sounds strange, but watch him. He's dying, but there's plenty of hate left."

"You don't like him, do you?" I asked quietly.

"I don't like him at all. He's a sick old man, and God rest his soul when his time comes, but he's evil."

"Who is it?" The voice rasped from the bed on the far side of the narrow, darkened room. I gasped at the smell, part urine, part feces, and part something else—decaying flesh, maybe, or even death itself. Faded curtains were pulled over the window, and the only light was from a fluorescent tube recessed into the headboard. It blinked on and off, intensifying the room's hellish quality. Nothing in the setting softened the harsh reality of sickness and advanced age—no carpet, no family pictures, no flowers.

Scronziak, I could see, had restraints around his legs.

The only bright thing in the room were his black eyes. They blazed fiercely out of sunken sockets. Wisps of ivory hair fell over his forehead. Spittle streaked down one side of his mouth, and blood stains spotted the pillow. Gauze and bandages covered his neck. Below them, his whole frame looked emaciated.

I had to fight back an impulse to bolt, not because Scronziak was old and sick, but because he looked so lizard-like and malevolent that I understood instantly what Nurse Brabham had warned me about. This man hated me and probably everyone who stepped through the door. I had no doubt that if he could get his hands on a scalpel, he'd drive it into my side the second I came within range.

I steadied myself with the reminder that he wasn't the one I had come to see. "Is Andrea here?" I asked.

He suddenly looked uncertain, confused. "Is it time to go? Time to go home? She said she was taking me home, taking me the fuck out of here." His voice was a harsh, broken rasp, somewhere between a hiss and a whisper, reinforcing his reptilian appearance. He focused more fiercely on me, taking in what I looked like and what I might be doing here. It was the practiced, wary leer of a man who had good reason to avoid lots of people over the years. Bill collectors, surely. Cops. Social workers. Angry landlords. Enraged husbands or boyfriends, maybe.

"Well, I'm here to help," I improvised. "When are we moving?"

His eyes narrowed. "Get out of here. You're a liar. Get out of my room. Get out." He couldn't quite shout, but his voice rose as he began chanting, almost as if it were a mantra, "Get out, get out, get out."

"There's no point in screaming at me," I said, more calmly than I felt. "I'm not a schoolkid. You can't drown my cat. You can't slug me or rape me, or whatever it was you did to those kids, you vicious old bastard. I never thought I'd ever want to see anybody suffer, but I hope your cancer takes you one cell at a time, and that each one hurts more than the last." I was horrified by the sound of my own words. If I could have taken it back, I would have—I think.

He was snarling now, like an animal caught in a trap, while I stood shocked by my own words. Benchley and I had spent long spiritual evenings talking about forgiveness and understanding. I didn't want to rejoice in anyone's pain. But all I felt for this man was raw hatred. Nurse Brabham was right; it reflected from him onto you, bouncing back and forth. I could not even imagine what growing up in this monster's household could mean.

But there wasn't anything I would learn from him. He barely seemed to know where he was, let alone what he'd done decades ago. As much as I loathed the sight of him, it suddenly seemed pathetic for me to be verbally abusing this sick, twisted old man. At long last, thank God, he couldn't defend himself.

I left the nursing home as quickly as I could, then drove to the apartment house where, Willie had told me, Lucca had signed a lease. But there was no Lucca listed on any of the doorbells. So I rang the manager's buzzer and was promptly clicked in.

Mrs. Holcomb was short and black and heavily made-up, overdressed for the job in a tight-fitting metallic sweater and snug ski pants. She wore lots of jewelry. She seemed oddly glad to see me.

"Come in, my friend. Sit down. Pardon my familiarity, but I have a thing for brown hair that falls over men's eyes."

I am not a vain man, especially with my face still swollen and purplish, but was this woman coming on to me? I could feel myself blushing, which is what I did in these rare situations. She was probably the type who would find blushing cute.

"I'm looking for Andrea Lucca."

"Oh, sure," she said. "F-8. Her realtor came in yesterday with her check. I'm expecting a call from her anytime now. She's moving in with her father. You are . . . ?"

I showed her my investigator's ID.

"Oh, my," she said flirtatiously. "I hope she's not in any trouble? Perhaps I shouldn't have talked to you?" Her coyness would sweeten coffee.

"No, no trouble," I said, reassuringly. "You did the right thing, Mrs. Holcomb. I'm just looking to talk to Ms. Lucca. There's this case that I'm working on. She may have some information for me."

Her eyes narrowed shrewdly. "And what if she doesn't want to give this information to you?"

I smiled. "She can just say no."

Not looking for any impediments to our budding friendship, she seemed to accept this. "I don't see the harm. Reason I'm so protective, you see, is that Andrea's down here to take care of her father, who's real sick. She says he hasn't got much time, so she's moving in here with him to spend his last days. I gave them F-8, which has a patio with access to the lawn. It's so sweet, it's really so touching. And she's so dear." She clasped her bejeweled hands, then leaned forward across the formica dinette. "Tell me, what is this case?"

I struggled to look apologetic. "Mrs. Holcomb, I really can't go into the details. But you're right; Andrea's a sweetheart. When did you meet her?"

Even if my questions were starting to bother her, even if she couldn't think of a good reason a private detective would be asking about one of her prospective tenants or any possible benefit that could accrue from having let me in the door, she couldn't help wading in. "Why, I've met her just the once. Three, maybe four days ago. She looked around for five minutes, leased the apartment, and then her realtor brought her check. Her credit and all has checked out fine." I knew that was true. "I haven't talked to her since, though I've checked her residential references and all." She looked a bit hesitant, moving some papers around in an accordion file. I bet she hadn't checked a blessed thing, not after Andrea had charmed her plants right out of their pots.

"Isn't that a bit unusual, for somebody who rents an apartment to spend such a short time here? Especially when it comes to finding a suitable place for her dying father?"

Mrs. Holcomb moved the papers around some more and rearranged her pink-and-silver sweater. "No, not really. Elaine Kramer, the realtor, met her; they became real good friends right away, she says." Oh, brother. Kramer was probably calling her divorce lawyers even as we spoke. "Told me that Andrea was one of the warmest, most intelligent girls she'd met in a long time. Said I'd really like her, and damned if I didn't. Elaine says we'll all have lunch from time to time. That would be nice, you know, because to be honest, even though I surely love it here, there aren't all that many interesting people to talk to. Especially men." She smiled again, glancing deliberately away from my wedding ring.

I stood up. "Is there a time that she'll be here to occupy the apartment?"

She looked disappointed. "Well, of course. Monday morning, nine A.M., is when the movers are due to arrive. Then around four P.M., the ambulance is supposed to bring her dad. Not many children would make a sacrifice like that," she added disapprovingly. "I have two from my first marriage. They sure wouldn't, I can tell you that."

If it's any comfort to you, Mrs. Holcomb, I thought as I made my escape, I didn't think Pete Scronziak would ever leave the Maple Shade Nursing Home, either, not alive and not to sit on the patio in F-8. But I wouldn't be sure until I looked into a few matters.

The newly emerging Deleeuw investigative philosophy: keep gathering all the information you can until all of a sudden, the truth sort of pops out of the thicket. File under all-clichés-are-true: you often really can't see the forest for the trees. I stopped at a phone booth on Main Street and placed a few calls, the last to set up a meeting in Chief Leeming's office at five P.M. But I sure as hell couldn't take any pleasure in busting the case open. Quite the opposite; I felt sick at heart, worse than I had last night when Stan Platt used me as a doormat.

CHAPTER 19

The new county jail where Marianne Dow was being held was seven miles west of Rochambeau and on another planet. At the nearest corner, New Jersey Transit buses disgorged weary women, mostly black and Hispanic, from Newark and Paterson. Suburbanites would have driven there to visit their loved ones, but few of them had any loved ones in residence.

It would, of course, have been unthinkable to build a prison in Rochambeau itself. Rochambeau citizens arrested for drunk driving or disturbing the peace were quickly out on bail, sprung by well-paid lawyers and embarrassed parents or spouses. Mostly, Rochambeau people went to prison for cleaner crimes—income-tax evasion, insider trading, stock manipulation, mail fraud.

So you could live your whole life right down the road and never know the jail was there, tucked behind its wall of evergreens and forsythia, if not for the women who lined up at the bus stop. On weekends the kids came along.

Though Marianne's lawyers (Eric Levin had signed up

several hotshots from big Newark firms; at least Marianne had some money) had been unable to get her freed on bail, they had argued successfully that she at least ought to be held near Rochambeau pending her trial, rather than in a more forbidding and distant state prison.

That morning the New York tabloids had dubbed her suburbia's "Murderous Mom." There aren't many murders in the 'burbs, but the media loves them when they do occur, although for reasons they are unlikely to concede or even think much about. In cities people are *supposed* to gun each other down. Suburbanites aren't. Suburbanites have all the advantages—money, education, good housing, prospects—so on the rare occasions they do kill one another, it is big news. Much bigger than babies getting shot through their apartment windows by Uzi-toting fourteen-year-olds. This is not a well country.

But I have to admit, it did feel strange to visit Marianne in the county jail. I bet there was no one like her in the whole complex, certainly not on the maximum-security floor where she was being held. Levin, as he had promised, had telephoned ahead to declare me part of his staff, which gave me official status and forced the prison officials to pretend to be civil. When I came in as an investigator, they didn't bother to pretend. The matron put my wallet, keys, and shield in a thick manila envelope.

In a couple of hours, I would be huddled in Leeming's office with Jane, Levin, the deputy county prosecutor, and the chief. Leeming had called to say that the prosecutor wanted to know why she should come off the golf course early to meet with a private investigator, on a weekend no less.

I told the chief to relay that the only reason I could think of was that I would present major new evidence regarding the murders of Gil Dow and Roberta Bingham, and if she didn't want to read about it in the papers, she probably ought to hop into a golf cart and ride over to the police department at five P.M. The prosecutor apparently had agreed that was reason enough. Leeming tried every which way—pleading, threatening, coaxing—to get me to reveal what I had, but I wouldn't, not until I'd talked to my client. Levin went ballistic when I wouldn't fill him in, either, but I held fast. Besides, I had to be sure. I could barely believe it myself.

The risks of screwing up were high; the consequences would be higher. "Don't come in here with some irrelevant bullshit that doesn't have a very major bearing on this case, Deleeuw," Leeming had warned hotly. "Because if you do, I will kick your ass all the way to Trenton. Levin and Rachel Mayer will be very unhappy if you've oversold the importance of your information, and I will look very foolish, which I'll deeply resent. I'll make you feel like a chicken fajita." This was perhaps the most bizarre threat I'd ever received. But I well understood the source of Leeming's discomfort. If there was new evidence in a murder case, he wanted it to come from his department, not from some relative amateur in an ancient station wagon.

By claiming to be on her legal-defense team, I was allowed to meet with Marianne in a conference room, rather than in the visitors' center, where inmates and visitors faced each other through two-inch-thick Plexiglas and spoke via telephones.

I was led down two halls, through three locked gates, to Room 4. The jail was more oppressive than its newness would lead you to expect. Green tiles seemed to cover almost every surface. The fluorescent lights made faces green-tinged, too.

Jane and I had gone over the questions I would ask Marianne, and the way in which I would ask them. Yet I could feel my hands trembling, hoping I was wrong, fearing I wasn't, at the last minute suddenly unsure of what I had known to be true just a few minutes earlier. It's the truth, I kept telling myself. You're after the truth. She'll be best served by it, and it's your job.

She was seated at the opposite end of the windowless room, facing me across a thick wooden table whose legs were bolted to the floor. I took the single chair opposite her. I asked her how she was. A bizarre question, under the circumstances, but these are the times when we hide behind good manners.

Had there been this much gray in her hair when I'd first seen Marianne at the American Way? And was it only a week ago? The light-blue prison jumpsuit she wore was so formless and baggy, it revealed nothing of the fit, attractive body honed at Buns of Steel. Her complexion had turned pasty; the hollows underneath her eyes were dark and pronounced. It seemed more like months, and I said so.

"Not months," she said dully. "It's been a lifetime." She put her face in her hands. "Sundays I was at soccer games. Or we would go to the Garden Center for seeds and annuals this time of year. We always had a family activity in the morning.

"Alan and Susie are in New York City now," she went on. Her voice was nearly expressionless. "They're using a different last name so people won't ask how it feels to have a killer for a mother." She shuddered.

"In just a few days, I've lost my husband, my children are gone, I've been put on indefinite leave from my firm—we really can't have an accused murderer in a law firm, can we? My best friend has betrayed me. I'm in jail. My lawyer tells me they have a powerful case, and we should consider a plea bargain. Maybe fifteen to twenty years for third-degree."

She hadn't looked me in the eye or even said my name.

She looked so stunned that I wasn't certain she had even focused on who I was or what my connection was to her. Outside the room we heard doors clanging and occasional shouting.

"Marianne. Do you know me? Do you know what I'm doing here?"

"Oh, Kit," she said, her head snapping up. "I'm so sorry. You have been out there all week trying to help me, I know that. I am grateful, believe me. . . ." She seemed sincere, appreciative, but then she suddenly drifted away. With difficulty she focused on me again, looked up at my still-swollen face, and registered the injuries. "Were you hurt? Were you in an accident?"

"Yeah, hit by a speeding vehicle named Stan Platt."

Her face didn't reflect anything—no guilt, recognition, or surprise.

"Do you know him?" I asked.

"I knew a woman named Platt. Donna, was it . . ." She shook her head, as if to clear it. "I'm not thinking clearly these days, Kit. I'm just a little, well, stunned."

Jane and I had gone over this in the short time we'd had to prepare. Hit her with it, Jane had advised. Hit her again and again with the truth. Keep on hitting her. You might get lucky. If you want to call it that.

"Not too stunned to buy furniture, though?" I said, hearing the harshness in my own voice. "Not too confused and shattered to go buy living-room furniture and store it. For what, Marianne? Why are you buying furniture when you're facing murder charges? What the hell happened to you this week? Where did you go? Why did you take off? Why did you run across the street to Sarah Lawson the night Gil was attacked and give her a gym bag with your aerobic weights, the weapon used to kill Gil? Why would you, a lawyer, disappear, when you know you're under suspicion? And leave me hanging out in space when you'd just hired me to help you?"

I was pacing behind the table now, too tense to sit still. "I want you to talk to me. I want you to tell me what's been happening. I have a right to know. I've been out there all week busting my chops for you, and all the while, at every step, I had to hear and face evidence that my client was hiding things from me, running away. C'mon, talk to me. Your life depends on it, Marianne."

She looked across at me, bewildered and silent. She seemed unable to grasp what I was asking or why. The questions bounced off her. I simply could not square the dynamo who had hired me with this passive, befuddled woman who didn't seem in touch with who I was, who she was, or why she'd done any of the baffling things she'd done this week.

I felt a pang at my brutality.

When she replied, she sounded almost dreamy. "Kit. Why are you shouting at me? Have you found out about Andrea? Do you believe me now?" She looked away, satisfied and nodding, as if I'd said yes. I had the sense that she was talking to me a bit of the time, and to someone else as well.

"The furniture, Marianne—you signed for it. The salesman described you. The warehouse says it's still sitting there. You went to Pennsylvania to buy furniture, to Mizpah. Did you see Andrea when you were there, Marianne? Isn't that why you went there? To see Andrea? To see Frankie?" I was raising my voice now, not quite shouting loud enough to attract the guards, but enough to startle Marianne.

She had narrowed her eyes, still confused but desperately trying to concentrate, almost as if she was fighting something off. Break through, Jane had urged. Shock her, keep shocking her. It will be difficult and you'll feel like a shit, but it's the only way. She was right. It was horrible, and I felt like a bucket of slime.

"Was it Frankie you were visiting? Frankie, who's stuck in his wheelchair—"

"I don't know. . . . Frankie?" She began sobbing softly. "I've never been to that place."

"You don't know Frankie?"

She shook her head.

I waited until the pain in my chest subsided. It was time to take my shot.

"You know Pete, though, don't you, Andrea? You know Pete very well. You were planning on living with him again, weren't you? You were going to take care of him, to be a family again, isn't that right, Andrea? Because you *are* Andrea. I mean, that's your other personality, isn't it, Marianne? You're Andrea. And you're Marianne. You're both. One of you has the family you always wanted, the other wants to destroy the family she never had. In Hollandale you were going to take your last chance at building a family, weren't you? You were going to have a place with your father, and do it right, especially now with Pete so feeble. He couldn't hurt any of you anymore, could he, Andrea? He was the person who made it impossible for you to have a normal family, but he was the one person you chose to make one with now. I guess he was the only one you had."

Tears were streaming down her cheeks. I was weeping too. My heart ached for Andrea, for her maimed brother and dead sister. And for Marianne, her other half, and that sweet life that was painfully built up and then destroyed. For the other families that were shattered too. Was I right? Could I be sure? Was there any other explanation?

"Go away," she sobbed, shaking her head as if to clear

away the fog. "You're not on my side. You're on their side. Get out!"

I reached inside my jacket pocket and clicked on the small tape recorder I'd put there. The guards had spotted it, but lawyers were allowed to bring tape recorders inside. She didn't seem to notice.

"No, Andrea. I'm on your side. I'm talking to you now, Andrea. Marianne has been away for a while. I'm sure she'll be back, but she's not available now. You are. And I know you. I know all about you. How you've moved from place to place. How you're drawn to women who have all the things you've never had. It's easy for you to make friends with them, because you've spent so much of your life fantasizing about being like them. You can slip into their lives without any effort, almost at will. You don't think they're worthy. Why do they deserve marriages and kids and homes and dogs when you are alone, when you never had anything but horror?

"I know that once you're inside, some part of you turns against them and you've got to take the family apart. You did it to the Platts. You did it to the Tannenbaums. You almost did it to the architect you worked for. But it's wrong, Andrea, and I think you know that. It's terribly wrong. What you're doing destroys people's lives, it hurts and scars their children, just like you were hurt and scarred.

"You know it's wrong. Marianne said it, you're a family stalker. You kill families, not with knives or guns, but with friendship. You're a serial killer. You want to stop, and I'm going to stop you. It's over now. I know you killed Gil, I know you set up Marianne. I know you killed Roberta and why. I know where you went this week, to Pennsylvania and then to Hollandale. I know a lot about you, both of you. You can end the lie now. It's over."

"No," she whispered. "No. No. No. No."

"It was you who invited Emily to that concert, right?" I could hear doors closing and cells clanging in the distance. "I didn't think you'd actually harm her. Was I right? I'd like to know that."

But I doubted if I ever would. She just kept on shaking her head.

There was probably one way to be sure, Jane had advised. I hoped she was right. *But do it with conviction,* she said. *Do it with clarity. Do it as if you know for an absolute fact that what you are saying is true, that you will never believe anything else. Don't waver or hesitate, no matter how much she crumbles.* I knew how dangerous this was, stirring things up I wasn't equipped to handle, but the alternative—twenty years in state prison for Marianne—had to be worse.

"Do you remember the kitten, Andrea? Do you remember when you brought the kitten home? What he made you do? In that room, while Frankie tried to help you?"

There was no sense of victory, no satisfaction or vindication, in seeing her break. There were no winners in a case like this. I had never seen a human being in that kind of pain. It was as if I were seeing someone split in two, and I guess I was. Her sobs turned to animal howls, piercing cries of anguish that brought the matrons running.

"God," she cried, suddenly looking up, angry. The fog had vanished. She looked alert, sharp, focused. "You're Deleeuw, aren't you—that asshole who's been running all over the place prying into my private life? Well, we finally meet. You wanted to find me, and you have. You had no right to do this. I'll have you in court."

She looked away, seething. "It was Marianne who hired you. I finally figured that out, stupid me. Who else would have? Marianne, that goddamn goody-goody. That holier-than-thou bitch. She thought she had everything. She

thought she was better than me. She was a phony, a hypo-
crite, the kind of fake person who gets everything by lying
and pretending and sucking up to men. I couldn't let her do
it. I couldn't." Her eyes blazed at me, fiercely angry, terrifying.

"I was going to quit, anyhow, to take care of my dad. My
dad's dying and I was going to take care of him and now
you've screwed it up. You bastard. You son of a bitch." She
spat out obscenities and insults as two matrons dragged her
out of the room. I clicked off my tape recorder, sat down at
the desk, and tried to fight off the nausea.

One of the matrons returned. "Hey, buddy, pardon me,
but you okay? You look like hell."

"I've just come from there," I said.

CHAPTER 20

Chief Leeming sat uneasily behind his shabby wooden desk, his office a vivid advertisement for a larger police budget. The green carpet was bare and worn, the pull-down map of Rochambeau dated to 1969. Tottering piles of manila folders covered a wooden table behind him. He even had a stack of much-used carbon paper on a corner of the desk, next to his old Underwood. I had never seen a piece of carbon paper on Wall Street, or a typewriter, either.

Several chairs were arrayed in front of the chief's desk. Next to a bemused Levin sat Rachel Mayer, the deputy county prosecutor, looking frosty and put out in her designer golf togs and an aqua-blue visor. "Deleeuw," she snapped, as contemptuous a greeting as she could muster. She leafed through a case file—probably Marianne's—in her lap, as if she were much too important to engage in chit-chat. She was not used to being summoned to rinky-dink police chiefs' offices on the whims of private investigators she'd never heard of. Jane took the seat on the right, dressed in her clinic working clothes: slacks, a pastel cotton shirt, and a khaki blazer with leather buttons. This wasn't her crowd either, but she probably looked the most at ease.

Leeming crossed his arms sternly over his chest, fixing me with a glum gaze. If I didn't have something significant to say, he would look like a horse's ass. If I did, he still might.

But everybody in the room had to feel better than I did. This was as dramatic a moment as I'd had in my fledgling career, but I couldn't feel triumphant. I was spent, haunted by the faces and stories of all the people who'd been scarred by this case. I felt as if I had just witnessed the most wrenching and horrible violation of a human being I'd ever seen.

Fortunately, I wouldn't have to be jovial. No coffee was ordered, no pleasantries exchanged. I introduced Jane as my wife and as a psychiatric social worker who had, as usual, been instrumental in helping me break the case.

"I know you're all busy. I appreciate your all coming here to meet me," I said, standing next to Leeming's old desk. In the adjoining room, the police radio squawked and crackled, then fell silent again. People who listened to police bands in towns like Rochambeau got plenty of sleep.

I pulled the tape recorder out of my pocket and set it on Leeming's desk. "This is a conversation between me and my client Marianne Dow, which just took place at the county jail. After you hear it, I'm turning it over to the county prosecutor."

In spite of their ill humor, they all leaned forward when I played the tape. Midway through, Mayer's mouth was wide open, Levin was dazedly shaking his head, and Leeming wore the same expression he might have if Josef Stalin had marched in and joined the group. They were paralyzed, disbelieving. If the conversation weren't so tragic, I would have savored the moment: they simply didn't believe what they were hearing, yet the voice on the tape was as convincing as it was tormented.

When the tape ended, the room erupted. "Son of a bitch, Deleeuw, I'll have your license!" bellowed Leeming. "This is incredible. How did you get this? Did you cook this garbage up to save your client?"

"I can't believe it," Levin kept mumbling. Mayer had pulled a cellular phone out of her briefcase and was cursing at someone over it. At least she believed me. The only true politician in the room, the prosecutor had gone past shock and on to practical questions like, was her ass covered?

Leeming held up his meaty hands for silence. "All right, all right," he shouted. "Let's be professionals. Let's listen to what the man says, then we'll talk among ourselves about what to do. Okay?"

What Leeming most cared about was that killers not run loose in his town, riling the taxpayers. Next to that, the chief did value justice. If I had something to offer, he wanted to hear it. But there was no way he was going to hear my story without being furious. I had broken a high proportion of the regulations covering private investigative work in New Jersey. I had withheld evidence, obstructed justice, interfered with investigations, maybe tampered with witnesses, to name a few that came readily to my mind and would surely come to Leeming's. Worse, I had embarrassed him yet again, taking a case he'd sworn was clear cut in a completely opposite direction. I hoped everybody would recognize that he'd been at least partially right.

A sergeant came into the room lugging a large tape recorder. Mayer pulled out one of her own, a much smaller pocket-size. Levin went out into the hallway to call the hot-shot criminal lawyers he'd retained to work on Marianne's case. Leeming mumbled something into his phone. Then everyone quieted.

"First, I think Marianne should be moved immediately to a hospital where she can get psychiatric care," I said without preamble. "Before we do anything else, she has to be under observation. I left her shattered, in great distress, and Jane thinks we should worry about what she might do to herself. I told the matron I was worried about suicide, and she said they would watch her closely until instructions arrived." Mayer nodded, made another call, then tucked her phone away.

Leeming was still shaking his head. "You telling me this woman is Marianne Dow *and* Andrea Lucca. A multiple?"

"That's right. One and the same. A multiple personality. A promising attorney with a successful family in suburbia, and a horribly abused woman with a psychotic need to destroy happy families, the kind she never had. A stalker and killer of families, and sadly, a killer of individuals as well."

"It's not as rare as people think," Jane interjected. "Especially in abuse cases. Severe, horrible childhood trauma often causes children to split their personalities; it's the only way they can survive."

As I recounted the family history Frankie Lucca had shared with me, the frosty look on Mayer's face vanished, I noted with satisfaction, replaced by an intense but business-like one. Her pen scribbled furiously across a legal pad.

"Motive?" she demanded.

"In Gil Dow's murder, I'm honestly not sure. I believe in part Andrea wanted to destroy Marianne's life, but there are other reasons. Over the past weeks, and certainly in the last week, the Marianne persona was beginning to crumble. Her husband Gil was a mean drunk, a philanderer. He was failing at work. She loved him, but the man she'd married was grow-ing cold and cruel, something that could obviously unsettle and terrify her. I've learned that he was in trouble at work. He was failing to meet his sales projections and was on the verge of being fired."

Jane picked up the narrative. "I suspect you'll learn that he deteriorated in some way, that he threw tantrums, or started hitting her or the children when he was drinking, or exhibited some other repulsive behavior terrifyingly reminis-cent of what her stepfather did to her. That was probably more than she could bear. Even if Dow wasn't nearly as abu-sive as her stepfather, he could have triggered feelings and emotions that she'd been struggling with her whole life, bringing her back to that horrible time and to the feeling she had to fight desperately to save herself and, now, her children, too.

"She'd spent decades constructing this completely new persona to try to escape the nightmare of her childhood, and now she was back in it again. I'm sure it's no accident that she killed her husband in a bathroom. That's where the worst abuse she suffered had taken place. From what Kit tells me, both personalities probably were breaking down at the same time. I don't think she herself knows what Marianne or An-drea was doing at a given time."

Leeming slapped his hand down on his desk, causing Levin to jump. "Jesus, this is fucking incredible. But it doesn't make any sense. They were friends. They both were in the same exercise class! Shit, I'm losing my marbles."

"I felt all week I was losing mine," I said. "Especially when I learned my client had taken off and gone on a shop-ping spree. It is disorienting," I acknowledged. "But listen, Chief, the basic point is that you were correct about Gil

Dow's death. She did have motive, opportunity, and means. She *was* the best suspect, in ways you couldn't even have really imagined. And if you're disoriented, think how she feels.

"But what made me start to wonder was that they were never seen together. They were in the exercise class at different times. None of the women who were friendly with Andrea were close to one another. And nobody, by the way, had a photo of Andrea. There were only two people who knew them both well—Gil Dow and Roberta Bingham. And we know what's happened to both of them."

"You're saying, Mr. Deleeuw," said Mayer (I had graduated to "mister" in under ten minutes), "that Gil Dow was killed because he had identified the two personalities?" Mayer was wading into the conundrum, but Levin seemed almost stunned. The expression on the lawyer's face suggested that nothing he was hearing computed.

"No. I think Gil was killed because he was turning into Marianne—or Andrea's—stepfather. He was becoming more disturbed as his business troubles mounted, and more abusive. Marianne had constructed a completely new identity, gone to college under a different name, gotten married. Virtually all of that time, I suspect, she was Marianne."

"Except," Jane added, "she retained an obviously compulsive and psychotic need to destroy intact families, even as she was carefully constructing one. Neat exteriors often mask very disturbed lives. Any psychologist or psychiatrist practicing around here, and there are lots, knows that. Eventually, Marianne—or Andrea—may have had a desperate need to destroy her own.

"It will take a long time to sort it out," she went on musingly. "One very plausible explanation is that Gil did somehow get wind of the double life his wife was leading. After all, it's very complicated, maintaining a separate life, an apartment, another job. . . ."

Leeming interrupted: "That probably wasn't so hard. There was hardly anything in Lucca's apartment. A bed, a drafting table, a phone and answering machine. It was like one of those furnished places you rent when you move to a new town. Didn't I mention to you, Deleeuw, how little stuff was in there when we searched it?" No, I seethed, you didn't. If you had, I might have moved a lot faster.

Jane picked up. "I don't think even the smartest, healthiest people could manage it for long. Sooner or later Andrea had to unravel. And Marianne would unravel with her. When a multiple is deteriorating like this, it isn't always possible to know which personality committed a specific act. Multiples don't always know about the other personalities, although in this case I suspect Marianne was increasingly becoming aware, or sensing the presence, of Andrea."

I jumped back in, since none of our audience seemed able to say much. "If you lay out their two lives, which I did late last night, it's like a puzzle; each fits into the other perfectly.

"Marianne worked in her law firm two, maybe three days a week. Gil was in the city five days and worked late many weekday nights, so that left a lot of time. Andrea's free-lance art work was done at her own pace, and she made her own schedule. At night and on weekends she'd do the sketches for the architectural firm. Some mornings and some afternoons, she'd go over to her other apartment, collect her mail, call her friends, maybe meet the men she saw." I filled them in on Andrea's affairs. "Notice that her liaisons never lasted very long. She always managed to be found out, so that the marriage would be the victim. So it wasn't as if she led a double life continuously.

"I remember Marianne mentioning how many hours her babysitter worked, and I was surprised when she said thirty or thirty-five, because Marianne had made a point of telling me she was only at her firm part-time. Two part-time jobs and a secret apartment adds up, of course, to a full-time job."

"Are you telling me she was trained both as a lawyer and an artist?" Mayer looked skeptical.

"Andrea spent two years at the New York School of Art, but according to the school's records she didn't finish. She met Gil Dow in the city, got married, went back to college, and then to Seton Hall Law School as Marianne Dow. But she was gifted and had some instruction as an artist, and the work the architect asked her to do wasn't that complex. She must have met Gil and decided to live her life with him as Marianne. . . ."

"A personality I'm sure you'll find she constructed in her early adolescence," Jane added. Leeming and Levin were looking from one of us to the other as if this were a ping pong tournament. "Somewhere in Mizpah you may find a woman, a former friend of Andrea's, who seemed happy and privileged to her, who probably had loving parents. Andrea fantasized about that person's life and eventually absorbed it. Multiples are not uncommon; we treat a half dozen at my clinic. Most of them split into several personalities when something horrible happens, when there is episodic or systematic abuse, or a parent is killed, or they are raped. They're amazingly resourceful at creating and keeping track of their separate identities. One personality is usually at least semiaware of the other. If you force it—as Kit did this morning—you sometimes can break through, especially if there are crises underway that are already unraveling the walls between them."

"Do you know which one killed Gil Dow?" poor Levin managed to ask at last.

I bit my lip on that one. I was way out of my league, yet I felt that I did know. "Andrea had to have done the killings, without the Marianne persona knowing. What I can't know yet is why; whether Andrea resented Marianne's success at building a life and her own failure to do so; whether violent or angry behavior in Gil triggered something violent in Andrea. Psychiatrists, not detectives, will have to figure that out." I saw a pained look cross Mayer's face: she was undoubtedly looking ahead to what a circus the trial would be.

"In this sense both the police and I were correct: Marianne couldn't have done the killings, yet she had to have. It's possible Marianne began to fear or suspect what was happening, and that that was one of the reasons she hired me. But I believe the killer in both cases was Andrea.

"It's just that I think Marianne was starting to lose it," I added, as much to myself as to the others. "Jane tells me that it's characteristic of the disorder, as the problems worsen, for two and sometimes even three different personalities to start colliding with one another. It must have been horrible for her."

"Pretty uncomfortable for Gil Dow, too," Mayer added sourly, still scribbling on her pad. Good prosecutors were not particularly empathetic.

Leeming buzzed his aide for some coffee and jotted a note, which he sent out with him. We were obviously going to be there awhile. A few minutes later two detectives, dressed a cut above the rumpled Rochambeau PD style and with military-style cropped hair, suddenly appeared. I would have said federal agents, but they were too young.

"State police," said Leeming, catching my glance. "It'll take months to sort through all this shit. So what about Roberta Bingham? Why do her?" A beefy sergeant came in with a tray holding a pot of sour-smelling coffee, powdered cream, and packets of sugar. The smell alone would have kept us awake.

"Well, Roberta was the only person other than Gil who saw both personalities at roughly the same time. And she saw them from a unique perspective. She saw their bodies, knew their stamina and movements and physical responses; she must have finally recognized one in the other. She may have been fooled for a while—like everybody else—by a scarf or a wig or different makeup, by the fact that Andrea and Marianne were never in class together. But eventually she caught on.

"I may even have triggered the recognition, myself; I may have been responsible for her death," I added sadly. Jane put a hand on my arm. But she didn't say I was wrong.

"When I told Roberta that Andrea was busting up families of some of the women in her class, I could see she was enraged. She might have contacted Andrea or confronted her with her suspicions that she and Marianne were one and the same person."

Mayer stopped taking notes long enough to rub one visibly throbbing temple. "But how could Bingham have contacted her? Wasn't Andrea already gone?"

"Well, Andrea may have checked her answering machine," said Leeming. "Or Bingham may have called Marianne with the same accusation, which, obviously, would be the same thing." I nodded approvingly but as nonpatronizingly as I could. The chief was getting it and apparently accepting it, too. I had worried that despite the tape they might just proceed to prosecute Marianne. I supposed they still could. Mayer might feel uncomfortable accepting an insanity plea. At least Leeming had accused the right person, sort of.

Leeming looked at Jane. "And this woman would have been capable of the kind of violence that killed Bingham? I mean, she was savagely beaten."

"Yes," said Jane. "It was not much worse than was done to her or her younger sister. And I'll almost guarantee that she also saw her mother beaten in something like this manner. Andrea is a woman who was brutalized, if her brother is to be believed. Her adult behavior certainly supports that conclusion. Making a child drown her own kitten is about as dehumanizing a thing as you could force her to do.

"Poor Roberta Bingham couldn't have known this, but in exposing the truth, she was threatening not only Andrea's life but Marianne's. The truth could destroy Marianne's marriage, her work, and her children, as well as force her to come to grips with the families she'd destroyed. This knowledge, conscious or subconscious, would have been devastating to Marianne, who had come to Kit prepared to fight to the end for her family.

"Now, to Andrea a lot depended on Roberta never repeating those suspicions—including, don't forget, the fact that she'd added murder to her crimes. Imprisonment would have never been an acceptable option for Andrea. She would have done anything to avoid that, perhaps even commit suicide, as her sister had. We don't know and may never know if she meant to kill Gil Dow or not. I suspect she intended to frame Marianne, whom the police would inevitably deem the most logical suspect, to divert attention from herself. But she surely meant to kill Roberta Bingham. And then, with the wall between the two personalities starting to crumble, she fled."

I dumped two plastic containers of fake cream into my coffee and recounted my visit to Sarah Lawson, Marianne's neighbor.

"But I don't get who it was that brought the murder weapon over," Mayer objected. "Andrea or Marianne?"

Jane answered before I could. "Remember the dynamic here: the distinctions between the two personalities were starting to erode. This was the period when each became fleetingly conscious of the other. Marianne would have recognized her house, found herself holding aerobic weights, realized she was somehow in trouble. This is when it all began to fall apart. After that night," added Jane, "Marianne never really acted rationally again."

Levin was returning to earth. "It wasn't even rational for her to return." I suspect one of the reasons he was spinning was that he probably didn't know which person to bill any longer. Maybe he could bill them both.

Jane said, "Marianne had seen her husband killed, her children taken away. Andrea was on the run, even reaching out to her stepfather. It's no longer so clear which personality was doing what."

"If you ask me, none of this is especially clear," grumped Leeming. "What do you mean about the stepfather?"

I explained about the apartment in Hollandale and my visit to that hateful old man in Maple Shade Nursing Home. The memory of his eyes still made me shiver.

"Deleeuw," said Leeming, rubbing the bridge of his nose and wondering who was going to type up the police report, gulping from a cup of black coffee, "what put you onto a multiple?"

I guess a part of me was pleased to have this battle-hardened ex–street cop interested in my reasoning, but it was a bittersweet triumph.

"A couple of things kept bugging me. I didn't understand why, if they were such good pals, nobody had ever seen

Andrea and Marianne together. I couldn't fathom why a lawyer like Marianne would disappear while she was under suspicion in a murder case. Andrea actually had more reason to bolt; presumably she feared what some of these women might do to her. But even then, wouldn't she say good-bye to somebody, or give notice at her job? Here were two former close buddies, both in love with the same guy, both gone.

"Then, Benchley Carrollton, at the Rochambeau Garden Center, had told me that he'd sold three young maples to Andrea Lucca. That was odd—Lucca had an apartment, no room for trees. But I visited Marianne right about that time, sat out on the porch and talked about Andrea, and I saw three little maples there in her yard. I saw them again when you guys were digging up the yard looking for the murder weapon, and that's when Benchley's comment finally clicked.

"When Marianne gave Evelyn a retainer for me, she filled out the standard form I give my clients"—I took it out of my pocket and dropped it on Leeming's desk. "She put her maiden name down as Jameson. I feel like a jerk, but I never looked into it until this morning. No matter how much I checked"—I was protecting Willie here—"I couldn't find any trace of a Marianne Jameson. It was as if she doesn't have a past. Her license and voting records and paperwork are all in her husband Gil's name. The only document with her name on it is a marriage certificate, but I think you'll discover she found a way to fake that."

"And how exactly did *you* check?" Leeming asked, sarcastically. "Especially on a Sunday morning? Employing all the vast resources of your part-time secretary?"

I merely smiled.

"How did you know to even go to Hollandale?" Mayer put in.

"Look, the police have their sources, I have mine," I said, a bit defensively.

"Are you saying you had evidence on a murder case you didn't share with us?" Leeming was suddenly growing more menacing than thoughtful.

"I'd mull a bit before answering that," Levin offered helpfully.

I nodded to him. "I *am* here sharing information with you, directly after talking to Marianne at the prison."

Leeming's expression made it clear he wasn't buying that, but he plowed ahead. "What about Stan, your boxing pal? Where do you see him fitting in here?"

I frowned. "I think Stan Platt just came by the Dows' that night, probably to beg for more time to pay Gil what he owed. Maybe nobody answered, although Marianne was at home. Possibly, Andrea lured Platt there for some reason—maybe to implicate him. Maybe he saw the body in the bathroom and bolted—I don't know. You could shake him like a dog with a bone and see what happens. I don't see Platt as a killer, just a scum. He'll crack, especially if he fears being drawn into a murder investigation. I've questioned him enough, thanks."

"And Frankie, Andrea's brother. Did he know of her life as a multiple?" Mayer was still taking notes.

"I doubt it," I said. "Andrea visited him faithfully. I think Frankie knew she was disturbed and was nervous about all the damage she'd done, but he had no reason not to accept what she told him—she was a graphic artist living in New Jersey. Since he never traveled, she wasn't really in much danger from him."

Mayer pulled out a new yellow legal pad. The rustle of the paper was the only sound in the room, which was silent for the first time, I realized, in an hour.

I looked up at the clock, haunted by the haggard face I'd seen that morning at the prison. "Look, I think the imperative thing is to get Marianne some psychiatric care. What seems to have happened was that as she cracked, she had this wish to re-create her home, to go back and rebuild it. She went and bought some furniture in Mizpah, Pennsylvania, and has been storing it near Bordentown." Leeming and Mayer exchanged puzzled looks. "She was going to redeem her stepfather and her own tortured childhood by making him a new home in which to die. I've met him. The man deserves to die right where he is."

But the questions and answers persisted for another hour, until I was exhausted. And I knew I would have to repeat these answers many times. Even Mayer seemed sympathetic when I told her about my own family's experience with being stalked by Andrea.

"Do you want to bring charges on that?" she asked. Jane and I both shook our heads.

"No," Jane said. "When I saw Marianne's picture in the paper this morning, I saw, of course, that she had been Pam, even though she'd disguised herself well. From what Kit has told me, I believe retaining him was one of the things that began to send Marianne—I think of her that way—over the edge. On the one hand, Marianne wants Kit to help save her marriage by hunting her other half; on the other, his investigation is threatening to expose Andrea and send both halves to prison. It isn't surprising that she targeted Kit's family. But it was extraordinary how together she seemed; how much I trusted her after a couple of lunches. . . ."

"When exactly did she surface at your clinic?" asked Leeming, gently. It was funny: he seemed to view me as a menace, but Jane was a citizen and a taxpayer.

"Well, I first met her a couple of weeks before I even mentioned her to Kit. She must have been planning to hire him for some time, and was scoping out our family." Jane shivered.

"You're lucky," Mayer commented.

"Maybe," I said, "but I don't think either Andrea or Marianne had it in her to harm a child. At least not directly." I was positive about Marianne. But to be honest, less so about Andrea.

Jane explained more about multiples, and I filled in some of the other details of my own investigation, including the trip to Providence. I thought Leeming would be pleased with all the legwork I'd done, all the evidence I'd presented. So I was unprepared when, at a nod from the chief, the state detectives, who'd been holding up the back wall of his office, strode over, read me my rights in front of my stunned and horrified wife, told me to stand up, handcuffed me, and placed me under arrest.

"What's the charge?" I stammered.

"Obstructing justice. Witholding information in a criminal investigation," Leeming said evenly. "Who knows? Maybe even obtaining information illegally. You knew more than you could possibly have found out legally, Deleeuw. I've warned you before: you can't become an independent law enforcement agency in this town. The regulations governing your work state quite clearly that you have to bring relevant information in a criminal proceeding to the local law enforcement authority immediately. But you haven't—you've run off following your own trails. I want to know how and whether you're bribing one of my officers." He started negotiating. "Talk to me and maybe we can skip formal charges—"

"Jesus," said Jane, as the skinheads snapped the cuffs

shut. "You ought to be giving Kit a ticker-tape parade down the middle of town, not arresting him. What's the matter with you?"

"There are laws, Ms. Leon," said Mayer tartly. "He's got to follow 'em the same as anybody else."

Levin came toward me with one of his cards. "Maybe you need a lawyer?"

"For Chrissakes, Levin, I don't need a card. You're hired. Get me out of jail."

EPILOGUE: SEPTEMBER

They stood almost catty-corner from one another: the young mother, waiting with her small boy for the school bus, and the fiftyish Gray Suit, staring through the chain-link fence at an early high-school football practice. I walked down the street between them, Percentage lunging this way and that on his leash. Despite three hundred bucks' worth of training, Percentage's response to "Heel" was to squirm enthusiastically and look at me with that stupid retriever grin. He knew the joke was on me. It was like shelling out hundreds of dollars to train a tree stump.

It was an almost perfect day, the kind that reinforces the crucible suburban notion that we and our neighbors have found one of the most comfortable and pleasant communities that humans have ever constructed for themselves and their families. The town glowed in the morning sun, yet there was a slight chill in the air, and a light breeze that set the towering trees rustling and swaying over the well-tended houses and yards. Fall was coming.

Everywhere, the town was cranking back into action—back to school, to dance and music lessons, soccer and football leagues, play dates and sleepovers. In a few weeks the trees would form a rainbow canopy over the houses, and pumpkins and bed-sheet ghosts would begin to sprout.

The boy on the street corner looked so expectant and his mother so nervous that I was sure this was his first day of public school and his first school-bus ride. I didn't know the woman, but I waved sympathetically, recalling what she was feeling. Ben and Em, waiting at their own bus stops, didn't want or need an escort anymore. She nodded, smiled back a bit sadly, then busied herself refastening the boy's Mets jacket.

I could already see the bus, red lights flashing, at the other end of the block. It would be here in a minute or two to take her child from one phase of his young life into another. "See, Robby," she said, in the way parents have of feigning excitement in the hope their kids will pick it up. "There it is, there's your bus. It must be the Purple Swan. Remember, the Purple Swan. That's the same one you take home. I'll be here when you get off. Good luck, sweetie. I love you like crazy." She couldn't quite take her eyes off the bus, as if she were willing it to take more time, pushing it back with her gaze. It wouldn't work.

Robby fidgeted, anxious to get on with it, to have the strangeness over with. He would probably never recall this scene. His mother would never forget it. By the end of the week, I knew, he would be lobbing spitballs at the bus aide and asking his mother to wait inside the house when he came home. That seemed right.

The Purple Swan had taken my kids off on that journey, too. They probably didn't remember it either, but I could still picture Em's red backpack bobbing up the bus steps, pausing as she took in the shouting and jostling in front of her. It was just a few steps, but it seemed to me that she was going farther away than she had ever gone. I knew that no matter how long our children lived with us, they'd never completely return; they would only grow more and more separate.

Jane and I knew it was our job to wish them godspeed and give them every encouragement and tool they could possibly use on the trip. There were moments when I would have given anything to freeze things for just a few months, but we knew that that was impossible. Robby's mother knew it, too.

The Suit across the street put his right hand on the chain-link fence, put his briefcase down alongside him, and glanced at his watch. He had ten minutes before the eight-fifteen to Hoboken pulled into the station a block away. If he was important enough, he could catch the eight-thirty and claim the train was delayed. Behind him, half a dozen middle-aged commuters had pulled their sedans and minivans over to the side of the street to join the Suit in watching the Rochambeau High Panthers working out on our field of dreams.

The local paper was awash in glowing reports about this year's team. I listened to the coaches bellowing one dumb homily after another about concentration, dedication, team spirit, and hard work.

"Play like a team, and you'll win like one!" shouted one thick-necked behemoth.

"You wanna play, you gotta sacrifice!" another thundered.

The coaches seemed to have no end of witless sayings and exhortations, all of which seemed to fall like a thud. I saw the kids smirking at one another, even as they jumped up and down in unison or dropped to the ground for push-ups. Kids automatically screen out lectures, conventional wisdoms, and hard-taught lessons from elders. They want to make their own way; they'll learn their own lessons.

The middle-aged men didn't look at each other, or at me. Several of the engines kept idling, as if the drivers were pretending that they were pausing for only a second or two. They stared intently at the kids and at the bellowing coaches, their faces unreadable. On Saturday these boys, ghosts of the Suits' former selves, would be strutting in front of two thousand townspeople, with the cheers of parents, classmates, and girlfriends echoing through the town.

I was pretty preoccupied myself these days. The Family Stalker Case, as the media had enthusiastically dubbed it, had finally wound down. The Brown-estate case earlier in the year had left me feeling like hot stuff: the Suburban Detective, entitled and ensconced. This one made me wonder how many more cases like it I could stand. The casualties had paraded through my mind all summer, one after the other—Marianne/Andrea, Gil, Donna Platt, Gay Tannenbaum, Roberta Bingham, Frankie Lucca, his dead sister, the old man in the Maple Shade Nursing Home. All those bewildered children. All those broken families and torn lives.

I was not much fun to be around this summer, as everyone in my family had pointed out regularly. I took long lunch hours at the mall, sitting in the crowded International Food Court, thoughtfully chewing my vegebean burritos and sipping iced tea. I took a delighted Percentage on two-hour walks through Rochambeau's streets, half-emptied by family vacations, summer camps, my neighbors' retreat into air-conditioned playrooms and backyard pools. Even the industrious Volvos, which squired children around most of the year like soldier ants ferrying bread crumbs, were scarce. The quiet deepened my own melancholy.

As for me, Levin had turned out luckily to be a sharper

lawyer than I'd given him credit for. The charges against me were dropped three days after Jane posted bail. Leeming later conceded what was almost instantly obvious: he was bluffing, trying to teach me a lesson the way Rochambeau grown-ups were always trying to teach their irresponsible kids. We had even resumed our monthly lunches, with the chief grumping at me about stingy taxpayers and meddling town-council members.

Benchley and I had also resumed regular chats in his greenhouses, now that his busiest season was slowing a bit. Luis and I had coffee most mornings. Whatever misery some people in Rochambeau were experiencing, the family in Cicchelli Furniture's window at the mall was prospering reassuringly. The mannequins had broken out their fall duds—flannel shirts and sweaters—and would be acquiring decorative corn husks soon, I was sure.

Our own family had returned to normal after the kids' camp and a two-week vacation at the Jersey Shore. Ben was rumored to be involved with a fellow ninth-grader named Amanda something-or-other (I was working on her last name), but no confirmation of this was forthcoming from him. According to Em's friends' older siblings, this Amanda was rumored to be *fast,* which to Em's mind meant she painted her fingernails.

Jane and I continued to make one another's new lives possible. Her salary and health plan had gotten us over the hump, my new caseload would help get her through the necessary coursework and training until she could become a full-fledged psychologist and could listen to even more disturbed people. My Volvo had just had its cracked engine block replaced and would break 117,000 miles soon. My mechanic swore I didn't need a garage but a papal dispensation, but I was far from ready to give it up.

Watching the Suits absorbed by football practice, I felt nostalgia for the first time for my cocooned Wall Street days, when I could glance at awful headlines in passing and leave them behind, hear tragic stories about neighbors' or fellow townspeople's mishaps without ever really absorbing them. I had lived on the run, always on the move, always in a rush. I never had to pay real attention to anything much but work. Now I was seeing the busted lives behind the headlines and the rumors and dinner-party tales. I hadn't anticipated that I would spend a substantial part of my life looking more closely into people's lives. I worried that the beauty of the suburbs would always seem somewhat shallow and false.

Yet the shocker was that this investigating seemed the right work for me. I was good at reading people, intuitive about their lives, increasingly confident of my instincts. I was better at being a private detective than I had been at anything else, and I was still drunk on the freedom. Now the only asshole I ever had to put up with, as Jane so lovingly put it, was myself. No, I wasn't going back. But I had a way to go before I got used to the kind of pain I had witnessed in the spring.

My case had ended successfully, if not happily. I'd gotten another round of publicity, a new wave of clients. Evelyn was after me to get serious about taking on a junior associate. I fantasized about it being Willie, but first I'd have to meet him. The problem was, how useful could he be without access to a computer? I suppose I could buy him one. Was I ready to take on a cyberpunk?

Marianne never did get out of jail and into a hospital. The state decided that it didn't matter which personality committed the murders; neither one should ever be free again. Fearing that a jury would agree, her lawyers pled guilty to two counts of first-degree murder. Pending some imaginative appeal, she would remain in the psychiatric unit of the state prison in Rahway for the next thirty or forty years. I visited Marianne there—she would always be Marianne, my client, to me—every other week or so, but she never spoke to me or acknowledged my presence. Still, I hoped some of what I said to her penetrated. What troubled me was that I wasn't sure either Marianne or Andrea had survived.

Despite the fact that she, or at least one part of her, had killed two people, I clung to the memory of a smart, warm, and loving woman who had walked into the AmWay mall looking for help. Only a barbarous society would stubbornly refuse to recognize that the devastated remains of that person belonged in a hospital. But this country clings to much simpler and more rigid notions of right and wrong. One file I never misplace is my growing correspondence with county, state, and federal officials and legislators on Marianne's behalf. In reply I have a two-inch stack of mostly form letters.

Marianne's children went to live with Frankie in Pennsylvania, one of the few happy twists the story had taken. I had driven over to see them, to check on their new home, as Marianne would have wanted me to. Their uncle is thrilled to have them. Frankie revels in the busy domestic life he is suddenly leading again. The kids had lost a mother and a father, but had ended up luckier than either of their parents.

Pete Scronziak, Marianne's stepfather, never got out of the Maple Shade Nursing Home. The nurse there told me he waited every morning for the truck to come and get his things, and wept and cursed for hours when it didn't. He shouted for Andrea as if she were his beloved and devoted daughter. Maybe at the end she had become the child he'd wished he'd had, and he'd turned into the parent he had really wanted to be.

One other perversely happy note: Stan Platt's financial life didn't withstand the scrutiny to which state auditors, at Leeming's urging, subjected it. Platt was charged with failing to file income-tax returns for six years, and for evasion on those he did file.

Teach him to mess with the Suburban Detective.

The train whistled in the distance, and the Gray Suit picked up his briefcase and hurried off. As if that were a signal, the other men started up their cars and drove off too. They would all be at work soon, pushing paper, making calls, their lives far from championship football and the simpleminded verities that governed it.

The mother was still there on her corner.

The bus pulled up with a squeal; the doors rattled open as Percentage and I passed. Robby hopped on even before the bus aide could climb down to get him. Kids are among the most heartless of creatures.

Percentage thought every school bus he saw had Em or Ben on it and tried, as usual, to jump on. I jerked the leash back sharply as I had been taught by the trainer. It made not a particle of difference.

The mother waved as the bus passed, and pulled her jacket close against the breeze. She waited just in case her son was looking back. I knew without looking that he wasn't. They never did.

DATE DUE	BORROWER'S NAME	ROOM NO.
OCT 9 1994	J-000477	
OCT 26 1994	G-000329	
NOV 16 1994	S-003281	
NOV 30 1994	C-013975	
DEC 28 1994	1005200003067	
JAN 11 1995	1005200001640	
SEP 12 1996	OCT 1 1996	
NOV 30 1998